BOOKS BY GLENN KAPLAN

The Big Time

All for Money

*Evil, Inc.**

*Poison Pill**

**A Forge Book*

POISON PILL

GLENN KAPLAN

A TOM DOHERTY ASSOCIATES BOOK
NEW YORK

This is a work of fiction. All of the characters, organizations, and events portrayed in this novel are either products of the author's imagination or are used fictitiously.

POISON PILL

Edited by James Frenkel

A Forge Book
Published by Tom Doherty Associates, LLC
175 Fifth Avenue
New York, NY 10010

www.tor-forge.com

Forge® is a registered trademark of Tom Doherty Associates, LLC.

ISBN 978-0-7653-7079-2

Forge books may be purchased for educational, business, or promotional use. For information on bulk purchases, please contact Macmillan Corporate and Premium Sales Department at 1-800-221-7945, extension 5442, or write specialmarkets@macmillan.com.

First Edition: October 2013
First Mass Market Edition: November 2014

Printed in the United States of America

0 9 8 7 6 5 4 3 2 1

To Marty Lipton
A good friend to all my books and
the original author of the title of this one

ACKNOWLEDGMENTS

First, the legendary Al Zuckerman of Writers House: editor, taskmaster, creative partner, tireless agent, indomitable advocate.

Thanks to the experts who gave their time and knowledge:

Marty Lipton, who advised on the *Poison Pill* and the takeover defense (of course).

Douglas Schloss, who helped me structure Josh Katz's empire and financial woes.

Todd Slotkin, for his insights into the world of private equity.

Josh Knerly, for extracting his partner's knowledge of criminal law.

Bill Vahle, for computer security and hacking.

Tony Glants, for Russian language and culture.

Dan Starer of Research for Writers. Again.

Special thanks to the anonymous Wall Street executive who gave me the industry credo that I gave to Josh: "Immoral we do every day, illegal never."

My former clients in the pharmaceutical industry, who had no idea they would be contributing to this effort (nor at the time, did I).

Any errors are strictly mine.

Gordon Bowen, one of the great artists of advertising, who led me to Jon Moe, whose genius with the camera made me look better than I deserve.

Jill Shaw Ruddock, self-help author and the visionary behind London's Second Half Centre, who led me to Baroness Helena Kennedy and her wondrously detailed descriptions of the House of Lords.

Alison Holtzschue, a reader of many early drafts of all my novels, whose enthusiasm and critical insight I cherish.

In this much-heralded era of the disintermediation of publishers and writers, three cheers for the people at Tor/Forge. Tom Doherty, who said "Yes, but it needs fixing." Jim Frenkel, the editor who guided the fixing with incredible insight, care, thoroughness, and dedication. Seth Lerner, whose cover designs and graphics took my breath away. And the rest of the people at Tor: Linda Quinton, Phyllis Azar, Patty Garcia, and their teams. They practice the business of publishing with passion and consummate professionalism, giving this author everything he could hope for in a publisher. And more.

First, last, and always, Evelyn, for putting up with this mad, unlikely enterprise all these years. Together we strive for Alec, *il nostro tesoro*.

PART ONE

1

Viktor Volkov stared at the encrypted satellite phone on his desk.

"Chort, nu zvoni zhe!" he barked in Russian. Ring, you damned devil, ring!

Suddenly, he hated the sight of its fat little antenna.

He was waiting for the most important call of his life.

Well, the most important call of the *last* phase of his life.

No, no, it was the start of his *new* life.

At fifty-five, he thought, he must have a good twenty—no, thirty—years left. With luck, maybe more. Why not? He was strong, fit, and vigorous. People told him he looked like a man ten years his junior—and not just people who were afraid of him or wanted money. Of course he might be older by a few years. He would never know for sure. The Leningrad orphanage to which he had been abandoned as a baby had no record of his birth or when he had arrived.

He grabbed the phone from its base as if that might make it ring sooner. It didn't. He slammed it back into place.

"I've never seen you so jumpy," said Artyom Zadorov, his business partner and friend of more than forty years. "My sons are on the job. We have nothing to worry about."

Viktor shook his head and stared out the soundproof windows of his white mansion overlooking Belgrave

Square. He stared into the night, pondering his master plan. Viktor, the orphan boy with no birthday, had come so far. Today he had great houses on three continents, yachts, cars, and jets bearing the name that an anonymous bureaucrat had made up for him. Viktor, the victor. Volkov, son of wolf, the great hunter. In his early teens, fatherless Viktor gave himself his own patronymic. Viktor Viktorovich, Viktor son of Viktor, father to himself, inventor of his own life. He had grown up to become Viktor the envied billionaire, Viktor the feared oligarch. Still, there was so much further he hoped to go. If only that damn phone would ring.

"Please, Viktor Viktorovich," Artyom said soothingly. "Everything will happen according to your directions." Even Artyom addressed him formally. No man ever used Russian pet names with Viktor Viktorovich. No Vitjok, Vitichka, Vitenka, or Vitunya. Even if Artyom had saved Viktor's life when they were teenagers— grabbed Josef, the rival gang leader, as he was about to choke Viktor to death. And cut his throat from ear to ear. Not even his lifelong blood brother dared to be too familiar with him.

Viktor had learned to command when he was a boy. He had more nerve and native intelligence than the others. Power radiated from his steel-blue eyes—cold, never the first to blink, always keeping his distance. Over the years, he inspired men to fear, to loyalty, and to the belief that with him they could accomplish more than they ever thought possible.

He took a deep breath. Viktor loved Artyom, this hulking bull yak of a man, who provided the brawn to his brain. Artyom was the force that allowed Viktor to issue an order or a threat only once and never raise his voice. But there was still so much he could not tell Artyom about his plans. So much Artyom would never understand about the new life he was determined to make.

"How many people do you think will die?" Artyom asked eagerly.

Viktor looked away. Artyom took pleasure in killing. Always did. Yes, Viktor thought, he *had* to break from his past, this old way of getting things done. It would be essential for the grandsons he meant to have. They must come into the world untainted. A dynasty of men with a completely respectable fortune. Like Rockefellers or Rothschilds, Hapsburgs or Windsors. All of his money had to be clean, not just the half that was legitimate today.

"You think maybe *thousands* will die?" Artyom asked, again too eagerly.

"No, Artyomchik," Viktor sighed. "Maybe hundreds, maybe just a handful." He was hoping for the handful. "Only a death or two are necessary. Once the first few people die, the company will have to recall every pill bottle everywhere, tens of thousands, more. People will be afraid to buy. The government will prosecute and slap new regulations on them. There will be lawsuits. This Percival & Baxter company will lose billions overnight. The stock will plummet."

"And you," Artyom smiled, "will buy it up at a lovely price."

Viktor nodded.

Artyom winked. "With a minority interest for your partner, as always."

Viktor nodded again. No reason to talk now about ending their partnership. It would happen soon enough. "Yes, Artyomchik, as always."

That was the plan, but only the beginning of it. Much more had to follow. Viktor checked his watch. It was ten past eleven in London so now ten past six outside

Philadelphia, where the factory was. The day-shift work-ers would have gone home almost two hours ago. Two hours, so why hadn't he heard confirmation? What could be the delay? He held his breath.

Finally the phone chirped.

Viktor sat up straight. *Now it begins,* he thought. Calmly, he folded his arms across his chest. His cool returned. The phone chirped again. He did not reach for it. He looked across at Artyom and raised his chin slightly.

Artyom grabbed the phone. "Sergei!" he said eagerly. Artyom listened to his eldest son but kept his eyes locked on Viktor's. He listened for several minutes, nodding and nodding. Finally, he snorted a little laugh, whispered a fatherly good-bye, and put the phone back in its cradle.

"*Gotovo, wse zdelano,*" he said. It is done, all of it.

"The poison?" Viktor asked.

"Yes, it was set. No one noticed anything. Our soldier entered the factory with his false identification. The com-puters authorized him coming and going. All worked per-fectly. No one saw the tube sewn into his sleeve, no one saw him pour his white powder into the white powder that makes the famous little pills with the yellow coating." Artyom laughed. "Enough sodium cyanide in that batch of Acordinol to kill a herd of oxen." He laughed again.

"And the soldier?" Viktor asked. "It was that young Ukrainian who spoke English like an American. What about him?"

Artyom smiled. "Erased."

Viktor felt a pang. "He was a loyal soldier. How did he die?"

"He was happy, counting his money. He never knew."

Viktor grunted approval. A good death. What more can a man ask for?

"I promise you, Viktor Viktorovich, my *sons* assure me

that every phase of this has been accomplished impeccably. They are *my* boys, after all." He added tenderly, "*Moi synochki.*" My dear darling little boys.

There he goes again, Viktor thought, *flaunting his sons. Rubbing them in my face.* Four sons, all with him. While Viktor had only one child. His Tanya. The only child he would ever father.

Tanya was key to his plan. Yet stubbornly resisting his matchmaking efforts with the English lord. He *had* to bring her around. He knew he would, even if he did not yet know how. Sooner or later, everyone did submit to his will. Even his spoiled, very English daughter.

Artyom poked Viktor's arm the way he did when he was about to tell a joke. "Sergei said the soldier told him something funny before he died."

Viktor was put off. "Funny?"

"Yes, he reported something funny."

"What do you mean, funny?"

"He said this company has a big sign above its parking lot. It says that the people of Percival & Baxter are proud to make Acordinol because," he paused to keep from laughing, "because it is the world's most trusted medicine for pain." Artyom cackled. "Ha, not for long!"

Viktor wanted to tell him not to be so goddamn amused. He wanted to tell him many things, but this was not the time. Later, when everything was done. Or maybe never. He studied his old buddy for an instant, forcing himself to put aside his close attachment. He looked at the thick, giant hands that could snap men's arms like twigs; the mouth that leaked spittle like an animal's maw; the riotously colored silk shirt left half unbuttoned to show off the collection of gold chains glinting in the bush of curly white chest hair. Yes, he loved Artyom, but Viktor knew he must leave him behind. He had transformed himself before. He knew he could do it again. He took a deep breath. "No, Artyom," he snapped, "it is not funny. There is nothing funny here."

The phone chirped again. Again Viktor did not reach for it. This time he extended his open hand across the desk. Artyom took up the phone and gave it to him.

Viktor held it to his ear. The voice on the other end spoke in the curiously accented Russian of a Yorkshireman raised by a mother from Vitebsk.

"Viktor Viktorovich," Tom Hardacre intoned respectfully.

"Tom, just a moment," Viktor said. He stood up from the desk and turned his back to Artyom. He walked to the window. "Now, please brief me."

Hardacre said, "My hackers have done everything we discussed. The Percival & Baxter computers now have no record of our soldier entering or leaving the plant. The surveillance videos have been altered, the images overwritten. It is like he was never there."

"Are you sure, Tom?"

"Absolutely, Viktor Viktorovich. No one will ever know."

"No one?" Viktor asked.

"Are you doubting my work, Viktor Viktorovich?" Hardacre was the only man who talked back to Viktor. Viktor tolerated his arrogance because Hardacre was the best computer criminal he had ever seen, one with the arrogance of a great artist. He commanded invisible troops of hackers around the globe. His zombie networks, like magic, hijacked computers, did their work, then vanished without a trace.

"No, Tom," Viktor said, "I'm not doubting you. I'm just thinking about every contingency."

"Viktor Viktorovich," Hardacre explained, "even if they discover their data has been tampered with—which is unlikely—the original data has been destroyed. Someday they may realize there is something they don't know, but they will have no way to know what it was."

"You are sure, Tom? Really sure?" Viktor knew enough about computers to use his own PCs, laptops, and smartphones. Still he mistrusted them. Too many mysteries inside them, too many surprises popping out.

"Viktor Viktorovich? Do you really doubt me?" Hardacre sounded indignant. "Didn't I hack into how many pharmaceutical companies to bring you their most confidential research projects? Didn't I bring you everything you asked for from this Percival & Baxter?" Hardacre took a deep breath and lowered his voice. "If you doubt my ability to deliver, maybe we should talk about calling this deal off."

"No, no, Tom," Viktor said. "Proceed. Proceed as directed." He was so glad he had not put the hot-headed Yorkshireman on the speakerphone. It would not do to have Artyom hear the man's insolence.

Viktor turned back to face Artyom, to include him now. He pushed the speakerphone button to "on" and held the phone away from him. "Tom," he announced, "you are now running this operation from the banker's house in America. Make sure he does what he is supposed to do. And make sure he knows nothing about what really is happening."

"No problem," Hardacre responded, "he's a greedy American banker. When he thinks he can see dollar signs, he sees nothing else. I have all his computers and phones monitored. Every room in his house bugged. He does nothing I don't know about, not even a fart."

"Good. We will talk soon. Tom, you are the best."

"Thank you, Viktor Viktorovich," Hardacre said, his respectful tone returned. "And yes, I *am* the best."

Viktor clicked off and walked the phone back to its cradle. But he did not sit.

Artyom took the cue and stood up. He loomed over Viktor, his broad shoulders like a brick wall. Viktor thought, *I will miss him*.

"This formula the American company has," Artyom asked, "could it actually become the key to the first female orgasm pill?"

"The chemists at my French company are convinced," Viktor said as he started for the door. Artyom followed. "But of course, they have no idea where the report they saw came from. Or who got it for them. But they say in their analysis that the molecule the American computational chemists have constructed could well be it. Its molecular dynamics—increased reactivity and its compatibility with solvents—could make it more powerful even than natural dopamine. So combined with the opioid stimulants, vasodilator, and synthetic oxytocin they already have, it should deliver both the triggers for woman's ecstasy whenever she wants it. Emotional and physical. A few touches to her favorite points on the pudendal nerve system and bang— orgasm!"

"You now speak this strange language," Artyom said as he broke into a wide grin. "But I think you are saying it will be a gold mine."

"No, Artyom, better, much better." Viktor reached up and patted Artyom on the cheek. "Come, old friend, I will walk you out. We did a good day's work, no?" He unlocked the door of the study.

As they walked down the hall, a white-gloved butler appeared. Viktor waved his hand slightly. The servant retreated, leaving them alone.

The two men stood for a moment.

Artyom turned to the ornately framed oil painting that

dominated the foyer. A larger-than-life-size portrait of a young English beauty in riding clothes—jodhpurs, breeches, tweed coat, silk cravat with pearl stickpin, riding crop and helmet tucked under one arm. She had long chestnut hair; high cheekbones; pale porcelain skin; and large, dark eyes. She radiated poise and aristocratic confidence. It was Viktor's shrine to his deceased wife, his one great love, Alexandra. He would not let anyone enter or leave his Belgravia mansion without paying homage to her.

"How old would she be today?" Artyom asked tenderly.

"Forty-one," Viktor answered in a sad whisper, "and one month. Her birthday was four weeks and two days ago." Viktor looked down. "I can't believe she is ten years gone."

"Tanya looks so much like her," Artyom said brightly, patting Viktor on the shoulder.

"Yes, Artyomchik, more and more each year. She just graduated from Cambridge, you know. Trinity, where the royals and aristos get their education. I see so much of Alexandra in her. The way she moves or says things or raises her eyebrow. Willful, too. Always a mind of her own. Like her mother. She has no idea how much she takes after her. No mother at only ten."

Viktor opened the door onto the square. Traffic noise and warm night air flooded in. He took Artyom's face in both hands. They kissed on the cheeks once, twice, three times. "*Spokojnoj nochi*," Viktor said. Good night. He ushered Artyom through the doorway, nodding to the bodyguard on sentry duty, barely visible in the darkness.

Artyom took a step forward, then turned back, index finger raised questioningly. "Viktor Viktorovich, we have many businesses together, you and I. Yet you invest so much of your clean money in drug companies. Big ones, small ones, all kinds. And all in secret. No one knows it's you."

"It's the greatest business, my friend," Viktor said. "Everyone gets sick."

Artyom wagged the finger, "I know you, Viktor Viktorovich. For you this is a passion. It's business, yes. But it's also personal, I can tell." He touched Viktor's arm gently. "Tell me, it began for you when Alexandra got sick, didn't it?"

Viktor nodded. "Yes, Artyomchik. Now go home to bed." He stepped back into the foyer, one hand on the door. He forced a smile. He knew he was no good at smiling. So he wanted to make up for his impatience. "Your sons did well today. I did not mean to doubt them. It's just that this deal . . ." He paused, not wanting to reveal too much. ". . . This deal is especially important to me." He waved good-bye and started to close the door.

"And important to me, too," Artyom called over his shoulder, "and to my sons!"

Viktor shut the door, then paused in front of Alexandra's portrait. He could never forget the day he got her diagnosis. Ovarian cancer. He'd searched everywhere for treatments, however experimental, for anything that might save her. But he'd gotten no time and no miracle. He'd stood by helpless, watching disease ravage her beauty and murder her at thirty-one, leaving him and ten-year-old Tanya adrift. He wondered, was Artyom right about his obsession with medicines? Was it more than a good business? Was he still trying to save Alexandra?

He tried to imagine the people who would soon die for him. He was sure he could feel the agony of their families. He remembered how he felt when he sat at Alexandra's deathbed and touched her withered, lifeless hand one last time. A tear formed at the corner of one eye. Slowly, he wiped it away.

All great causes sacrifice lives, he thought. *Everyone lives in pain.*

2

SATURDAY, JULY 11

Emma Conway got up from her weeding when she heard the bleeps of the video game from inside the house. She brushed off her knee pads, kicked dirt from her clogs, and wiped sweat from her forehead with the back of her gloved hand. She was sure she had just created a streak of dirt across her forehead. *Not the look of an authority figure,* she thought. But Peter did need a talking-to. She tromped across the stone patio to the open door to the den.

"You were late for work yesterday," she shouted, trying to get her son's attention as he waved the Wii remote at the big screen. He was standing in pajamas on the edge of the couch, maneuvering an alien invader through a dark tunnel. Her tall, lanky sixteen-year-old with long coltish limbs looked like he might shoot up to six feet by dinnertime.

She put hands on her hips. "Peter Conway Katz!"

Her short, light brown hair, once naturally blond, was matted with sweat, accentuating her high cheekbones and big blue eyes. Having recently turned forty-two with a shrug and a romantic weekend away with Ned, she hoped that her good bones and hardy genes would keep her looking more or less like herself without much artifice through the next decade. She stamped her foot. "Peter, I am talking to you!"

The boy howled as his alien got zapped into oblivion. He fell to the floor in a crumpled ball, letting the remote fall out of his hand, dead like his space creature.

How odd, Emma thought. She could give orders at Percival & Baxter and move tons of pharmaceuticals, millions of dollars. She could command mega-factories and direct thousands of lives. But in the face of her son's adolescent behaviors she felt helpless. What happened to the dear little boy who would jump into her arms for snuggles every chance he got? Abducted by aliens, she decided. Men were such mysteries, going from wanting everything to wanting nothing, with never a warning or a clue why.

He was now back on his feet, invading another space station. She moved in front of the TV. "You were late for your job, young man. That is not acceptable."

But Peter remained back in the space station fighting for his life, trying to navigate around her, not even looking at her. He never looked at her any more, even when he was muttering what little he had to say to her.

She stuffed her gloves into her back pocket, and turned off the set. "Damn it, Peter, look at me!"

"Aw, come on!"

"What makes you think you can waltz in at nine when it's your job to be there at eight? People depend on you."

"Mom, that summer job, it's like a dollar fifty over minimum wage. I'm just one of the robots on the production line. It's a stupid waste of time. Geez, Dad says the portfolio he runs in my trust fund can make more in a month than those guys make in a year."

She saw him wince as soon as the words escaped his mouth. Yes, he knew he was going to get it. She charged over to the couch and looked up into his face. "Don't you *ever* talk that way about honest, hardworking people. This is not about money, it's about responsibility." She stared into his eyes—his father's burning brown eyes, the same eyes that had led her to fall in love with Josh Katz back when they were students at Wharton. She could also see her own high cheekbones and pale complexion in his face. And, in his burgeoning height and broadening shoulders, traces of her late father.

He looked down, guilty as charged. She was sure he was hoping he could weather this storm without getting grounded again.

She gave a weary sigh. "Your father set up that trust fund without discussing it with me. And I think it is not a good idea. Besides, the money isn't yours 'til you turn eighteen. I *told* him not to tell you. I didn't think it was a good idea for you to even know about it."

As she looked at her son, she saw stop-motion flashes of his life from newborn to now. It made her ache with indescribable love. He had no idea how she adored him, even in his difficult, trying stages like this one. "Oh, sweetie, having all that money dumped on you without having to work for it, without appreciating what it means, without understanding what normal people go through," she reached up and touched his cheek, trying not to be too possessive. "Well, it could ruin your whole life."

He looked down.

She withdrew her touch. She knew enough not to prolong displays of affection with him, even in private. "I'm just trying to balance that crazy world of your father's with some sanity." She knew she was not getting through to him. But he had to hear it. Eventually, she so hoped, he would understand.

He looked up. "Dad says money is the only scorecard that counts. All the Wall Street guys say that. The game is net worth. Only chumps work for a salary."

She shook her head emphatically. There he goes again, parroting his father. "That's not true, honey. I know it sounds like a cliché, but money really isn't everything. It's like food. If you're hungry, you can't stop thinking about it. But when you have enough so that you don't have to worry about it every day . . ." She paused, trying to reframe her plea. "Honestly, the things that make you happy and fulfilled as a person don't come from having more and more money. Someday you'll . . ." She paused again, pretty sure she was wasting her breath on him. "Peter, I'm just trying to show you how fortunate you are." She shook her head with frustration.

She watched him look down again. Was that a little smirk he was trying to hide?

Now that the anger was gone from her voice, she guessed, and he hadn't been grounded, he must have stopped listening. He started in again, spilling out a jumble of impulses, fantasies, and addled convictions that constituted his sixteen-year-old worldview. "Geez, Mom, I don't see why we have to have such a boring lifestyle."

She watched him sweep his arm to indicate their house, a 1920s fieldstone colonial with three bedrooms and a pool on two acres in the leafy suburb of Wynnewood, just outside Philadelphia. "Dad says you do pretty well yourself. He showed me how to look up your P&B compensation on the Internet. You know, the EDGAR filings with the SEC. Anyone can, like, see them. You were there with the other senior executives. I saw your base salary, bonus, restricted stock, long-term perks, the whole thing."

She blushed as if her son had just seen her naked. "Peter!"

"We could afford to live *so* much better than this. I mean, all I've got here is one lousy room. At Dad's house in Greenwich, I've got four rooms all to myself. He calls it my West Wing—you know, like the White House. I've got my own media room with four screens, my own gaming arcade . . . ."

She felt her jaw clench. "Your father's life in Greenwich

has nothing to do with reality. *That's* what I'm trying to teach you."

"What do you mean? Like it's, you know, not *real*? He's got seventy acres, two pools, three tennis courts, all these, like, fancy hedges and gardens, a screening room with better seats than a multiplex. And this safe room! Wow. In the basement. It's got this hidden secret door. You could walk past it a hundred times and never see it. There's this whole wall of framed black-and-white pictures of the mansion back in the 1920s. And there's one picture right in the center. It's these preppy guys in white suits beside this humongous Rolls-Royce. You slide it about six inches up, and bingo, there's the keypad. Then you press the code. It's a secret—Dad made me promise not to tell anyone." He paused. "It's his birthday, backwards and inside out."

She hoped he did not see the grin she worked to suppress. Secretly she was proud her son still shared some confidences with her, however unintentionally. It proved that he still felt a powerful bond with her, even if he would never admit it.

He rambled on, "And the room's got cement walls triple-wrapped in Kevlar, with a battery-powered ventilation system. You could stay there for days and be, like, totally secret. Hey, Mom, why don't we get a safe room? It would be so cool. I could help design it. I mean, I could put it in our computer systems for, like, gaming and news reports while we're inside it and it could be so-o-o . . ."

She raised her hand. "No, we are not getting a safe room. Peter, that's another one of your father's ridiculous status symbols. He is obsessed with proving, well, I don't know what exactly." She was not about to let herself fall into the subject of men and penis size with her adolescent son. If Josh Katz were trying to compensate for something, it was not a small penis. "Your father," she said, hunting for the

right words, "your father is obsessed with proving something about money and manhood that . . . that . . . just isn't
true." Even if her message was not getting through, he *had*
to hear it. If he heard it often enough, she hoped, maybe
someday it would penetrate.

Peter looked up. "Yeah, well, *you're* obsessed with that
freakin' Acordinol!"

Again his standard counterattack, she thought. Since
she and Josh had divorced just after Peter's eighth birthday, he had grown into a master at playing the guilt card.
She bit her lip.

"I can remember as a little kid, all the time. 'Mom's got
P&B work to do. Sshhh, Mom's got a conference call,
Mom's got a report that's due.'" He struck a mock-feminine
pose—one hand on his hip, the other pointing a finger insistently. "Peter," he said, doing a sly impersonation of her,
"don't you know how *important* Acordinol is to people
around the world? It's not just a product, it's a bond of trust.
That's why I work so hard."

She felt her stomach tying into knots. A part of her
wanted to smack him, another part wanted to cry.

She felt grateful when Ned walked in from his studio
over the garage. His potter's apron was smeared brown
with wet clay, but his hands were clean. He made it a point
never to leave his studio with muddy fingers. Ned was tall
like her father but thinner, with longish hair befitting a
professor of ceramics at an art school. She sought those
warm, sensitive, deep, dark eyes, then looked again at his
strong, subtle hands. Oh, those hands. Two years after her
divorce, she took that pottery course at night school. Just
a whim. But the handsome teacher changed her life. Ned
Myers had healed the pain of her divorce.

Most of it.

Well, much of it.

Okay, enough of it to make this second marriage feel like a wondrous new beginning and a chance to enjoy grown-up fulfillment with a loving, caring husband. It was almost six years now. Ned had slipped so naturally into the role of Peter's stepfather. Even after Josh decided to insert himself back into the boy's life when he'd moved from London to Greenwich, Ned showed no resentment. He had a way of letting Peter be himself, no matter how awful the phase her son might be going through.

He gave Peter their usual fist-bump greeting. At forty-five, Ned still had the boyish energy and bounce of a teen-ager, which, to Emma's delight, made him as close to a pal for her son as a stepfather could be.

"Dude," the two guys whispered in unison in that silly testosterone-soaked way. *Men,* Emma thought, and felt another wave of gratitude for just about everything about Ned.

Ned looked back and forth between them. "I think we need a time-out here." He made a "T" gesture.

Peter looked down, nervously passing the Wii remote back and forth between his hands.

Emma sighed. No, her son had no idea how much she loved him and cared about his true happiness. How could he? He was swept up in the fury of being sixteen.

"I'm going to go visit my mother," she said. "She raised two teenage boys and lived to tell about it." She gave Peter a little smile of forgiveness. He quickly looked down. But she knew he saw it and was pretty sure he felt the love she beamed his way.

3

Josh Katz inspected himself in the triple full-length mirror.

Yeah, he liked what he saw.

He was trim, fit, and forty-four, with a full head of wavy brown hair touched by only a few strands of gray—just enough to give him that bit of gravitas that helped in tough negotiations. He felt confident of his looks, especially his big, dark eyes. Women often commented on his eyes.

But his height bothered him. Even though five-foot-eight was only slightly shorter than average, it was enough to make him feel, well . . . not defensive, no, not him, no way . . . but sometimes at a disadvantage. Even in private, here in his mahogany-paneled dressing room at Ledgemere Farm, with its rolling lawns, formal gardens, and old-growth forests on one of the most prestigious roads in Greenwich.

He felt nervous about the interview he was soon to have with the magazine reporter. He'd had mostly bad experiences with journalists. They'd all looked for ways to take cheap shots at his humble background. Like that snotty bastard from the *Times* he'd invited to his housewarming gala. The guy was all gracious and complimentary. Then he made Josh the lead in a condescending piece about the new millionaires of Greenwich titled, "The Great Katzby." Fortunately, that name never stuck. Josh was certain it was Charles Brody, his public relations man, who made it go away.

For ten minutes, he had been trying on one combination after another of designer jeans, slacks, and casual shirts—Armani to Zegna. Nothing looked right—too edgy, too young, too old. He left the discards in a pile on the floor. A distant voice sounded in his head—his mother, dead twenty years—chiding him to pick up his room. *No need, Mom,* he thought. *Don't you know I have a crew of maids?* God, how he wished she'd lived to see this.

He inspected himself again, this time in chinos and a light blue Oxford button-down shirt, the preppy work "uniform" of the contemporary hedge-fund star. Fine. Done.

He left his cavernous bedroom suite and walked across the second-floor landing to the main staircase, a wide marble balustrade of Gothic arches. He bounded down, one finger skimming the banister. He moved quickly, as if powered by little jolts of electricity. As he headed for the library, he passed under his timbered ceilings, past walk-in fireplaces, stained-glass windows, and carved woodwork. Looming behind it all, he saw something no one else could.

It was the derelict triple-decker three-family house in shabby South Boston where he grew up. He could still hear the grown-ups screeching at each other about money, still smell the putrid garbage rotting in trash cans on the curb, and the disappointment in the air. He'd left all that when he won his scholarship to the Wharton School. But that old world had never left him.

His father, Sid, retired in Florida on an allowance from Josh, had bequeathed him a mixture of absolute confidence and permanent anxiety. "You can do it, kiddo, you can do *anything*," he would say when Josh brought home another all-As report card. Meanwhile Sid was dodging collection agents or on his way to bankruptcy court. To little Josh, the world appeared always on the verge of collapse. And so from his teenage years onward, he'd devoted himself— heart and soul, mind and body—to making money.

He made his first fortune, a small one, as an investment banker in London. Then he returned to the States and started a private equity firm, Anglia Partners, with the intention of making a big one. Josh considered himself a master of the LBO, the leveraged buyout, the means by which the financier buys companies with money borrowed against the value of the to-be-acquired companies. It was a great business as long as the markets kept Anglia's numbers heading upward. His wealth on paper was heading for the $400 million mark when he bought Ledgemere in 2005. The estate was much more than just a home. It was an aggressive statement in one of the most competitive towns in the world, a declaration of his net worth and his self-worth.

But part of Josh still feared he might wake up and find himself back on the derelict street in Mattapan. When the global financial crisis triggered by the subprime melt-down hit, his nightmare began coming true. His equity positions turned to dust. The magic of leverage, the bor-rowed money that multiplied profits beyond all imagining, exploded into staggering losses. The businesses Anglia had borrowed so heavily to buy were tanking, crushed by sagging sales, a shattered economy, and their massive debt load.

A lesser deal maker would have lost everything. But Josh remade himself into a master of fancy footwork. Un-like many whose fortunes were wiped out, he "recapital-ized" discreetly, privately. He even refinanced Ledgemere when its market value fell $7 million below the balance on his mortgage. He got the money, a $500 million loan, from Viktor Volkov, the Russian he had helped turn into a billionaire back in his UK days. Josh had syndicated Viktor's deals and made the Russian a star in the City of London.

Josh stopped at the bottom of the staircase when he heard his name over the house intercom. "Mr. Katz, call from London on the satellite." It was the thick Yorkshire accent of Tom Hardacre, the estate manager he hired shortly after Viktor refinanced him. Hardacre was one of three British candidates Viktor had referred.

"Now that I hold the paper on your house," Viktor had said, "I say you need fancy English houseman. Make Greenwich people think you big shot like Duke of Westminster. Good for making deals." Hardacre—young, personable, and very tech savvy—was Josh's hands-down choice.

Hardacre's disembodied voice asked, "Shall I bring you the extension?"

"No, Tom, transfer the call to the library. I'll take it in there."

It had to be Viktor. The secure, scrambled satellite line was another thing Viktor had insisted upon. No one but Viktor, Josh, and Hardacre even knew it existed.

Josh opened the door to the library, a half-timbered shrine almost the size of the gym at his old high school. Beneath towering shelves of antique volumes bought by the yard, Charles Brody stood at a side table. He was arranging trophy pictures of Josh with the famous and powerful.

"Hey, Josh," he called, "what took you so long?" He turned to inspect his boss. "You look good, man. Hey, we've got a decision point here." Brody gestured at the lineup of expensive frames. "In the front row, do we put Josh Katz with the presidents or movie stars?"

He gave Brody a distracted wave as he headed for his desk. "Just let me take this call. Five minutes, eh, Brodes." Josh used pluralized nicknames for his intimates, a habit he picked up in England.

Brody, a portly man four inches taller than Josh and fifteen years older, closed the door as he left. After Brody's footsteps faded, Josh picked up the handset with its fat, stubby antenna. He looked at the screen. No other extensions active.

"Viktor," he said, "what's up?"

"I see you register with SEC."

"I told you," Josh said, "we had to as soon as we hit five percent. That's automatic."

Even though Josh had ceded control to Viktor, to the world at large, he was still in charge at Anglia. That was the beauty of the "private" part of private equity. He well understood how the line between bullshit and reality blurred on Wall Street. He knew how to bluff away the predatory bastards. Besides, he told himself, he still knew how to manage Viktor.

"What they think, this management at P&B?" Viktor asked.

"I don't know what they think. Our papers say our only intention is to be a passive investor. They didn't issue a statement. But I know they hired Mike Saltzman. He's the big gun in takeover defense law."

"Our lawyer is bigger gun, yes?"

"Of course, Viktor. Dietrich Willoughby are the biggest guns around."

Anglia had fronted several corporate takeovers for Viktor's global empire since getting the giant loan. Anglia took over the target companies, with the world unaware that Viktor's money was providing the cash. Then Josh would break up the companies and sell off the pieces, with Viktor and his unnamed partners acquiring the assets they wanted. Always behind the veil of shell companies and offshore trusts. Viktor never told Josh why he wanted those companies. And Josh never asked, until now. Until the Russian gave the order to start buying Percival & Baxter stock.

"Say, Viktor," Josh had said, "Percival & Baxter will be complicated for me. My ex-wife is a senior executive there. Taking over this company is going to create personal problems for me. And when the press picks up this ex-spouse angle, it could make things messy as hell." Josh had then squirmed, waiting for Viktor's response. He was sweating missing the next scheduled $55 million payment on his loan.

"Is *your* problem," Viktor had said, "not mine."

Josh had had to bite his lip. But he had no choice. With the spoils from just one more takeover, he'd pay Viktor back and get him out of his life. He hated that it had to be Emma's company. And that this might destroy his relationship with her once and for all. Worse, Emma might then turn Peter against him. Even worse, Peter might naturally side with his mom and turn against him on his own. *That* could be impossible to fix.

So he thought he might bring it up again today. Get Viktor interested in a sexier drug company with a bigger upside. He could still sell the 5 percent stake in P&B as easily as he had bought it.

"Viktor," he said, straining to sound casual, "we have looked at a few of the most attractive pharmas out there. I brought you Advantix, GeneQuest, Equinome, and Healthvision. All with bigger upside than P&B. And I did show you the numbers. Why P&B? It's an old-line blue-chip stock. Viktor, the price is just too damn high."

"I have reasons," Viktor said, just as before. "You get

deal done, you pay back my loans. Then . . . ," he added with a sneer, "then you get me out of your bed."

Josh knew that settled it.

Viktor was referring to an event years earlier. After a late night of crunching numbers at the Belgravia mansion, Viktor had invited him to stay over in one of the guest rooms. During the night, Viktor's silky little Tanya snuck into Josh's room and climbed into his bed. The fourteen-year-old girl was naked and drunk. She snuggled up against him, clumsily trying to seduce him. Josh threw a shirt on her and whisked her out the door. Viktor heard the commotion and stuck his head out into the hall just in time to see a woozy Tanya staggering from Josh's bedroom in nothing but a man's shirt.

At breakfast the next morning, Viktor asked about it.

"Nothing happened," Josh insisted. "Tanya must have made a wrong turn in the dark." He turned to the girl. "Tell your father the truth, Tanya. Tell your father that *nothing* happened."

"Nothing happened, Papa," Tanya said obediently. Then, turning back to her toast and tea, she muttered something in Russian that made Viktor glare.

Josh would have loved to tell Viktor to shove it. But for now, he had to suck it up and take it.

"Yes," Josh said softly, swallowing his punishment, "I will get your deal done. I will pay you back and *we* will get out of bed." It couldn't happen soon enough.

Viktor hung up.

Josh wondered if he might get lucky. Maybe one of the gigantic global pharmas would step in and outbid Viktor. Once P&B was in play, anything could happen. One of the monoliths like Novartis or Roche or Johnson & Johnson might pay a whopping premium. Having tried would fulfill his obligation to Viktor. And maybe, just maybe, get him off the hook with Emma and Peter.

But no way could he count on that happening.

So if this had to be the deal that would do it, hell, he'd figure out a way to get through it.

4

"He never talks to me anymore," Emma said as she followed her mother around the garden of the small, comfortable ranch-style house where she lived happily by herself. "He won't even make eye contact. Sometimes when I walk into a room, he gets up and leaves. And it's not like I even said anything."

"Now don't get melodramatic, sweetie," Diane Conway said. An older version of her daughter, Diane had the same short hair, now white, the same high cheekbones, somewhat finer features, and wrinkles that gave her face warmth and wisdom. With mother and daughter both dressed for gardening, in clogs, jeans, and old shirts, they rhymed even more than usual. "That's teenage boys for you," Diane said with an amused sigh.

"Were John and Gil like that?" Emma asked, referring to her two older brothers. John, now a professor of English in Seattle, Gil, an engineer in Baltimore, both married with kids.

Diane nodded. "I think they were a little more obnoxious than Peter. Depending on the phases they were going through. Gil was, for sure. He was impossible. John not so bad, but the oldest usually hides it better." She crouched down effortlessly into a deep full squat to pull some weeds.

Emma sat down beside her. She admired her mother's fitness and flexibility, hoped she had inherited those genes. "But I can't stop worrying about Peter," she said. "I'm afraid he believes all that money-is-everything talk he gets when he's with Josh. He's just a boy. He doesn't know *anything*."

"Of course he doesn't," Diane said. "Teenage boys are physically incapable of thought. But it's not their fault." She winked. "There's no blood left over for their brains."

Mother and daughter laughed.

"Listen, honey," Diane said, "you've got to relax a little. Stop trying to control everything. Peter's a good kid. You've done a great job with him, divorce or no. And Ned's wonderful. No one can ruin that boy, not even Josh Katz. Now I must say, Peter does play those computer games an awful lot. But I think that's just a phase. Shall I remind you of some of *your* more trying times? Like when you threw yourself so passionately at Henry Mills on that lacrosse team."

Emma winced.

"By the way, I never breathed a word to your father about you getting birth control."

"Really?"

"Never. You don't think he would have been able to spend all that time with Henry talking about those matches if he had known what the captain and his little angel were doing?"

"I guess not." Emma brightened.

"Let him be," Diane said. "Cut the boy a little slack and you'll become friends again when he matures."

"From your lips . . ." Emma said, shaking her head. The BlackBerry in her waist pack started to chirp. She looked at the screen ID. Bradley Johansen. "Sorry, Mom, I have to take this." She stood and walked a few steps away.

"Brad?" Emma said, wondering what the CEO would want from her on a Saturday morning.

"Emma, sorry to bother you," Brad said.

"Not at all," she said.

"At the close of trading yesterday, one of those corporate raiders filed a 13-D. They'd been quietly acquiring our stock and yesterday they hit the five percent mark. Officially, they are just passive investors, but that's what they always say. We're having a conference call with our key board members this afternoon. We're preparing a strategy before they go any further."

"Well, if there's anything you think I can do, just tell me," Emma said, wondering why Brad would be consulting her about a matter far removed from her responsibilities as a divisional president. He had defended Percival & Baxter against takeover attempts before and never consulted her. "But why," she asked, "are you calling *me*?"

"Uh, Emma, we, er, uh . . ." Brad stammered. Strange, he was rarely at a loss for words. "This raider runs a private equity fund." He paused again. "Anglia Partners. I assume you're familiar with it."

Her heart sank. "My ex-husband," she said. Here she was struggling to rescue their son from him. Now her company? No, this was too much, way too much. She believed in P&B, in the lives it saved, the good people it supported. And goddamn it, she *loved* her career, loved belonging there, being one of the leaders. Her dad had been priming her to be a Percival & Baxter leader, like he was, since she was a teenager. Emma wanted to scream. That *bastard*! He had to know about this. What the *hell* was he doing? She stood clutching the BlackBerry, as if by tightening her grip on it she could choke Josh Katz.

She still could feel the sting of that afternoon years before in London, when Peter was just a baby, when she was pushing the stroller down Mount Street and she turned the corner. There was Josh, tongue-kissing the svelte Italian countess right outside the Connaught Hotel. Emma a sleep-deprived mess, still carrying baby weight that was supposed to have melted away but hadn't. Josh picture-perfect in his pinstripe suit, only his tie slightly askew.

She stood there, wanting to cry, to scream, but couldn't make a sound. Baby Peter broke the silence. He shrieked because he dropped his pacifier.

That was the day she realized she'd have to forge a life independent of Josh.

"Emma, if this turns into a fight," Brad said hesitantly, "it, uh, could get complica—"

"Brad," she cut in, "this is Pete Conway's daughter you're talking to. If there's going to be a fight to keep us independent—absolutely—count me in."

"That's what I thought you'd say. Next step is the poison pill. The board vote is coming up. No raider has beaten a poison pill in the thirty years they've been around."

"That's reassuring," she said.

"We certainly hope so."

The call ended.

Diane walked up to her. "What's wrong, sweetie?"

"Mom, first he's trying to ruin Peter," Emma said, shaking her head. "And now he wants to destroy Percival & Baxter."

"What? Josh?"

"That fund of his, Anglia Partners. They're buying up P&B stock. I've read about what those guys do. They take over companies, perfectly good companies, and destroy them. They fire half the people and sell off the parts like scrap iron."

"Honey, P&B has fought off raiders before," Diane said. "I remember your father talking about that fight with the oil patch guy. And Dad said that Brad's a born fighter. It'll work out, I'm sure."

Emma stared into the distance.

"Emma?"

Diane tapped her.

No response.

Diane took her by the shoulders and gave her a little shake. "Emma?"

"What, Mom?"

"I said, it'll work out."

"Yeah," Emma said distractedly.

"They're sharks, those Wall Street guys. Predators. It's just what they do."

"But why come after P&B?"

"I have no idea, sweetie. Isn't it always about money?"

Mother and daughter stood silent, arm in arm, for a long moment.

Diane spoke first. "You know, if it turns into a war for the company, *you've* got an unbeatable advantage."

"I do?"

"Yes, you do."

"Really?"

"Absolutely. You used to be married to this particular raider. You don't just know the son of a bitch. You know him better than he knows himself."

Emma dropped her BlackBerry back into her waist pack and forced a smile. "I hope you're right."

"Of course I'm right. I'm your mother."

5

Josh pressed the intercom again. "Brodes? Brodes?"
Nothing.

"Hey, Brodes, come back. Let's finish prepping for the interview."

Still no answer.

"Brodes? Where are you?"

"On my way," Brody mumbled through the speaker. He sounded like he had a mouth full of food. In the kitchen, as usual.

He and Brody went back almost twenty years. Brody had gotten him his first deal publicity when Josh was still a novice. As Josh's deals grew, he'd helped his loyal flack establish Brody & Company. He watched with pride as the PR firm and its owner got fatter.

The library door opened. Brody appeared, out of breath. "The reporter should be here soon," he said, rebuttoning the navy blue suit jacket he always wore.

"I-I don't know about this interview," Josh said, feeling his anxiety return. "Maybe it's not such a great idea."

"I tell you, Josh, this will be different." Brody patted him on the shoulder. "This is *Town & Country*. They appreciate your accomplishments, your taste. This will be different, I promise."

"I hope so, Brodes, I hope so." Josh scanned his library, as if looking for any flaw that might betray him. He did a mental inventory of the mansion and its contents, the gardens, grounds, and their key appointments. It was perfect, all of it. Josh had paid experts top dollar to make sure there was not one false note, not a single lapse in taste anywhere—from the artfully untrimmed wisteria climbing up the gothic colonnade to the naughty Picasso etchings in the guest bathrooms.

He took a deep breath. No, not another public embarrassment. "I don't need another reporter taking cheap shots."

"Trust me," Brody said. "After this piece comes out, you'll sail right through membership committee at Greenwich Links." The old-money club had rejected Josh twice. It galled him, especially since he lived in the house of the very man who had built the damn place.

Brody walked back to the side table to finish his picture arranging.

"Brodes," Josh said, "put the celebrity ones in the back. I like the one of me and Peter digging wells on the water project in Tanzania." He smiled. *What a great time we had on that trip,* he thought. *Just us, two guys sharing an adventure. Peter was so wide-eyed. How close we felt in our own little father-and-son bubble.*

"That's just what I was about to suggest," Brody said and moved that picture in front of all the others.

Josh grinned. "We just won't mention that two minutes after the shot was taken, His Nibs got the runs and had to be helicoptered out." Calling his son "His Nibs" was another British-ism Josh was fond of.

"How *is* Peter doing?" Brody asked.

"He's great," Josh said, then shook his head. "He's sixteen. What can I say?" He stared out the window, wishing he understood Peter. "He's a mystery. Always alone with those computer games. But I guess that's okay. All the kids do that, right?" He paused again. "I'm, uh, pretty sure he likes girls. I try to get him invited to parties with kids his own age on his weekends up here. I got him into this club for well-fixed kids. It's called Kroesus Kids. That's some name, huh? They've got a party coming up at Angus McLeod's place. Kids flying in from all over the world."

Josh loved the miracles money could create. It did heal the hurt of a lifetime of failure for his father. Snap! Just like that. He was sure it could give his son a sense of expansive possibilities he himself could never have imagined when he was growing up. It could instill in his boy the kind of confidence that only came from being rich. At least he hoped Peter was getting all this from the money he showered on him. But it was hard to know, hard to tell where his own guilt left off and his teenage son's normal moodiness began.

He turned back to Brody. "Say, how's *your* boy doing? Does his house need anything?"

"Nah," Brody said, "all fine." Thirty-year-old Sean Brody was mentally retarded and lived in a group home on Long Island. Josh made regular donations to the foundation that ran the place, and gifts of new televisions, furniture, and chocolates.

The cell phone in his pocket started vibrating. He checked the screen. A Percival & Baxter corporate cell number. Had to be Emma. Oh shit. He pushed answer.

"Josh, this is Emma," she said curtly.

"Emma," he said, forcing a smile as he turned his back to Brody. "Nice to hear from you. What a surprise."

"Surprise? *Surprise?* You *know* what I'm calling about."

He had no answer. His troubles with Emma had officially begun. Thanks, Viktor, you fucking monster!

"Why are you going after Percival & Baxter?" Emma enunciated each word slowly. Josh shriveled from the chill in her voice, the icy tone she used to take at the end of their worst fights—after she had recovered from crying.

"I'm not going after your company, Emma." He hoped he sounded innocent. "I'm just an investor looking for opportunities."

"Josh, I've seen what you do in your hostile takeovers and it's—"

"Emma, Emma, just a minute," he heard himself talking over her. He realized he was falling back on how he'd pleaded when his cheating broke up their marriage.

He'd loved Emma then.

He loved her still, but in a way he did not understand.

He was just starting to get rich back then. A new world was opening up, tempting him with possibilities he would never have dared to dream about. Suddenly women—gorgeous, hot, new women—who wanted to play with him.

He had not wanted to leave Emma and Peter. Just needed a few other women once in a while. The way he needed Ledgemere, the way he needed his sleek Bentley. To prove to himself—and the world—that he actually could have them.

Still, he kept that snapshot of Emma in the secret compartment of his George I desk. That old honeymoon picture with her love note scrawled on the back. And the lock of her straight blond hair. Emma smiling at him in front of that lost pond in the New Hampshire woods. Just seconds after he'd snapped it, she'd peeled off her hiking clothes and stood there naked, teasing him, daring him to relax and let loose for once. He could still see her, his wood nymph, as she dove into the water. She haunted him. He stared at the inlaid panel that covered the secret drawer.

"Emma," he said, "this is just business. I'm a shareholder, a passive investor. That's what the SEC filing says. And it's true." He knew his words were empty. When the moment came, his lawyers would file another paper stating revised intentions.

"Uh-huh, right, Josh. Should I dig into this with someone from one of the now-dead companies you destroyed?"

"Emma, come on."

"Josh, tell me this much. What put it in your head to start buying Percival & Baxter? Don't you know we have defeated takeovers before? Is one of the big pharmas putting you up to this? Is it Pfizer, Roche, Novartis?"

"Emma, Anglia is making investments in a number of companies." He was trying to act as if this was not the woman with whom he had shared a bed, a baby, and countless memories. "Our analysis put P&B high on the list. After all, I think that, uh, with executives like you, P&B *must* be a great investment."

"Oh Christ, Josh, don't bullshit me."

What else could he do? His relationship with Emma, such as it was, was about to get crushed. And as for Peter, well, who knew what would happen?

"Emma, the last thing I want to do is create more bad feeling," he said. And that he meant. "This is just business."

"Is that so?" she said flatly.

He could tell that their talk was about to end. "Really, I mean it," he said, trying to sound earnest. *Lame,* he thought.

The line went dead. He put the cell down.

Brody looked at him questioningly. "You knew this would happen. Are you sure it's worth it?"

Josh dared not reveal the real story. "From a personal standpoint, I knew this was going to be a goddamn disaster," he said. "But from a business standpoint, I believe it's the right decision."

Brody gave an obedient nod.

Hardacre's voice sounded on the intercom. "Mr. Katz, the reporter has arrived."

Brody answered. "Please, Tom, let her in."

"Aye, sir. You want me to bring her to the library?"

Brody leaned over the house phone. "No, Tom, just escort her to the front entrance hall. I'll bring Mr. Katz."

"Aye, sir."

"And Tom," Brody continued, "please let Miss Longstreet linger long enough to, you know, take in the grandeur of the space and the architectural details."

"Anything specific I should point out?"

"No, just let her stand there. She's a journalist and a snob. She'll get it."

"Aye, sir."

Brody gave Josh a wink as he shut off the intercom. "I promise you, she's not your traditional ink-stained wretch."

6

As Penelope Longstreet made the turn toward the gates of Ledgemere Farm, she clutched the wheel of the silver Maserati even tighter. Her hands were sweaty. She would make sure they were dry by the time she went inside. She felt nervous about meeting Josh Katz. After researching him for three weeks, she felt as if she knew him, that he was not a typical Wall Street blowhard. Yes, of course a player, a powerhouse, a man to be reckoned with. But she also entertained the possibility that perhaps he was not shallow and obsessed with money and appearances like so many of the hotshots she had dated and been used by. Not like Barton, that blue-blood banker she had almost married last year.

She wasn't nervous about the article she was supposed to write. She was nervous because she'd become convinced Josh Katz might be more than the too-obvious symbols of success that surrounded him suggested. She didn't know why exactly. Or maybe she did. The feeling had overtaken her one night at her desk at the magazine, looking at pictures of him with his son Peter on the website of the Water for Africa Project. There was something about the way he gazed at the boy. That gaze looked to her like love and pride and a need to be connected. She was sure of it. Well, almost.

She had gone over his life in detail. He had been married for eight years to his first wife. This Emma Conway was a seriously independent woman with a serious career of her own. Penelope thought she could see how their lives had gone in different directions, but she felt that it said a lot about Josh's character to have been married to a woman of substance like Emma. And he had not done the usual rich guy thing and married a vapid young trophy wife on the rebound. Sure, there were lots of party pictures of Josh with girls who were clearly arm candy. But none of them had lasted. She felt he must be searching for a real grown-up partner. Plus, he not only supported his father in Florida with a nice condo and new car every year, he also gave him a generous allowance for losing at the race track. He indulged his old man, spoiling him like a child. Penelope thought she knew why he had that kind of family loyalty. Like her, Josh was from the wrong side of the tracks in Boston. They had both made it into to this high-style world without forgetting what they'd learned growing up. So there would be more they would share, much more. She loved imagining the life she could have with him.

But she was also nervous about anything happening to the fancy car she had borrowed from Jill, her best friend from their years as "Ford girls" at the modeling agency.

"Go on, take it," Jill had insisted, after fetching Penelope at the Greenwich train station. "Todd's in Singapore at another investor conference. I'm telling you, he won't mind."

"But what if someone bangs into it?" Penelope had asked as she and her friend stood in the four-bay garage beside Jill and Todd's new mansion. The shingle-style house had two turrets, one on either side of the second floor, and a central tower with a widow's walk protruding from the roof over the third floor. It had ells sprawling out in three directions and four double chimneys. A lovely house, Penelope thought, but it left her cold. It looked like it had been built more to impress people outside it than to cuddle the people inside it. Josh Katz, on the other hand, had lovingly restored a historic landmark.

"Don't worry," Jill said, giving her friend a hug and pressing the car key into her hand. "You're going through the gates of Ledgemere Farm. You've got to look like you belong. Besides," she said, waving at the green Aston Martin and the red Ferrari flanking them, "those two are the only cars Todd really cares about. I know because he won't let me drive them. Ever. The Maserati is his run-around-and-do-errands car if he doesn't need the cargo space in my Range Rover."

Penelope smirked, "He uses *this* for errands?"

"Welcome to Greenwich," Jill said, opening the car door. "Seriously, it only looks like a sports car. It's got four doors and an automatic shift. Anybody can drive it."

Penelope steered the Maserati close to the intercom box alongside Ledgemere's towering gates. She leaned her head out of the window, pushed the call button, and announced herself. "Penelope Longstreet for Mr. Katz."

"Just a meeeenit," a woman with an indeterminate accent replied.

A long moment later, a man spoke, "Welcome, Miss Longstreet, we've been expecting you. Please drive up to the porte cochere." Penelope recognized the odd British accent of Tom Hardacre, Josh's estate manager.

The gates made an ominous clunking sound and swung open. She took a deep breath and drove forward.

This anticipation was the best, she thought. You could idealize how perfect everything would be. How incredibly perfect. But what if things didn't work out that way? No, no, don't think like that, she told herself. Besides, she would be testing Josh Katz to see if *he* had the stuff she thought he had.

She was surprised at the racket the tires made crunching over the perfectly raked gravel. She knew that Josh was between girlfriends. Yes, she had double-confirmed that. She also liked that Josh had been turned down by the old-money golf course that bordered his estate. Same awful club Barton had dragged her to.

As she reached the porte cochere, she hit the brakes a little too hard and got thrown forward, almost bumping her chin on the steering wheel. She looked around. She was pretty sure no one saw her. She took a tissue from her prized vintage Birkin bag and dried her hands. She yanked the rearview mirror to one side to take one last look at herself. Brush the hair back in place. Touch up the lipstick. A confident smile. Dab that bit of lipstick off her front teeth and smile again. Yes, she still had the looks that once made her a top Ford girl, only now more womanly. And wise. Yes, she had the glamour the outer Josh wanted and the substance the inner Josh really needed. She slipped off her ballet flats and pulled out her Christian Louboutin pumps.

She had it all planned. Be bold. Be aggressive . . . but charming. Be sexy and seductive. And if you feel him responding, let nature take its course. One more breath strip on her tongue and off she went.

7

Viktor finished knotting the solid blue tie that matched the bold blue stripes in his spread-collar shirt. He then slipped on the single-breasted jacket of his gray chalk-stripe suit, and looked himself up and down. Every stitch had been custom made for him. Yes, fine British tailoring did give a look of dignity. He turned from the mirror in his mahogany dressing room.

"*Nu kak?*" he asked Artyom. How is it?

"Like an English nobleman," Artyom said, "like you just came from the most exclusive club on Pall Mall."

"It will be a private dining room at the Connaught," Viktor said. "Everything perfect for her. Candlelight, champagne." He looked down to inspect his black Chelsea boots from John Lobb. He'd had the valet polish them four times. "Seriously, Artyomchik, do I look all right?"

Artyom nodded emphatically as he stuffed two pastries into his mouth. Crumbs tumbled all around him.

No, Viktor thought. *Take Arytom with me where I am going? No, I couldn't.* He fidgeted with his suit jacket. "Adeline's family goes back a thousand years to William the Conqueror. No money left, but she has the taste and breeding. It's in her blood. She's invited to the Duke of Westminster's. Imagine, the duke himself." Viktor sighed. "I think tonight I propose to her. Yes, tonight."

"Propose?" Artyom said, nearly choking on his last

mouthful. "I've never heard you talk marriage since Alexandra died. Not once in ten years. Viktor Viktorovich, what in the name of God does this Adeline have?"

In business, Viktor's decisions were clear-cut and logical. But with Adeline, he felt his mind tumble into a fog. She had everything he needed for his new life. The perfect woman to accompany him and make his great fortune noble and aristocratic. Elegant, refined, and so very well-connected. He felt attracted to her like a moth to the light. And if—no *when* Tanya married Adeline's younger brother Percy, they would have sons, sons with Viktor's blood *and* the Montifer title.

"She is most beautiful," he said, unsure how much to reveal.

"Ah, a beauty." Artyom now was eager. "How young? Twenty-five? Young bodies, they are so thrilling. That young skin . . ."

"No, no, no! Not young," Viktor snapped. "Maybe forty, maybe a little older. I'm sick of the young ones. All silly and empty."

He folded his arms across his chest and took a deep breath. "She knew Alexandra," he said solemnly.

"Oh, I see." Artyom looked down.

Viktor paused, letting the memory of his beloved Alexandra resonate for a respectful moment. "Yes, like Alexandra but only in some ways. Also very different."

"How long have you been seeing her?"

"Ascot last month. I walked into the wrong box by accident. Suddenly, I'm surrounded by these English aristos, all too proper. I decide to stay a minute just to see. These people, they really know how to ignore you. You could set yourself on fire and they pretend not to see. So I stand, alone in this crowd of snobs. Even the waiters avoid me. Then she walks up and introduces herself. Gets the waiter to get me a drink. Very confident, this woman. Said she had been a school friend of Alexandra's. Met me once when Tanya was a baby. I did not remember. But now . . . now? I can't get her out of my mind."

"Viktor, could be you are in love."

Viktor shrugged. "Believe me," he said, "she is the rare one who understands how much better a man must be to make a fortune than to inherit one. She says I am like those men who built the British empire. Yes, men with the balls to take what was theirs for the taking. She said she knew I *had* to be away from Alexandra during the Yeltsin years. Too dangerous in Russia for mother and baby in those days. If Alexandra had been more mature, she says, she would have understood."

He peered into Artyom's eyes. "She says if Alexandra had lived, she would have come to forgive me." He gave his old friend a sad glance, remembering Alexandra's anger at the separate life he'd lived in Russia.

Viktor's mood suddenly brightened. "I have an idea, Artyomchik." He walked to his house phone and dialed.

"Roger," he said to his majordomo, switching to his heavily accented English, "I need most beautiful orchid in London for my dinner with Lady Adeline tonight. How quickly you find me most beautiful orchid in London? I no care what she costs."

"But sir, the shops are closing just now."

"Roger, you find most expensive shop. Most expensive shop with most expensive orchid. You do this now. You pay them to stay open. You pay them anything they want. You get me most beautiful orchid on island of Great Britain. Pay anything. Understand?"

"Yes, sir, right away." Roger hung up.

Still holding the phone, Viktor gave Artyom a wink and spoke as if Roger were still on the line. "Roger, make *sure*

you pay too much. Make good gossip for newspaper."
Viktor smirked as he hung up. He loved to drive the hard
bargain in business. Breaking the other guy's balls was
the joy of it. But other times, he enjoyed overspending.
One of the pleasures of paying too much was tossing off a
staggering price tag as if it were pocket change.

Artyom smirked in return. "And after the poisoned pills
my sons arranged make our deal happen, we'll all splurge
together. You said, it will be better than a gold mine, yes?"

"Yes, Artyomchik, I did," he replied, distracted. He was
fretting about Adeline and the orchid at the moment. He
turned his back to Artyom and stared out at Belgrave Park.

"Viktor Viktorovich," Artyom said.

Viktor remained facing the windows.

"Viktor Viktorovich," Artyom repeated.

Viktor turned back to face him, trying not to show his
annoyance. "Yes?"

"Viktor Viktorovich, my sons are asking if they can
maybe get a bigger share of the deal for their contribution."

"Not now, Artyom, please. We can talk business
later." The phone rang and he grabbed it eagerly. "Yes,
Roger?"

"Sir," the servant said, "I've contacted the florist that
supplies Her Majesty's private apartments at the palace.
They have a rare hybrid, a cross between a Sweet Vengeance and a Princess Kalitia. They say it is very rare indeed and quite spectacular. They are keeping the shop open
for us. At great expense, just as you instructed."

Viktor nodded at Artyom. "Good, Roger. You get this
rare orchid from queen's special florist." He was talking
more to Artyom than to Roger. "Go in Daimler. Take bodyguards in Land Rovers, too. No, no. Go in Rolls and take
bodyguards. Make more impressive scene, yes?"

"Yes, sir, much more impressive."

"Go!" Viktor commanded.

He felt good for a moment. Powerful. Masterful. Brilliant. Then a pang gripped him. Was he overplaying his hand? Were his shoes too shiny? His tie too bright? The stripes on his shirt too bold? Was his suit too new, too pressed, too perfect?

That's why he needed Adeline. She knew all this stuff and so much more.

He felt adrift, the ticking clock of mortality drowning out everything. Adeline, with her beauty, bloodline, and titled little brother. They could be the last chance for his dynasty. His very last.

8

Josh started taking in Penelope Longstreet well before he and Brody reached Ledgemere's entry hall. His eyes followed her long legs up to the short skirt, then on to the plunging neckline of the skimpy summer blouse. Her back was arched, throwing her breasts forward, her long neck curving, what looked like double-process blond hair cascading behind. She appeared to be studying his intricately carved ceiling.

Somewhere in her mid-thirties, her striking looks told Josh she was once a model. He could tell. He had dated models. He paid scant attention to fashion, but he did recognize her two expensive items, the black Hermès Birkin handbag on her arm, and, judging from the red soles of her towering heels, shoes by Christian Louboutin.

"Penelope!" Brody called as they approached.

She turned and seemed to light up. "Charles, I'm so glad we could finally get our schedules to click." She offered Brody her hand like a queen greeting a subject.

"Penelope, allow me to introduce Josh Katz," Brody said.

She stood a moment with hands on her hips, looking intently at her interviewee. "So, we finally get to meet the owner of this town's finest old estate. I have been researching you for several weeks." Josh felt her eyes riveted on his. "I must say, I feel as if I already know you."

To Josh's ear, her accent rang of old money, private

schools, and debutante balls. "Well," he said, hoping to turn on the charm, "I think it's only fair that I get the chance to get to know *you* just as well." He felt an immediate attraction to her. He just wished to hell she were not a goddamn journalist.

"I will tell you absolutely anything you want to know about me. Shall we make a deal, Mr. Katz?" She offered her hand.

"Please, it's Josh," he said as he took it. Penelope did not shake his hand. She held it, her fingers nestling into his, making the most of the touch of his skin against hers, lingering, then slowly, letting go.

Josh was transfixed. It felt like her eyes were looking inside him. He liked the feeling. "Uh, when Brodes told me to forget the stereotype of the ink-stained wretch, I had no idea."

"Oh please," she said, placing her fingertips between her breasts, as if directing his gaze there, "inside, I am completely ink stained and thoroughly wretched."

She's flirting, he thought. *Perfect.* He loved flirting. Even when it went nowhere, flirting made you feel so alive.

"Me too," he whispered at her ear.

"Ink stained?" she whispered back.

"No," he smiled, "wretched." He made a comic frown and tapped his heart.

He wanted to continue their banter, but a thought of Viktor crossed his mind. He looked at the floor instead. Fucking Viktor.

Brody interrupted them. "Penelope used to be a fashion model before she became a writer," he said.

I knew it, Josh thought.

"Achhh! Another life," she said dismissively. "You know that pout the girls on the runway have?" She puckered her lips and faked a haughty glance. "They're not being stylish. They're just hungry. As in, I haven't had a full meal since middle school."

She led the men in a little laugh, let a silence develop, then spoke as if making an announcement. "You know, they say a great man's home is a reflection of his inner self. Wouldn't you agree . . . Josh?" She spoke his name softly, cooing it, giving it almost two syllables.

He lowered his eyes to appear modest. In fact, he was imagining all the delights of her. In those heels, she was almost two inches taller than he. So what? Having a taller gorgeous woman on his arm had always been part of the thrill of dating models.

"For instance," she said as she arched her back again, throwing her breasts forward. "This fanned gothic ceiling reminds me of Wells Cathedral, the chapter house."

He nodded, impressed. "I see you've done your homework. As you probably know, I lived in Britain. So when I saw this property, well, it just resonated with m-m-m-my inner self." He had a feeling this woman would be perfect for his mild British stammer.

Brody turned to leave. "Penelope, your office will work with Tom Hardacre to schedule the photo shoot?"

"Yes, they're on it," she said, keeping her eyes on Josh.

"Okay, looks like you guys don't need any more help from me."

Brody opened the great gothic front door to reveal the silver Maserati. He did a double take. "Is that *yours,* Penelope?" he asked as he stepped outside.

"Uh, it's not my cah," she said, sounding uneasy, "it belongs to a friend. I'm, uh, in between vehicles of my own."

Josh started at the sound of the "r" dropped from "car." As a native of South Boston, he knew that low-rent accent. Penelope was no debutante. And as for being "in between vehicles," well, probably she was broke and spending her last dollar on keeping up her high-end look. So, her charade was like his own. He felt drawn to her even more.

Brody said "so long" as he closed the door. Neither Josh nor Penelope responded. Their eyes were locked together. He thought her gaze was saying she was interested in him as a man, not just as a story. At least he hoped so.

They smiled at the same instant with their eyes locked. *Yes,* he thought, *there's a spark.* To hell with the magazine article. He would find a way to date her. He was good at falling in love. And he did it with panache. His problems came with the follow-through. Relationships required, well, work. And his work plate was always too damn full. What was worse—and he hated himself for it—he found himself measuring every woman he tried to love against Emma. And sooner or later, they all came up short.

Penelope took a step back and crossed her arms across her chest. She stared at him as if inspecting a piece of furniture. "You know, I am very angry with your Charles Brody." She cupped his jaw firmly in her hand.

"Why?" he asked, enjoying the commanding way she held him.

"Charles did not tell me about your eyes. You have beautiful eyes. Dark and mysterious, Mr. Josh Katz." Her breath was sweet in his face. "Women have told you that before."

He looked down, embarrassed. Yes, women had told him that. Most of all Emma, when they first fell in love. "Uh-huh," he mumbled.

She had taken control of him. And he did like it. Oh, yes, he did.

She let go of his face. He wished she hadn't.

"You are a very interesting man. More interesting than most men in your position."

"What makes you think so?" he asked playfully.

"I just know it," she said. She tapped her heart again—and her left breast. "Most Wall Street men are one-dimensional moneymaking machines. Net worth is all they care about. But I can tell you've got more character and depth. For instance, your choice of this estate. For most, it would have been a teardown. Replace it with something postmodern, overdone with architectural geegaws that scream 'I'm rich.' Your restoration shows respect. And something else we see very little of in Greenwich."

"What's that?"

"Restraint." She gave him a sly smile. "You strike me as a man who can . . . hold himself back when it's appropriate."

Josh found her little double entendre outrageous and encouraging.

"Yes, as a matter of fact, I can," he said with pride.

She reached into her Birkin and pulled out a tiny digital recorder about the size of a stubby cigar. She waved it in a way that Josh could have sworn made it seem like a sex toy. He had no idea what she might do next. And he could hardly wait to find out.

"We're not going to use this today," she said as she dropped it back into the Hermès sac. "Today is not our interview. I want to meet the man behind those dark eyes . . . off the record." She took hold of his face again, keeping their eyes locked.

He loved how forward she was. And outrageous. "You, uh, still want to bother with the house tour?" he asked.

"We could, but really, I'm more interested in the man than the manse."

"Clever phrase."

"Not mine. I borrowed it from my editor." She gave a deep sigh. "I've borrowed quite a lot to become the person I am now, Josh Katz." Suddenly, he heard no more debutante in her voice. She turned and faced him with a new, more penetrating gaze. "Same as you."

"Yes," he said as he took both of her hands in his, "I think we have a lot in common, Penelope Longstreet."

Penelope gave his hands a little squeeze. Their shared touch felt good. It felt right. That was a good sign. *No, a great sign,* she thought.

She leaned into him and whispered in his ear, "I saw you flinch when I said 'cah.' I didn't mean for it to slip out, but it did." She brought her lips close enough to kiss his earlobe. Then she let go of him. She was sure she could feel his excitement.

"That's how my relatives talk. Know those triple-deckers in the back streets of Somerville?" She repeated the word with a full Boston intonation. "Summaah-ville. That's where I grew up. Kind of like your Mattapan. It was the modeling in New York that drilled the accent out of me. Well, most of it. They sold me as their girl with the society look. Couldn't talk that way if I wanted speaking roles in commercials. But my accent slips out when I get nervous. Didn't you ever talk that way?"

"No," he said, "I never really picked it up. My mother was from Ohio and she did most of the talking in our house."

She smiled, then turned serious. "She died twenty years ago, didn't she? Do you still miss her?" She watched his reaction closely.

He paused and looked away, as if reviewing fond memories but with sadness. She liked that.

He turned and looked into her eyes. "I would have liked for her to see all this."

Penelope could not stop herself from taking his hand again. "She would have been so proud," she said. She pulled him toward the door that opened onto the gardens. "Let's go outside, okay? I'm really *not* interviewing you today."

"I'm glad, Penelope," he said as they walked through the door. "Say, do you like being called Penelope? Or do you pre—?"

She put a finger over his lips. "Pen. Like a pen. I'm a writer now."

"Okay, Pen it is." He said it again, "Pen." He gave her hand a little squeeze.

They walked out onto the flagstone path. She stopped and leaned against him to reach down and take off her shoes. Now they were eye to eye. And casual. And intimate. "Will you carry these for me?"

He seemed glad to take her shoes. It was almost the right moment for the first kiss, she thought. Almost.

Holding hands, they toured the gardens in comfortable silence. *We don't need to talk,* she told herself. *We're communicating just fine.*

Finally, they sat down on a bench under one of the towering oaks. She stretched out her bare legs and wiggled her toes. She watched him watching her. She let her thigh rest against his pants leg. Yes, she had his complete attention. It was time to get him talking. Really talking.

"You know, Josh," she said, looking deeply into his lovely eyes, "I learned something when I started modeling."

"What?" He held her gaze. She liked the way he did not flinch.

"I learned that being beautiful is like being rich. It gives you power. Power other people don't have. It also isolates you. People don't see the real you. They just see the face. Or the money. You never know who really likes you or who's using you. You must know the feeling."

He nodded emphatically.

She let her forearm rest against his. "Suppose you and I started going out," she said.

"I'm already supposing," he said. "I have been for some time now."

She felt there was an electric charge passing between them. She withdrew her hand and arm, breaking their touch in anticipation of her next question. "Well, if we went out, would you be using me for my looks like a Wall Street trophy hunter?"

As she had planned, the question caught him off guard. "Uh, no . . . honest . . . ."

"Just as bad, would *I* be using *you* for your money?"

He seemed doubly flustered, just the way she wanted.

Before he could answer, she put a finger to his lips. She was sure she could feel him trying to resist the urge to kiss it. "More than all this," she gestured at the grounds of the estate, "I'll bet the thing you're most proud of is how you support your dad in Florida."

He nodded. "How did you know?"

She smiled. "And I'll bet the thing you worry most about is your teenage son, who you see only once a month."

He nodded again. She knew it was time to move in for the kill.

"And when you think about it, you realize that you are still the kid working harder than the other kids to get the best grades from whoever is handing out the As—the teacher, the management committee, the stock market." She paused and smiled. "Or Greenwich Links."

"Pen, I'm afraid you have me nailed." He smiled. She thought he looked captivated. Just as she hoped he would.

"Let's play a game." She moved her thigh back against his. She ran her fingertip up and down the pants leg her bare leg was touching. "What if you told me I don't have to be your arm candy? What if I said you could be broke?

Wouldn't it be amazing," she purred, "if the rich man and the beauty found a way to be just their real selves?"

"Nothing would make me happier," he whispered.

She felt him put his arm around her waist. She turned her face to his, presenting her mouth, lips just slightly open.

For Josh, that first kiss with Penelope was as natural as taking a breath.

He felt a little delirious. This woman, a miracle, had appeared at just the perfect time. In the weeks and months ahead, he would have a lot of Emma. And there would be more pain and mess with her than he had ever known.

9

Viktor, when he had inspected it, liked parts of the décor of this private dining room at the Connaught Hotel. The silver accents on the crown moldings and bits of filigree were pleasing. But there wasn't enough of it. This Georgian Room had so much bare white wall, and white on white, cream on white, and more white. And so much empty space between the rich bits of intricate carving. If there was silver, he felt, there ought to be gold, too. Gold leaf. And colorful inlays. And ormolu. And crystal. The way he had livened up his house in Belgravia and his estate in Kent. But the English style, he knew, confined vibrant decoration to little bits. No Russian architect would let himself be held back this way, he thought. But never mind what he likes. What counts is that Adeline likes it and feels at home.

The lead waiter opened the door to usher them inside.

"How lovely," Adeline said, touching Viktor on the arm.

Viktor had ordered the sconces and chandelier turned low so that the riot of antique silver candelabras he told the manager to bring in would bathe the room in soft, flickering light.

"For most special woman in all of Britain," he said, "a man must make very special dinner. Make her feel at home." He escorted her to her end of the smallish oval mahogany table and held out her chair.

"Is beautiful your dress," he said. And he meant it. Adeline looked elegant in the silvery-gray crepe de chine column dress that was dramatically bow-tied around her narrow waist. "You look like Greek statue," he said as he smiled and kissed her cheek, "but warmer and softer to touch."

Viktor loved Adeline's angular good looks. She was tall and svelte, a whole head taller than he, with sharp angles everywhere. She had high cheekbones, a high forehead, firm jaw, and a noble, aquiline nose. To Viktor, she looked every bit from centuries of privileged blood lines.

"Like goddess," he said as he took his seat at his end of the table. The waiter popped the champagne, poured two crystal flutes, and disappeared behind a swinging door. Viktor raised his glass. "To beautiful Greek goddess Adeline."

She smiled and took a tiny sip. "Well, I'm not sure the crew on Mount Olympus would accept me, but I'm awfully grateful for this elevation to divine status, if only for the evening."

Viktor took a little sip, paused, then drained his glass. He reached for the ice bucket, poured another, and drank half of it, readying himself for his next move.

He cleared his throat. Then he spoke as if about to make an announcement, "I ask myself, what can I bring you that is worthy? Beautiful enough? Special enough?"

"Why, you needn't bring me anything," she said, "truly. I don't deserve anything special."

He waved away her polite modesty. "I think hard about this. For you is necessary a gift of nature, something greater than just expensive thing, something—how you say?—one of a kind. Like you." He reached down for the corsage that had been placed, out of sight, in a box on the footstool beside his chair. He stood up, proudly holding the large pure-white orchid flecked with red and gold. He walked over to her. "Is rarest orchid in all Great Britain," he said as he slid the silk ribbon around her wrist. "Is combination of two rare breeds. Make this rarest and most unique of all." He took her hand. "Like you."

He raised her hand to his lips and gently kissed it. He loved Adeline's hands, the way her long elegant fingers contrasted with the short, fat sausages of his hand.

"Oh, Viktor," she said, holding out her wrist to view the flower, "it *tizz* very unusual indeed."

Viktor marveled at the ability of the English to conceal everything they were thinking and feeling. Tanya had it, too. She was so completely English.

He took her hand again. "You tell me truth. You like it, yes?"

"Why, of course I like it," she said. "It's exotic . . . and beautiful. Yes, beautiful."

"That means you no like it." He let go of her arm. He had become used to snooty English people pretending not to condescend to him while doing just that.

"I didn't say any such thing."

"Really?" he asked, trying not to show how vulnerable he was feeling.

"Truly, I said no such thing." She sounded sincere to him. His mood brightened again. He wagged a finger at her.

"Message in what you *don't* say. Is how English say everything."

"Well, I'm telling you right now that I love it. Furthermore, I think you are highly creative and thoughtful to bring me something special that has more value than a mere price tag can express."

"Exactly!" he declared. He leaned over to kiss her on the cheek again. "You know what I thinking." He loved

the way Adeline seemed neither impressed nor cowed by
his wealth. She seemed merely pleased by it. Or, amused.
That came as a relief. After Alexandra's death, he had had
a parade of women hotly pursuing him, trying any and all
tricks to get their claws into his fortune. "You and I, we
understand each other, no?"

"Why no," she teased, then giggled, "I mean, yes! Of
course, we do understand each other."

He gave a big sigh. He couldn't wait any longer.
"Adeline," he said, sighing again, feeling the weight of
everything he was hoping to accomplish before he died.
"Adeline."

"Yes, Viktor?"

"I make confession. You are woman I want, woman I
must have. For rest of my life."

He leaned down and took her face in his hands, kissing
her gently but ardently. They kissed for a long moment.

"There now," she said, stroking his cheek as they dis-
engaged, "what a lovely surprise."

"Is no surprise," he said, relieved at having managed to
say it.

"No, I suppose not," she said, smiling and looking up
into his eyes.

He moved quickly back to his end of the table, refilled
his champagne flute, took the bottle from the ice bucket,
and came back to Adeline. He topped off her glass. He
wished it were vodka.

"Thank you," she said and took a little sip. He topped off
her glass again. "Viktor, I don't know what to say, I . . ."

"You say yes. This is what you say. But wait." He put a
finger to her lips. "First, you hear everything I tell you."
He picked up his chair and brought it beside hers. He took
her hands in his. "Alexandra, before she die, she tell you
why we no have children after Tanya?"

"No, Viktor, she never did." Adeline sounded tender. Caring, he thought, yes, caring and sincere.

"Problem was me," he said. "Doctor did tests." He looked down at the floor. He remembered that day in humiliating detail.

He gave her hand a squeeze. He felt her squeeze back. He looked her in the eye again. Yes, definitely a caring and sympathetic expression. He had shared something so personal and devastating. And they were fine, the two of them. Yes, fine.

"Adeline, when I see something in here," he tapped his temple, "I make it happen out there." He made a sweeping gesture. "I make big plans, make big life."

"Yes indeed, you certainly do," she said. She reached for her glass and took another small sip.

He drained his flute and refilled it. "For us, I see big life. I bring money, great fortune. You bring important family with history and noble title."

"Well, the title belongs to my little brother Percy actually."

"I know. You have Percy. I have Tanya. They know each other from Cambridge. Both Trinity, yes?"

"Yes, apparently so," she said.

He had been devastated when Tanya broke up with her Trinity boyfriend, Alban. It would have been the perfect match. The boy's grandfather a hereditary peer in the House of Lords, his father vice chairman of the London Stock Exchange. Viktor had gleaned from Tanya's tone that Alban had dumped her. She must have scared him away. He now saw Adeline's Percy as his next best hope. Probably his last.

"Adeline, my family," he said haltingly, "your family. Could be *our* family, Adeline." He paused a moment, then continued in a whisper, "I am fifty-four." He gave his guess at his age in the lower of the range of possibilities. "I live twenty years more? Thirty? Maybe more?" He paused again and looked into her eyes. He felt he saw understanding there. "I was orphan, you know this?"

She nodded. Again, he felt she looked full with caring.

"Is important to me to make legacy. Most important thing in my life. Legacy of men with my blood!" He tapped his heart. "You understand?"

"Oh yes, we Montifers certainly understand legacies and bloodlines."

"I cannot make sons. But Tanya and Percy can. Sons with Montifer title. And my fortune. A legacy."

Yes, he thought, in twenty years, he *could* begin to see grandsons getting ready to succeed him. But he must start making them now. Immediately. That is, Tanya and Percy must. It was set in his mind. He just needed to get both Montifers on board. Then Tanya. "Adeline," he said, taking her hand again, "please, you tell me. How you feel?"

Adeline looked into Viktor's pale blue eyes, trying to imagine what living with him might be like. Beyond the vast riches, she wanted to imagine her life—the intimate details of his personal habits, his moods, his noises and smells, his generosity, his parsimony, his relationships with her relatives and friends, her relationships with his nouveau plutocrat comrades.

"Of course you want to create a dynasty," she said, giving his hand a little squeeze.

He nodded solemnly.

"You are so right to look at what you will leave behind." She knew one could never go wrong telling men they were right. No matter how many times. Especially men like Viktor.

She pondered the particulars of their cohabitation.

Would they have separate bedrooms? Possibly. Definitely separate bathrooms. That would be nonnegotiable. Would they take vacations just the two of them, or would he bring some retinue? Might it be a nightmare? Or mightn't it be fun? At his age, it might take not all that much to please him physically. And less with every passing year.

She then thought of the amusements that would come with being married to a billionaire. Oh yes, and the freedom from drudgery. A fortune of billions could compensate for . . . just about everything. "Should we arrange for Percy and Tanya to go out on a proper date?" she asked.

"Yes, this week! Yes!" He stood and took her hand again.

And Percy, she thought, dear Percy, her little brother. More like her child. Mum had died giving birth to her late, accidental baby. So Adeline, at fifteen, took over caring for what became her own little one. Then, when she was about to enter Cambridge, Daddy died in that car crash. So she'd had to become Percy's dad as well as his mum. And with no Montifer money left, she'd had to sell the London properties and the estate. And, instead of university, start working at that awful bank. She was fed up now with playing the sycophant to rich, vulgar clients not remotely her social equal. And with two divorces behind her, including one ex-husband whose family trusts kept his money far out of reach, she barely got by on her paltry salary.

Yes, Viktor could be just the ticket. And the particulars of their domestic life, those could be worked out.

"Viktor," she smiled, "I shall call Percy tonight and have him ring up Tanya first thing tomorrow."

Percy would do whatever she damned well told him to do. Dear boy, he was an angel, but not one skill with which to survive in a materialistic world. With Viktor's backing he could at least pretend to be someone. And if he sires sons with Tanya, he will have earned his keep and then some. Percy Montifer, lord of the marriage bed, the family stud. The thought made her want to laugh.

"You call," Viktor said, squeezing her hand, "you call Percy now!"

She let go of him and reached into her purse.

She asked herself again, *do I dare marry this man?*

She tapped Percy's speed-dial button and held the phone to her ear. As it rang, she realized she did not have to decide right away. If things between Tanya and Percy worked out, she could give it a try. Meanwhile, she could play with Viktor as the drama unfolded and keep him on tenterhooks.

Yes, no man holds all the cards with a woman he wants, not even a billionaire.

Percy answered after three rings.

"Percy darling," she cooed, "I have something terribly important for us to discuss."

She smiled at Viktor and blew a little kiss at him.

10

Tatiana Volkov was well aware that her townhouse just off Sloane Square was an act of youthful rebellion, even if it did involve her buying £7 million worth of prime London real estate at twenty-one.

As her graduation from Cambridge had approached, she rejected her father's plan to buy a mansion just for her next to his Belgravia residence and knock down the walls between them. "That's a sweet thought, Papa, but I'm buying my own house with my own money," she explained, trying to sound gracious. "Mummy did leave me that money in her will."

She gave a sniffle, a real sniffle, for the mother she'd lost at age ten, and another sniffle (not so real, to see if she could inflict a little guilt on her distant, withholding papa) for her exile to boarding schools where she grew up with other wealthy girls who'd also been abandoned by disinterested parents. "Mummy would want me to have it, I just know she would."

She dared not mention her real reasons. Among them, that many of her cheeky pals thought Viktor a lowlife. That she was repelled by the Russian tarts he sometimes cavorted with and the goons who guarded him and lurked about the ormolu-encrusted residence she called the "White Elephant." Worst, she cringed at the thought of what he might do or say to any young man she brought home.

Her house on Sloane Gardens near the fashionable square was one of a row of sedate Victorians in the Dutch style, topped with fanciful gables. She had had her designer give the interior the minimalist look of a downtown Manhattan loft. The very opposite of the gilded excesses of the White Elephant and her father's other abodes.

On this July afternoon, she was casual in J Brand jeans and Versace T-shirt. She planned to change into something more stylish before Viktor arrived with the young lord he was trying to foist upon her. But she was eagerly awaiting a much more special guest who was scheduled to come and go first.

She paused in front of the foyer mirror. As she often did, she looked at herself to inspect for traces of her beloved Mummy. Tanya felt certain she got almost all of her DNA from her mother, the beautiful Alexandra Yardley. In particular, her long legs, elegant facial structure, and wavy chestnut hair. She wished that she owned the stunning portrait of Mummy that hung in the foyer of the White Elephant. Being able to view it was the main consolation of her infrequent visits there.

She remembered Mummy telling her, "You are all mine, my own little girl. I made you all by myself." This was usually when Mummy would come to cuddle in bed with her, sniffling and teary-eyed after noisy fights with Papa. The only traces of Viktor she could see in the mirror were her pale skin, crystal blue eyes, and, when she turned and inspected her backside, the horrifying prospect of developing a "wide Russian bum."

The doorbell rang, sending one of the maids scurrying from their preparations in the dining room. Tanya reached the front door first. "Never mind, Lucja," she called, "I know who it is."

She pulled the bolt and swung open the heavy

nineteenth-century door. Before her stood Fiona Alford, her best friend from Cambridge, a Baby Björn baby carrier strapped around her chest and Fiona's six-month-old niece Maggie bouncing inside.

"Hullo, my darlings," Tanya said as she ushered in Fiona with a kiss on each cheek. She gave little Maggie's pudgy baby feet a squeeze. "Come to the living room, we have just a few minutes before the dreaded *they* arrive."

Fiona was shorter and curvier than Tanya, with hair as pale and fine as corn silk. They were a contrasting pair, tall and short, brunette and blond. On the couch, Fiona unstrapped little Maggie from the carrier. Tanya scooped up the infant, bouncing her, kissing her, and squeezing her.

"You remember me, luvvy?" Tanya cooed.

Maggie gave a drooly smile.

"She remembers me!" She did more kisses, bounces, and pinches. The touch and smell of Maggie's soft baby flesh sent bolts of pleasure through Tanya's whole body. It felt so sublime, it was almost unbearable. "I do wish she were mine," she said as she showered more kisses on Maggie.

Fiona opened the bag of baby gear at her feet and rooted around inside it. "Some days, my sister might actually oblige you," she said as she plunked Maggie's pacifier into her little mouth. "Motherhood's making her rather ragged about the edges. When I left them just now, she and John looked like zombies."

Maggie sucked contentedly in Tanya's arms. "Tell them I'll take their little munchkin any time they need a break." She planted more kisses on the baby's head. "You have two aunties who love-love-love you, don't you? Mwwwah!" Maggie made a happy little sound.

"We can only stay a minute," Fiona said, looking at her watch.

"I know, I just needed a bit of comfort before the ordeal."

Tanya looked deeply into her best friend's eyes. Fiona had been her "mother" at Trinity College, the upperclassman assigned to show her the ropes when she first arrived. They had been inseparable ever since. Born into a family long on heritage and short on cash, like Tanya's mother, Fiona now worked as an assistant in a toney art gallery and struggled to keep up appearances. Tanya, with the bounty of her late mother's trust fund and the investment trusts Viktor had put in her name, was happy to help her pal with cash whenever she could. On their weekend excursions, Tanya made a point of paying the bills out of sight.

"Oh *gawd,* Fiona," Tanya said, "he's bringing over Percy Montifer."

"Not *the* Lord Percy we knew at Trinity?" Fiona asked with gossipy delight.

"Yes, penniless Percy of the lineage."

"Sweet boy he was," Fiona said, "but the unfortunate chin is rather a deficiency."

"Papa wants me to go out with him *again*. At the Groucho Club two nights ago, Percy walked us over to the prince's table first thing, apparently to show me that the young royal greets him like the cousin he is. Afterward in the taxi home, he tried to give me the most awful French kiss." Tanya giggled. "I can't bear him."

Fiona whispered, "Does Viktor have some awful plan for the two of you?"

"He hasn't said so outright yet." Tanya lowered her voice as she signaled approval to the maid walking by with a large vase of flowers. "But since Mummy died all those years ago, he's had his nose pressed up against the glass, as it were. A titled son-in-law would be exactly the entrée he thinks he needs. Chin or no. And grandsons, of course. Male heirs for his empire."

Fiona paused. "I know what! Tell Percy you've got teeth in your lady parts. I'm sure he's the original twenty-three-year-old virgin." The girls giggled.

"Do you think Maggie needs . . ." Fiona asked with a look of horror, ". . . a fresh nappy?"

"Oh, squeamish you," Tanya said. She raised the baby into the air and gave her little bottom a sniff. "No, luv, not yet," she said.

"She will as soon as we leave," Fiona said with a shudder, "that's always my luck."

"Oh, tut!" Tanya gave Maggie another big kiss. She could now move on to the item that had been gnawing at her. "Listen, Fiona, I'm going to the Kroesus Kids meet-up in America next week. It's in this Greenwich, Connek-tee-cut place. Near New York. Won't you come with me, luv? You could see your dear Oliver-in-exile."

Kroesus Kids was the social network for teens and twentysomethings of the international plutocrat class. Membership cost $5,000 and was by invitation only. Tanya had been networking on its website and going to its lavish parties around the globe since she was sixteen.

Fiona sighed, "Oliver did mention it. His parents have sentenced him to an entire year with that American supermarket company. He's supposed to be learning supply chain management, whatever that is. He would *so* rather be back at Cambridge, reading Chaucer. But I'm afraid his mum and dad don't much approve of me or old Geoffrey. I miss him terribly. And it is tempting . . . but I can't quite swing the air ticket at the moment."

"You must come as my guest," Tanya pleaded, "you *must*. Please, Fiona!" Tanya was scared to go alone. The thought of it turned her stomach into knots.

"No, luv," Fiona said, "I can't let you do that. You are already far too kind to me."

"Oh sod, it's only money. I'm borrowing the smaller of Viktor's jets, so it's absolutely free." *Well, not quite,* she thought. Nothing was ever really free when it came from Viktor. "Please, Fiona, I can't go alone, I just can't."

Fiona was silent. Then she said tenderly, "Ah, it's Alban, isn't it? Alban is going to be there."

"Yes," Tanya sniffed, "I saw it on the website. And with that American. She's now his fiancée! Sweetest, I need your support."

Her wound still felt raw. Viktor had approved of Alban, especially his family. He blamed *her* for the breakup. "Please, Fiona?" She had given herself to Alban, heart and soul. She'd imagined a whole brood of little Albans, all alpha males who would grow up to be just like him. She even had names for them. But when he'd found himself a tennis star, Alban left her in the dust.

"You must be strong," Fiona said, "and show him absolute indifference."

"I won't give Alban the time of day," Tanya declaimed. "Just be there to help me." To lighten her plea, she assumed the tone of an elderly governess: "My dear young lady, this party is your moral obligation. It is an errand of duty!"

"Well, I suppose," Fiona teased back, "since it's a duty, I shall *have* to bear it—dear Oliver, vintage champagne, dancing, and all."

The girls giggled. Tanya felt hugely relieved. The house phone rang. A maid in black uniform ran into the living room. "Meester Volkov on his way!" she announced. "They leave five minutes ago."

Tanya shook her head. "Viktor the Terrible and Lord Chinless are about to make their entrance."

"We've got to run, dearie," Fiona said as she stood and

scooped up little Maggie and began snapping her into the harness. Tanya planted one last kiss on the baby's head.

"*Courage,*" Fiona called from the doorway.

"*Merci bien,*" Tanya called back, feeling shaky and alone.

Little Maggie started wailing. Tanya was sure it was because the darling baby was already missing her *most* favorite auntie.

11

Tanya bolted up the stairs. She had hardly enough time for hair and makeup and to change into the black silk Prada blouse and capri pants she had picked from her huge wardrobe closet.

As she kicked off her espadrilles and crossed her arms to yank off her T-shirt, she noticed something awry on her canopied bed. On top of the layers of embroidered damasks, Tanya kept a family of twenty or so precious baby dolls, all exquisitely dressed and arranged just so. But she saw one missing. She ran to the bed, confirmed her worst fear, and jammed down the button on the phone that triggered the intercom.

"Where is Little Mummy?" she howled, her voice echoing in every room of the house. "Where is my Little Mummy? Somebody get up here and bring me Little Mummy. *Now!* Right this *fucking* minute!"

Then her face crumbled. "Li-li-little Mummy?" she stammered, tears starting. "My lovely baby with the tattered dress." She bent over the bed and reached into her family of dolls. "Little Mummy, you're supposed to be right *there*!" With two frantic scooping motions she sent the other dolls flying about.

Crying, she collapsed to the floor. The dolls lay spread around her like tiny lost corpses. "Little Mummy, my little Mummy, my poor Little Mummy," she sniffled, as if becoming the little girl she was when her dying mother, emaciated from ovarian cancer, gave her the tattered dolly she herself had grown up with. "Keep it always, darling," Mum had wheezed, "Keep it *always*."

The portly Polish maid appeared, took in the scene, then smacked her forehead. "The new girl," she gasped, "the new girl. She must throw out by accident. Must be why she go home sick." The woman got down on the floor, gathered up Tanya in her arms, and rocked her gently.

"Lucja, Lucja," Tanya sniveled, crying into her maid's bosom, "Lucja, she threw out Little Mummy, didn't she? Mummy gave her to me before she died. My poor Little Mummy."

Lucja hugged her tighter. Tanya was oblivious to the hubbub of people arriving below.

Viktor stopped as he neared the top of the stairs.

"Masha," he spoke into his cell, "*milalya tyontenka,*" my dear little aunt. He spoke in a tender voice he used with no one else.

Maria Gavrikov was neither his aunt nor his mother. To Viktor, she was both and more, the woman who took him off the streets of Leningrad when he was a teenage runaway. "Yes, Auntie, Tanya will be making us so happy. Soon marrying a nice English lord and making noble grandsons. Just a minute, I put her on the line."

"*Vitunya,*" the old woman said tenderly, little Viktor. She was the only person on earth who used diminutives with him. She alone remembered him as the terrified child he once was. He called her often, visited her whenever he went to Russia, and lavished her with gifts that, she said, embarrassed her. "But little Tanya can hardly understand me," she said, "she speaks hardly any Russian."

"She speaks enough to tell you she loves you." Viktor had now finished climbing the stairs. He stopped in the doorway and took in the scene. Tanya sobbing on the floor, her head buried in her maid's bosom.

"*Masha*," he said into the phone, his voice now crisp. "Tanya cannot speak just now. *Do swidaniya, milaya tyontenka*." See you again, my dear little aunt. He deposited the phone into the pocket of his suit jacket.

Viktor looked down at the maid. "Leave us alone."

Tanya shuddered and grabbed Lucja tighter.

Viktor glared at the maid. "I say, leave us alone."

Lucja squirmed, trying to free herself. Tanya held on, burying her face deeper into Lucja's bosom.

"Get out, woman," he hissed.

Lucja kissed Tanya's head as she pulled herself free, scrambled to her feet, and fled.

"Tanya, what is this?"

"The new maid threw out my Little Mummy doll."

"Get up. Is just a toy. You buy another one."

Tanya made no move to rise. No daughterly embrace. The last time he remembered her voluntarily hugging him was at Alexandra's funeral.

"You look a mess," he said, reciting one of his favorite British phrases in his thick accent. He folded his arms across his chest. "Stand up. Get ready. I bring Percy Montifer."

Tanya slumped back onto the floor in a teary ball. "Bring me a Kleenex, Daddy." She pointed at the box in a mother-of-pearl holder on her night table, as if getting a tissue herself was *too much* to ask in this awful moment. "Please, Papa, pleeeeease."

Viktor did not move.

"*Papachka*," Tanya sniffled in Russian. "*Moey papachka*," she said through her tears. My dear sweet darling daddy.

Well, that was a peace offering, he thought, even if a small one. He got the box and handed it to her.

Tanya blew her nose and wiped her eyes, leaving balls of

wet tissue on the carpet. Then she stood to her full height and faced him. Suddenly, he realized, she was looking down at him. Like Alexandra, she was half a head taller than he.

He took a step backward. "Clean up now. Lord Percy waiting downstairs."

"Papa, I did go out with Percy as you requested. He's a perfectly nice chap, but he's not my type."

"What you mean, not your type?" He raised his arms to indicate the town house. "I give you big life." He still thought of the inheritance Tanya got from Alexandra as *his* money. He, after all, had given it to Alexandra. He had given Alexandra everything she had ever asked for. *Everything.* Well, almost.

Viktor waved away her objections. "This Montifer, I tell you, he is like that other Trinity boy you almost marry, Alban."

Tanya flinched.

"Our family make important connections with Montifers," he said firmly.

"Daddy," Tanya protested, a new flood of tears starting. "I'm not ready to get married. I'm only just twenty-one."

Viktor folded his arms across his chest. *Well, at least we're talking about this issue,* he thought. "Princess Diana," he said, ignoring his daughter's waterworks, "she twenty when marry Charles."

She moaned, "Look what *that* produced!"

"Two sons," he said.

Tanya fell back into a heap on the floor and howled in protest.

Viktor clenched his jaw. *I'll keep going until she comes around,* he told himself. *I will try one strategy after another until something works.*

. . .

Tanya sneaked a look up into her father's eyes. She saw the pale blue eyes she had inherited from him. But none of the fire and vulnerability she felt in herself. Maybe they really were the "ice-blue, killer eyes" the tabloids wrote about.

She had heard him rail against the accusations, that the English aristocrats were the criminals—built their bloody empire on theft, extortion, and murder. Like all big shots everywhere. And laws? Laws were made by the criminals who ruled to keep themselves in power. Hypocrites, all of them! He would get so furious. How dare they accuse me? How *dare* they?

But Tanya knew otherwise.

She remembered *that* night in Viktor's Moscow house two years before. She'd snuck out of bed and hid on the stairs, saw a sliver of the dining room through the half-open door. She could hear and understand. She'd never let Viktor know how good her Russian was.

Artyom calling the meeting to order. Viktor spoke quietly, saying each man's name and city and how well he thought each man's business was doing. He talked, using odd names like "roofing" and "trucking" and "candy." The sounds felt burned into her memory, most of the men's names and where they worked: Leonid Cherkin, St. Petersburg; Dimitri Chervonenko, Novograd; Sergei Archipenko, Riga; and others. Finally, a Sergei from Odessa. She could not remember his last name, she must have blotted it out.

Viktor spoke calmly. "Sergei, how have I treated you these years?"

"You have been good to me, Viktor Viktorovich."

"And where would you be if I had not taken you in and trained you in roofing?"

"Dead in an alley."

"But instead, you enjoy protection from the highest ranks of government. Right?"

"Yes, Viktor Viktorevich."

"And you live like a Romanov."

"Yes, Viktor Viktorovich."

"And who do you have to thank for this life of yours?"

"You, Viktor Viktorovich, you."

"Then why?" Viktor paused. He lowered his voice. Tanya had crept closer to hear. "Then why have you been stealing from me?"

Silence.

"After all I have done for you," Viktor said calmly.

Sergei sputtered excuses. Higher costs, much higher, more bribes to police and politicians.

Viktor sighed. Then sighed again. It was the same sigh of disappointment he used with Tanya. "Artyom," he said, "make sure he suffers."

Sergei started crying and blubbering. Horribly. Tanya ran back to her room and buried herself under the covers, never let Viktor know what she had overheard.

Tanya looked up from the floor. She massaged her forehead. "*Papachka,* I have a headache. Please get me my headache pills. Please, *Papachka,*" she pleaded, "they're in the medicine cabinet. The yellow ones. And bring me a cup of water, too." She sniffled. "Then I'll change and go see Lord Percy. I promise."

As she watched Viktor head for her bathroom, she felt that need again. For the sensation of holding little Maggie. It was a dull ache all over, like hunger and lust combined. She realized that it wasn't the ragged dolly she wanted, dear as it was. It was a longing for a real baby. And not a baby from silly Montifer. Or any of the prissy men she knew. But a baby all her own.

She counted the days since her last period. Aha! The

Kroesus Kids meet-up would be right in the middle of her cycle this month. She would almost certainly be ovulating in Greenwich.

Suddenly, she had a plan. Find a boy at Kroesus Kids, the perfect boy to make her baby. He'd have lovely eyes and strong hands. And she would never tell him. She would keep the baby all for herself. She just knew it would be a girl. And it would be hers. All *hers*.

Tanya felt she had always been good at making plans. And now she had one that would truly make her happy.

Viktor stood before Tanya's open medicine cabinet. He saw his grown-up daughter's life in intimate detail. Many drugs, messy rows of beauty and hygiene products, birth control pills, and condoms. A woman like her mother.

Suddenly, he remembered his Alexandra as the twenty-year-old assistant to an attaché of the British commercial mission. He had just taken control of Russia's biggest aluminum company. He and Alexandra spent two days locked in passion such as he'd never known. Then suddenly, she left and returned to England. For a month, he called, wired, wrote, and showered her with gifts. No response. Then finally she did call. Pregnant. He flew to her side and, without thinking twice, married her.

Viktor rummaged through the cabinet until he found the bottle of Acordinol. He scanned the label for the lot number and the date. Almost one year old. No matter, he thought. He unscrewed the cap and poured the pills into the toilet. He flushed and threw out the empty bottle. Then he found the Boots ibuprofen. He grabbed two pills and a cup of water.

Tanya was still curled in a ball on the floor. He got down on his knees to be at eye level with her. "Here, darling," he said, trying to be tender.

She looked with one eye through a crack between two fingers, then quickly covered herself again. "No, Papa! I said the yellow pills. The . . . *yellow* . . . pills!"

"Was empty the bottle," he said softly. "This better for headache. Go ahead, take."

She sighed, took the pills, and gulped some water.

He took Tanya by the shoulders and gently pulled her toward him. He had to bring her around. Eventually, she would understand and do as he wanted. Eventually, everyone did.

"I never have family," he whispered in her ear, "never know father and mother. You my only blood, my only family. We must work together." He kissed her forehead gently, hoping he was starting to get through to her.

12

Peter Katz was almost finished shooting his way out of the martian space station in this online session of *Death Star*. He was playing against ten other gamers from who-knows-how-many countries. *Got to be a couple of Koreans in there,* he thought. They're always the best and they've got, like, no clocks in Korea so nobody sleeps over there. Peter was making kills left and right, dodging deadly ray bursts.

Then it happened! From around the corner, before he could swerve, a burst of deadly laser beam! One explosion and a sick ripping sound. His warrior's head was severed, the body torn into pieces and flung into a dark corner. Green blood freakin' everywhere. Shit! That's what happens when you lose concentration, even for a nanosecond.

He logged out of *Death Star*.

His leg tapped wildly under the desk. He was thinking about the upcoming Kroesus Kids meet-up. Dad had arranged for him to join the stupid club. The kids he'd met there sure weren't *his* friends. Their dads were friends of his dad or just rich kids from all over. But he hung out with them on his weekends in Greenwich. Most were assholes. But it was more fun than at Ledgemere all by himself, which was how it was, since his dad was usually busy with meetings and business and that Wall Street stuff.

He looked at the wallpaper image on his computer's home screen, that picture of him when he was a baby. Mom and Dad next to each other, smiling. Mom had an arm around Dad. They were outside somewhere, probably in one of those parks in London. He couldn't remember any of this; he was too little. Dad was holding up his baby son. To Peter, he looked really, really happy. Like he was holding a trophy he'd just won. Peter liked the picture. It kind of irked Mom. But he also knew she didn't dare say anything about it. He hoped his dad still felt that way about him. But he was so busy all the time, Peter couldn't tell.

Sometimes he felt Dad was disappointed in him. Like on that big trip to Africa with the water project. He'd had Dad all to himself the whole way over to Tanzania. Riding in that timeshare G5 just him and Dad, that was incredible. Except for a few emails and phone calls, Dad *really* paid attention to him, asked him questions and totally listened to everything he said. Well, most everything. Then, when he got so sick on the third day, they had to call an emergency helicopter. He remembered the look in his dad's eyes. Sure, he was concerned. But more like he was disappointed. Maybe even angry. What with the photographers from the charity and all these guys writing what was supposed to be this famous moment for father and son. Digging wells for humanity. And then, in front of the freakin' cameras, his son gets the worst diarrhea . . . ever. Yup, Peter just knew he had ruined it all.

That was their last big trip. Now it was just these weekends once a month in Greenwich. Peter did love his dad. But he was mad at him, too. Really freakin' mad. For the divorce, for not being around, for a lot of things. But he also did love him. The weird thing was—sometimes he felt both at the same time.

He logged onto Kroesuskids.com. His avatar was Katman. All the Kroesus Kids had made-up screen names for networking on the part of the site called FriendVault. It was strictly anonymous until you chose to reveal yourself.

He went to the general message board, trawling. He scanned down the usual rich kid crap about hitching rides on private jets, code language about getting laid on yachts, or some hot new five-thousand-dollar handbag. Then he saw a message flashing on the screen in real time:

"A chin! A chin! My kingdom 4 a chin!" Pause. "Maybe my naughty bits 2!" The writer's avatar popped up at the end: Tsarina Alexandra.

Peter recognized the quotation. He had been forced to read *Richard III* in English class. He kind of liked the nasty hunchbacked king; at least he wasn't constipated like most of the characters in the books he had to read. Why not? He decided to take the Tsarina's bait.

"I have a chin. Big chin. Superhero chin! All 4 U." Then he added, using the Tsarina's odd language. "And your naughty bits 2." He assumed that meant what he thought it meant. He waited, watching the screen intently.

"Yum," Tsarina typed back, "Hungry 4 superhero chin."

Wow, Peter thought, this girl has a thing for chins. Chins? He never imagined his chin as part of anyone's sexual fantasy.

He typed feverishly, "My big sexy chin make U feel good all over!" Then, when he saw his stupid words, he asked himself, *what the fuck am I doing*? She's going to blow me off.

He waited. Nothing. Yup, blowing me off. I'm such an asshole. What idiot brags about his freakin' chin?

He could never stop thinking about girls, about all their delicious parts, especially the incredibly mysterious part he had not yet experienced, all the way. Pussy. Vagina. Vadge (like he was so familiar he could give it a nickname, ha!). He had come close once or twice with his finger. But just a drive-by. He just knew he was the only sixteen-year-old boy on Earth who had not been laid. The only one! And the way things were going, in six months, he was going to be the only *seventeen*-year-old virgin. He was about to log off when he saw Tsarina responding.

"U going 2 KKids meetup in Greenwich?"

Immediately, he typed, "YES!!!! I M chin king of Gwich!!!!!!" Then he blushed at his uncool urgency. Okay, now she's definitely going to blow me off. He held his breath. Even his budding hard-on was in limbo, half hard, waiting for Tsarina to give it the green light. Waiting. Waiting.

Then Tsarina typed, "C U in Gwich, CHIN KING!"

"Yyyyyyes!" Peter shouted, raising his fist. Then he covered his mouth, afraid his cry might bring someone knocking on his door. He was at Mom's, he remembered, as he came back to Earth. He took off his headphones and listened. Nothing. Whew!

He sat back, trying to imagine this Alexandra. What she looked like. What it would be like to kiss her. Touch her breasts. Take off her clothes. Taste that mystery between her legs and for the first time ever—finally put his dick inside . . .

Then it occurred to him. Tsarina Alexandra *might* be the pretty girl he was imagining. Or *not*. She might be a loser girl. Hugely fat or eight feet tall with buck teeth. Worse, she might not even be a she. His delicious fantasy was turning into a hairy nightmare. Oh fuck!

He *had* to find out about her. At the very least, whether she was a girl or not. If only he could hack into the data. He knew it was somewhere on the website. He just had to crack through the security. He knew from his own Kroesuskids.com profile that her real name, addresses (K-kids all have more than one home, of course), cell number, and pictures of her were there in the source data.

Hmmm. Think, Peter, think.

Kroesuskids.com had to be like any website, always working up new features and enhancements. And when they tested out stuff, they used copies of the source data to see if the new stuff worked. So they often couldn't have all their security in place on the test site, because the developers were the only ones who went there. So the truth about Alexandra could be sitting right there as part of some new application they were testing. Of course, only their web developers knew how to get to their development site. Okay, Peter thought, what URL did they type in to get there?

He took a shot: www.kroesuskids.developers.com

Nope. Nothing. Okay, try another.

www.kroesuskids.testsite.com

Again, nothing.

Peter had once pirated a software program (Mom would kill him, if she knew about it) that could throw a jillion possible URLs at a site to find the one that would crack it open. But before he went nuclear, he tried once more with something obvious. Maybe he would get lucky. He typed: www.kroesuskids.test.com.

And there it was! The homepage of the developers' site.

They looked to be working on a bunch of site improvements. Peter scanned the list. Nah, internal modifications mostly. Peter wanted projects that would link to the member database at the root level, where all the personal information would be. At the bottom he saw a new "meet-up" function and an enhanced mobile function to let members track each other on the go. He went to the mobile page and entered his own Katman information, including his password.

There he was. Katman, plus all the Peter Katz info behind the security wall. But of course he did not have Tsarina Alexandra's password.

Think, Peter, think. Then it hit him.

He could try a buffer overflow attack. He had used these before. Again, if Mom knew, she would kill him. He went to the "name" tab on the mobile development page and typed in a few lines of code $(\text{Sin}(\pi^{\wedge}12345) * \text{Tan}(3^{\wedge}54321))$ that would multiply by itself over and over and over in a loop until . . . until . . . Yes! He watched the buffer overflow with his endless repeating code. And yep, the program crashed. Then, he knew, what he had to do was overwrite the opcodes stored in memory. The overwrite was easy, just code to tell the program to query the database for "all users" info instead of just himself. If the code worked, his second request to the "name" field should give him the master list.

He waited briefly. Five, six, seven, eight. Bingo! The mobile program crashed and showed him a screen that held . . . the copy of *The List*. The members and all their data. He searched "Tsarina Alexandra," expecting to bring up her information in a nice little package. It ought to have come up in a second or two. But it started taking too long. He searched again.

Suddenly his screen went blank. All the data was gone, vanished.

Then letters blinked into view: "Dude, you are not authorized!"

It had to be the site administrator, the Kroesuskids.com webmaster, logging in from who knows where, finding someone invading and snooping around.

"Nice try, Katman," the administrator typed. "Thanks for reminding me to program against buffer overflow attacks like yours. We are protecting YOUR data, too, dude. Now SCRAM!"

Abruptly, Peter found himself looking at a big flashing screen that read ACCESS DENIED. Shit, he was so freakin' close.

Well, maybe I'll get lucky anyway. Maybe she's looking for a guy with a major chin. Or just a guy who wasn't chinless. Suddenly, he couldn't wait for the party in Greenwich.

13

MONDAY, JULY 13

ONE PERCIVAL & BAXTER PLAZA · FRANKLIN CROSSING, PENNSYLVANIA

Brad Johansen welcomed Emma and Steve Upshaw into the den beside his inner office. "Please, have a seat." He sat on the couch that overlooked the woods of the P&B land preserve.

Emma liked Brad. She remembered when her father was his mentor and he was the eager young star in product management. Now he was the wise elder statesman of the company with nearly two decades as CEO. The sixty-year-old did not look his age, or any age, for that matter. He was tall and lean with salt-and-pepper hair that he wore in a short, military chop. A lifelong runner, Johansen had the hollow cheeks and taut neck of a man who had never carried an ounce of body fat. Yes, she found him a little bit cold, but guessed that it was partly his nature and partly his job to keep a bit of distance. As usual, he sat on the edge of his seat, as if ready to leap up at any moment. "I want the two of you to hear this first, before word gets out," he said.

Emma sat across from Steve Upshaw, wondering what was up.

Had Josh's fund bought more shares of P&B? Were they preparing to defend against a hostile takeover attempt?

And why did Brad want her and Upshaw, the darling numbers boy of finance, to be here together? To Emma, she and Upshaw were like oil and water. He was the quintessential bean counter, a cost cutter, who didn't give a rat's ass about the values that made Percival & Baxter the kind of company it was. A forty-five-year-old accountant, he seemed to Emma a cold, gray, robotic white man who would shoot his own mother if he thought it would help him make his numbers.

Brad looked at his watch. "If you two don't mind waiting, Hal should be here momentarily."

Hal was Harold Percival, great-grandson of the founder of Percival & Baxter. He was the company's largest individual shareholder and chairman of the executive committee of the board. Emma had known him since she was a little girl, when her father used to bring her to P&B annual meetings to give her lessons in how the company worked.

Voices sounded from the outer offices. Then Hal Percival walked in. To Emma, he looked the same as he had when she was a girl. Round, bald, and jowly, he wore the same rumpled Brooks Brothers suits, probably twenty years old, plain white shirts, and skinny regimental-striped ties that Emma thought might have gone to Groton School with him fifty years before. Hal was among the last of a vanishing species—a highborn American WASP who used his inherited wealth to cultivate his finer sensibilities and do good works.

"Sorry I'm late," he said, taking his place beside Brad. "When the fates conspire to make one tardy, there's little we mortals can do." Emma had always wondered about Hal's lockjaw accent. Did they have elocution classes at Groton where they taped the boys' mouths shut and forced them to recite long passages of Kipling? With Hal Percival, it seemed not an affectation, but a well-worn part of who he really was. Like his brown English oxfords, enduring and unchanged, resoled for the umpteenth time.

"No problem," Brad said. "Hal, would you like to open this meeting?"

"Oh, no, please," Hal said, "go ahead."

Brad nodded. He looked first at Upshaw, then at Emma. "We're all familiar with our succession planning process."

Of course, Emma thought. Every year, P&B sorted through performance reviews and shuffled the deck of top executives to see who stood in line behind whom to take each one's place—should that whom get hit by a bus, run off to Fiji, or get lured away to another job.

But why, she wondered, would she and Upshaw be here together in the inner sanctum?

Brad cleared his throat. "Joe McKeen has decided to take early retirement. He's leaving to head up the Juvenile Diabetes Foundation. We want to line up his successor well in advance. And so," he paused for a moment, "at the end of this year, one of you will become chief operating officer. Next in line to succeed me."

Emma took a deep breath to maintain her outer calm. The time had finally come. Her shot at becoming chief executive. She stared out the window. Inside, she felt cheers, high fives, and explosions of pride. Validation of all her years of hard work. Her father had said to her time and again, "I could see you running this whole company one day. Emma, there's nothing you can't become if you put your mind and your heart to it."

"Of course," Brad said with a little laugh, "I'm not planning to go anywhere for quite some time. My mandatory retirement isn't for another five years." He winked at Hal. "And it's possible that the board could decide to extend it, right, Hal?"

Hal nodded.

"I want you two to work together and transition from your current jobs. You should each recommend a successor. And we'll move you up to offices on this floor."

"I believe they call it 'Mahogany Row,'" Hal mumbled.

"Huh?" Brad said, having not quite heard.

Hal smirked. "They call this executive floor Mahogany Row."

Brad shrugged. "It was built long before the rain forests became—"

"Yes, of course," Hal said, still amused. "If my grandfather were alive today, he would no doubt have used more ecologically correct building materials."

Upshaw raised an index finger. "I'd like to clarify something, if I might. If only one of us will be left standing after Joe retires in December, then what does the other—"

"Pardon me, Steve," Hal interrupted. "This is not a gladiator match in ancient Rome. The two of you are, obviously, our most promising leaders. There will be plenty of work and responsibility to go around, regardless of the outcome."

But it *was* a contest, Emma knew. Upshaw, she was convinced, had it all backward. If he were in charge, he would slash and burn and do whatever it took to feed Wall Street's endless hunger for quarterly profits. In no time, he could destroy the trust P&B had built over more than a century.

"You two are like our yin and yang," Brad said, opening his arms as if embracing them. "Emma, you with your dedication to our products and our P&B culture. Steve, with your sharp-penciled financial discipline."

"Indeed," Hal said, "we've all watched Emma lead the team that has built Acordinol into the world's number one pain relief medicine. Acordinol, it's your baby, Emma."

Yes, Emma thought, *one of my two babies. Maybe someday Peter would understand.*

Brad reached across and patted Upshaw on the knee. "And in Steve Upshaw, we have a relentless realist who is not afraid to ask the toughest questions and go wherever the hard answers take him."

Upshaw smiled. "Thanks, Brad. Without keeping our stock price high, the company would be crippled."

"That's true, Steve," Hal said, looking at Emma, "but without uncompromising quality and the values our people live by, there would be no company."

"Uh, of course, Hal, of course," Upshaw said. "I certainly meant that. Our values always come first. Always." To Emma, his agreement now rang false. She saw him glance nervously at his watch. Maybe, she thought, because he was lying. Or maybe he was just nervous.

Brad stood. "Good. Let's go to the boardroom. Mike Saltzman, that lawyer of ours, will talk about adopting a poison pill. In the thirty years they've been around, no raider has beaten a poison pill."

Emma was relieved no one mentioned Josh by name.

"Great strategy," Upshaw said.

"Indeed," Hal said, "I must say, that New York lawyer of ours is one smart son of a bitch."

"Sounds like my kinda guy," Emma said, preparing herself for the two biggest fights of her life—against Steve Upshaw and Josh Katz.

14

Viktor walked through his corporate headquarters on the forty-eighth floor of the tallest building in the United Kingdom, the steel-and-glass, pyramid-topped One Canada Square at Canary Wharf. From these sleek offices he ran his legitimate interests around the world. Guardian Capital employed executives and corporate staff here and in Moscow, Bermuda, Abu Dhabi, and Lichtenstein. Not one in them, Viktor felt certain, knew about the dark side of his world.

He nodded at the rows of pretty secretaries outside his imperial corner office, now sitting down to morning cups of tea, booting up their computers. "Good morning, Mr. Volkov," each said, one after the other.

Cell phone to his ear, Viktor was talking to his auntie. "*Tyotya Masha,*" he said fondly, "yes, I think we are finally making progress with Tanya and the English lord. I say I *think* so, because, well—" He paused to consider the doubts he still had. Tanya had been warm and polite to Percy after her little scene, but polite in that English way that revealed nothing. "I just don't know what she will do. Always a mind of her own, that girl." If Tanya could only have been raised among Russians, he often thought. That would have made her heart so much more open.

"Give her the time she needs," Masha said. "She is a woman now, not a little girl."

"Yes, dear Auntie," he said, feeling that time was the one thing he could not afford.

"Yes, I promise," he said, and bid Masha good-bye.

He stood by the rosewood door to his office, looking back at his secretaries. "I am not to be disturbed," he announced as he closed and locked it. Sitting behind his black granite desk, he turned a switch that lowered the window blinds and turned on the electronic interference. He sat staring at the satellite phone beside his regular one, the same model he kept at the Belgravia house. At precisely 9:00 AM GMT, it chirped once. Viktor grabbed it and jammed it against his ear.

"*Kakaya informatsiya u tebya est dlya menya?*" he barked into it. What information do you have?

"Viktor Viktorovich," Tom Hardacre answered in Russian. "Right now, it is four in the morning. Katz is sleeping next to his new girlfriend, Penelope. She is beautiful. But she snores like a horse. I hope she doesn't break the microphone behind the bed. It is very sensitive."

"What does Katz think about the price of the stock?" Viktor asked.

"He is convinced that P&B shares will go higher now that Anglia's position has been registered. The market, he says, smells a takeover. The stock was overpriced before, but now it will go even higher. He complains about having to do this deal."

"Good," Viktor said, "we want him to be surprised when the pills do what they will do."

Hardacre snickered, "He suspects nothing."

"Tom, if Katz becomes uncooperative, you must let me know. I have a way to keep him in line."

"You want me to . . . uh? . . ." Hardacre hesitated.

"No, no, no killing, not useful. I mean those pictures from years ago."

"Ah, *those*."

"If I should tell you, you send them to every financial newspaper and every website that fights child abuse, yes?"

"Oh, yes, just say when."

"But Tom, not unless *he* forces us. Not without my direct order. Understood?"

"Yes, Viktor Viktorovich."

For a long moment, neither spoke.

Then Hardacre broke the silence, taking a more casual tone. "Viktor Viktorovich, how long will I have to pretend to be this American's butler?"

"Until this deal is done."

"But how long is that? A few more weeks, a few months?"

"Tom, just be patient."

"I have been patient."

"Be more patient."

"How much more?"

"A little more," Viktor said gently, hiding his irritation. "A few more months, maybe six at most."

"Another winter is coming, and I'm sick of the cold weather here. I want to be in that villa on the beach in the Seychelles."

Viktor could feel Hardacre about to angle for more money. He played dumb, as he would in any negotiation. "It is waiting for you," Viktor said. Then he decided to hand Hardacre the plum he was after. "And your one million dollars in the Seychelles bank."

"*One?*" Hardacre sounded outraged.

How much more would the fucking hacker ask for? Four, Viktor thought. But he knew Hardacre would be happy with two. He would have to be.

"It should be four million, Viktor Viktorovich. Do you realize the complexity of the computer operations I am running to make this deal happen for you?"

Viktor smirked but kept his voice flat. "We agreed to one."

"But you keep adding more things to the job. How about four?"

Viktor waited.

Hardacre jumped into the silence. "Just watch how everything I've done will work out. As soon as the first people die from the poisoned pills, everything you wanted will start to fall into place. That should be any day now."

Viktor waited in silence. Through the phone, he could feel Hardacre's impatience. He waited still more.

"Please," Hardacre said, almost pleading. "I don't know what you want to do with this fucking pharmaceutical company. But whatever it is, I'm sure you're going to make billions from it. You wouldn't put me to all this trouble otherwise."

Viktor grumbled, "How about I give you one and a half?"

Hardacre exhaled noisily. "You know, Viktor, I could push a button and make your whole operation public. Send every last detail of your black operations straight to the FSB . . . ." That was the Federal Security Service of the Russian Federation, the fearsome force that had evolved out of the KGB. That could be a huge scandal for Moscow. The Kremlin would disavow him. "Plus Interpol, the FBI, and the French Police Nationale. You know, those Frenchies will give you a rude greeting next time you dock in St. Barths."

Hardacre then spouted names of some criminal enterprises Viktor knew he knew about. Then some Viktor was surprised to hear him mention—drug importing in Riga, arms in Somalia and the Philippines, all the businesses he shared with Artyom and would soon leave behind. Viktor was impressed and disturbed.

"Viktor Viktorovich, I'm not kidding," Hardacre said, sounding tough again. But Viktor knew that he was just another worker pleading for money that to Viktor was pocket change. "Viktor, you *know* I can do it."

"And *you* know," Viktor said softly, calmly, "I push a button and you will be dead." Viktor would never admit to fear of any man, although he was a little afraid of Hardacre and his mysterious computer skills. Hardacre was capable of carrying out his threat. But Viktor also knew that Hardacre was well aware that Viktor would kill him if he did. And not a good, swift death. Both knew that Viktor would not be the one to back down. Viktor sat silent. Waiting.

Finally, Hardacre said, "Viktor Viktorovich, by the time we're done with this, you'll be so happy you will *want* to give me a bonus of another couple of million."

"Bonus? You talk like an American banker." Viktor laughed.

"Viktor Viktorovich, everything is going according to plan. And I want to be in the Seychelles before winter comes to this fucking place. I can't stand these people. They think they are smarter than everyone. But they're lucky, that's all. Vultures picking on the carcass of the dead American empire. Come on, make it four, eh?"

Viktor laughed a real laugh. "That's why I like you, Tom. We hate the same kind of people."

"Viktor Viktorovich, please. Four. The job is worth it. You know it is."

Viktor said, "I make it two million," Viktor said and he knew that Hardacre knew that would be his best offer.

"Thank you, Viktor Viktorovich," Hardacre said. Viktor liked the gratitude he thought he heard in the man's voice. He wanted him unsuspecting if it became necessary to have him put away.

15

Emma made a point of meeting Linda Farlow outside the door of her new office suite on Mahogany Row. She wanted as little ceremony and hierarchy as possible. Just two women colleagues, long suffering, overworked and underappreciated, having a chat.

She knew this was risky. Linda had been her rival for almost twenty years. And Emma had beaten her for every promotion. Now she was co-chief operating officer with a fifty-fifty chance of becoming CEO. And Linda was still sidelined as a senior group product director. Famously angry, embittered. But famously competent. No, better than competent. Linda was a walking encyclopedia and she was part of the P&B ethos.

Emma was feeling tense. Could she turn Linda Farlow into an ally? "Glad you could make it on such short notice," Emma said. She gestured for Linda to go in first. As they walked through the outer office where her secretary sat, then through her private conference room and, finally, into her actual office, Emma watched the jealous look on Linda's face as she took it all in. *Oh shit,* she thought, *we should have done this in the cafeteria. Yes, coffee in paper cups in a quiet corner of the cafeteria. That's what I should have done.*

Linda sat on the couch. Emma took the chair facing her. Linda crossed her arms across her chest.

Emma smiled.

Linda did not.

"Linda, remember when we had cubicles near each other down in Consumer Products? And Steve Farricker said everyone in his group had to have their desk completely clear last thing before going home every night?"

Linda nodded.

"Well, it was hell for me." Emma pointed across the room to the big desk. The gleaming mahogany surface was covered in piles of documents. Well organized by her assistant, with every corner of every sheet of paper arranged in perfect right angles, but piles nonetheless. Lots and lots of piles. "I'm, uh, a messy desk person by nature."

"Yes, Emma, I remember." Linda tried not to smirk. She uncrossed her arms and seemed to relax a bit. "You realize, of course, that everyone knew you took the mess from your desk and stuffed it into interoffice envelopes every night so you could get it all back with the first mailroom delivery in the morning. Farricker knew it, too. Joked about it behind your back."

"He did?" Emma wondered if she was blushing.

"Uh-huh." Linda's face seemed to say *gotcha*.

This wasn't at all how Emma wanted the meeting to go. She waved her hand, as if to erase the tape so far. "Ah, so many years ago. Can you believe how long we've been at this?"

Linda folded her arms across her chest again. She gave the big suite another once-over. "Time sure flies when you're having fun."

Emma knew she would have to strain to break through the wall of Linda's anger. After considering this from a lot of different angles, she still felt it was worth a try. Yes, Linda had issues. But she was capable, and, well, the devil you know and all that.

Emma leaned forward. "Linda, let's make a fresh start, okay?" Deep breath. "In my opinion, you have not gotten the promotions and rewards you deserve. I want to fix that, right now."

Linda sat back, visibly shocked.

Emma, the tennis player, pressed her advantage. "I want you to take my former job as divisional president. I need someone who knows what to do without having to struggle up a learning curve. Someone who knows this company." Deliberate pause. "And *cares* about it." Emma watched for Linda's reaction. A faint nod. Now it was time to move in to the net and get the point. "Linda, I've gotten approval to award you the extra stock grants you should have been getting, and put you in the top-level compensation pool that will bring you up to parity with your peers. You have been undervalued for too long. I want to get you doing the kind of things for this company you should have been promoted to a long time ago."

Emma paused, watching Linda's eyes. "Are you with me? With *us*?"

Linda stared down at her lap, then looked up. "Yes, I, uh, of course."

Emma couldn't read her. Was she happy? Surprised? Relieved? Emma had more up her sleeve. That was one of the beauties of being the boss. You knew what the boss has in mind; the employee has to wait to find out. "You know the way Farricker roadblocked my career?"

Linda raised her chin and seemed to smile ever-so slightly. Emma wondered. Was she gloating just a bit at the mention of their old boss?

"Well," Emma said, "he did a number on *you*, too."

Linda's smug expression evaporated. "He did?"

Emma nodded. "I've seen some of the crap he managed to get into your file. I don't know whether he had it in for the two of us or women managers in general. But he was destructive and unfair to everyone but his favorite boys."

Linda looked shocked. "He always told me he was my biggest supporter."

Emma shook her head emphatically no.

"Why that lying, two-faced . . ."

". . . bastard," Emma interjected. "He was a bastard. But he got away with it because he played politics so well." She leaned forward, pressing her case. "Linda, sometimes good people get used badly, no matter how hard the company tries to be fair. But one of the nice things about my new job is I get the chance to right some old wrongs." She looked into Linda's eyes and thought she saw the venom draining out of them. At least she hoped so. Emma had one more olive branch to offer.

"I want you to know something. When I got transferred out of Farricker's department, I had no idea my father had pulled strings to make it happen. Really, I did not. I only found out years later, during my divorce. Dad had passed away by then. I'm not sure what I would have said to him."

Linda answered quickly, "How about 'thank you'?"

"Uh, I'm not so sure. I had been prepared to tough it out."

Emma read Linda's look as skeptical.

"Were you now?" Linda said. "Really?"

"Yes, I was. Well, for long enough to see if I could . . . uh . . ." Emma realized this was going to sound lame. "Listen, Linda. I'm sorry. I got an unfair advantage. But you have to understand that at the time, I had no idea where it came from or why. Life isn't fair. Not to anyone. But for what it's worth, I'm sorry for the injustice. Let the company make it up to you now, okay?"

Linda looked down.

"Linda, I want you on my team," Emma said.

Linda looked up, staring full into Emma's eyes with what seemed like a new openness. She took a deep breath. "And that means *not* on Steve Upshaw's team, right?"

"I didn't say that," Emma added quickly.

"You didn't have to," Linda said quietly, still looking into Emma's eyes. Emma held her gaze steady. Yes, this was the bottom line between them, choosing up sides for the big game. "There's no love lost between me and Steve Upshaw," Linda said. "I think he's an empty suit. You'd be better for the company. And better for the women who work here."

"Linda," Emma said, "I need you to pull together a report on our consumer products division."

"Okay, what do you want to focus on?"

"Long-term payout of our extra antitampering packaging. Not just the short-term costs, but the big picture. Factor in the market share growth we've had since we started and add the growth projections from the brand equity studies. Nobody knows that data like you do."

"And this to demonstrate what?" Linda asked.

"Why more antitampering packaging across more product lines will drive even more growth in market share."

"That's weird," Linda said. "Upshaw said he was thinking of asking me to do a similar report for him. Except he wants the opposite conclusion." Linda made a little cutting gesture across her throat. "Cost cuts." She smiled.

Emma smiled back. "Yes, I heard. So tell me, which conclusion do you think is right for the company?"

"Yours," Linda said.

Emma stood. "Welcome to the team, Linda. And the good things you've earned."

"Thanks, Emma, I . . . er . . . I . . ."

Linda seemed happy. Emma shook her head. Thanks were not necessary. A hug would have been the nice female gesture to seal the deal, she felt. But it would have been inappropriate at this moment. So she took Linda's hand, man-style, and shook it. It was damp and limp. She realized that, in almost twenty years of working with Linda, she could not remember ever touching her.

16

"We have a mole deep inside P&B," Brody said.

"We do?"

They were in Josh's corner office at Anglia, overlooking Park Avenue in midtown Manhattan. Josh was proud of the plain, white minimalism of the two floors Anglia occupied. And the décor looked far more expensive than it was.

"What's more," Brody said with pride in his voice, "our guy just got a big promotion so we'll know even more and faster."

"Isn't that illegal?" Josh asked. He was glad to have such a source, but worried that it could get him in trouble.

"Since when is talking to someone a crime? We're absolutely *not* asking for financials before they're released. And we are *not* going to trade on what we learn. We just want to know what they're saying about our takeover. This person is merely being a bit of a two-face, which is not unusual in a big corporation."

Josh felt concerned that he knew too much already. "Don't tell me more about him, okay: I don't want to know." Josh shuddered, imagining a subpoena from the SEC. "Remember, Brodes," he said, reciting the words of his investment-banking mentor, "Immoral we do every day. Illegal never."

"Ah yes, the Eternal Credo—'Immoral we do every day. Illegal never.' Absolutely, Josh. Old Brodes is taking care of everything. No money trail to Anglia or even to me, for that matter. You don't know anything. Hell, *I* don't know anything. I get my information out of thin air because, well, because that's how I get my information." Big grin. "For instance, I didn't tell you that our mole is in tomorrow's meeting of the takeover defense committee."

"No," Josh said, "you didn't tell me that." Brody was making him damned uncomfortable. Should he talk to his lawyer? What if he did not like the answer his lawyer gave? What if the lawyer asked questions that led to Viktor?

"Aren't you glad?" Brody said.

"Yes," Josh said, fidgeting in his chair, "ignorance is bliss. But somehow, I don't feel blissful." He looked nervously at his watch.

"Listen to me, Brodes," he said, rising. "Do not, repeat *do not,* cross any lines with this mole. Got that?"

Brody nodded. "I promise."

Josh hoped to hell he wasn't lying. Lying was what Brody did best.

17

WEDNESDAY, JULY 29

Mighty Death Dealer was about to deliver the final smack-down. Mighty Death Dealer flexed his muscles and roared. The crowd roared. His enemy roared.

Suddenly Peter felt his left headphone yanked away from his ear. "Earth to Peter," his mother's voice intruded. "Earth to Peter." She spoke in a funny robotic voice, "You have arrived at your destination."

He looked up from the PlayStation Portable. Yes, they were in the parking lot of the heliport. He could see the Delaware River, dark blue under the clear summer sky, and hear the traffic roaring behind them on South Columbus. "Come on," Mom said, "your father's helicopter is waiting." He watched her scan the back of their four-year-old Volvo wagon. "Got anything else besides your backpack?"

"No, Mom," he said, packing away his game. They walked to the small terminal and the helipads beyond.

Peter was used to having Ned drive him here. As a professor, Ned had a more flexible schedule than Mom. And Ned made things less awkward when Dad was there on the helicopter, although he hardly ever was. That was okay. Peter knew Dad was busy. Besides, he had gotten to know the pilots who worked the charter service. Cool guys. If it was Danny, he knew he'd hear some new stories about the Gulf War. Danny had a million of them.

He also didn't mind that Dad wasn't there to greet him most times when he landed at Ledgemere. Actually, Dad was hardly ever there either. Instead, Tom Hardacre would meet him at the helipad. Tom was a cool guy, too. Funny English accent that sometimes was hard to understand. He and Peter both loved computers. Tom would take him into the cold room in the basement where all the servers were; Tom kept all the systems humming and was up on the latest software. The house Tom lived in on Dad's estate was called a cottage. But it was almost the same size as the house he lived in with Mom and Ned.

S tanding beside the Sikorsky S-76, Josh saw Emma and Peter emerge from the terminal. He quickly ended his cell phone call and bounded over to meet them.

"Hi, Nibs!" he said, tousling his son's hair.

"Emma," he said in a more restrained voice, "always nice to see you." Just seeing her set him off-kilter. A million memories exploded before him. The hideous secret shadow of Viktor loomed. Everything he could never say to Emma, never say to anyone. Maybe when it was all over, he could explain it all to her. Maybe someday he really could make things work out, turn all this into a win for all of them. That *had* to be possible. He'd thought of what he wanted to say to Emma on the flight down, mouthing the words to himself. But now, his mind went blank.

Emma forced a polite smile. "Hello, Josh."

At a loss, he turned to Peter. "Here, Nibs, give me your rucksack."

"This is America, Josh," Emma said curtly. "It's called a backpack. And your son's name is Peter."

Josh bit his lower lip.

"You know, Josh," Emma said, "we should not be talking to each other without lawyers present." She turned to Peter. "Your father is planning to take over Percival & Baxter. A hostile takeover."

Josh smiled, struggling to turn on the charm. "Don't be silly, Emma. Of course we can talk." He touched her gently on the sleeve. She withdrew her arm. "I'm just a stockholder."

Emma shot him a frosty look.

He put an arm around Peter's shoulder and ruffled his hair again. "So, Ni—I mean, Peter, did you tell Mom about the big party?"

"Uh-huh," Peter mumbled, and looked down.

"Kroesus Kids?" Emma said. "Organized conspicuous consumption by people too young to appreciate how lucky they are. Really, Josh?"

"Come on," he said brightly. "He should learn to be comfortable with his economic and social equals."

"You mean spoiled brats from around the world?"

Emma stood straight and raised her chin to show that, in heels, she was a bit taller than he. Josh knew this move too well. She did it when she was pissed off at him.

"Come on, Emma, you think being rich is some kind of disease?"

"I'm trying to teach our son some values. To give him grounding," she shook her head, "in reality."

"So am I. Hey, I don't recall you taking him to Africa to dig wells and build schools. I'm trying to teach him how the world really works. What the score really is. Kroesus Kids is kind of silly, I know, but they can relax when they're around their peers. It's at Angus McLeod's private island off Greenwich. Hell, I've done deals with the guy and I've never been invited to his house. But Peter's going as a first-class invited guest, aren't you?" He gave Peter a fond little nudge. "All part of his worldly education."

Emma folded her arms across her chest.

Josh copied her gesture, even though he had not meant

to. "Emma, we're not going to win any prizes for pretending he has no money."

"Oh, Josh, that's not—"

He dropped his arms. "Listen, I grew up poor. It requires no special training. You just suck up your pride and stare at all the things you can't have. Being rich is more complicated. Peter deserves to understand the whole deal." He prodded Peter toward the helicopter. "Come on, kiddo, let's go to Greenwich."

Peter went up the airstair. Josh went after him, then hesitated.

Emma blew a kiss at Peter and turned away.

"Emma, wait!" Josh called urgently. This minimeeting had not played out the way he had wanted it to. What the hell had gotten into him? Emma had a way of making him feel defensive. And guilty. Once again, he'd been saying all the wrong things to her and not knowing why. In front of Peter, that often happened. This time worse, so many complications, fucking secrets, and so damn much at stake. He had to give it another try. He stepped down from the airstair and hurried toward her. "Please, give me a minute, that's all."

She stopped without turning around. He came around in front of her and touched her arm.

She moved it away.

"Emma, please."

"Please what?"

"Can't we work something out?"

"What are you talking about? What could we possibly work out?"

"A deal for the future." Josh had thought about this and he liked what it might promise. Maybe I can convince her. "Please, Emma, hear me out. I think with your pharma operating experience and my deal making, we could make a bloody fortune together." This was the win-win he had imagined.

"I am not interested in making a *bloody* fortune with you." She seemed to spit his British adjective at him. "Not with you or any other corporate rapist. Excuse me, I mean raider. This conversation is inappropriate on every level. *You* were the one who showed up out of nowhere and started a fight. You want to fight? Okay, let's have at it. I promise you, the good guys will win."

"Emma, uh . . . I really . . ."

"Josh, I'm late for my next appointment. It's with Mike Saltzman, by the way, our poison pill attorney."

"Emma . . . I . . . uh . . ."

Well, at least he had planted that idea, he told himself, put it into the air between them. He could come back to it again when she had seen the light.

She looked away.

"Emma?" he said.

She did not look at him. "What?"

"Just so you know . . ." He paused. "Emma?" He was trying to read her. She was putting up a cold wall. He had thought about this part, too. This would be tough, but he had to say it. He knew what was coming and she didn't. Or maybe she did. In any case, he had to say it. "Uh, if there's ever a proxy fight?"

"Are you planning one?" she asked.

"No, Emma, I'm just saying . . ."

She looked over his shoulder at something behind him.

"Sometimes with these deals," he said hesitantly, "well, nothing that might be said, nothing you might read in letters to shareholders, well, it'll all be business, just business." He touched her arm again. She turned away again. "None of it will be personal. Please understand that. Please understand that, Emma. None of it will be personal."

She turned back to him, glaring. "Josh, anytime one person does anything to another person, it's personal."

She turned and walked at a fast clip toward the terminal.

18

After spending the first ten minutes in the helicopter with his PlayStation, Peter felt Dad squeeze his arm. He looked up and saw Dad motion for him to take off the headphones.

"Kiddo," he said, "I want you to know something. I put a chunk of your trust fund into Percival & Baxter. We can all make some nice money on this play. It wouldn't hurt if you helped convince your mom. But don't tell her I told you. That's important. Understand?"

Peter felt his stomach knotting up. He could just hear Mom freaking out when she heard this.

Dad raised his index finger, the way he did whenever he had a lesson for Peter. "The only way you're ever going to learn how the market works is to have some skin in the game." He tapped Peter on the chest. "Your mother is right in a way. Money *isn't* everything. It's the *only* thing."

Peter muttered, "Okay, Dad." Then he said tentatively, "Mom says when you take over companies, you fire all the people and sell off everything."

Dad looked surprised. "Uh, no I don't. Not always."

"Mom says that's what you do." Peter had to hear this out from his dad. He had heard it all from Mom, over and over in recent days.

"Well, sometimes, yes. When that plan makes sense. You'll learn about business someday. That's what I'm starting to teach you now."

Peter replayed what Mom had said. "She says you destroy good companies."

"She's wrong," Dad insisted. "I build shareholder value and create wealth for a lot of people. Like you, for instance."

"Mom says it's greed to buy things you don't need, like a big mansion and a helicopter."

"I happen to need this helicopter for my business, Peter. And if I'm not mistaken, you like it, too. And the West Wing at Ledgemere? Right?"

Peter went silent. Of course, he adored his West Wing media arcade, even if it was kind of lonely most weekends, and these rides in the Sikorsky, too. Of course, nothing was as great as that trip to Africa in the timeshare G5, even if his getting sick had ruined it. This was one of those times when he loved Dad and was pissed off at him at the same time. He didn't dare speak.

"Look, kiddo, I'm not out to hurt Mom," Dad said, patting Peter's knee. "I'm out to help her. Wait and see how much money we'll be able to make out of Percival & Baxter. All of us. Mom, especially. She's a really talented executive, we all know that. I've got an idea. I was just trying to tell her about it. After we're done with P&B, Mom could lead Anglia's pharma-buyout division. We could be partners. We could buy up pharmas, have Mom run them, take them private, spin them off, take them public, take some private again, then public again. It's how the LBO business works."

Peter wasn't sure what Dad was talking about. He just knew Mom would have no part of it.

"We can make fortune on top of fortune on top of fortune, all of us. You, too. All of us together."

Suddenly, Peter's words just spilled out. "But Dad, Mom cares about P&B. It's her company. It was Grandpa's company. She really loves it." She hadn't actually said "love," but Peter could tell that's how she felt.

"Peter," Dad said, "you have so much to learn."

Peter knew that Dad must be really serious. He hardly ever called him Peter.

"Son, you can't love a company. You can love your family, you can love your dog. But you can't love a company. A company is just a thing you use to make money. Work on her to convince her, okay, kiddo? Will you try for me, please?"

"Okay, Dad," he said. He knew he would get yelled at by Mom. He knew exactly how it would go. Trying to please both of his parents was im-freakin-possible.

Dad looked down and reached into his attaché case for a file. Peter knew that his time with him for the weekend was over. It seemed like most of the time they were together, Dad found ways to ignore him. Or maybe it was because he really did work all the time. Still, it bothered Peter. He missed the feeling of closeness they'd had on the Africa trip . . . until, of course, *he* had ruined it by getting sick. *Maybe I blew it forever back then*, Peter thought. *Or worse, maybe I'm just not that interesting to a high-powered grown-up like Dad.*

"Listen, Nibs," Dad mumbled. "The pilot's going to drop me at the midtown heliport first, then take you to Ledgemere. I've got some business and a benefit in Manhattan tonight." He pulled out some papers and started reading.

Already Peter felt alone. He hated being put in the middle of his parents' worst fight ever. And why the hell did Dad have to start it in the first place?

19

Emma watched Mike Saltzman make his presentation of the shareholder rights plan, the strategy known as the "poison pill." She was one of six around the table in Brad Johansen's private conference room, along with Brad, Upshaw, general counsel Jack Hupper, and Eric Abernathy, the investment banker from Bernhardt & Co. Saltzman was a laser pointed at Hal Percival.

She marveled at the energy of the fabled takeover defense lawyer. He looked somewhere between seventy and eighty, probably closer to eighty. But he talked with the kind of passion Peter had when describing a hot new video game. With his full head of curly gray hair, bright blue eyes, and vibrant body motions, he seemed like a young man masquerading inside the body of someone much older.

Saltzman had first gone through the governance arguments that the board would need to understand, then the legal precedents, and finally the mechanisms of how the poison pill would work in the stock market. He then closed his thick binder and began his wrap-up.

"So, the minute Anglia buys so much as one share beyond the fifteen percent ownership our plan allows . . ." he said, and paused. He made a chopping motion. "Then the pill is automatically triggered. All current shareholders are issued warrants to buy P&B shares at a significant discount below the market price. All current shareholders, that is, *except* one: Anglia Partners."

Hal looked at Brad. They exchanged a glance and a nod. Emma could see in them the smooth communication of people who have been working together for years. *Like a couple with a strong marriage,* she thought.

"In that instant," Saltzman said, opening his arms, "the flood of new P&B shares will dilute the raider's position. His fifteen percent ownership will plummet. The cost of their takeover will skyrocket."

"It would skyrocket," Hal said, repeating Saltzman's word, "beyond any price Anglia Partners might be willing or able to pay."

"Yes, exactly, Hal."

"You know," Hal mused, "there have been chances to sell this company for a quick buck before. And I, as the chap born with the silver spoon in his mouth and the largest chunk of inherited shares in his trust fund—well, I have stood to gain the most. But that's not what we're about, is it?"

"No," Emma chimed in emphatically, "it's not in any way what this company's about."

Hal gave her a proud smile. Almost fatherly, she thought. "These Wall Street bastards care only about money," he went on. "To them, there's no greater good. The only purpose a company serves is to squeeze out the last nickel of profit. Of course, we too make money, lots of it. But money isn't our product. Money is the *by-product* of making medicines that are beneficial. That's why our executives must share—and I apologize for sounding old-fashioned—must share a set of *values* beyond mere dollars."

"Exactly," Saltzman said, patting his document. "The poison pill is protecting P&B's independence *and* its values."

Hal nodded. "Yes, exactly." He glanced at Emma. She gave him a smile. He smiled back. *Take that, Josh*, she thought.

Hal looked back at Saltzman. "Now Mike, you promise this poison pill will keep the raider at bay." It was half question, half statement.

Saltzman nodded.

"And you say that no raider has ever beaten a poison pill." Another half question.

The attorney smiled. "Not really. Not since the first one in 1982."

"And the board can enact this preemptively now and still allow for a vote of the shareholders, say, a year from now?" This one was all question.

"Yes, Hal," Saltzman said. "The board must act decisively now to avert a possible threat. Once you let one of these raiders get even a foot in the door, they can bring down the whole house."

Hal stood and extended his hand to Saltzman. "You have my support and, I'm confident, the support of the full board today."

Everyone else stood.

Hal picked up Saltzman's thick document. He seemed to weigh it, then let it fall to the table with a thud. "I must say," he added with a grin, "I do enjoy the irony of the name 'shareholder rights plan.' That's a nice bit of spin wizardry, uh, since it denies the rights of a major shareholder."

Emma jumped in. "A shareholder who has no place trying to seize control in the first place."

Hal gave her another big smile. "Exactly," he said, again borrowing one of Saltzman's words.

"So, that covers our prep," Brad said. "The board meeting starts in an hour. Steve and Emma, you have your presentations ready. Eric and Jack, you'll set the stage for the plan. Mike, you'll walk the board through it. Then Hal will call for the vote."

"Yes indeed," Hal said brightly, "we do seem to have

everything in order." He turned to Brad, who had suddenly turned away. The CEO stood facing the wall, massaging his temples.

Hal tapped him on the shoulder. "Something wrong?"

Brad turned around. "Fine," he mumbled, "just a little tension headache." He shook himself. "Nothing a couple of Acordinol can't fix. Excuse me just a second."

He walked to his private bathroom down the hall. He returned a moment later, holding a sealed Acordinol bottle. He waved it in the air. "I get Stephanie to keep me stocked with samples from the latest production runs," he said.

He started wrestling with the layers of plastic around the bottle.

"I think of you, Emma, every time I try to open one of our packages." He looked up and smiled. "You made P&B the first pharma to exceed FDA tamper-proof standards with two extra layers." He pulled the top tab and tore off the first wrapper, then began working on the next one, then the next.

"And all the majors followed our lead," Hal said. "Emma shamed them into it. Now it's the industry standard."

"Not only me," she said. "It was their customers who demanded it, once they saw how safe our new packaging made them feel."

Emma remembered how bitterly Steve Upshaw had fought her on this.

"Why on earth spend the money to *exceed* what the government demands of us?" he had said repeatedly in executive committee. "Makes no financial sense."

"Because we're Percival & Baxter and it's the right thing to do for our customers," she had argued. "And they will reward us with their loyalty. They'll tell their family and friends. And in the long run, that will translate into bigger market share and more profits."

"Wall Street will hammer us," Upshaw had warned. "There's no reason to do anything more than we're required to do."

But Emma had been proved right. Sales of the company's over-the-counter medications, Acordinol in particular, had grown 10 percent by that year's end, thanks to her new packaging and the "Safer Choice" marketing campaign she masterminded. After a small dip in the stock price following two tetchy quarterly earnings reports, sales, profits, *and* the stock finished the year at an all-time high.

Brad finally got the bottle open and spilled two yellow pills into his palm. He offered the open bottle to the group.

"Anybody else need a little headache relief?"

He got a round of "no thanks."

He popped the pills into his mouth, turned around, and started back toward his bathroom.

20

Peter stood outside the caretaker's cottage, waiting for Tom Hardacre to come out and drive him to the Kroesus Kids party. He held Dad's little gift-wrapped package with the gold ribbon. "Check your medicine cabinet before you leave for the party," Dad said before he ran off to his meeting. The box looked like the right size for a watch or something. Dad was always giving him presents, especially when he had to go off and leave him alone.

This weekend, Peter would have liked to spend time with him and maybe ask him some stuff about girls. Or maybe not. If Grandpa Sid had been here, he wouldn't be shy about asking *him*. He loved his grandpa. They could talk about *everything*. They would play together all weekend long, shooting pool, video games, cards. They'd watch movies in Dad's screening room 'til late at night. He'd tell all these stories—he called it "shooting the shit"—about how smart Dad was growing up in Boston. And about his buddies at the race track in Florida and all the trouble they liked to make. But Grandpa Sid wasn't here this time.

He was worried about the party. He knew only a couple of the kids who'd be at the party. There was Scott McLeod. It was at his house. Scott's dad was the big-deal guy who owned the whole private island. Dad had told him all about Angus McLeod. He was like the richest guy in Greenwich, practically invented the hedge fund. So rich he didn't work for clients anymore, just invested billions for his own account.

Scott was okay, Peter supposed, but not exactly friendly. He never really made Peter feel welcome. In fact, a couple of times at parties, he had made Peter feel like some kind of charity case. "Here's Peter Katz," he would mumble. "My dad does deals with his dad and he's visiting from Philadelphia for the weekend." Made it sound like Philadelphia was some Third World country where they had no computers and people went to the bathroom in a ditch.

He wondered about this girl, Tsarina Alexandra from the FriendVault. If she even was a girl. And how the fuck was he going to look like someone with a superhero chin? He cringed at his stupidity. Why did he type that? It was one thing to be Katman. He liked his avatar. Katman could say and do things Peter Katz couldn't. But what was he supposed to do *now*? Walk around with his chin sticking out like Dudley Do-Right, that cartoon character from the old show on TV Land?

He kicked the gravel in the driveway. He was always nervous before parties.

Tom stepped out of the front door and let the screen door slam behind him. He was a big man, taller than Dad, with broad shoulders, a wide face, and thick strong hands. And younger than Dad, maybe midthirties. He was wearing the black Armani sport jacket, white shirt, black tie, and gray slacks that were his "uniform" when on duty as the number-one staff person at Ledgemere.

Tom raised a little remote in one hand and pointed it at the stables that had been converted into a six-car garage. The six doors opened all at once.

The first bay was empty. "I'm afraid your dad's gone in the Bentley so I can't run ye to the party in that," he said in that thick accent of his. "But we got the Porsche," he said, pointing at the customized green 911 Carrera with the huge spoiler swooping off the back. "The Merc or the F430 perhaps?" Tom meant the Mercedes convertible or the red Ferrari. "Or maybe the Land Rover? Or the Suburban? We could crash the gates and arrive through the woods," Tom said with a laugh. "Off-road, eh? Now tell me, Mr. Peter Katz, which car would ye like to arrive in?"

Peter didn't care about the cars. He was worrying about the Tsarina and fretting that he would never in his whole life get laid.

Suddenly one of the Mexican gardeners ran up to them.

"Meester Tom, Meester Tom!" he said, out of breath. "The raccoon, the raccoon! Is in the trap!"

Peter had heard about a raccoon that was raiding the garbage and destroying plantings around the estate. Tom thanked the gardener and, with a wink, told Peter he'd be right back. He went into the cottage and came back holding a big handgun.

"Let's have us a bit of fun," Tom said. He motioned with the pistol for Peter and the gardener to follow him into the woods behind the cottage. Peter knew nothing about guns—real guns, outside of video games—but this one looked even bigger than the ones he'd seen city cops carry in their holsters.

In a clearing in the woods behind the greenhouse, an angry and confused raccoon hissed and struggled inside the wire-net trap. Tom offered the gun to Peter. "Would ye like to do the honors?"

"Uh, no thanks." He stared at the weapon. He had never shot a real gun. Of course, he had eviscerated, decapitated, and slaughtered with brutality and creativity countless people and space creatures. But all his courage and murderous pleasure was make-believe. Like little girls playing with dollies. He was afraid of the big gun in Tom's hand. Really afraid.

"Ye sure?" Tom asked.

Peter took a step back. The angry raccoon was creepy. And pathetic. It did not know it was about to die. Or maybe it did. Peter shook his head no.

"Watch this," Tom said, unlocking the safety. "We keep a bit of firepower for security purposes here, lad, just in case. All registered with the Greenwich police, of course." Tom paused and watched the raccoon struggle for a moment. Then he lowered the pistol beside the cage. The shot was the loudest thing Peter had ever heard. He winced. When he opened his eyes, he saw a hole in the cage and a mess of bloody bits inside. The raccoon's head was mostly gone. The stink of gunpowder and animal guts filled the air.

Peter looked at Tom.

Tom was smiling. "The next one can be yer kill, eh, lad? I'll show ye how she works." He held up the gun proudly.

Peter shrugged. He thought he might be getting sick to his stomach. "I think we can go now," he said. All he wanted was to flee.

Tom lowered the gun to his side and put the safety back on. "Before we go," he said, "don't ye think ye should open the present from yer father?"

"Oh, yeah," Peter said dimly. He had forgotten that he was clutching it in his hand. The wrapping paper was soggy with his sweat. He had almost crushed the box. He pulled off the ribbons and undid the wrapping paper. It was a box of condoms. "Extra Sensitive for Extra Pleasure" the label read. Peter opened the envelope and read the card Dad had scrawled, "Nibs, Here's to getting lucky at your big weekend. Love, Dad."

Tom winked and nudged him. "All set then, lad?" he asked.

"All set," Peter said, trying to sound macho. All he wanted to do was get the hell away from the dead raccoon, the gun, and Tom Hardacre.

21

Was it a few seconds after Brad popped the pills in his mouth and turned his back? Or was it a full minute? Or maybe more?

Emma would never be sure. Time had become something new. It was slow and fast at the same time. An alien dimension through which Emma found herself moving. Like a dream, like a nightmare. But she would never forget those awful sounds. The thud as Brad collapsed, the crack as his head smashed into the floor.

She ran, with Hal, Saltzman, Abernathy, and Upshaw to the corridor.

She saw blood pouring from the side of Brad's head. He was shaking, arms and legs flailing. His face was contorted, eyes rolled back into his head, his mouth open, gasping for air.

Emma remembered it as a blur. Panic. Confusion. Fumbling about. Hal on his knees beside Brad. Saltzman, Abernathy, and Upshaw huddled over Hal. Hal calling Brad's name over and over. Trying to stop him from shaking.

Emma dashed back toward the secretaries' desks. "Stephanie! Jeanette! Get medical! Our nurses, our doctors from downstairs! Call 911! EMS! Brad's having a seizure!" She watched Stephanie call medical while Jeanette got on the line with 911. Emma felt as if she could not get enough air. She was breathing hard. And trying to catch her breath at the same time.

She ran back to the corridor. Brad lay motionless. Looking like he was not breathing. The men stood over him, gaping. In one hand Brad still clutched the open bottle. A spray of little yellow pills littered the floor around him. His other arm was extended, hand open, as if grasping for something that wasn't there. His mouth was wide open, eyes horribly glazed and vacant.

Emma remembered saying, "We've got to call the police, too." She shouted, "Stephanie, call the police! The police!"

The medical team from the company infirmary burst in carrying EMS gear—oxygen tank and mask, defibrillation paddles, a big satchel. A doctor with two nurses, one man, one woman. Emma and her group stepped out of their way and back into the conference room. The medical team got down on the floor over Brad, turning him over onto his back, holding up his head, trying to rouse him. As they took the scissors and began slicing off his shirt, Emma had to turn away.

The lifeless person on the floor did not look like Brad anymore. Brad's moving presence took up a lot of space, she realized. This pale waxworks imitation of him was smaller than the Brad she had known until moments before.

Stephanie shouted from the outer office, "EMS is on the way! The police too!" Amid the noise and chaos, Emma had a sickening feeling in her stomach. Some evil instinct told her what had just happened. She just *knew*. It was not a seizure or heart attack or stroke. She wanted to scream. Who could have done this? How? Why? To destroy P&B? A thought of Josh flickered in her mind. What, to help his takeover? Then no, not Josh, not Josh even at his absolute greedy worst.

She had bottles of Acordinol . . . in her desk drawer, in her purse, in every medicine cabinet in their home. So did everybody else everywhere. Her crowning achievement had been to get those bottles . . . everywhere. Building in extra tamper-proofing for safety. Brad's bottle was sealed. She watched him open it. The seals all intact. Even the slightest attempt at tampering made them turn red. If someone had poisoned the pills, it had to be before the seals were put in place. That would have to be at the factory. Right here under their noses.

She ran back to the corridor where the medical team was working to revive Brad. She reached down and picked up the bottle he had held just moments before. The lot number was EQDD8574 and the date told her it had been made just days before, on July 12. She felt that number burn into her memory. She set it back on the floor.

She had to protect the people she loved, protect everyone . . . protect P&B. She dashed back to the conference table and grabbed her BlackBerry. She fumbled dialing the number. Her heart pounded as it rang once, twice, three times.

"Alex!" she half-shouted when the head of production picked up. "Alex, something terrible has happened to Brad. It could be a foreign substance in the Acordinol he just took. Lot number EQDD8574. Got that? EQDD8574! Where has product with that lot number been shipped? We've got to find it and get it out of people's hands! Please, Alex, this is an emergency! Stop all production immediately. Take samples from every lot number we have in inventory and have our labs test them for contaminants. Test them for poisons! Same at our distribution centers. Immediately! It could be deadly. And Alex, be prepared in case we announce a recall of *all* product. I'm not saying we will. But in case the worst happens, we need to be prepared. Get the logistics lined up and ready if we have to pull the trigger. I hope to high heaven we don't have to."

"Emma, can I ask? . . ." Alex tried to say.

"Alex," she said urgently, "we can talk about why later. Please just do it. Do it *now!*"

"He's gone," the doctor called from the hallway, "there's no reviving him." Stephanie started crying.

She heard Upshaw saying something to her, but his voice sounded distant and unclear, as if he were on the other side of a wall. She felt hands on her shoulders. She thought she heard Upshaw say, "Emma, before we start a panic, let's think about the money."

22

"I thought a Zamboni was a little *dolce*!" Tanya giggled to Fiona, "you know, one of those yummy Italian sweets."

"Me, too," Fiona said, slipping her arm through Tanya's as they walked out of the frigidly air-conditioned ice-hockey rink into the summer heat. "Who knew it was a steamroller for smoothing the ice?" They giggled.

Tanya loved being half of a contrasting pair, short and tall, brunette and blond. Fiona was in a lime green mini sundress by Chanel, Tanya wore black silk pasha pants, black bra, and a gold camisole by Marc Jacobs. Both wore Gucci sunglasses. Fiona's were narrow tortoiseshell with rhinestones, Tanya's were big and oval in the Jackie O mode.

Tanya guessed there were one hundred or so Kroesus Kids in full party mode under the brilliant, cloudless sky. They milled about the sprawling mansion and outbuildings, chatting, dancing, playing all kinds of sports, drinking and munching treats from trays proffered by a small army of waiters who followed them everywhere. She saw much flirting, with couples of all sexual orientations forming and vanishing from sight for private indulgences in sex or chemicals or both.

She and Fiona had vowed to stay with each other until Oliver showed up.

Ever the art critic, Fiona gestured at the overgrown new mansion modeled after Versailles. "It's such an oafish attempt at copying," she said. "They got the glitz but none of the grace. I tell you, Le Vau, Le Brun, and Le Notre must be spinning in their graves." She was referring to the architects and designers of the French royal palace. She shrugged and shook her head at the vast indoor sports complexes, ball fields, tennis courts, basketball courts, gardens, and pools over the rest of the island. "And how odd to build what looks like the site of the next Olympic games right beside one's great house."

"But not in Disneyland," Tanya said with a smirk. "Nothing is odd in Disneyland. Maybe they have their own private Space Mountain. Think we'll have to queue up for a long time?" They giggled again.

Tanya was having random thoughts about the boy with the superhero chin. How on earth would she find him? Would she even want to? Her goal was to find the right boy to be the father of her baby girl. The chin business was just chat-board nonsense. Tanya was on a mission. She would inspect all the available young men and apply her considerable experience with boys to find just the right sperm donor.

Arm in arm, the two girls wandered to the deejay by the giant marble fountain. They danced with each other for half a song when Fiona grabbed her buzzing phone from her Burberry studded-leather sling bag. "Oliver's just arrived!" she said, reading the text. "Says he's sorry he's late. Damn trains from New York. He wants me to meet him under the chandelier in the foyer of the main house." Fiona was breathless.

Tanya kissed her friend on both cheeks.

"Now if you see Alban," Fiona said, raising a warning finger, "you show him a heart of stone: granite."

"Obsidian," Tanya said with a wink, hoping she really could pull it off. "Obsidian is harder, shinier, and goes better with my eyes."

"Obsidian," Fiona called as she dashed off toward the house.

Tanya wandered among the Kroesus Kids, just observing. Hiding behind her sunglasses, she told herself she was like an anthropologist, or even a zoologist, cataloguing the social and premating rituals of this tribe or colony or whatever this collection of pampered creatures like her was. Or maybe she was a cat on the prowl for prey. Yes, she decided, she would think of herself as a big hungry cat.

She felt a tap on her shoulder. "Tanya?" a familiar male voice asked.

She turned. It was Alban Abbott-Reade holding the hand of a pretty young woman. It was inevitable! And awful! She looked at the girl. Or maybe not. At least it wasn't that horrible girl he took to the May Ball.

Tanya took in her old boyfriend. Alban was as tall, handsome, and haughty as ever. Thick blond hair, chiseled aristocratic features (yes, the jutting noble chin, how ironic that she had chins on her mind). And those green eyes. He was the boy who had everything and knew it. Champion rider, fencer, rower, and champion fucker.

She vowed to show him nothing. She gave him a big fake smile and kissed the air beside him. "Alban," she said, not quite coldly. As she stood back, he looked a bit smaller. She noticed a little pimple starting to erupt near the cleft of that noble chin. Yes, she could do this. *Obsidian,* she thought, *obsidian.*

"I was hoping we'd run into you!" Alban's girlfriend said, in a plain American accent. "Alban's told me so much about you."

"Not everything, I hope," Tanya said. She wagged a finger at Alban. "You didn't tell her *everything*?"

"Fortunately," Alban said, "my memory is a sieve. I can barely remember what I did yesterday."

"I'm Sandra Wolcott, Alban's fiancée," she said warmly. "I'm so happy to finally meet you."

Tanya inspected the girl. She was quite beautiful, with an oval face, wide cheekbones, large brown eyes, a cascade of honey-colored hair, full lips, and a gap-toothed smile that was sensual and, Tanya had to admit, friendly.

Sandra looked earnestly at her. "Alban said he wasn't sure if you would come to our wedding. But I'm hoping you will. I really do. We're taking over the Capella resort in Telluride for a week next January. We're hoping *all* the people from our lives will be there with us to help us start our new journey. Won't you come? Please?" She gave Tanya's hand a little squeeze.

Tanya decided that she liked her. She felt bad for the pain Sandra would feel when Alban betrayed her. Which was inevitable. Soon enough, they would be sisters in heartache.

"Of course I'll come," she said to Sandra. She glanced at Alban. Yes, he *was* getting smaller. "What fun it will be. I've always wanted to ski Telluride."

She gave Sandra a real hug and a real kiss on the cheek. She watched Alban out of the corner of her eye. She could see him looking a bit uncomfortable at the sight of "his" two women bonding. She liked that. She decided she could push things and make him positively squirm. She locked arms with Sandra and pulled her to one side.

"Now you must let me *fete* the two of you when we're back in London." She watched Alban's lips tighten. She had a sudden realization about the future. His mouth is going to become mean and miserly as he gets older. Not the kind of mouth one wants to live with. No, definitely not. "Let me arrange a little party at my new house. I'm just off Sloane Square. I'll gather as many of our old mates as I can. I'll have gondolas filled with ice in my garden, overflowing with bottles of champagne. We'll make the May Ball look positively paltry."

She watched with delight as Alban flinched.

Sandra gave her a hug in return. "Yes, we'd love it, wouldn't we, Alban?"

He smiled. A forced smile, Tanya could tell.

She felt him getting shorter still. Less imposing than he was a moment ago. Less imposing than her memories of him. There, before her very eyes, Alban Abbott-Reade was fading into . . . ordinariness.

She touched the two of them. "I'm so happy for you," she said. She was actually feeling happy, but for her own relief. "We'll see each other in Chelsea and on the slopes of Telluride then."

"Definitely!" Sandra said as she wrapped one arm around Alban's waist.

"Happy to see you, luv," Alban said with a meek little smile. Tanya was sure she saw a burden of guilt lifting off his shoulders. Now they could be, if not friends, friendly acquaintances.

"Me too," Tanya said and mostly meant it. "Got to run off and meet someone," she said, thinking that she was not lying, she was a woman with a plan. "I fear I've already kept him waiting too long." She meant, of course, her little baby-girl-to-be.

She turned with a wave and headed for the squash courts and the screening room. Stepping inside to the cool air of the glassed-in atrium, she heard the rumble of the movie sound track from behind the closed doors of the screening room and the electronic babble of a row of arcade video games along the opposite wall.

There she saw a tall, lanky boy lost in concentration in front of an arcade video game of an intergalactic battle. He was wearing plain, nondesigner jeans and a black T-shirt.

He did not notice her noticing him. She watched him. She was taken with his dark eyes and his intensity. Like her, he seemed determined to ignore the party. She wondered if she could get him to pay as much attention to her as he did to his game. He was handsome in a callow way. He looked . . . sixteen, maybe seventeen. She studied him. Yes, he definitely had a virginal aura. Sweet. A sixteen-year-old virgin. Ah, they are so randy at that age. And so curious, so insecure. And once unleashed, so utterly insatiable. She could teach him the ropes, be his first woman.

Perfect! She felt a happy hum deep inside her. Her body and stars were aligning. All the elements of her grand plan were coming together . . . perfectly.

She brushed up against his arm and took off her sunglasses. "Will you show me how to play? You make it look like a lot of fun."

"Huh?" the boy looked up, startled. Oh yes, such lovely dark eyes, Tanya thought, and nice strong hands with long elegant fingers. Once again, she counted the days since her last period as she inspected him more closely. "Lovely," she said and slipped her arm through his. Yes, she decided, *I have* found my sperm donor. His eyes are lovely. His hands are lovely and strong. And his innocence and virginity? Well, what could be better? She could have sworn she felt something throb deep inside her womb, telling her that the stars and the moon and her mysterious female cycles were all coming into alignment tonight. Yes, Tanya decided, I have indeed found my sperm donor.

She could almost see her baby girl, almost smell her delicious flesh. *I shall love you perfectly and forever,* she thought, *my dearest little Alexandra.*

23

"Our laboratory tests confirm," the Miami police detective announced over the speakerphone, "it was sodium cyanide in the Acordinol pills those people took."

Emma stared at the speakerphone shaped like a spaceship on the conference room table. Her worst fear confirmed. She looked around the room at the executive committee, convened in emergency session. The board of directors was meeting down the hall. She looked at her watch. Just past 1:30 PM. Brad had collapsed at about 10:30 AM. It felt like weeks ago.

"We're autopsying the two victims now," the police chief droned in his monotone. "A female Caucasian aged fifty-one, and a male African-American aged sixty-eight. They bought from the same store. She last night, him early this morning. Same lot number, EQDD8574. We're impounding all the Acordinol in our jurisdiction. FBI and FDA are joining us in this investiga—"

Emma tapped on the speakerphone as if it were the policeman's shoulder. "What were their names?" she asked urgently. She needed to know their names. She wished she could see their faces.

Papers rustled over the line. "Uh . . . Anne Womrath," the policeman said, "and, uh, Steven Drake. As I said, we have impounded all the Acordinol in our jurisdiction and put out a bulletin. Because this crosses state lines, the feds are taking over. You'll be hearing from them momentarily."

"Yes, thank you," Emma said, "we're awaiting their arrival any minute now."

"Then I'll go back to my end," the police chief said and hung up.

There was a moment of stunned silence in the conference room.

"We can't wait for Brad's test results," Emma said, suddenly out of breath. "Brad will make it three. There will be more. Oh God, there will be more. We need to announce a nationwide recall immediately."

"Emma's right," Steve Upshaw said. "We need to recall everything from that lot number."

She turned to him. "No, no, Steve, we need to recall *all* the Acordinol."

He shook his head emphatically. "No we don't, just that lot number."

"No, Steve," she insisted, holding herself back from saying "No, goddammit!"

"Emma, I totally disagree," Upshaw said, sounding irked. "May I remind you, we are *co*-chief operating officers. And under the circumstances, uh, with Brad . . . uh, Brad . . . gone, we need to act as co-chief executives. We need to make this call together. I'm telling you, we can contain the damage and the financial impact. We *have* to. It's our fiduciary responsibility."

Emma shook her head angrily. "We don't have time for this. Lives are at risk. Steve, imagine yourself in a drugstore. You see two packages of Acordinol side by side. One could kill you and your entire family. The other one is fine. The only difference is a little number buried somewhere on the back label. Are you really going to stop, check out the lot numbers, and pick up the one that's EQDD8573 not

EQDD8574? Or are you going to be scared shitless of anything labeled Acordinol that hasn't been certified a million times over to be absolutely safe?"

"Emma," he snapped, "recalling all the Acordinol out there could bankrupt us."

"Steve, lack of trust will bankrupt us an awful lot faster."

Upshaw's eyes darted around the room, the top sheet from his notepad was scrunched up in a ball in his fist. "Emma, can we take this offline?"

Before she could answer, the door opened and Hal Percival stepped inside. "Emma, if you'd come with me, please. The board needs to see you right away."

24

Peter Katz had just plain given up. This rich-kid party at Scott McLeod's was a bust, a flop. Totally. Okay, some kids were having a good time. No, a lot of them. But not him. He had stopped trying to find Tsarina Alexandra after the first hour. He had no idea how to advertise his superhero chin. Three (or was it four?) times he had approached girls he hoped might be his Tsarina. Three times (no, it *was* four times) he had tried a different opening line about his superhero chin. Trying to be clever. Trying to be masterful. Trying to sound in charge. Trying to be all those things the cool guys who got laid managed to be. Trying, really, *really* trying.

And he just got laughed at. Or looked at with that expression that said, "What the fuck?" And seeing them run off to tell their girlfriends about this weird guy. Or texting a warning to watch out for the creep who wants to brag about his chin.

I am a fucking loser. No wait, I can't even say "fucking." I'm just a loser.

Then *Mighty Death Dealer Arcade Version* came to the rescue with its giant screen. Two joysticks. Death, destruction, split-second timing. He could stay here all night. Maybe he would. Pull an all-nighter. Something. Anything. Just forget about Tsarina Alexandra. Forget about his stupid chin. Forget about, well, just forget about it.

"Will you show me how to play?" he heard a girl with

an English accent ask. He felt her arm brush up against his. "You make it look like a lot of fun."

"Huh?" he looked up, startled. She was pretty. With nice blue eyes. Very blue. Taller than most girls. What could she want? He didn't dare think too much. If he did, he knew he would blow it. He would probably blow it anyway, but, geez, never mind. He looked at her blankly, frozen with . . . not fear . . . not resignation . . . but hope, hanging by a thread.

She smiled. "I said, you make the game look like a lot of fun. Will you show me how to play?"

Cover your panic, Peter. Don't think. Just do. "Uh, sure."

She wrapped her hand gently around his forearm. With a nudge of her hip against his, she moved him a bit so that they were sharing the big screen.

"There now," she said brightly, talking over the raucous sounds of the video game, "are you going to give me a tutorial?"

He held his breath for an instant. He had made up his mind. He was a loser. And now, suddenly, a pretty girl was touching him on the sensitive skin of his inner forearm and banging her hip against his. *OMFG! Oh my fucking God.*

He quickly pushed the reset button. The game went quiet. He looked at the girl. She kept her hand gently on his arm, her hip still just barely touching his.

"You're English," he said, feeling a smile bubble up from his confusion and spread across his face.

"In part," the girl said, returning the smile.

"Can I ask which part?" Peter had no idea where his clever response came from.

The girl gave his arm a squeeze. 'You are very naughty indeed."

Had he actually scored with a good line? He couldn't believe it. That had never happened before. Whatever he was going to say next—and he had no freakin' idea—he was *not* going to say anything about his chin.

The girl squeezed his arm ever so lightly. The sensation was thrilling. "I've got an idea," she said, "since we are all Kroesus Kids here, let's not go through all that baggage of who one's parents are, where one's money comes from, how one's trust funds are structured, how many houses, how many yachts and planes, and so on. Wouldn't it be lovely just to meet and have a bit of fun? With no baggage?"

He nodded, unable to think of anything clever to say beyond "Abso-fucking-lutely!" which he did not want to say. He thought about the awful pecking order of rich Greenwich kids and their parents, and the complicated explanation of how he got here and how he really did not fit in, except where he could escape into video games. And, well, this girl was really cute. The way she smiled at him with those pretty pale blue eyes of hers, and how her dry, warm hand against the inside of his forearm felt really, really nice. She was older, early twenties for sure. *She must know what she's doing,* he thought.

"Fun with no baggage," he said. "Good idea." His words just spilled out and they sounded . . . they sounded just fine. Could it be he was relaxing and starting to feel confident?

"There now, isn't that a relief?" She released his forearm and took his right hand in hers. "My name is . . ." She gave him a sly grin, "is . . . is . . . Kroesus Girl. And you must be . . . ?"

"Kroesus Boy." He smiled back. This girl made it easy.

"We were fated to meet. Don't you agree?" She clasped her left hand over their two hands, making a little sandwich.

She's leading me, he thought, with a combination of relief and throbbing sexual excitement. *She knows where she wants to take this.* Suddenly, for the first time, he felt clearheaded about how to behave with a girl. Excuse me, a woman five or six years older. *Peter*, he told himself, *all you have to do is* not *be a jerk. Just be yourself and stop trying so hard.* "I'm really happy to meet you," he said with no self-consciousness, just letting his words and a smile come out naturally.

"Me too," she said and released her hands from his. "Do you think I could lure you away from—" she glanced at the flashing screen, "*Mighty Death Dealer*? And get you to dance with me?"

"Sure thing," he said instantly, turning away from the screen to show how much he meant it. Peter felt his phone vibrate. His mother? Oh cripes! He saw the text from her: DO NOT TAKE ANY ACORDINOL! I WILL EXPLAIN LATER!! *There she goes again*, he thought. Who gives a shit about her freakin' pills at a time like this? He turned off his phone. Something amazing was about to happen.

25

A t 2:30 PM, the press conference began in the main lobby of the corporate headquarters. Reporters, cameras, microphones, and chaos filled the bland, usually empty space the size of a suburban train-station waiting room. The only decoration on the cream-colored walls of travertine marble was a large P&B logo symbol in bronze. On a nearby television monitor, Emma saw the type beneath her live picture—*Emma Conway, Percival & Baxter CEO*.

She read the prepared statement that had been vetted by P&B's attorneys and PR people and the representatives of the FBI and the Food and Drug Administration, who had rushed to P&B from Philadelphia and Washington. It concluded, "We are working with local police, FBI, and the Food and Drug Administration around the country and around the world. We have mobilized our field sales forces to pull product off the shelves. We are putting announcements in all media, warning people not to take Acordinol and instructing them where to bring in packages for refunds. Do not under any circumstances open any bottle with the lot number EQDD8574.

"Our deepest sympathies go out to the families. We have suffered this terrible criminal act here among our own as well. Our CEO, Brad Johansen, died from the first of the tainted doses here this morning."

In her mind's eye, she saw a sudden flash of memories of Brad. Twenty years of her life and his blurred together. Young Brad and her father, encouraging her at the start of her career. Brad taking her father's place after he died, giving her advice, encouraging her. Brad in meetings, Brad talking at town halls, proudly showing off pictures of his newborn grandkids.

Emma had to catch her breath. "We do not yet know who did this or how. Our security is second to none in the industry. But rest assured, we will redouble our efforts to make sure it never happens again. Percival & Baxter will do whatever it takes to keep your trust. Right now our highest priority is to keep you and your families and all our families safe."

She stepped back from the microphone.

Greg Toland from PR touched her shoulder approvingly. He stepped up to the mike to take questions. Emma went back upstairs.

Hal Percival had asked to see her privately. They sat in her office, on facing couches.

Hal looked shaken and pale in a way Emma had never seen before.

"You know, Emma, taking this chief executive job could be the worst decision of your life."

She shook her emphatically no.

Hal shrugged. "This company could be headed for ruin."

She shook her head again. "Not on my watch," she said and meant it.

"We believe you, Emma. That's why we chose you today."

She knew she did not have to reply.

Hal looked out the window and mused, "You know, it's rare for a company to endure for fifty years, let alone more than one hundred. I hope you understand the sense of responsibility I feel toward P&B. It's a combination of things—the good we do with our products, the lives we make better, the people we support, the communities they live in, all of that. I believe it deep in my soul."

"Yes, Hal," she said softly, "and I do too."

She felt sad that her father was not here to see her realizing the dream death stole from him.

She looked at her watch. Ten minutes before three. In just over four hours, her entire world had been blown to pieces. And she had no idea where the pieces would fall. "I have to do the town meeting for the employees in ten minutes. It will be webcast to our locations all over the world." She took a deep breath. "Hal, I haven't even prepared for it."

"Don't worry, Emma," he said, "you've been preparing for it your whole life."

26

After a few slow dances by the fountain, Tanya let Kroesus Boy know when it was the right moment to kiss her. She snuggled against him and presented her mouth. And he kissed her right on cue. She liked this boy. She felt her plan moving forward inside his arms. She showed him how to be gentle, how to tease and tempt and turn up the heat of desire. He was a good student. No, an excellent student. He took every cue without a single word from her. Cooler is hotter, see? Now move to that little hollow between my collar bones and, yes, down toward my breasts. Yes, you can touch them, first one then the other. That's a good boy. Now back up to my mouth for more kisses.

Finally, she took his hand and walked him away from the plaza. "Let's go find some privacy," she said.

They walked in silence, fingers intertwined. They stopped at the door of one of the pool houses beside one of the three pools. The curtains were drawn behind the window. She knocked on the door. Nothing. She gave him a deep kiss.

She opened the door. Inside were a couch and two easy chairs in front of the cabanas, showers, and bathrooms. "Perfect," she said softly, giving his hand a squeeze. She just *knew* it was his first time. And that he was the right boy to make her pregnant. *Take that, Alban,* she thought, as she led him inside.

She closed the door and locked it. The room went dark. "Open the curtains just a tiny bit," she said.

"Uh, okay, sure," he said. A thin ribbon of light ran across the floor to the couch. In a flash, she stepped out of her shoes, pulled her top off, then her bra. She walked up to Peter, put her hands on his waist, and pulled his shirt off over his head. As she kissed him, she took his hand and slid it into her panties and down to the waxed landing strip of her pubic hair.

"Uh . . . I've got condoms," he whispered, trying to sound masterful.

She wrinkled her nose. "Silly boy," she said, guiding two of his fingers inside her. "Would you rather feel the inside of a rubber balloon or the inside of me?" She was wet and there was no faking that. "Don't worry," she lied, "I'm on the pill." She did like this boy and found him appealing. *He's a better kisser than he knows. And his touch is naturally sensual. He doesn't realize it yet, but he is going to be wonderful at lovemaking.*

She undid his belt, slid his jeans and undershorts down to his ankles. His hard-on bobbed up and down.

She noted that he was circumcised, nicely formed with no odd bends, and rather thick. *Lovely,* she thought, *and auspicious.* "You don't want to keep your socks on, do you?" she whispered as she stepped out of her panties. He fumbled to get his feet out of his jeans and quickly peeled off his socks.

She stood in the dim light, presenting her naked body to him, arms out, palms up. "All yours," she whispered.

He gasped. His eyes darted all over her.

She smiled at his gawking. "You like?" she asked rhetorically. *He* is *a lovely boy,* she thought. She was watching the tip of his penis for the first drop of pre-ejaculate fluid. She had read everything about the mechanics of making a baby. Absolutely everything. She knew that she needed to get the man's first ejaculation into her womb. That was by far the most fertile shot he had, even a randy teenager who could come over and over again. She also knew from messy experience that boys, especially the less experienced ones, tended to fire off early, unexpectedly, and outside the target. She was determined to capture that first teaspoon of semen with every last one of his most-able-bodied sperm cells.

She put her arms around him. She grabbed his butt with both hands, and pressed against his erection. She tried to feel if the tip of his willy was releasing anything. She couldn't tell.

He stroked her back and grabbed her butt in return. She reached down and grasped the end of his penis, checking for that first leaky trace of fluid. There it was, clear and slightly sticky. The mother lode, so to speak, could be released any moment now.

"Do you want me to, like, go down on you?" he asked.

"No need," she said, "I'm already wet. Let's get you inside me now."

She took him to the couch. She lay down with her legs open and hips raised as she pulled him down on top of her.

"Just slide it in," she whispered. He pressed against her with an awkward thrust. Oh yes, definitely a virgin. "No," she said sweetly, "it's lower than you think it is." She raised her hips and guided him inside her.

She wrapped her strong legs around his hips and locked her ankles together. She knew that a boy on his very first shag was likely to slide out accidentally. And she would have none of that.

His whole body began to rumble and flutter.

"Come, lad," she whispered, her tongue in his ear, "just

let it all go." She tightened her legs against him. "Close your eyes, and let it go." She was confident she could hold him in place, no matter how excited he got. He did indeed feel good inside her, but she kept her focus. This was business, not pleasure, she told herself. Although this boy was giving her a fine dose of pleasure.

He closed his eyes and began rocking harder. He quivered and twitched and shook frantically. She held him tight against her. Gradually, his thrusts began to grow softer and slower.

He gave a short thrust, then another even shorter one, and exhaled. All the tension had gone. He lay his head down beside her face. She felt him wither and slip out of her at last. Yes, she had kept him inside the whole time.

"There now," she said with a little kiss, "you're a grown-up now, my man." Quickly, she slid out from underneath him and stuck her legs straight up in the air, resting them against the back of the couch as if about to ride an upside-down bicycle. She pressed her legs together and wiggled her toes. Happy thoughts of her baby girl were filling her up.

"You were splendid, luv," she said. She was suddenly chatty and matter-of-fact, looking up at him from this odd position, her head almost off the edge of the couch. "You are going to be an excellent lover. You are going to make many girls happy. As a woman of some experience, I want you to know that."

"Uh, thanks," he said, totally confused. His breathing was still shallow. "What are you . . . uh?" he asked, gesturing at her legs in the air.

She knew from her research that gravity is a sperm cell's best friend. Rather than making them swim upstream toward the cervix and her egg, letting them swim downstream would speed the journey and increase the chances of one lucky cell scoring a goal. She knew that married people who had been working at getting pregnant were accustomed to this drill, putting the woman's pelvis in the air upside-down. But what would she tell the boy?

"Just a little thing with my lower back," she said dismissively. "Keeps it from going out after a lovely ride like we just had. A little stretch for a few minutes is all."

He shrugged. She thought, *how could he know better?*

They were silent for a while, smiling at each other.

She was imagining millions of sperm swimming downstream to help one lucky fellow win. Finally, she blew a little kiss at him and reached out her hand to tickle his swelling penis. "Dare say you're almost ready to go again."

He smiled.

She continued stroking his penis, making it grow. "You've got a fine, strong willy. Nice and thick. And such handsome dark eyes." She was happy to have found him. She had accomplished her objective. But she had also enjoyed it. Yes, thoroughly.

And it made her happy to have given someone a wonderful first time. Hers had been brutish and short—that handsome Frenchman with the sullen wife and two toddlers at Petit Cul-de-Sac beach on St. Barth's. She had seduced him behind the seafood shack. It was rushed and rather nasty. She was twelve and had just read *Lolita*.

He opened his legs to make himself more accessible.

She began stroking him harder. They could do it again, she decided, this time for fun. "You know, luv," she said idly, "I was supposed to hook up with another boy. We'd swapped some silly messages on FriendVault about his superhero chin. But I'm so glad I found you instead."

Peter gasped. She felt his willy go soft in her hand.

She gasped too. So, she had found her Chin King after all! She started to giggle. She tried not to, but she could not help it. She let go of him. "It's so funny, don't you think?" she said, looking at her mortified naked boy. He seemed frozen with what she guessed must be injured pride, crushed confidence, and much embarrassment. She felt bad for him. She wanted to give him back his brand-new manhood.

"So, *you* are Katman," she giggled, "and I am Tsarina Alexandra!"

The boy mumbled something and looked down.

She pulled her legs out of the air and righted herself. "Come give us a kiss, Katman." She wrapped her arms and legs around him, sitting on his lap, kissing him with a combination of desire and compassion. With no more words or guidance, he was soon inside her again. Coming.

When they sat back, she could see the flush of happiness on his face. "You are a fine fuck. An absolutely first-rate shag. I want you to know that." She leaned forward and planted a flight of kisses around his chin. "You and your superhero chin."

The boy had another hard-on. "Do you think we should tell each other who we really are?" he asked. He began kissing and gently sucking one nipple, then the other.

"Not yet," she said tenderly, kissing the top of his head. "We are Katman and Tsarina Alexandra. We'll find out who we really are when the time is right."

27

Emma entered the auditorium just after 3:00 PM. She was running on pure adrenaline. She hadn't eaten since the morning. She had lost her sense of the hours. Things were happening so fast. She would have to wait until later to try to make sense of it all. In the meantime, she moved like an athlete, giving her complete attention—mind, body, and soul—to each new test.

She looked at the people filling the amphitheater.

She recognized faces in every row. She knew names and bits about their families. She knew what many of them were good at and also what they needed to work on. She had watched them grow, heard them bitch and gossip and work hard.

This was a community. *Her* community. And it was under a double threat. Suddenly, from a monster with cyanide. And from the man she had once loved and thought she would share her life with.

She started by reading the statement she had read to the press. The poisonings, Brad, the recall, the campaign to win back trust. The paper was a good crutch. It kept her from having to think. And let her hold her feelings in check, at least for the moment. She took a deep breath after reading the last sentence and turned the paper over.

She looked down at the podium. Suddenly, more images of Brad fluttered through her mind. Happy times with

Patty and their grandchildren at the annual company picnic on the big lawn right outside this building. The last one was just a few weeks ago. The names of the two other victims echoed in her mind. Anne Womrath. Steven Drake. Their faces were all over the television news. They had children. And families. Was that her jaw starting to quiver? *Don't go there now,* she thought, *you are the leader here.* She bit down on her index finger for a second, then looked up. *There now.*

"We are in a serious crisis mode," she said slowly and confidently. "But we will get through it, I pledge to you with all my heart and every bit of my strength.

"Now you're probably asking, who is this new CEO? Well, let me try to answer. I'm a lifer here at P&B. Except for some odd jobs in high school and college, I've never worked anywhere else. I'm a wife and a mother. I have a wonderful husband who is an artist and a teacher. I have a normal, happy sixteen-year-old boy who completely ignores me and everything I say." She paused and got the ripple of laughter she was hoping for—especially from the mothers in the auditorium.

"I think of myself as a hard worker. What I may lack in brilliance I make up for in dedication and discipline. And I expect no less from the people I work with. Like anyone in a new job, I know I've got some learning to do. I'm not afraid to admit when I don't know something and go to the people who do know." She pointed a finger at her audience.

She scanned the amphitheater from one side to the other. "Hmm, what else should you know?" She collected her thoughts for a second. "I'm not afraid to make a mistake. When I do, I'm not afraid to admit it, take responsibility, and change course. And this is important—I have no tolerance for dishonesty. None. And I can't stand to see anyone getting treated unfairly."

She leaned closer into the microphone so she could speak softer and let her voice ring louder. "Someone is threatening to destroy us. But we won't let them win. Another someone is threatening our independence. And we won't let them win either. Today, our board of directors adopted a strategy to protect our independence. It's called a shareholder rights plan." Given the events of the day, she had decided not to use the term "poison pill." "Since it was invented thirty years ago, it has never failed."

Emma picked up the second press release, crafted with Mike Saltzman's guidance, and read it aloud.

28

Josh sat behind his antique partners desk at Ledgemere. He was stunned into open-mouthed silence.

He had been watching the news coverage of the Acordinol deaths on television with Penelope. She tried to get him to say something—anything—about what the poisonings might mean. After all, she had insisted, this was the very company he was, possibly, about to take over. And now the CEO was dead from poisoned pills. "Jesus, Josh, your ex is the new chief executive," she had pleaded. "Don't you have *anything* to say?"

Josh had just stared at the screen, shaking his head. He had no idea what to think or what to say. He was afraid to think the unthinkable and more afraid to speak it—that his secret partner Viktor was somehow behind these deaths.

Had his Wall Street mantra failed him? "Immoral we do every day. Illegal never." He tried not to think about where this might head. He dared not say anything to Penelope for fear of what might slip out.

"Say something, Josh! Anything!" she cried. "Please, say something!"

He shook his head and covered his eyes with both hands.

Penelope left in a blur of upset and frustration, saying she was going upstairs to sleep with her other lover, Ambien.

Josh was finding it hard to breathe. Maybe the library was too stuffy. To let in the evening breeze, he opened the windows overlooking the formal gardens. The beauty of it all did not touch him tonight. The fresh air did not help. He still found it hard to breathe, feeling like metal weights were pressing down on his chest.

He wanted to talk to Viktor this minute. And he did *not* want to talk to Viktor ever again. He was questioning whether to wake Viktor up in the middle of the night or wait until morning in Britain. Could Viktor, with the murky, forgotten, criminal past, be responsible for this? No, he can't be, Josh kept telling himself. Impossible. You, Josh Katz, have certified to the whole financial world that Viktor Volkov is the legitimate businessman he purports to be. You, Josh Katz, have put your credibility on the line for him in deal after deal. You have told every major bank to believe in Viktor's absolute honesty and probity. Because you know it's true. Right? Right? Then Josh's mind seemed about to seize up. *Don't go there,* he thought, *don't even start to go there*.

The satellite phone rang. He lunged for it.

"Why you no call me with news?" Viktor asked. He sounded a bit annoyed to Josh. "Is important to deal."

Josh said, "I thought you'd be asleep now."

"Is big news, this poison in pills. Chief executive dead."

Josh listened for Viktor to say something more. Anything. He heard only silence. Viktor was waiting for him.

"Viktor, this is just too creepy," Josh said with a shudder. "Is there anything about it that you want to, uh . . ." Josh stopped himself. He cleared his throat. Then he spoke formally, like a lawyer to a witness on the stand. "Is there anything you have to say about what happened?"

Viktor said nothing.

"Well, do you? *Do* you?"

"What you mean, Katz?"

"I think you know what I mean, Viktor. Tell me now. Before we go any further with this deal."

Viktor took a deep breath. "You insult me. This I expect from tabloids. They write stories say Volkov is criminal, always criminal. Is how they sell their dirty newspapers. But you? *You?* You my banker. You do my deals. I save your ass when you have problems. Why you insult me?"

"Viktor, I . . ." Josh tried to interject an apology.

Viktor went on. "Is terrible thing these people die. Make me very sorry." To Josh, he sounded sympathetic. "Bad thing, terrible thing. Innocent people die for no reason. Like in war. Very bad. Tragedy."

After a pause, Viktor continued solemnly, "Is tragedy, yes. But also . . . is business. Stock will be cheaper soon."

Josh exploded. "Viktor! Do you realize the hours and money we're burning on a company that soon won't be worth taking over? There's a murder investigation going on, for Christ's sake. They're going to have to recall tons of product. I say we just walk away from this one. I've shown you other deals. GeneQuest, remember GeneQuest? The future is genetic medicine." Viktor's threat notwithstanding, he thought he saw a chance to get them off this deal. "Let's regroup and take another look at those. I can find us more deals, too. Doesn't have to be in pharma—"

"*I* say what we do, Katz."

Josh said nothing, trying to think.

He heard Viktor breathing calmly. He knew that the man would not say anything more. Nor would he need to.

Josh sighed. "Okay."

"Yes, okay." Viktor paused. "I remember old days. You remember? You teach me lessons of capitalism. Give me books, magazines. Remember?" Suddenly, he sounded warm. *Was he being nostalgic?*

"Yes, of course I remember," Josh said, confused and impatient. "Teaching my Soviet client." Josh shuddered now at the recollection, the scrupulousness with which he and his colleagues pretended not to know what they all goddamn well knew about their clients.

"You teach me quotes how success works in business world. From this *Forbes* magazine. Capitalist tool, yes?"

"Yes," Josh said, wondering where this was going.

" 'The harder I work, the luckier I get.' You remember this? This you said, 'Underline this one, Viktor, underline it.' "

"Yes," Josh said, feeling hopeless, powerless.

"Well, we work hard, *you* work hard. Now we get lucky."

"But Viktor . . ."

"Is capitalist way. We wait. When stock good and low, we take over. No problem. No problem beating poison pill now. Bad luck for other guy, good luck for us. We work hard, we get lucky. You wait for instructions." He hung up.

Josh stared at the phone as if it were radioactive. He stared at his hand, wondering what malignant condition it might have just picked up. His mind was bursting with suspicions he tried to suppress but couldn't.

Could Viktor be connected to this crime?

No, no, no, it could not be.

Oh, yes it could.

Should he call the police, he wondered.

And tell them *what*?

He closed his eyes and stared ahead. What he saw was darkness deeper and blacker than anything he had ever imagined. It plunged down into a pit that was probably hell. Or maybe it was not hell. Maybe hell was nothing but the endless plunge into that horrifying darkness.

He shuddered and opened his eyes. He grabbed on to his magnificent George I desk as if to keep from falling.

He felt like he didn't belong here. He was an imposter, a burglar in some rich guy's library, waiting to get caught, waiting to be sentenced, waiting to plummet into eternal hell.

He had to get out from under Viktor. He didn't know at this moment how he would do it or where he would get the financing to buy out the Russian. But he knew it's what he had to do. After all, the credit markets had loosened up considerably since he had approached Viktor for the loan. He would figure out a way. He always did. Not right this second. But soon.

The landline rang. He sat up straight, preparing for the worst. The police, the FBI, maybe Satan himself.

"Hello," he said, hoping his voice did not betray how helpless he felt.

"Big news day for Percival & Baxter, eh?" It was Brody.

"Yeah," Josh said listlessly.

"In-fucking-credible, no?"

"No." Josh quickly corrected himself. "Uh . . . I mean, yes. Awful, terrible, horrifying." He had no more words. He held the phone in silence.

Finally, Brody spoke. "So, what's the plan, boss? What about P&B?"

"We wait and see," he said quietly.

"Got it," Brody said.

Josh hung up.

29

After the town meeting, Emma led the committee planning the recall. It was some time past midnight when Linda Farlow shouted from the far end of the long table, "Holy shit! Holy shit!" She was holding up her BlackBerry. "Check your P&B email! It's the message with 'FUCK P&B!!!!' in the subject line!"

People grabbed their handhelds and punched into their inboxes. At first one by one, then as a unified chorus, they groaned.

Emma read the email in the palm of her hand.

Addressed to the "P&B Corp. Inclusive" list, basically everyone in the entire company worldwide, and from someone named Loralee Eaton, who had a P&B email address that appeared to be real:

HI EVERYBODY

I BET YOUR WONDERING WHO PUT POISON IN YOUR LITTLE
PILLS.

ME LORALEE EATON.

THE VOICES TOLD ME TO DO IT. I HEAR THEM A LOT NOW.

I SAVED A LITTLE TO SEND ME ON MY WAY 2.

I AM WITH JESUS NOW WHERE I BELONG.

SOON WE ALL BE TOGETHR AT END OF DAYS.

C U THERE.

THE END

Emma slammed her BlackBerry down on the table and looked around the room. "Get our IT experts on this! Find out who she is! Where she is! If she's real; if she really worked here; get her file, her records. Where she lives. Get the police to her. If she did work here, since when. Where inside our facilities has she been? Get all the facts."

People came and went around Emma, making phone calls, bringing in messages, conferring, checking emails. In short order, word came back confirming that Loralee Eaton was indeed real. A real P&B employee who had worked in the main plant for ten months. Her email was real. And she was really dead, apparently of her own hand, and from the cyanide powder that police found on her dead lips and fingertips, and spread around the mobile home she inhabited in the trailer park outside Jenkintown, Pennsylvania. Lab tests followed soon with confirmations of exactly when and how she died and how good a match her deadly chemical was to the stuff that murdered the six—the number had risen over the evening—unlucky people.

The room fell eerily silent. Everyone sensed that the worst of the worst had just happened.

"We have no choice," Emma said to the group around her, "we recall everything we've ever manufactured in our plant since that woman's first day on the job. No questions asked. Everything. We'll figure out how we handle the reimbursements. But first, everyone needs to know that we will do absolutely everything to keep their trust."

"But Emma, that could bankrupt us," Steve Upshaw said. "We don't have to go *that* far. We can parse this, calculate where we do and don't have a problem. We can manage the losses, we can spin our story—"

Emma sighed. Angrily. "No, Steve, we can't *spin* anything!" She almost said "fucking can't" but restrained herself. The word lurked there in her sharp tone, though. "We can't parse it or calculate it and try to shave the dollars here and there. People will either trust Percival & Baxter coming out of this crisis, or they won't. This isn't about saving money. It's about saving the company. You can't put a price tag on that."

The company, of course, could be headed for oblivion. But something told her it could be rescued, should be rescued, *would* be rescued. The mother in her would save her baby.

But at this awful moment, she had no idea how.

She stood and called down to Linda Farlow. "Can I ask you something, uh, offline?" She motioned to the door and the corridor beyond.

"Sure," Linda said, joining her outside in the hall.

"Can you double-check—no, triple-check—this Loralee Eaton confession for me?"

"You suspicious?"

"After all that's happened today, I'm suspicious of everything. This is all happening so fast. I want us to be sure, really sure."

Linda nodded. Together they went back to the crisis meeting.

30

FRIDAY, JULY 31

61 COYLE STREET • HAVERFORD, PENNSYLVANIA

As dawn peeked through the living room windows of Diane Conway's house, Emma and her mother sat side by side on the couch. Emma was in the blouse and skirt of her business suit. Her shoes were cast off by the couch, her suit jacket flung over a nearby chair. Diane was in a bathrobe and slippers. They drank tea and honey.

Emma sighed. Whatever is left over after absolutely everything has been wrung out of a person, that's what she felt. It wasn't much. She had a distant sensation that she was still breathing, that her body could still move around. That was about it. She was an empty vessel, an exhausted empty vessel.

She had called Ned. Several times. She had tried Peter and got his voice mail. Finally, she just texted him her warning. At the end of the long day and even longer night, she had called her mother. Diane said she had hardly slept, that she had been following all the news reports on TV and online. She let Emma recount the day's horrifying events. She just let her talk and talk. And talk and talk. Until finally, Emma had nothing more to say.

"That it?" Diane asked after Emma had gone quiet for a couple of minutes.

Emma nodded yes.

Diane took her hand. "You'll get through it. You and Ned and Peter. You and the company. All of us. You know that, don't you?"

"Yes," she said quietly, "I do."

"Your father would be proud of how you handled today. Everything you did. He always said you had big shoulders, big enough to carry the heaviest burdens for others. He was right, you know."

"I hope so," Emma said.

Her mother squeezed her hand. "Yes, Mom, I know it."

"That's right, you *know* it. And don't ever forget it."

"No, Mom, I won't."

Another silence. Solemn but peaceful.

Finally, Diane spoke. "Honey, would you like something to eat?"

Emma shook her head. "No, thanks, Mom."

"You sure?"

Emma sighed. "No, really."

"I could make you something."

"No, really. Nothing, please."

Diane picked up Emma's chin to turn her and capture her gaze. "Of course I know you don't feel like eating, sweetie. But as a mother, I'm required by law to ask that question, no matter what the circumstances." She gave Emma a mock *tsk-tsk*. "As a mother, *you* should have known that."

Emma gave her a little smile. They shared a little laugh.

"That's my girl," Diane said.

They sat for a while, just holding hands.

Again, Diane was first to speak. "Do you want to lie down for a while?"

Emma shook her head no. She knew she would have to go home to freshen up and change and go back to the office. "I like just sitting here." She leaned back and snuggled against her mother, their heads just touching.

Another comfortable silence. Emma couldn't tell how long it lasted, maybe two minutes, maybe ten. It just felt good. Calm. Reassuring.

Finally, Diane whispered, "Do you feel like crying, sweetie?"

Emma sat up. "I wish I could. But I just can't. A part of me thinks if I started, I couldn't stop."

"It might help, you know. A good cry."

Emma shook her head no again. "I don't have it in me right now, I just don't. Maybe when all this is over. Maybe then. But not now." She felt no tears building up, no sniffles trying to get out. She took a deep, calm breath. No, there was no flood in there. "I just couldn't cry now. Not even if I wanted to."

She stood up and shook herself, ready to leave and face whatever would be next.

Diane walked her to the front door. "Well, would you like a hug?"

"Oh yes, Mom," Emma sighed. "A big one."

31

After sitting at his desk through the long night, Josh sat watching the dawn come up over the oak forest on the eastern edge of his estate. The phone rang. He grabbed it on the first ring.

"Heard the latest, Josh?" It was Brody.

"No."

"They found out who poisoned the Acordinol. My mole just tipped me off."

Josh held his breath.

"You still there?"

"Yes, goddammit," Josh snapped, "who did it?"

"Some pissed-off P&B hourly worker," Brody said. "Kooky white-trash babe named Loralee or Tammy Jean something. Confessed in an email blast to half the Internet, then killed herself with the same poison she used in the factory. They found all these rants and postings of hers. Angry at everybody from her supervisor at the factory to the secretary general of the United Nations. In her note— get this, she emailed it to the whole fucking company— said she did it for Jesus and all this crazy shit about 'end of days.'"

Josh gave a huge sigh.

"You there, Josh? You hear me?"

He closed his eyes. "Yes, Brodes, I hear you."

"Josh, listen, later today we can—"

"Thanks for calling. I'll see you at the office." He hung up.

He closed his eyes and sat for . . . he did not know how long.

He opened his eyes. Looked around his library again.

So Viktor was right. The billionaire bastard was lucky, that's all. Josh's suspicions began to evaporate. Suddenly, his magnificent surroundings regained their color. The world was coming back to life. He felt his fingertips rubbing against the antique mahogany. He was regaining the sensation of his own physical being. He could feel his heart pounding, he was aware that he was breathing hard. His clammy right hand moved to the knob of the secret compartment. He did not turn it. He just pressed his fingertips against the drawer. He did not have to open the secret drawer to feel its contents inside—the envelope with the picture of Emma from their honeymoon, her passionate love note on the back, and the lock of her golden hair. He felt the presence of these objects through the panel. It was as if they were pulsing and beating like a living creature locked away in there. Emma. What on earth did she still mean to him?

He stood up, taking an inventory of the sensations coming back to him after his trip to hell. He ran out of his library, over the vast marble floors past the minstrel's gallery, and up his magnificent sweeping staircase to the master bedroom.

As he opened the door, he again had the strange feeling that he had merely borrowed all this grandeur from its true owner. Or even stolen it. He tiptoed into the master bedroom, undressed quickly, and climbed into bed.

Penelope did not stir. She lay sleeping, snoring as usual, her mouth open and sticky.

He took her face in both hands and pressed his lips

against hers. Snapping awake, Penelope tried to jam her fingers over her mouth.

"Josh, my breath!"

He yanked her hand away and pressed his tongue inside. He began to devour her in every way he could— touching her, inhaling her; feeling the smooth of her skin, the prickliness of her hair, the hardness of her bones, the softness of her flesh, the heat of her blood, the taste and smell of every part of her. Kissing her, sucking her, gnawing her, drinking her, devouring her with the abandon of a starved beast.

Penelope seemed startled and happy at his ardor. She wrapped herself around him. He thrust into her with a life force he had not felt in a long time. As he was about to explode, he cried out, "I . . . love . . . you . . . !" Then he bit down hard on his hand and swallowed the word "Emma!"

PART TWO

SEPTEMBER 2009

ANGLIA WANTS PERCIVAL & BAXTER BROKEN UP IN ASSET SALE

The cat-and-mouse game between Anglia Partners and century-old pharma P&B is at a standstill, with Anglia's ownership position holding steady at 14.9%, just under the threshold that would trigger P&B's poison pill.

Meanwhile P&B continues to hemorrhage red ink from the massive recall of product, after real poison pills of its star product, Acordinol, killed three people, including the company's own CEO, the late Brad Johansen. P&B stock closed yesterday at a 50-year low of $22. Shorts are counting on the nosedive to deepen.

According to its most recent filings, Anglia is seeking two board seats and asking the P&B board to break up the company and sell off the parts, in particular the very profitable pediatric division and the company's portfolio of exclusive drugs still under patent, said to produce in excess of $180 million in EBITDA. Anglia contends that the damaged reputation of P&B is hurting the value of many of its otherwise healthy businesses. Anglia is conducting a raider's typical campaign of slings and arrows aimed at management in order to convince shareholders to vote for its proposals at next month's annual meeting.

P&B CEO Emma Conway and the board have so far refused to consider a breakup. They say P&B will weather the storm and can produce more shareholder value in the long term by keeping the company intact.

An interesting sidebar to this battle for control of P&B is that the two main combatants, CEO Conway and Anglia General Partner Josh Katz, used to be husband and wife. So far the fireworks have been confined to proxy statements and press releases.

32

"Can you believe what Anglia is saying in today's letter to our shareholders? This is the third one since last month! There's practically a new insult every day."

Emma waved the paper over the kitchen table and flung it down, just missing her plate of half-eaten lamb chops. She saw Ned and Peter wince. She hardly ever showed such anger.

"'Complacent management!'" she spat. "'A culture of inbreeding! Feathering the nests of entrenched management at the expense of shareholders!' What a load of lying crap! What . . . what . . . fucking bullshit!"

She watched Peter mouth the word "fuck" at Ned, who shrugged in reply.

"Yes, *fucking* bullshit! I mean exactly that." She looked directly at Peter. "All of it under your father's signature, as head of Anglia Partners."

She remembered Josh's entreaty not to take this battle personally. But how could she *not*? These attacks were directed at the leadership of P&B. At her!

She grabbed the paper and read on. "'We can only have doubts about their research pipeline, given management's secrecy and lack of transparency.'" She took a deep breath and said, "Well, of course, you bastards, that's because it's none of your damn business!" She pointed to another sentence. "And get this, 'We also have doubts about management's determination to cut costs in order to harvest cash flow in mature business lines like the pediatric division.'"

She shook her head. "Hell, it's like they've been reading our internal reports. This is exactly what Steve Upshaw has been proposing. I wonder if that son of a bitch is feeding them confidential material. Maybe even secretly working for them. I wouldn't put it past him." She shuddered. "I'm going to watch that fucker like a hawk."

"You know, Emma," Ned said softly as he patted her hand, "it's not personal. It's a proxy fight. They've got to prove that they're right and you guys are wrong. They have to get a majority of the shareholders to vote against you. It's an election, they'll sling mud. What else do you expect?"

"I know, I know." She took a deep breath, yoga-style. Then another. *There now.* "It's just when you see it there in black and white, see them lying about everything we've all worked for and believe in, it just infuriates me."

She paused again, then brightened. "But you know, with our poison pill in place, *they're* the ones facing an uphill battle. Mike Saltzman says no raider has ever beaten a poison pill."

"Who's Mike Saltzman?" Peter asked.

"Our lawyer. A very smart and powerful lawyer who defends companies from bad guys."

Ned glanced at Emma. "That's his father," he said.

"Against raiders," she said, correcting herself. "Against hostile, unwanted takeovers."

Ned interjected, "Let's change the subject, okay?"

Emma shrugged okay, but she knew her face still showed how angry she felt.

Peter attacked his lamb chops again, chewing insistently.

Emma finished first. She pushed her plate away. "You

guys can have some pie, if you like. I've got some work to do." She moved her chair back and started to get up.

"Uh, Mom?" Peter asked.

"Yes, honey?" she said.

Peter was sure this was a mistake, but he did not know what else to do. He felt like now was the moment, even though he knew the right moment would never, ever arrive.

"Yes, Peter?" She sat down.

He took a deep breath. "Mom, uh, so now *you're* the one who could decide to sell the company, right?"

She stared at him.

He pressed on, feeling this might lead to disaster. "Well, you know, like, *will* you?"

"I told you. Absolutely not. P&B is not for sale."

"Why not, Mom?" Peter flinched at her clenched teeth.

"Peter, selling the company would be a terrible thing for everyone. For thousands—no, millions—of people who depend on it."

"Not according to Dad. He says—"

"Peter, he's wrong!" She leaned across the table. "I'm going to fight your father tooth and nail and I'm going to win. P&B is. P&B will win."

"But don't you think people will want to make all that extra money?"

"What on earth are you talking about? There's no extra money. It's all a lie. It's a short-term gain that loses money in the long run. It's a horrible, destructive, greedy thing! There's no way I will let P&B sell out. Do you understand, young man?"

"But I'm supposed to get you on board!" he blurted. *Here goes,* he thought. He heard his words spill out, but distantly, as if it were someone else talking on the other side of the room. "If you don't sell out, it's going to cost *me* money in my trust fund. Dad made me a shareholder. He showed me numbers." Peter knew Dad had not shown him any numbers, but he had overheard that expression in so many business conversations that he threw it in for good measure. Then he said, "We can all get superrich together, with you and Dad making deals. I'm supposed to convince you."

He regretted all of it the instant he spoke. "Oh shit," he muttered and put his head in his hands.

"What?" Mom cried out.

He mumbled, "I'm supposed to get you on board."

She stared at him. "How dare he put you in that position." Then she turned to Ned. "How dare that man put his own son in that position? He's a monster!"

Ned patted her arm, trying to calm her down.

Peter knew he was in way over his head but he plunged ahead, just to get it all out and over with. "But I'm supposed to help you *and* Dad. Help *all* of us. We could all work together. Dad explained it to me. He's asked me, like, lots of times. You could make all of us a fortune running his pharma division, lots of fortunes, like, you know, buying and selling pharmas. Then buying them back and selling them again. It's how LBOs work. He said so."

Peter watched her bite down on her lower lip. She was so pissed off. Oh shit. "Your father is lying," she said. "I have no intention of working for him as his private-equity hit man. That's what he's talking about, you know. A mass executioner, a corporate rapist."

She leaned forward again. Ned put a restraining hand on her arm. She took a deep breath and looked at Ned. Then she turned to Peter and, in a calmer voice, said, "Listen to me, please. You will tell him nothing you hear in this house from now on. Nothing. Do you understand? Besides the legal implications here, well, the personal and ethical ones are just horrible." She turned to Ned and got upset again. "Oh! That *man*! That *man*!"

She rose in her chair. Again, Ned put a restraining hand on her. "Emma, please."

"Oh fuck!" Peter cried out. This was even worse than he had feared.

He jumped from the table and ran upstairs to his room.

He slammed his door shut and jumped in front of his computer. *Secrets,* he thought, *oh fuck!* Grown-ups! Secrets! He turned his speakers on and kicked up the volume. *Fuck Mom and Ned and their rules. Fuck Dad for making me do this. Fuck the whole fucking world.* Then he put on his headphones to escape as far away as he could.

33

Peter was playing a game of *Galactic Destruction* while listening to the new Green album in his headphones. The noise and chaos were just what he wanted. To drown out, well, to drown out everything.

Somehow, the little *ping* sound effect cut through the music and battle noise. He looked down at the corner of his screen and saw the little message icon from FriendVault. He clicked on it. Tsarina Alexandra had just left a message for Katman to contact her so they could video chat. He clicked through immediately. He felt his dick getting hard even before the connection loaded.

"Greetings, Katman," Tanya said playfully, as her face filled the screen.

Peter removed his headphones and beamed at the green light of his webcam. He looked behind for a moment, to make sure his bedroom door was good and closed.

"Greetings, Tsarina," he replied brightly, wondering what was up. Her face was as pretty as he remembered. He wished he could be naked with her again. He remembered almost everything about her body. He was sure that finally getting laid had made him a changed man, he just wasn't sure how. Doing it again might help him figure it out, to say nothing of how much fun it would be.

She cleared her throat, visibly attempting to get serious but unable to wipe the grin from her face. "I swore to myself that I would not do this, but my friend Fiona—she was my mother at Trinity, not my *mother,* of course, that's just our college name for it. Well, anyway . . ." She took a deep breath. "She told me no, you must absolutely let him know. Not to alarm him. But to inform him that one of his little whiptailed spermies scored a goal. He was your stud, after all. I mean, *my* stud." Pause. Bigger grin. "Katman, my man, my stallion, I want you to know that I am . . . pregnant."

"Oh shit!" Peter said, feeling more alarm and confusion than he had ever known. "Shit, shit, shit!" He dropped his head, covering his face with both hands. This was the worst thing that could have happened. The worst. Well, not like getting AIDS. But next to that, it was the freakin' worst thing. All he wanted was to have sex like the other kids, and now his whole life would be fucked up.

"No, no, no!" she trilled. "Don't worry, silly boy. Come on now, pick up that superhero chin."

Peter looked up at the screen, petrified.

"That's a good lad," she said. "Now, I don't expect you to do anything, nothing at all. I don't expect you to be a daddy. I'm quite independent and terribly rich." She added under her breath, "Of course we all are at Kroesus Kids, aren't we? But you're just a lad. And I . . ." she paused, then said in a throaty, seductive voice, ". . . I am an *older* woman."

Peter had no idea what to think. "You're, you're, you're . . . going to *have* the baby?"

"Well, of course I am. It's what I planned all along." She rattled on at high speed. "I don't want to get all Marxist with you—but you were, I fear, just the means of production. Charming, delightful, ardent, sweet, all those things. But still, just a sperm donor. Carefully selected, of course. I'm going to raise the baby all by myself and the two of us are going to be so-o-o-o happy. This was your first time, I could tell. *You* need to go off and shag a lot more. And I? I'm happy, rather, *we're* happy. . . ." She leaned back in her chair and patted her perfectly flat tummy. "We're happy to have met you."

He sat silent, mouth open, superhero chin frozen.

"You did yeoman service, Katman, but your job is done."

"Uh, shouldn't I, uh, see you again?" In his haze, he wasn't sure why he asked. He wasn't sure of anything.

"Mmm," she said, pausing, "probably not. But we can check in on the FriendVault from time to time. No need to tell your mum and dad, either. You're a grown-up now. High time you had a secret or two. Remember what I said. Secrets are what make us grown-ups. Things we never tell another soul about. This one is yours."

"Uh, shouldn't we tell each other our real names?"

She shook her head and wagged her finger no. "Ta, luv. I made a man of you. And you have made me the happiest girl on earth." She gave a little wave and clicked off.

Peter felt like he'd been run over by a freight train. And somehow survived. Unless he was dead and just did not realize it. He buried his head in his hands again. He did not dare look up at his computer.

Tanya stared dreamily at her home screen. She was so happy. From the moment she missed her period, through the excitement of peeing all over the home pregnancy test kits, to the confirmation at the doctor's office, she felt like her earthly body had been transformed into a miraculous instrument that resonated with music of the heavens.

Her baby girl! Tatiana, the lonely and loveless, was to

be the mother of her very own baby girl. She had started walking all over London. Well, *her* London—Chelsea, Mayfair, and the other posh parts of the West End. She was watching mothers with new babies. She sat in the parks and observed them, rode the buses, studying what went on inside the magical bubbles that mothers and babies inhabited together.

It is so perfect, she thought, *a love affair like no other.* They gaze into each other's eyes, they babble to each other in their own secret language. Their bodies and souls are one. The mothers anticipate their baby's every move, fulfill their every need, and their babies expect it like air. That was how she would be with her baby girl. She would be the perfect mother. And she would not disappear the way her own dear Mummy did.

Finally all the crushing, complicated gift-curse of being rich had a purpose, something she could *do* with it. Her baby would make everything all right. Yes, together she and her beautiful baby girl would fix everything that was ever wrong. Everything.

"Thank you, Katman," she said aloud, "whoever you are."

34

Charles Brody pulled Josh out of the "P&B War Room," formerly conference room A, at Anglia Partners' Manhattan offices. The deal team—lawyers, proxy servers, investment bankers, accountants, and all their assistants—was huddled around the long table.

"You look worried, Josh," Brody said as he escorted him down the hallway. "What's the matter?"

"The press is going to have a feast on this," Josh said. "Ex-husband, ex-wife battling over wife's company. A woman CEO? A nasty raider? Talk about tabloid drama. I'm going to be so fucked in the press, Brodes, so completely fucked."

"No, you won't. I promise you, I won't let that happen." Brody put a protective arm around him. "Old Brodes will take care of things. In a hostile takeover, both sides have lawyers and investment bankers to set the strategies. They have PR guys like me and proxy solicitors to manage opinion and get the shareholder votes. Then they have private investigators like Kroll Associates to uncover dirt the other side would like to keep hidden. Even-Steven so far, right?"

Josh nodded. He thought about the money he owed Viktor. He tried to focus on Brody. If his flack had a way to do damage control, he needed to hear it.

Brody smiled and whispered in his ear, "Well, I've got us a politico trained by none other than Karl Rove. His talent is uncovering dirt that doesn't even exist. He makes it real and he makes it stick."

Suddenly Josh felt disgust. Brody was talking about smearing Emma. "No," he said shaking his head emphatically. "We don't do that kind of thing."

Brody raised his eyebrows. "Do you want to win? Or do you want to win?"

"Yes, of course I want to win," Josh snapped. He knew he had to dress up his lie and pursue it as if it were what he really wanted.

"Then hear what the man has to say."

He thought of Viktor and felt trapped. He thought of Emma and Peter and how much he did *not* want them to know, how he wanted to protect them. He waved Brody away. "I'll hear him out," he said angrily, "but I'm telling you, there are certain lines I will not cross. You got that?"

Josh heard him mutter something under his breath. It sounded like, "That's what they all say."

"Where we going?" Josh asked.

"Your office," Brody said brightly, "to meet our secret weapon. We've got the best experts lined up for the public battle. Now," he said, opening Josh's door, "Drew Pawling is here to work behind the scenes." As he closed the door behind them, Brody leaned in toward Josh and lowered his voice. "Like I told you, he's the dirty-tricks genius of the Republican party. Remember the black baby smear campaign that Bush's people used to sink McCain back at the convention in 2000?"

Josh nodded, thinking, *yes, that certainly was a dirty trick.*

"Sure, Rove got credit for it. He got credit for everything. But I'm telling you, it was Pawling. It was *his* idea, his execution. The secret placements, the whispers in the right ears, the whole thing. Guy's a genius at what he does."

Brody stood at the door while Josh sat down behind his desk. "Know his nickname at the RNC? Captain Underpants." Brody guffawed. "Isn't that great?"

Josh thought of the kids' books by that name that Peter used to find so hysterical when he was little. He did not find the comics or Brody's joke funny.

Josh was skeptical. But this was trusty old Brodes talking and he had to hear him out. "Okay, let's meet him."

"Great!" Brody opened the door and called down the hall past Josh's two executive secretaries. "Missssster Pawling! Please come in."

A small, round, very pale white man appeared in the doorway. Fat and soft. With little hands and little feet. "Thank you, Charles," he said. Pawling reminded Josh of the character Peter Lorre played in the classic black-and-white movie *The Maltese Falcon*. Joel Cairo, the creepy, murderous double-crosser who was a bully when he had the upper hand and a sniveling wimp when he didn't. No funny accent, though. Drew Pawling had the pure velvet diction of a TV news anchorman. Expensive suit. French cuffs, big gold cuff links. Tassel loafers with a gleaming spit shine. And the pin on his right lapel—fat red elephant and the words "Rush Is Always Right."

"Josh," Brody said proudly, "I'd like you to meet Drew Pawling, political strategist par excellence."

"Mr. Katz," Pawling said, pumping Josh's hand, "it's always a pleasure to meet a successful capitalist. You men are the leaders and visionaries who make it all possible. In spite of those who would take our freedoms away."

Josh removed his hand before Pawling seemed to be done with it. Pawling's hand was not just hot and damp, it was downright oily. Josh noticed the fingernails. Bitten down so short that the skin above the torn little half-moons looked like it had long ago given up hope of ever seeing a nail again.

"Please sit down." Josh motioned for Pawling to take a chair.

Brody sat down beside Pawling to preside over the matchmaking. "Josh, like I told you, Drew has been doing some prep work on the P&B deal."

Josh nodded and smiled politely at Pawling.

"*Mister* Katz," Pawling began.

"Please, it's Josh."

"Thank you." Pawling lowered his eyes in reverence. "Josh." Pause again. Then in a stage whisper aside, "It really is an honor to work for the people who safeguard our way of life."

"You mean rich deal guys?" Josh asked louder than necessary. Sid Katz had taught his son to hate and mistrust sucking up in all its forms and in whatever direction it was flowing.

Pawling gave Brody a confused glance. Brody, with a shake of his head, signaled that Pawling should ignore the remark and go on. Pawling rubbed his little hands together, then opened them with a flourish. *Like a magician producing a fluttering white dove out of nowhere,* Josh thought. But there was no dove. Just his oily little hands. "Now, before we get into the strategies and tactics, I always ask one question." Deep stare into Josh's eyes, stubby index finger pointing. "Do you want to win? Or do you want to win?"

Josh shrugged. "Of course." Little did they know he *had* to win. Viktor's loan was like a gun to his head.

"Are you ready to be completely objective about your opponents?" Pawling asked. "And I mean completely."

Josh nodded.

Pawling gave a thumbs-up. "Now, if there's one thing we've learned on the battlefield of politics, it's that there's always something *wrong* with anyone who becomes your opponent. The fact that they oppose you on issues is an indication of problems that run much, much deeper. I'm talking about character flaws. Moral deficiencies. Dark, shameful secrets that your opponent will try to hide. But that *we* will uncover. And bring into cleansing sunlight for all to see. So people can judge for themselves."

Brody beamed at Josh. He seemed to be proud of the competitive firepower he was bringing to him. Josh just listened.

"Now, I'm not inside this deal yet," Pawling went on. "But my preliminary investigations tell me we can really help. You know, shareholders are just voters in a different kind of election. And what voters care about, when all is said and done, is character. Character! That's where my organization can make the winning difference."

He paused and looked around. "Any questions?"

Head shakes from Josh and Brody.

Deep breath from Pawling. Hands rubbed together and popped apart. *Still no magic dove.*

"Now, when you look at the personal life of this opposing CEO, well, I think it's pretty clear what you see. First, her husband is a teacher at an art school. An *art* school?" Pawling shook the fingers of one hand as if he had just touched a scalding hot surface. "We all know what kind of people are attracted to the *arts*. And what kind of behaviors they like to engage in, using *art* as their cover. I think we'll find some rich discoveries in what this . . ." Pawling winked, ". . . *art* teacher leaves in his trash. Easy to imagine the magazines and, uh, toys we could find." Then under his breath, "And of course, we *will* be sure to find them." Pause. Leer. "One way or the other. People with these perversions buy them by mail order and the Internet. Ah, the Internet. Even under hostile administrations in the White House, we have patriotic friends in the Bureau who could help us document the kind of, uh, special-interest websites some *art type* would be likely to visit. Pictures he would download for his perverted plea-sure. Very damaging pictures that might even be ille-gal . . . uh, if you would like them to be."

Brody leaned on his elbows, listening with apparent relish.

Josh sat dumbstruck. He was appalled. He stared with growing horror at the little man.

"And from our preliminary work on the woman CEO, we can pretty well conclude what kind of an . . ." Pawling cleared his throat, ". . . arrangement their so-called mar-riage is hiding. She has that short hair, short nails. Dresses mannishly. So many women friends, all single. Competes in a masculine arena. Domineering. Husband of dubious masculinity with a secret life in a world famous for per-verts."

Pawling sat back, little hands in his lap. The prosecu-tion rests. "Of course, none of these revelations would come from anyone connected with Anglia Partners. They would just have a way of surfacing here and there. Bits of evidence, random at first, that will build and build into . . ." Pause. Hands rubbing again. Poof. *Still no bird.* ". . . ines-capable conclusions."

Brody spoke up. "You know, Josh, we've already got our business arguments against P&B management lined up and ready to pull the trigger on a takeover. We've al-ready started our campaign, detailing their mismanage-ment for the business press. I see what Drew has to offer as a complementary strategy."

Josh had to work to catch his breath. His eyes darted from Pawling to Brody and back again. He stood up. "That's my ex-wife you're talking about slandering. You're propos-ing a trumped-up gay-baiting character-assassination cam-paign against the mother of my son and his stepfather?"

"Mr. Katz," Pawling said, again pointing the stubby

index finger, "as I asked you at the start of this meeting—do you want to win? Or do you want to win?"

Josh turned away. He could not look at Pawling. He did not want to look at Brody. "Charles," he said to the wall, "get this guy out of here."

All Josh wanted to do at this moment was to go away somewhere to collect his thoughts. And take a shower. He did not know how to make Viktor's threat go away. But at least he could get rid of this nasty little extortionist.

Brody and Pawling stood.

"Josh," Brody said, "I don't think you understand the—"

"I understand completely," Josh said, still not looking at Brody. "You and I will have a talk later. In the meantime, I want it understood that we will do this proxy fight aggressively. But we will fight it clean and win it strictly on business issues."

"Josh," Brody said, "you can't win a proxy fight like this one that way."

Josh turned on his heels and headed for the door. "Oh yeah? Just watch me." He slammed his office door for good measure. At that moment, he decided he *had* to get out of this deal. He had thought about it before. Now he was sure. He would find a way to refinance his debt, repay Viktor, and get him and this deal the hell out of his life.

35

Emma sat at her desk across from Hal Percival and
Mike Saltzman.

"My fundamental question, Mike, is this," Hal said to
the takeover defense lawyer. "What do you suppose it is
that Anglia actually *wants*? Certainly not to try their hand
at curing the sick."

Saltzman snickered. "No, I didn't see that objective in
any of their filings."

Emma smiled. She was starting to feel right sitting
where Brad had always sat. In the month and a half since
she had moved in, Emma had changed the wallpaper from
dark gray to pale yellow, changed the rugs from dark er-
satz Orientals to plain light-toned rugs, and swapped the
heavy leather couches to pale seating that was spare and
modern. She hadn't feminized the space, just transformed
Brad's traditional men's club feeling to something light
and airy—plain, simple, and serene. God knows she could
use a little serenity with the pressure she was under.

"Well," Saltzman said, screwing the cap back onto his
empty water bottle, "based on Anglia's recent track record, they take over companies to break them up and sell
off the pieces. Or like other raiders, they could use their
takeover threats to produce a quick run-up in the stock
price. And then get out with a profit. Both are fast-buck
strategies. The point is, whatever they want, it's all for a

quick buck. If we can do nothing but make them wait, that in itself is a strategy. Most raiders have no patience."

Hal nodded. "And we at Percival & Baxter are famously patient." Emma saw him look her way. "We have an unbroken chain of CEOs who lead with the long-term good of the company foremost in mind." Hal raised his plastic bottle, as if toasting Emma, and downed the last of it. He stood. "If you'll excuse me, I have to get a meeting of the museum board downtown."

"Thanks, Hal," Emma said as he left.

"Yes, thanks," Saltzman said, not budging from his seat. He waited for Hal to leave and close the door to Emma's office.

Saltzman leaned forward. "One more thing, Emma," he said in a confidential hush. "I'd like you to speak to our private investigators."

She knew what was coming. "I already did, Mike. You know that."

"Yes, they told me," he said.

Emma clenched her jaw. "And they are disappointed, right?"

He nodded. "Emma, this is no time to hold back information about Anglia and Josh Katz. You must have potential dirt we could use against them. You must know things that—"

"No," she said. "No means no. I will not divulge information about things that happened in a marriage or that were shared me within the confidence of that marriage. Tell me, how is that any different from your attorney-client privilege? Or a priest and a parishioner in confession?"

Saltzman shook his head emphatically. "Emma, this is different. Trust me, it's different. If this becomes a full-scale hostile takeover—no, I mean, *when* . . . there are no rules, there are no confidences. Aren't you the least bit concerned about confidences of *yours* that the other side might betray?"

"No," she said. She regretted it the second she said it. "Well, yes, of course I am. But not until they actually try something underhanded. Until that happens, I want to fight fair. I could be wrong, but I think there are lines Anglia won't cross."

"Emma, as your takeover defense attorney, I strongly disagree. I have given you my best counsel."

"Okay, Mike. This is my call, right? A business decision. If they cross the line at some point, we can revisit it. Fair enough?"

"Fair enough," Saltzman said. To Emma, he sounded unconvinced. She hoped Josh would not prove him right.

36

"More tea, Papa?" Tanya asked brightly.

She wanted to please her father today. She felt as if she might float up into the air over the couch. In fact, she was happier than she had ever imagined she could be. She just *had* to tell Viktor her news. But then he would be upset. And she didn't want him to be. Not today, not with the heavenly way she was feeling. She so wanted him to be happy for her. Could she, maybe by cozying up to him somehow, possibly bring him around?

"Lord Montifer," he said and paused to see her reaction. "Lord Montifer, he very interested in you, eager for you."

Tanya leaned toward him. *I'm going to be calm and sweet,* she thought. *I'll bring him along step by step.* "Daddy, I wish I could find a way to love Percy, but I just don't know how I ever could."

"His family important. Nobility. Connections at highest levels. Business, government, everything most, most important," he insisted.

"I do wish I could find a way to make you happy," she said. And she thought she meant it. "Percy's not a bad sort. God knows we've tried going out together often enough. I have come to like him, sort of. And I do wish I could think of him as husband material, but I just can't." With that clearly stated, now might she be able to get her announcement out gradually? Somehow, yes, gradually.

"You are no more little girl." He placed a hand over his heart and bowed his head. "I accept this. You are woman now."

She nodded in a way she hoped expressed gratitude. She *was* grateful to him. For all his money, for all the privilege it had given her. Her baby would be the beneficiary. His money was why she could have this baby on her own and not worry about support. She *was* lucky. The way she was feeling today, she could be the luckiest girl on earth. She smiled warmly, thinking she would tell him soon.

Viktor inhaled deeply. He looked around the room. "We are alone?"

"Yes, Papa," she said.

"Is something interesting for you in pharmaceutical company. My French one."

"Daddy, I didn't know you owned a French pharmaceutical company."

"Is complicated. But I control, yes. Someday, I teach you these things maybe."

"I'm afraid I don't have much of a head for business, Daddy." She had no idea what he might be getting at. When nervous like this, she tended to chatter. "You know, Daddy, I'm much better at *spending* money. It's a talent, you know, having good taste and an eye for quality. I'm awfully good in that department, wouldn't you agree?"

"This company," he said, cutting her off, "making drug for women. Make every woman happy, so happy." He pointed a finger at her emphatically. "You, too. Make you happy with *any* man." Viktor made a sweeping gesture. "Any man."

Tanya sat back. "What on earth does it do?"

"Will be like Viagra for women. Only better. Much better." He stared into her eyes. "We talk like adults, no?"

"Yes, certainly." She was stunned.

"First, it put you in mood for sex. Any time. Like that!" He snapped his fingers. "This part very difficult. Emotions. You know, you are woman."

She nodded.

"Then it make you wet, nerve endings go crazy. Clitoris. G-spot. One touch. Anywhere where pudendal nerve system working. Orgasm, orgasm, orgasm. With man, without man, make no difference. You happy. Glow from inside out. How many times day you want?"

"Well," Tanya cleared her throat. "I must say you have got my attention. Uh, when will this be out on the market?"

"Still work to do. My company has half formula. American company got other half. Molecules built on computers, very modern." He leaned forward and whispered, "But see, Americans don't know what they got. I buy this company soon. Stock was too expensive. But now price is down, way down."

Tanya had never heard her father talk about business before. Or at least, she never remembered listening to him if he ever did. "How lucky is that?" she asked.

"Is no luck here. Never luck." He pointed at himself. "I *make* luck happen. Is lesson I teach you." He pointed at her. "Say it."

"Say what, Daddy?"

"Say, 'You make luck happen.'"

She was puzzled, but no matter. If this would make him happy. "You make luck happen," she recited.

"Say again, is important."

Tanya gave her delivery great oomph. "You *make* luck happen!"

"Right! Is why Viktor Volkov never lose. Is how *we*," he gestured at his daughter with open arms, "our family, we make billions."

"Oh yes, that part of business I do understand. Lots of ducky billions." She smiled broadly. This conversation was not getting her any closer to her goal. She might have to just spit it out.

Viktor smiled back at her. "This drug," he said, taking a big breath before coming to his conclusion, "is why man you marry does *not* matter."

Tanya lunged forward and put her hand on his chest. She had to stop him right there. Yes, this had to be the moment! It was as if he'd brought it to her on a silver platter straight from the window at Asprey.

"Daddy, I can't possibly marry Percy. And I'm quite sure he won't want to marry me now. No, I am certain of it." She took a deep breath and exhaled noisily. "You see . . . I'm . . . I'm already pregnant. *Pregnant!*"

She studied his reaction. His lips clenched, his eyes opened wide. She'd now charge further ahead before he could explode.

"I'm going to *have* the baby. I've made up my mind and that's final. Final! We are going to live happily ever after together right here in this house. And I'm *not* going to marry Percy. Or anyone else, for that matter. It's going to be just me and my wonderful little girl. Oh, I know she's a girl, I just know it. I've got it *all* worked out. Life is going to be ducky for the two of us. Perfect, actually." She sat back and patted her flat tummy. There now, she'd said it.

Viktor took several deep breaths. Tanya expected him to explode. She was waiting for him to scream at her. Instead, he was silent. He rose slowly and walked around to her side of the coffee table. He bent over her, hands apart. Tanya flinched, fearing he might hit her. If so, it would be the first time, but she had felt for years that it was going to happen. But instead of hitting her, he took her head gently into his hands and kissed her forehead.

"*Ti ne znayesh zhizni*," he said. You don't understand life.

Tanya looked up at him.

"*Dorogaya, moya. Ya zhelayu tebe tolko dobra*," he mumbled, then quickly translated for her. "Darling, believe me. I am only thinking about your happiness."

She knew that Viktor thought she could not understand. Even though she understood his every word, she had no idea what he meant.

37

"What means this?" Viktor asked Josh.

Josh gripped the satellite phone tighter, so tight he thought he might break it. "It means that I am pulling out of this deal and ending our business relationship. As of right now. I'm working on a new refinancing plan to get you your money. I'm calling it quits between the two of us. I'll work it out in the next week or so. In the meantime, let's just put this P&B thing on hold. Nothing can happen until the annual meeting, anyway. The poison pill ensures that. So let's just cool our jets, you and I. I will make you whole, and then some. And then, we will go our separate ways."

Silence on Viktor's end. A long silence.

"Do you understand, Viktor? Do you?" Josh felt a new lightness in his voice. His grip on the awful little phone loosened. "It means I'm getting out."

More silence.

Finally, Viktor spoke. Coldly, calmly. "No, Katz, we finish deal. *You* finish deal."

"I just told you, Viktor. No."

"No, Katz, *I* say no. You stay. You finish deal for me."

"Viktor, I'm going to have to hang up. As soon as I get the new refinancing package, we'll unwind this arrangement. In the meantime, I'll help you find another banker to do the P&B deal. From now on, we can talk through our lawyers."

Viktor laughed. Josh was so glad he would not have to put up with this crap much longer.

"Katz, you at computer?"

"Yes," Josh said tentatively, wondering where this was going.

He heard a faint clicking sound, like Viktor's fingers at a keyboard.

"Okay, Katz, I send you email. Just now. You look. Computer is on, yes?"

Josh heard the little *ping* announcing a new message. He stared at the screen. There was no sender listed and no subject line. Just a PDF file attached. He opened the picture file. A series of a dozen black-and-white photos filled the screen. The pictures were smudgy and a bit blurred, infrared photos taken in the dark. But they were more than clear enough to reveal what was happening.

It was a night-vision view looking down into a bedroom. There was a man wearing nothing but boxer shorts. He appeared in various poses of close contact with a naked teenage girl. From her little budding breasts, narrow hips, and faint smudge of pubic hair, the girl looked to be, maybe, thirteen or fourteen. The man in the boxer shorts was Josh Katz. The naked underage girl was Tanya, Viktor Volkov's daughter.

Josh did not have to ask where the pictures had come from. They must have been taken by a camera hidden in the guest bedroom at Viktor's Belgravia house that night years before. Josh replayed his recollections as he studied the photos. The freeze-frame images matched what he remembered. But the order in which the pictures were displayed presented the action backward. Instead of showing Josh yanking the drunk, naked girl *out* of bed and putting his shirt *on* her, the carefully selected images showed Josh taking the shirt *off* the girl and pulling her *into* the bed.

All he could do was breathe into the phone.

"Picture worth a thousand words. Is expression, no?" Viktor said.

In his mind, Josh tried to assemble the elements of Viktor's blackmail. He wondered how much of it was an accident and how much had been planned all along. There had been the drunken party the teenagers were having in one end of the mansion while he and Viktor crunched numbers late into the night in Viktor's study. There was Viktor's seemingly offhand invitation to stay over that night. Viktor had insisted they take a break from their deal analysis. Together, they had made a quick visit to the kids' party. There they met the older boy Sergei, the twentyish son of one of Viktor's partners. Sergei was leading the gaggle of school girls in drinking games. Sergei had given Josh a wink. At the time, he had thought nothing of it. Just a wink between guys. After Josh had gone up to bed, the kids must have played a Truth-or-Dare game of some kind to get Tanya, who was home on vacation from her exclusive boarding school, drunk enough to strip and go upstairs to seduce the man in the guest room. Had Sergei goaded her into it independently? Or had he taken orders from Viktor? It seemed like the stunt had to have been planned. However, if it was a mere accident of drunken follies, it meant that Viktor had hidden cameras recording everything that went on under his roof. And he could scan everything his friends and guests did in private for material that could be used for blackmail.

An even more sickening thought loomed over all the others exploding in Josh's brain. Viktor was using pictures of his own daughter, naked and sexually compromised, to blackmail him. His *own* goddamn child! Josh had spent his life among ruthless men who were driven to win at all costs. But this was a new low point. Just how cold and calculating a monster was Viktor Volkov? At this moment, Josh knew he could not even begin to answer that question.

These photos could ruin him and his reputation. Even if, by a miracle of criminal defense lawyer magic, it did not get him arrested, it would turn him into a pariah. It would not matter what actually happened that night. The visuals were completely damning.

He heard Viktor's voice again over the static of his own thoughts. "Katz, you only person I send these pictures to. Just you. But I can send to more people. Like *Wall Street Journal, Financial Times*. Maybe FBI and Scotland Yard. Is up to you."

Josh took a deep breath, then sighed. "What do you want, Viktor? Just tell me what you want." He thought of the history of Viktor's career. Josh, like all the bankers who worked with newly rich Russians back in the Yeltsin days, went to great lengths not to know how their clients' fortunes had begun. But of course the rumors must have come from somewhere. *We all had suspicions,* Josh thought, *but we had to pretend otherwise.* It was a necessary legal fiction. *Immoral we do every day. Illegal never.* It was whispered but never proven that Viktor had been a kingpin of the protection rackets, extortion. Roofing, it was euphemistically called. Extortion was Viktor's first trade. And now he was using it against Josh.

"What I want is you do this deal," Viktor said calmly. "You start it, you finish it. Now."

"And then?" Josh shuddered at the thought of being Viktor's permanent slave.

"Then?" Viktor asked with seeming innocence. Josh

could feel him toying with him. Stick and carrot, cat and mouse.

"Yes, Viktor, what then?" Josh had a terrible vision of unending midnight phone calls and unwanted deals continuing indefinitely into a dreadful future. He supposed he could try to fight the photos and rescue his life and reputation. But what a fight it would be. The odds seemed overwhelmingly stacked against him.

"Then," Viktor said, sounding almost kind, "when is paid back loan, you go away."

"I go away? You don't, uh . . . ?"

Josh wanted to delete the horrifying email, but he knew that was pointless. He resisted the urge to click the X button. The file was now on his server. Things don't really get deleted for a long time, he knew, they just get moved to one side until they finally get overwritten by something else. Anyone with a little computer savvy could access it and forward it or God knows what. That one little message sat there in his inbox, a deadly infectious thing waiting to contaminate his entire life.

"I want this deal, Katz. I no want you."

"But what about the pictures?" Josh spoke slowly and carefully, enunciating each of his words. "What . . . do you plan . . . to do . . . with . . . the pictures?"

"Look in computer again, Katz. Tell me what you see."

Josh peered into his inbox. The strange message with no sender was gone. He scrolled frantically up and down. Yes, it was gone. Where, he did not know. But through some kind of computer legerdemain, Viktor had made it disappear.

"What pictures you talk about?" Viktor asked, sounding playful.

There were a million things Josh wanted to say, no, to

scream. But in that moment, he had no idea. He sucked in his breath.

"Is gone email, yes?"

"Yes."

"Is good technology, yes?"

"If you say so, Viktor."

"Listen me, Katz. I no interested in you. And I no want hurt my daughter. You think I want that? Huh?"

"What do you mean?"

"You think I happy to use photos of my daughter—*my* daughter—being stupid with man like you?"

"I don't know, Viktor. I don't know."

"You force me when you say no," Viktor said. He sounded almost regretful. He paused and began again quietly. "I no like this kind of thing. But *you* make necessary when you say you quit. Katz, you do my deal. Then you go away. I leave you alone. Understand?" Viktor hung up before Josh could answer.

He leaned back in his desk chair. His stomach was churning. He asked himself, *what have I become?* He had no answer.

He thought back to the night before the syndication dinner for his first deal for Viktor, when his bank would be presenting the Russian to the elite of the City of London. He had had to coach Viktor on table manners. Here's how you hold the fork, here's how you take smaller bites, pausing between them, not chewing with your mouth open.

Emma had given Josh those same lessons when they had started dating at Wharton. Civilizing the crude boy from the wrong side of the tracks, making him fit for polite company. "Do you want people to think you were raised by wolves?" she had asked him when he balked at being told how to do something as basic as eating. When

Josh had asked Viktor the same question years later, Viktor had surprised him. "Is good, raised by wolves!" he cried. "My name, Volkov, is son of wolf. Wolf great hunter. Always eat, always have kill, no matter how bad is winter."

Yes, he thought, *Viktor is a great hunter. A greater hunter than me. A greater hunter than I had ever imagined.*

38

Emma was so grateful to have made it home for dinner with Ned and Peter. She had not seen them much since the crisis began. The simple domesticity of sitting around the kitchen table with the men she loved was such a comfort. She enjoyed bringing everyone's dishes to the sink, rinsing them, and arranging them in the dishwasher. A simple task, a loving task . . . completed and done. Unlike anything she faced at work.

Best of all, she had Ned's surprise gift ready. She had the moment all planned out. Right after Peter went upstairs, she would give Ned the envelope. Inside was the letter of the prepaid contract with the architect and construction firm, to let him design and build the studio of his dreams, whatever he wanted. All paid for. He would be so thrilled to finally get the studio of his dreams. And they would go make beautiful love together on Ned's beat-up old couch. Just the way they used to. It had been a while, she thought wistfully.

She brought servings of the apple crumble their housekeeper had made to the table. Ned finished his first. "You know, Peter," he said, "Mom's not the only one with a new set of work pressures."

Emma looked up. What was he talking about?

"I got a call from the Los Angeles Museum of Contemporary Art last month. We've been talking and we finally reached an agreement. They've commissioned some pieces for a show next year on the theme of ceramics as sculpture. It's going to be called 'Fire and Form.' The curator saw my *Earthborn* piece last year in Herman Askadian's collection out there."

Emma knew Ned's series of monumental abstract pieces he called *Earthborns*. He had started making them two years ago. Only that one adventurous collector had ever bought any of them. But Ned had kept making them and they kept not selling. She had tried to appreciate their primitive, geological strength. But they were just too masculine for her taste. She liked Ned's softer, more traditional works, the ones he turned on the potter's wheel, the ones that looked more like, well, traditional ceramics.

She was startled. She had no idea.

She was delighted. She was proud. She was thrilled. Of course.

She was also angry. *And* hurt!

What? A museum show? A curator who saw Ned's Earthborn *piece last year? Talking for a few months? Reached an agreement last week? Talking since last year? How could all this be happening without him saying a word until now? Not one word!*

"Those *Earthborn* pieces are so-o-o cool!" Peter said, jumping in before Emma had a chance to say anything or figure out how to express her upset. "They look like magma exploding out of a volcano, like the way it freezes when it hits the ocean, only more jagged. And then you make all those crystals run through it like swords and laser beams! Geez, can we all go out to L.A. for the opening? That'll be so cool!"

Emma reached across the table and took Ned's hand. "Congratulations, honey. Why did you wait so long to say anything?" She wanted to ask—no, *demand*—to know why he had been holding out on her all this time, hiding such important news. Instead, she squeezed his hand and said, "I'm so proud of you." She would ask him later. In a calm, undemanding way . . . she hoped. After she gave him the envelope. Yes, afterwards. Then it just spilled out. "Why did you wait so long to tell me?"

"You've been preoccupied," Ned said, "I didn't want to bother you. They're not your kind of thing, I know. But I like them. And so does the curator."

"Bother?" she said. "What are you talking about?"

Peter jumped to his feet. She could tell he wanted to escape. She saw his eyes darting back and forth between her and Ned. "Got an online championship round of Death Star tonight," he said as he headed for the kitchen door. "Gotta run." He vanished.

Ned stood. "I should get back to work. With my deadline and all. You mind finishing cleanup?"

Emma shook her head as she watched him go. She sat for a moment. Then she left the kitchen and went to her home office in the den. There were piles of work papers everywhere. She searched under one pile, then another, then another.

Then she found it. *Yes,* she thought wearily, *there it is. Right* under *my new job.* She grabbed the envelope and followed Ned to his studio. She would follow him to the far side of the moon, if that was where he had gone.

She walked to the breezeway that connected to the garage. It was original with the 1920s house, a two-car structure that had been built with a nineteenth-century carriage house in mind. The attic on the second floor that might have been a chauffeur's modest apartment was Ned's studio. Emma clomped noisily up the stairs to announce herself.

The studio was crammed with all the paraphernalia of a busy potter—shelves of pots in all stages of finish, buckets of clay, cans of glazes, two potter's wheels, a boxy kiln that looked like a medium-sized deep freezer painted blue, and Ned's beat-up old couch in the far corner beneath the skylight. In the center of the loft was Ned's new *Earthborn* work-in-progress. A big bricklike block with a saw, or a saber, or something like a lightning bolt crashing through it. Ned could do such glorious pots, she thought. And riffs on pots that were elegant round shapes in wonderfully mad combinations, ablaze with astonishing glazes and colors. They were poetic, they were beautiful, graceful, and surprising. Not like this thing.

"This is my latest *Earthborn*," Ned said over his shoulder. He dropped tools into a drawer, making more noise, she thought, than necessary. She wondered, *had he thrown them in there angrily?*

"It's beautiful, Ned." She thought she sounded convincing. She hoped so. "Just beautiful."

He turned to face her. "Really?"

"Yes, it's . . . it's . . . great. Powerful."

Ned gave her a skeptical glance.

She walked over to him and put her arms around him. "I'm sorry for being so distracted lately."

"Well," he said. "You've got a lot going on."

She kissed him once. A little peck.

He gave her a little peck back. "You're lying about the new piece, aren't you? You don't like it."

"No, I'm not."

"Yes, you are."

"I am *not*. I really love it."

He raised one eyebrow skeptically.

She smiled and took his head in her hands. She gave him the kind of deep, lingering kiss that usually initiated their lovemaking. "All right, I'm lying," she whispered, then kissed him the same way again but more ardently. "I'm lying in order to get sex. Men do it all the time."

They shared a little laugh and let go of each other.

She hoped she had rescued the moment. She took the envelope from her pocket. "Ned, I want you to have something you've always wanted." She put the envelope in his hand. "I want you to build the studio of your dreams. Here, it's all arranged." She watched him open the letter and read. "It's the same firm that designed that new studio space at U Penn."

"You paid for this? For everything?"

"Yup, everything." She studied him, unsure what he was feeling. "You deserve it. And we can easily afford it now."

"Well," he said, "*you* can."

"No, *we* can." She touched his arm. "*We* can." She tried to embrace him again. He stood rigidly in place, arms at his side. "Don't you know that I couldn't succeed without you, without your love and support and patience and understanding."

"You make it sound," he said, withdrawing from her, "like you're the one who's succeeding and I'm the one who, uh . . ." Ned bit his lip and looked down.

"No, Ned!" she sputtered. "I have never, never once, never, *ever* said that!"

The issue of her big income and Ned's small income did come up from time to time. Their unspoken agreement seemed to be to ignore it as much as possible. When she got her CEO contract, with its guarantees of millions, he congratulated her with a big hug and never brought it up again. She had been so preoccupied since then, she and Ned barely had the chance to talk about anything, let alone this delicate issue. This uncomfortable moment told her the time had finally come to settle it.

She took him by the shoulders and shook him. "No, goddammit!" She was so angry she thought she might cry, but she fought that urge. "We succeed together. You are the man who gives me the strength to face all that shit out there and stand up to it. The only reason I can make all this money is because of you. We are in this job together, don't you feel that?"

"Well," he muttered, "since you became CEO, it does feel like we are both in your job. It's all you ever talk about."

"That's not true, and you know it!" She felt that she had to defend herself. But the more his remark sank in, the more she realized he was probably right. No, more than probably. For some reason, she could not bring herself to apologize. Not now. Instead, she heard herself going on the offensive. "Ned, I can't do my work without you. And I assume, you can't do your work without me. We're a couple of worker bees, that's who we are. It just so happens my work makes us a lot of money."

"And mine doesn't." He looked down.

"So what? It's art. You're an artist." She touched his chin to recapture his glance.

He looked away.

"Who cares who makes money and who doesn't? Let's enjoy it. Isn't that what it's for? With a better studio and more freedom, who knows how your work will advance? With that museum show coming, you could be on the verge of your own breakthrough. Let's make the most of the advantages we have . . . because . . . because we love each other."

This had come out wrong. All wrong. Against her will, she could feel tears welling up in her eyes. "Goddamm it, Ned, I love you. I want you to have everything." She struggled to catch her breath. "If *I* can't make your dreams come true, who can?" She was almost in tears. She looked down so he wouldn't see. "It's called a gift. A gift from my heart."

Ned took her in his arms. They were silent for a long moment.

"I'm sorry," he whispered into her ear. "I don't mean to be ungrateful. I'm blown away, really. My dream studio. Presto, like magic."

"That's right," she said. "For you. You deserve it."

"Emma," he said a bit formally, but not letting go of her. "I can't accept this."

She stepped back out of his embrace. "What do you mean? It's the studio of your dreams."

"I can't let you do this."

"Yes, you can. It's just money."

"No, Emma. I can't."

"What do you mean, you can't?"

"I just can't. It's a matter of my . . . uh . . ." He hesitated, sounding like he was searching for the right word, ". . . my . . . uh . . . independence."

"Independence?" She sniffed back tears. "Who's independent around here? We *depend* on each other. What good is money if we don't use it for things that mean something to *us*?"

She thought of Josh, who was crazy for money, insatiable, more in love with money than with anything, including her. And Ned, for whom money was, well, she wasn't exactly sure. For Ned, money was a complicated prickly thing. Sure, it was appealing, buying nice things. But it also had dangerous thorns that could really hurt anyone who touched it in the wrong way.

"I'm sorry, Emma. But I can't let you do this. I'll build my own studio someday. Or not. It's no big deal."

Emma felt her shoulders droop. She did not know what to say.

Ned put his arms around her. "All that matters," he whispered, "is that I love you. I'm very touched that you thought of it. I hope you understand."

She buried her face in his shoulder.

She felt confused, conflicted, exhausted, and yet strangely relieved. Ned hugged her tighter. Suddenly, she let go of all her tension and worry and frustration and fear. She let go of everything that had been building and burdening her since that terrible day in July. And began to cry.

39

Josh watched his father carefully chalk the end of his pool cue. At eighty-five, Sid was starting to look frail. He seemed to be shorter each time Josh saw him. He was as alert as ever. But there was visibly less of him and his voice was getting thinner.

"Josh," he said, not looking up from the delicate task, "I told you you'd love havin' a pool table in your house. Now was I right or was I right?"

"Yeah, Sid, you were right," he said. Since buying the table, Josh had not gone near it, except when his father came for visits. The pool room was in the basement, down the main corridor from the cold room for the computers, the wine cellar, and the hidden safe room.

"Great way to relax while keepin' you sharp," Sid said. "Sure you don't want a game?"

"Sorry, not now, Sid. Pen's due any minute."

"Afraid your old man'll beat you again? That's it, huh?" Sid cackled.

"Yeah, that's it," Josh said. Sid racked up the balls, carefully inserting the fingertips of both hands into the back of the wooden frame to make the balls form a snug triangle. He walked to the other end of the table with cue and cue ball in hand and began planning his break shot. "You know, kiddo," he said as he scanned the green felt, "you must have inherited the touch from me. You just gotta practice more. You're practicing, right?"

"Sure I practice, of course," he lied. "When Peter gets here, we can all play a game." He was not lying about that. He was looking forward to it.

"He on the chopper?" Sid asked as he tried a few practice strokes.

"Yeah, he's on the chopper." It amused him that Sid insisted on using that word for the S-76, as if it were the traffic girl on local news.

Sid leaned forward to make his break shot. His baggy shirt spilled open to reveal gold chains dangling from his neck, white chest hair, sagging skin and a shrinking frame. Josh felt a wave of affection touched with sadness; his father was on his way to becoming a memory, like his mother. Sid thrust his cue gracefully and sent balls scattering around the table. Two balls disappeared down pockets. "Ha-cha-cha!" he sang out.

Josh was appalled at his father's shirt. It was shiny and cheap-looking with a loud abstract print in a riot of strange colors. "Where'd you get that shirt?" he asked, trying to sound casual.

"Like it, huh?" Sid answered distractedly. He was walking around the table, planning his next shot. "One of my buddies from the track showed me this place in Lauderdale. Called 'Sharp as a Tack.' Closeouts. Cheap. But real, uh, sharp. I'll get one for you?"

"No, that's okay," Josh said fondly, "I'm all set in the clothes department."

The sound of footsteps hurrying down the cellar stairs announced Penelope. She burst into the pool room, wearing jeans and a black T-shirt with a little "D&G" in sequins. "My two favorite men," she said cheerfully as she kissed Josh on the cheek.

Sid looked up. "Hey, gorgeous," he said.

"Hi, Sid." Penelope blew him a kiss.

Sid lowered his head and drove the cue ball down to

the far end of the table. It hit one ball, then another, then another, knocking a third ball, then a fourth ball into pockets. He looked up and grinned.

"You're showing off for me," she teased.

"Don't you know it," Sid said proudly.

"I've got the advance pages of my article on Josh," she said, waving them in the air. "You guys want to see?"

Josh took the pages.

He'd always protected Sid's secret. That he could barely read. Yes, Sid could read road signs, but by form more than by letter. Text was almost impossible. He once admitted—bragged, actually—that he got through high school by cheating, though he'd threatened Josh with certain death if *he* ever cheated in school.

Since Josh was little, Sid had had his son read aloud to him. First, he had Josh read kids' books. Then, from fifth grade onward, Sid had him read him back issues of *The Wall Street Journal, Forbes,* and *Fortune* that he "borrowed" from the barber shop. "Read to me, kiddo, read to me," Sid would say. "Read to me about the big money guys. I want to hear all about 'em. And you, kiddo, you're gonna be one of 'em someday. Ya hear? You're gonna be one a them big money guys. *Bi-i-i-i-g* money. Now, read for your old man."

This had been Josh's first education in the business world, beyond Sid's disastrous attempts at being an entrepreneur. While his father failed at one half-baked, low-rent venture after another—the used-car lot, the brake and transmission franchise, the plus-size dress shop, the convenience store beside the housing project—Josh learned how to play dumb with collection agents who made angry phone calls and pounded on the door of their apartment. Josh saw his family's televisions, appliances, and furniture get repossessed, with notices from courts waved in their faces by strangers who stripped the family, not just of things, but of their dignity. He remembered the big gold Cadillac Eldorado convertible Sid came home in one summer evening. He arrived with the top down in full glamour mode, ribbons of chrome glistening, white leather interior glowing under the street lamp. People around the neighborhood came to gawk and listen to Sid boast about its many luxury features. The next morning, collection agents towed it away.

One day when Josh was fourteen, he stopped calling his father "Dad" and started calling him "Sid." Not defiantly the way a kid might, testing for limits and expecting to get yelled at or slapped. Just calmly, as if he were one of Sid's buddies or the shyster lawyer who escorted him to bankruptcy court time and again. It wasn't anything he'd thought about, he just did it. "Hi, Sid," he said when he came home from school that day. His father and mother sat at the kitchen table, poring over the *Daily Racing Form,* the sign that Sid was out of work yet again. Josh's mother had been reading the names of the horses aloud, with that stricken look of worry and patience she so often wore. She turned around, visibly upset and starting to say, "Josh, don't you dare—" but Sid raised his hand to stop her.

He gave Josh a look he still remembered. It was a grown-up look. A look deep into his eyes that recognized something without ever having to say it out loud. "It's okay," he said, "he can call me Sid. That's my name." He nodded, never taking his eyes from Josh. From that day forward, the son never used "Dad" or "Father" again.

Josh put his arm around Penelope's waist and headed them toward the stairs. "We'll show the article to Sid later." He would spare his father the public embarrassment, the way he had their whole lives. "He's got to practice to beat the pants off Peter and me later on. Right?"

Sid nodded and went back to scoping out his next shot.

Outside in the morning sun, Josh read the advance print-out of Penelope's *Town & Country* article as they walked arm in arm.

"The New Traditionalist" by Penelope Longstreet, with photographs by Tim Leach, was every bit the glorious puff piece Brody had promised that day when Penelope first exploded into Josh's life. Penelope's breathless text recounted the taste and elegance of Josh's show palace, quoting Josh, his A-list decorator, and several A-list antiques dealers. It was a glowing showpiece for the impeccable taste of Ledgemere Farm and, most of all, its lord and master— the titan of finance, who, with no mention of his simple roots, was living the life of a true modern artistocrat, complete with well-worn Persian carpets and works of noblesse oblige.

Josh was delighted and proud. This would show them, he thought, as he flipped through the pages, savoring the captions under the perfectly lit pictures of his domain. Like this one: "Ledgemere's staff of five gardeners takes pride in their combined 100 years of service at the estate. These towering wisteria vines were planted by the head gardener's grandfather." Josh, his head gardener, and Penelope all knew that was not quite true. But Sal's grandfather had worked as a gardener around Greenwich and had probably planted wisteria vines like this one on someone's estate. Probably in this very neighborhood. Hell, maybe even this old vine right here. Who could say otherwise?

They neared the cement slab of the helipad at the edge of the forest that bordered on the Greenwich Links Association. Josh stopped and let go of Penelope's arm. He pointed into the dense shade of the old-growth oaks.

"You know, in the winter when the leaves are gone, you can see the pitch and putt over there at the club. And they can see over here to Ledgemere. There are always people out there practicing, except when there's too much snow."

"I know," she said. "Devotion to pointless sports is another one of their *rah-ther* endearing traits, along with ancestor worship and alcoholism."

Josh stared into the woods. "Pen," he said, shaking his head, "your article has made me change my mind. I am *not* going to try to get into that goddamn club again."

"Oh, I'm so glad to hear you say that!" She gave him a little hug. "Just let those people be by themselves. They're a genetic dead end. Really, it's no fun over there. When I met Sid, I could see that *he's* where you got your energy and drive."

"I love the guy, but those outfits of his are too much," Josh said.

"Well, his clothes may be out of place here, but I'll bet he looks normal with his buddies at the track. He didn't have the advantages and the education he made sure you got. And now, you take care of him. That's beautiful. I'd love to write about *that*."

"You didn't put that in the article?" he asked. He flipped back through the pages, afraid that he had missed something.

"Of course not, silly, it's *Town & Country*. It's all la-la and la-dee-dah. I'm talking about real life. What you got from your dad and what he gets from you, that's real. Shows the kind of man you really are."

He smiled and took her hand.

She put an arm around his waist. "Josh," she whispered in a serious tone, "tell me where you want us to go."

"Go?" Josh was playing coy.

"You know what I mean. *Us*. Where do you see us . . . ?"

He put his fingertip on her lips. "Pen," he said, removing

his finger and planting a peck. "I have to get past this P&B deal."

"You mean, *Emma*."

"No, Pen, I mean Percival & Baxter. I have contractual obligations. Business stuff. It's complicated. But I'll be free soon."

She took a step back. "What's that supposed to mean?"

He knew he was being evasive. But also truthful. He didn't know. He just knew that things would be somehow different once he finally had this deal behind him. Everything would be over and done. Maybe even Emma. Or maybe not. "It means I want you to stay here with me. Together we'll figure this out. Like I said before, just give me a little time, eh?"

He leaned forward for a kiss. She turned away. "A little time means just that," she said. "A *little* time."

He heard Tom Hardacre shouting from across the great lawn. He was grateful for the interruption.

"Mr. Katz!" he called as he neared them, running at a good clip, his black Armani blazer flapping. "Call from London." He came to a stop, not in the least winded from his run. "Sorry, Mr. Katz," Hardacre said, "but they called me on the house line when you did not pick this up." He held out the satellite phone from Josh's desk.

"Thanks, Tom," he said. Taking the phone in one hand and covering the microphone with the other, he turned to Penelope. "Sorry." He walked toward the forest to get out of earshot.

"Josh Katz here," he said after a few strides.

"Please hold for Mr. Volkov," an officious English woman said.

There was a wait on the other end. To Josh, it felt like a long wait. He wondered if the wait was punishment for making Viktor wait. Or was the delay because Viktor's secretary was conferencing him in from someplace far away, like his ocean-liner-sized yacht cruising in the middle of God knows where? Finally Viktor picked up.

"Katz," Viktor said, "is time." The connection sounded good, wherever it was coming from. "Stock price good and low."

Viktor paused.

Josh said nothing.

"Nineteen, maybe lower?" Viktor waited for Josh to chime in. But Josh said nothing. "Katz? Katz?"

"Viktor, are you asking me or telling me?" Josh did not hide his irritation.

Viktor snorted a little laugh. "Both. Is my opinion stock will go below nineteen next week. Is your opinion, too?"

"Do you care what my opinion is?"

"Josh," he said, switching to a sincere, respectful use of his banker's first name, "of course I care what is your opinion. You are my banker. Is time we make full tender offer. Like you say, we beat poison pill this way. We make offer so good stockholders no resist. At same time, we make new proxy fight. Remove whole board of directors. New board will remove poison pill. Stockholders happy to sell. We buy all shares. How you say, 'Done deal!' Katz, is time we take over Percival & Baxter. Now. How much premium we offer to close deal? Pay enough but not too much. What price?"

"Viktor, I'm standing on my lawn on Saturday morning. I have to get my deal team together. My bankers, accountants, lawyers, PR guys, proxy solicitors, you know. It's a big fucking deal."

"Make announcement Monday morning when market opens," Viktor commanded, with a grimness that made Josh think he was channeling Joseph Stalin. "You do this, yes?"

Josh sighed. "Yes, Viktor, Monday morning." The end was in sight. One final sprint to the finish line. And maybe, when it was completed, Viktor would remove the gun from Josh's head.

Peter was due any minute. Josh had been looking forward to spending time with his son and Sid this weekend. Seeing Sid deteriorating gave his wish an urgency he had not felt before. He felt himself missing him already. It pained him to imagine life without the cackling and irreverence of this man who was more like a child to him than a father. But still, Sid was his father.

"You go to work now," Viktor said. "Is time you make deal."

"Yes," Josh repeated, "is time I make deal." He had no idea if Viktor would pick up on the sarcastic way he repeated Viktor's awkward English. And he did not care.

"You wiseass, Katz. Maybe you try make business in Russian someday. See how far you get. Now go make deal. Call my private number any time, twenty-four-seven. They find me. Soon, Katz," Viktor snickered, "you get out of bed with me."

He cringed at the oblique reference to the incriminating pictures.

"Then you be free. I promise this."

Josh felt he could only hope so.

Viktor hung up.

The clamor of the helicopter arrived well before the S-76 came into view. He walked back to Penelope and Hardacre and handed the phone to Hardacre. "Thanks, Tom." He turned to Penelope. "I'm going to have to take the helicopter back into the city right after Peter lands. Sorry, Pen. Deal emergency. Can you babysit Peter and Sid while I'm gone?"

She shook her head, disappointed but understanding.

"No problem. But you're not coming back. Let's get real."

"Probably not 'til Sunday night. You don't have to baby-sit them the whole time, just get them started. They'll stay occupied, between my dad's pool table and Peter's video games. In fact, why don't you come into the city tonight and stay with me at the apartment?" He was referring to the corporate apartment Anglia owned near the office. "You can do some shopping and when I have to come back for a shower . . ."

She stopped him. "Josh, honey, you'll only have enough time for a shower and then it'll be back to the office. No thanks. I can play with the boys here for a while and then fend for myself. You've got work to do. Go do it."

Josh nodded to her as he switched into his deal mode. All business, maximum efficiency. Clear the decks mentally, physically, and emotionally for money making. He could check off Penelope and forget about her for the moment. She knew it, too.

He turned to Hardacre. "Can you give Charles Brody a call for me? Tell him it's all hands on deck for the weekend. He'll know who to call."

"Aye, sir," Hardacre said. "I already did. When the call came in from London, I gave him a ring on the other line. I figured you'd want me to. Brody says he's put yer team on standby."

As the helicopter appeared over the treetops, they walked away from the helipad to give it clearance. Josh thought of Peter inside the cabin. He would buy him something really nice to make up for yet another fatherly visitation weekend without the father.

And he thought about Emma.

How could he not?

He knew he was going to smash Emma's world to

pieces. But he had no choice. It was his world or hers. Why couldn't she understand that it was just a company? An empty vessel that served no purpose beyond making money. Why did she care so much about it? It couldn't just be her father's influence. Yes, they had been close and all. But he was long dead.

He could take her into his world and give her a taste of what she could do. He could take this awful situation Viktor had blackmailed him into and make it come out right. He could turn it into something positive. Couldn't he?

Yes, of course he could. And then, when Viktor left him alone, he could write a new chapter in all their lives. All their lives together . . . yes, together . . . somehow.

They would be business partners.

Friends, even.

Well, maybe later on, after he had shown her the way.

He would find a way to show her. Give her the means to do all the good works she wanted to do from the top of the mountain of money he would build for her, *with* her.

Why couldn't she understand that?

The deafening noise of the helicopter matched the noise inside his head. The windstorm it created matched his turmoil as he prepared to destroy this thing that Emma loved.

40

A s usual, Emma arrived first in the Defense Committee war room Monday for the 8:30 meeting. She did not like the name "Defense Committee." It sounded weak and, well, defensive. On the tennis court, she liked to play offense. But that word would have been even worse. She also did not like the name "war room" for this conference room, even though she had given it this unofficial moniker the day of the poisonings. The description was just too grim a reminder of what they were doing.

The charts on the wall told the story. Tons of product recalled and destroyed. Everything manufactured in the headquarters plant since the day that woman was hired. New security measures were being put in all the factories to screen employees and manufacturing lines multiple times. New product would soon be going out with new, multiple layers of seals of the latest tamper-proofing, new oversight by the FDA, and a whole new security department. Bill Renner suddenly had one of the biggest jobs in the company. The costs would soon break the $1 billion mark. And keep on rising.

Then there were the graphs of sales. Plummeting. Across the board. People were afraid of medicines from P&B. Would the company be able to win back consumer trust before the hemorrhage of losses bled P&B to death? Emma had plans for public relations, advertising, and marketing to rebuild consumer confidence, once the recall was over and the new security measures certified. But all that was still to come.

She had had to admit to herself that it was possible that, under the worst, the *worst*, possible scenario, the company could go under or have to be sold off. *But I'll be damned,* she thought, *if I'll let anyone hear me say that.* Not even to Ned in the dark in bed. No, not ever. As the leader, her confidence had to appear unshakeable. Even more, it had to *be* unshakeable.

She heard Upshaw and a woman laughing from down the hall, but could not make out what they were saying. She could recognize Upshaw's annoying machine-gun laugh anywhere. When the pair walked through the door and saw Emma seated at the far corner of the room, they went silent. It was Linda Farlow at his side.

"Hey, guys," Emma said. "What's the joke? I could use a good laugh."

She wondered if they had just bumped into each other by accident or if they had met deliberately. She wondered if their laughter was from an innocent joke. Or if it was something she was not supposed to hear.

"Just something from a stupid TV show," Linda said.

The sudden parade of executives filing in behind them kept Emma from wondering any more about Upshaw and Linda. This was going to be a tough meeting. Everyone knew that layoffs were coming. What they did not know was the surprise Emma had for her leadership team—her test of character and commitment. As she thought about what she was about to ask of them, she vowed that she would not—absolutely not—talk about it like a marriage. I may think it, she told herself, but I will *not* say it.

The group settled in at their usual places. She looked around the room, taking time to let her eyes meet the eyes of every person. She took a deep breath, then announced,

"As we all know," she shuffled the papers on her clipboard, "we're going to have to make some sacrifices. . . ."

Upshaw jumped in before she had a chance to finish. "Emma, I've already run some numbers. I'm thinking we can lay off ten, maybe fifteen percent of our middle managers and maybe twenty percent of our hourly workers. Hire some back on a temp basis and save a bundle on benefits."

"Same here," Joe Fredericks added, his hand half-raised like a student reluctantly volunteering from the back of the classroom. "I can make similar cuts."

Emma shook her head no.

Pause. Another deep breath.

She looked around the room again. "I don't know about you, but when I walk into a business that's having big layoffs, I can feel it. You can smell the fear. You can see it in the faces. People start to do their jobs at arm's length, like their job has become a nasty little animal that might turn and bite them at any moment. Sure, layoffs make some numbers look better on paper for a while. And maybe you get a nod or two from Wall Street analysts—guys who've never managed anything. But the price the company pays is just awful. And the trust you lose with your employees, well, I don't think you ever get it back." Pause. Deep breath. "Yes, we are going to be forced to make some layoffs. But first, I want to talk about cuts we can make right here in this room."

She looked around and saw puzzled expressions.

"You mean fire ourselves?" Upshaw asked, trying to sound incredulous, respectful, and slightly condescending, all at the same time. "Emma, excuse me, but you can't be serious."

"Yes, I am completely serious. And no, I don't mean fire ourselves."

More confused faces.

She sat back in her chair. "We are a pretty prosperous group, would everyone agree? We have nice houses, nice cars, we take lovely vacations when we can, BlackBerrys notwithstanding. The company rewards the people in this room more generously than any other group of employees, no?"

Affirmative nods, but their gazes were cautious and wary.

"Let me ask, does anyone in this room live paycheck to paycheck? Where every cent you take home is already gone for rent and heat and groceries and shoes for the kids and you're staring at a drawer full of coupons and that box of Hamburger Helper, hoping it's going to get the family through dinner without any hamburger? Anybody in this room live that way?"

They shook their heads no.

"I didn't think so.

"Before we ask how many jobs you can cut, I want to ask how many jobs you can *save*." Emma grabbed her calculator from her purse and began tapping away. "Let's see, if I gave up my bonus and cut my salary in half, I figure I could save fifty jobs on the production lines for this quarter. In fact, if I cut my comp to a dollar a year for this year and lived off my savings, I could save over one hundred jobs this quarter."

Emma put her clipboard and calculator on the table.

"I want you all to go back to your offices and do some calculations. Think about your people and your businesses. Think about what *they* need. Think about what *you* can do to preserve them after all they have done for you. This is a short-term emergency. *I* believe this company will rebound quickly and we can all get back to growing the business and building wealth. The question you need to ask is, do *you*? I want each and every one of you to look at your numbers. Then look inside yourselves. Then make some decisions. Then we'll come back tomorrow and talk about the employees we have to sacrifice."

"But Emma," Upshaw said, "isn't that just symbolic? I mean the numbers we're looking at—"

"It's not *just* symbolic, Steve. It's a symbol of our commitment. We are going to have to lay off workers. They are not just numbers. They are people who have been loyal, people who did not create our problems, people who have counted on this company to be there for them and their kids. And now they are victims, just like those poor people who died in Florida. You bet what I'm asking for is symbolic. It's a symbol of something called leadership."

Upshaw leaned forward to speak. Emma raised her hand and shook her head no. "I'm not telling you guys what to do. I'm asking you to look inside yourselves first."

There was a knock at the door. Greg Toland from PR bolted into the room. "Anglia just made their big move," he said breathlessly, waving papers. "They're making a pre-emptive offer at forty dollars a share."

Upshaw jumped out of his chair. "That's more than twice the price of the last close!"

"What about the pill?" Linda asked, "What about the poison pill? They can't buy any more shares without triggering it."

Toland shook his head. "At the same time, they are launching a new proxy. They want to have the entire board of directors removed. The new board they would install would revoke the pill and let the tender offer go through. It's a richer offer than anyone else is likely to make. And it's all cash, not contingent on financing." He waved the paper again. "It's all in here." Toland passed out copies of the documents. "The annual meeting is October nineteenth. We have less than a month to convince the shareholders not to sell."

Emma scanned her copy, her mind racing.

Hupper, the general counsel, started speaking without looking up from his BlackBerry. "I've got an email here from Mike Saltzman. Says he's on his way on the next train out of Penn Station. He says yes, Anglia can beat the pill this way. It's the only way they can. If they can convince the shareholders that this is the best deal they can possibly get, they can do it."

"That offer is insufficient," Emma said firmly.

"Insufficient?" Upshaw tried to say.

She silenced him with a raised hand. She continued, "The company is worth more than their offer. Significantly more." She kept her face a mask of calm, her voice steady and slow. She was surprised and relieved that she felt the calm and was not just putting it on. "We have to demonstrate that their offer is inadequate. The shareholders can do better in the long run by rejecting it."

"But Emma," Upshaw said, "the stock has been hovering at nineteen dollars. Anglia is offering more than double. . . ."

"It's still inadequate," Emma said, looking out the window, finding it easier and easier to maintain her composure. "We'll fight it. And we'll win."

Matt Deering, from Toland's department, hurried into the room. "Greg, I just got a call from Jeanine Holloway's producer. He wants to know if Emma will appear on her show along with Josh Katz." He looked at her. "Just the two of you. This Friday on their market wrap-up show. It's their biggest audience night of the week. And they're going to promote it like hell all week to make sure the audience is even bigger."

Emma knew immediately that she wanted to do the show. It would be a great opportunity to fight for what she believed in. She wanted to fight, she wanted to tear Josh, his arguments, and his deal to pieces. Maybe him too.

"Greg and Matt," she asked out of courtesy to her PR counselors, "what do you recommend?"

"Well, it's high risk," Greg said, always cautious.

"But it's also potentially high reward?" she asked. "This is like a political campaign, right? We're campaigning for votes." Toland and Deering nodded.

She stood. "Then how could we *not* do the show?"

"Yes, Emma," Toland said, "we can reach a huge number of stockholders and analysts. If it goes well, it could help. Definitely. But if it goes badly, it could, uh, it could . . . be a big risk."

"I've got a lot of experience debating Mr. Katz," she said with a little smirk. "Bring the bastard on."

41

Tanya came back to Sloane Gardens after another happy morning of watching mothers in the park with their babies. The weather felt brilliant, so clear and balmy. This morning it was Green Park. She was mapping out walks she would take and playgrounds she would visit when her little girl arrived. In the meantime, she was actually enjoying the occasional morning sickness, and eagerly awaiting the second trimester when she would finally begin to look pregnant.

Lucja opened the front door as she approached. The maid wore a big, wide smile and her eyes were bright with excitement, so different from her usual glum deference.

"What is it, Lucja?" Tanya asked.

"Come. You see."

As she entered, Lucja took her in her arms and hugged her. She mumbled something in Polish, then kissed the top of her head. As Lucja let her go, she turned Tanya toward the living room. "From your father," she said. "He have delivered when you in park."

Tanya gazed into her normally spare, minimalist parlor. It looked like a warehouse of baby equipment. A crowded warehouse, chockablock with cribs, playpens, bassinettes, changing tables, carriages, strollers of the walking and jogging varieties, high chairs, and enough toys and playthings to take all the infants of a small city through their first three years.

"Oh my gawd, Lucja!" she said with happy confusion. "My father sent all this? Really?"

The maid nodded emphatically and gave her another hug. She turned Tanya by the shoulders to face the gigantic floral arrangement in the foyer, a riot of all-white blossoms. "Look, Miss Tanya!"

She reached for the envelope sticking up from the sea of white calla lilies. "Tanya," it read in Viktor's tight, crunched, uncomfortable English scrawl. She opened the envelope, and read, with some effort, Viktor's handwritten note:

My Dear Tatiana,
Come to Kent this Friday and spend the weekend.
* It is time to make everything all right.*

Love,
Papa

Lucja said breathlessly, "Say he send the Rolls for you Friday morning. Take you to the country. Miss Tanya, I pack for you already. Is okay?"

"Yes, Lucja," she said, trying hard to believe that this was not a dream. Could he really be accepting her baby and all her plans? Dare she believe him? "Yes, that's all okay. Everything." She was pleased and possibly, just possibly, thrilled at the acceptance and (dare she hope?) love that might, just might, maybe, impossibly, possibly be coming her way.

42

MSNBC • ROUTE 9W, FORT LEE, NEW JERSEY

WNBC • 334 GRANT STREET, PHILADELPHIA, PENNSYLVANIA

LEDGEMERE FARM • LEDGEMERE FARM ROAD,
GREENWICH, CONNECTICUT

Behind the wheel of his Bentley, Josh collected his thoughts as he drove to the television studio on the New Jersey side of the George Washington Bridge.

He hoped—no, prayed—that the Russian would keep his word and not use the blackmail threat after Josh had gotten him what he wanted. He could not imagine why Viktor would want to. But he would have to figure out that negotiation then. Yes, after all this was done.

Once again, circumstance and momentum had combined to give Viktor just the tailwind he needed. Josh remembered the Siberian gas-pipeline deal he'd syndicated for Viktor in the mid-1990s. Plans for two competing pipelines somehow toppled off their drawing boards, for reasons that appeared as conflicting as they were confusing. Like magic, the competition evaporated just as Josh was bringing Viktor's deal to market. His shares skyrocketed; lenders and investors couldn't get enough of them. Yes, Josh had to admit, Viktor was good. Very good. But the bastard was too lucky. Viktor had the balls for giant bets that can produce giant wins or colossal losses. And yes, he'd had some giant losses—the Latvian shipyard deal, the communications satellite network that failed in orbit. But his wins outnumbered these. And it looked like Percival & Baxter would be another one.

Josh still had no idea why Viktor wanted this particular company so much. And at this point, he did not care. He just hoped that by being and acting civilized in this take-over, he could still salvage some sort of relationship with Emma. Maybe even keep her in his life as a business part-ner. It just might be possible. But first, she would need some time to get over losing P&B.

Brody was meeting him at the studio. They had dis-cussed his wardrobe. No suit jacket, no tie. Just khakis and crisply pressed light-blue cotton shirt, the classic Brooks Brothers. Casual, confident, unthreatening. A young tycoon cast in a new mold. This deal would come across like a senior thesis on the greater economic good. Not a stock-market mugging.

Jeanine Holloway had been good to him on previous deals. He was hoping for one of her softball questions straight down the middle, the kind he could hit out of the park. And he'd be calm, reasonable, and even express a little sympathy for P&B's tough times. Yeah, he would do it, sell his deal to the analysts and shareholders who unquestionably would be tuned in.

Emma would be doing *The Real Deal* from the net-work's affiliate in Philadelphia. Josh would be a talk-ing head on a monitor, not an actual man sitting nearby whom she might be tempted to strangle.

Ned drove her to the studio and volunteered to wait out of sight in the greenroom. Her prince, always.

This was a fight she felt she could win. Because she had to. And she would win it on the numbers. On the business strategy. And on being right and doing what's decent. Yes, that could happen. It *would* happen. She thought of the strength, fury, and determination of a mother lioness protecting her cubs. That was how she would fight. Like a lioness, yes. Combined with being a killer tennis player. Emma Conway would not let P&B be destroyed.

Peter Katz was finishing a microwave pizza alone in the breakfast nook of Ledgemere's vast kitchen. All day, his dad had avoided talking about the TV battle with his mom. As he was heading out the door, he mumbled something to Penelope about the time and channel of the show.

As Peter was about to toss his paper napkin into the garbage, the butler's door swished open. Penelope strode in. She was wearing short-short cutoff jeans and a T-shirt. Her hair was pulled back in a ponytail. She was barefoot, sporting a new pedicure with red nails. Peter had to admit that she looked great. She was way too old for him, he thought. But she was definitely hot, which made him a little uncomfortable when he was around her. She was Dad's girlfriend, after all.

"Hey, Nibs, want to watch your dad on TV with me in the screening room? I'll make us some popcorn. We can have a little party, you and me. I'll let you have a beer or two. No one'll know about it. What do you say?"

"Nah," he muttered as he scooped up his plate and fork and headed for the nearest of the kitchen's three dishwashers. The maids had gone home.

"Come on," she said brightly, "it'll be fun. We can watch the fireworks and goof on your parents and this whole crazy world."

He shook his head. "No thanks, really."

"I'll put real butter on the popcorn. Yum."

"Nah, I'll hang by myself. Maybe I won't even watch."

"Well, if you get lonely, I'll keep a seat warm for you in the screening room. Or if you like, just press the intercom and I'll come up to the west wing."

Peter walked past her, faking a smile.

She put her hands together and curtseyed. "Your wish, sire, is my command."

"Yeah, thanks," he mumbled as he fled.

"Tonight *The Real Deal* is all about . . ." Jeanine Holloway paused for effect, ". . . the battle for Percival & Baxter. Here in our studios in New York and Philadelphia, we have the principal combatants. Josh Katz, general partner of Anglia Partners, and Emma Conway, chief executive of Percival & Baxter." She leaned in toward the camera. "And in case you've been on another planet, let me point out that these two people used to be married to each other."

Emma and Josh spoke simultaneously, saying precisely the same words in almost identical cadence, "That's not relevant!"

The effect was stunning. They both sat back, tight-lipped and silent, knowing that they were sharing the same embarrassed thought. They had behaved like two *very* married people.

Jeanine milked the uncomfortable silence, committing the broadcast sin of letting dead airtime linger. Her intent was to frame this moment, a moment that was sure to become a YouTube classic by midnight. "Well, how about that," she said finally. She couldn't help the little smile that formed at the corners of her pretty mouth. Already this interview had given her career a gigantic boost. And it was only just starting.

Peter cringed at what his mother and father had just done. "Oh fuck!" he howled at the giant flat-screen mounted on the wall above the complex of video game screens and consoles that filled his personal arcade. He was tempted to turn it off. Instead, he threw the remote across the room. It crashed into a Wii balance board on the floor in a corner, one of five. Josh kept giving him Wii systems as guilt gifts, never remembering that he had already given him those before.

Like a caged beast, Peter paced around his arcade, turning on video games, making a racket to compete with the painful sights and sounds coming out of the television.

Jeanine read from the teleprompter, "Since the tragic poisoning of a batch of Acordinol pills by a disgruntled employee who confessed and committed suicide, Percival & Baxter has instituted a massive, unconditional recall of all products manufactured in the factory where the woman worked off and on for three years. Millions of consumers have turned in their P&B medicines at a cost to the company that could go into the billions. Before the tragedy, the stock was trading around ninety-eight dollars. This week it went below twenty dollars. Anglia had been acquiring shares but was stopped by the poison pill at just under fifteen percent." She paused and said parenthetically, "That's the, uh, corporate governance kind of poison pill. Now Anglia has made a dramatic two-pronged offer. One, to remove the entire board of directors in order to remove the pill, and two, to acquire the company at a premium of forty dollars a share."

She paused. "Emma, first to you. How much more can P&B afford to pay out and when can you stop the bleeding?"

Emma smiled at the camera. Confidence. Warmth. "Jeanine, at Percival & Baxter, we know you absolutely can*not* put a dollar amount on trust. Once trust is gone, no amount of money can buy it back." She glanced at Josh's face on the monitor in front of her. As she said "trust" the second time, she saw in her mind a flash of him kissing that countess in front of the Connaught. Trust, indeed.

"This is a temporary rough patch," she said, clearing her head of those memories. "Getting through it will require discipline. Intelligence. Financial resources. And above all, strength of character." *Take that, you cheating bastard,* she thought, against her will. "All of which we have in abundance at Percival & Baxter. Taking the long view, this period will be remembered as a short hiccup from which the company emerged even stronger. We see a great future for Percival & Baxter and our shareholders. They will be rewarded for their loyalty. As will all our partners. Richly rewarded. That is why we have rejected Anglia's offer as insufficient by every measure. Forty dollars a share grossly undervalues the future of P&B."

Jeanine smiled and raised her eyebrows. "Now, to you, Josh."

Josh saw the green light on the camera facing him. *Easy does it,* he reminded himself. Pointers from his media-coaching sessions. *Not too aggressive. No big gestures. The camera magnifies every movement. Remember. Slow. Calm. Unthreatening.*

"Jeanine, I believe in the truth of the marketplace. And the marketplace is telling us that Percival & Baxter is . . . toast. This is unfortunate. Because P&B *was* one of America's great companies. But it is clear that the enterprise as it is currently structured is damaged. Permanently and irreparably damaged. That's what the market is telling us loud and clear.

"Here's what Anglia proposes. Percival & Baxter has many businesses within it that are in great shape. What's hurting them is being part of Percival & Baxter. We believe that the pieces of the company are worth more without the P&B name."

Jeanine simply said, "Emma?"

Emma smiled at the camera. "Percival & Baxter is not for sale."

Josh saw that the monitor now showed his and Emma's face side by side with Jeanine's face in a much smaller box in the upper right corner.

"Every company is for sale," Josh said, working hard not to sound like a bully, "especially when the market tells you the price is right. The market does not lie."

Emma came close to a sneer. "The market lies all the time. Look at all the bubbles and how they burst. The dot-com bubble, the real estate bubble, the derivatives bubble, the list goes on. They were all lies. Lies with slick packaging from people who were manipulating markets to make a quick killing."

Josh fidgeted in his seat and said nothing. He was not about to let himself be painted as the poster child of financial bubbles.

Emma was on a roll and she knew it. "A company cannot do business if there is always a 'for sale' sign over the door. You can't make commitments. You can't make long-term plans. You can't invest in the future. And our business—the business of healing and helping and finding cures where there have been none—is all about making . . ." she paused and looked at the image of her ex, ". . . making and *keeping* long-term commitments."

Was she overdoing it? No, just being emphatic. She was talking about her company, *not* her former marriage, right? "When you think of all the promises Percival & Baxter makes to the tens of millions of lives it touches around the world, it could be dizzying. But it's actually very simple. It all comes down to the commitment one person makes to another. And the trust that binds them. If your company is always up for sale, you cannot look any of those people in the eye and say, 'We will be here for you. You can depend on us.'"

Jeanine looked left, to the side of the screen where Josh's head was floating, even though he was sitting to her right in the studio. "Josh?"

Josh thought, *How do women manage to make everything so fucking personal? All women. They can be so exhausting that way.* But he smiled for the camera, hiding his exasperation rather well, he thought.

"Jeanine," he explained, trying to sound kind, "there's only so much we can promise each other as human beings. We are all subject to forces beyond our control. Earthquakes, volcanoes, tsunamis, hurricanes, asteroids on a crash course with our planet, the list is endless. If you look at the history of mergers and acquisitions since the dawn of the industrial age, you see that there are larger forces at work, shifting and reshaping the landscape of industry. The same way that shifting tectonic plates reshape the landscape of the earth."

He knew Emma had heard this argument from him before. But it was the truth of the market, he told himself. He had to play this game for keeps or face personal ruin. His audience was shareholders who wanted their goddamn money back. He was talking to *them*.

He watched Emma pause for a moment, then crack a tiny little smile. Just the way she prepared for that killer serve of hers on the tennis court. "So, let me get this straight," she said. "You are saying that earthquakes and tsunamis and asteroid collisions are *good* things?"

"No," Josh said with studied calm, forcing a little smile in return, "I am saying that they are unavoidable. We cannot resist their consequences."

"But, Josh," Emma said. Josh sensed a hint of condescension. Maybe the audience could sense it too. Or maybe not. He knew he was all too aware of every little nuance of Emma's behavior and every tiny clue to her emotions. She went on, "There is nothing inevitable about a hostile corporate takeover. It's not like the weather or cracks in the Earth's crust moving underneath us. It is raiders—armed with investment bankers and lawyers and PR firms—mugging, assaulting, attacking a company for no reason other than to make a fast buck for a tiny group of people who already have much more money than they can possibly spend or put to good use."

"Capitalism," Josh explained, trying to sound professorial in return, "rewards the exploitation of economic opportunity. And that economic gain ultimately translates into economic gain for society's greater good."

"Really?" she asked. "Even if it does all sorts of bad things along the way? Like putting thousands of people out of work, not just in the company being taken over, but in the companies that depend on it for their own work? Like shattering the well-being of communities where those people live and work? Like shattering the hopes of families and their children, destroying an enterprise that has provided not just wealth, but *health,* to millions of people decade after decade?"

Josh leaned forward in his chair, then held himself back. "It is the process of creative destruction. The irreversible power of change that, in the end, does serve the greater good." *Listen to me,* he thought, *dear shareholders, please listen to me!*

"Whose greater good?" Emma asked. "The tens of thousands of families that will lose their livelihood? Their children whose aspirations will be dashed? Their hometowns that will be devastated? You know, there's a reason they call it 'making a killing.' And men like you don't do it for the greater good. You do it for your own selfish good. For a bigger yacht, a bigger mansion, a bigger helicopter or private jet. Human beings are not like earthquakes or the weather. They make choices. And they know when their choices will produce good, and when they will produce evil."

"I'm not the devil, Emma. I'm an investment banker."

"Really?" Emma asked, suddenly very calm. "Just ask the people whose lives you hope to destroy in order to make your next deal. Ask *them* what you are."

Inside, Josh cringed. He searched for a comeback.

Then Jeanine Holloway cut in, "I'm afraid we have to go to a commercial break."

Emma and Josh sat silent while the commercials ran.

When the director cued Jeanine, she gave Josh an unusually big smile. "Josh, in Anglia's proxy materials, you talk about P&B management being too insular, a corporate culture in need of outside infusions of talent. Now we all know that Emma Conway is the daughter of the late Pete Conway, one of the top executives at P&B for thirty years. Can we read between the lines here?" She leaned forward. "Aren't you saying, based on your own firsthand knowledge, that there's favoritism and even nepotism at P&B?"

Josh took a deep breath. He thought, *so* that's *the reason for the big smile*. How the hell did she find that out? Who could have told her about *that*?

Early in her career at P&B, Emma had a bad boss, Steve Farricker, who took out his grudge against Pete

Conway on Emma. Emma could do no right for this man. Emma was beside herself, but insisted to Josh that she must tough it out. Josh made a secret call to his father-in-law about the unfairness of Emma's situation. Pete arranged to have Emma transferred to a new assignment. He and Josh swore each other to secrecy. Emma's career took off after that. Pete took the secret to his grave. The truth of what Josh and Pete did came out during the divorce. Emma was both furious at Josh and grateful to him for doing for her what she refused to do for herself. Worse, being caught between these conflicting emotions made her even angrier at him.

Josh looked at Brody standing off camera behind the set. Brody nodded emphatically and fired an imaginary gun with his thumb and index finger. So, Josh realized, Brody had fed it to her. But how the hell did *he* know?

Josh turned quickly back to Jeanine and shook his head, "No, Jeanine, I'm not saying that at all. And I have no specifics to cite from my personal experience—by which you mean, when I was married to the current chief executive. No. In our proxy materials we do talk about infusions of outside talent. But if you read carefully, you also see that we cite the fact that there are many talented executives at P&B, including their chief executive. I would hope that, in the scenario we propose, we can retain their best people for our team."

Emma was shocked that Josh did not use the weapon he could have used to destroy her. Suddenly, the picture was changing. She remembered her mother's admonition, "You have an unbeatable advantage. You know the son of a bitch better than he knows himself." In that moment Emma knew, for reasons she could only guess at, that Josh was not willing to go all out against her. Even though the odds were terribly against P&B, she knew that she *could* win.

"Emma," Jeanine said, "would you sign up to work for your ex-husband at Anglia if this takeover happens?"

"Executive retention will not be an issue," Emma replied coldly, "because, as I said before, P&B is not for sale. Anglia's offer will be rejected because it does not reflect the true long-term value of the company. Anglia has no idea what we have in our pipeline."

"Josh?" Jeanine asked.

"Well, maybe if P&B gave us a look inside," Josh said, sounding a bit testy, "it might influence the offer we are prepared to make."

Emma folded her arms across her chest. "Anglia has no right to see our confidential trade secrets."

"Anglia is P&B's second-largest investor," Josh said, "after the family trusts of Harold Percival. Like any shareholder, we want our investment to grow."

"Anglia is a raider, pure and simple," Emma said calmly and emphatically.

"Investor," Josh said insistently, not meaning to snap the way he did. Emma could still unnerve him.

"Raider," Emma repeated.

"Investor," Josh said.

"Raider," Emma said, maintaining her calm.

"Inves—" Josh said.

Emma betrayed no emotion in her face. Inside, she was smiling.

Peter wanted to scream. He wanted to smash the television. He wanted to smash his parents. He wanted to smash himself out of his own life and into another one. He stormed out of his empty, lonely West Wing. He ran down the long corridor to the grand stone staircase, flew down the stairs, and headed, for no particular reason, to his father's library.

He fumbled in the dark for the light switches. They were not regular light switches. After all, this was Ledgemere Farm. They were fancy buttons that controlled the computerized dimmer system. You had to activate the system first, then choose the program number of the lighting scheme you wanted, then fine-tune it if you cared to. This was usually fun for Peter. But at this moment, he found it annoying.

I just want to turn on the freakin' lights, he thought, as he jabbed at the buttons. The soft mood lighting appeared, bathing the soaring ribs of the Gothic ceiling in a mellow glow. This was "program four."

"Yeah, right," Peter muttered, unimpressed, as he headed for his father's antique desk in the far corner. He fell into the chair and spun around, not sure what he wanted or what to do next. No, he did not want to play with his father's computers. They had all those stock market graphs and charts. He reached forward and turned on the brass desk lamp. That must be antique, too, he thought, inspecting its patina and imagining how much trouble it must have been to wire this skinny tube for electricity. Dad's got a thing for antiques. Hey, what exactly is the difference between an antique and something that's just somebody else's old junk? Peter had no idea.

He sighed. There were folders of papers arranged just so on the surface of the desk. *Don't mess with that shit. Dad will notice.*

He slid back in the chair. He had already inspected the big center drawer on previous weekends. Just the usual office stuff. But that funny little indentation on the far left. What was that? How did you turn it to make it do whatever it's supposed to do? Yeah, that was the mystery Peter was going to solve. He tried moving it up, then down. No.

Then clockwise. Nope. Then counterclockwise. Okay, that did something. He felt a bolt turning slightly under his touch. It stopped. He pulled it forward. Progress. Stop. He tried counterclockwise again. No. Okay, try clockwise. Yes. It turned. He pulled. Out came a long narrow drawer.

A secret compartment! Cool.

He wondered what Dad kept here. He wondered what he would keep in this secret compartment if this were his own desk.

He looked into the long narrow box in his lap.

One envelope. That's it. Squarish. No writing on the outside. Unsealed.

Inside he saw a snapshot. The kind they used to make when they had photo stores where you took your film to get developed. Like way before everyone had digital photography and printers. And something else inside. A lock of blond hair about three inches long tied with a little red ribbon. That's weird.

He pulled the snapshot from the envelope. He left the lock of hair inside. He wasn't sure if the hair thing was creepy or not.

It was Mom. She was young. Early twenties. Dressed for a trek in the woods—University of Pennsylvania sweatshirt, khaki shorts, wool socks, hiking stick, and hiking boots. Standing in front of a little pond in a forest of pine trees. Big smile. Really big smile. She looked so happy.

Peter turned the picture over. He recognized his mother's handwriting:

> *Dearest Josh,*
> *I love your dark eyes*
> *I love your arms around me*

I love your passion
I love your impatience
I even love your anger (we'll work on that)
I love you big and strong inside me
I love you inside every part of me
I love you always
Emma

Holy shit. A real love letter. A real hot love letter. He was embarrassed, even though no one was around. He was fascinated. Horrified. Like he had walked in on Mom and Dad having sex. Which he had never done, at least that he could remember, because they had split up when he was young. But this must be what it would have been like.

He had fucked a girl—finally. That pretty Tsarina Alexandra. It was amazing, *she* was amazing. He just wished he hadn't gotten her pregnant. He should have used the condoms Dad gave him. He had practiced putting them on like a thousand times before. That was fun and weird. But Tanya had persuaded him. Persuaded? Yeah, right. She took his hand and slid his fingers inside her pussy. Uh-huh, persuasion. She got him so hot and so hard he stopped thinking. That's sex, he thought. Everyone does it. Even my parents.

He stared at the smile on young Emma Conway. Maybe this was taken on their honeymoon. When they went hiking in the woods in New Hampshire. Dad must have been behind the camera. He remembered their stories. Before they split up.

He reached into the envelope and pulled out the lock of hair. Geez, that must be Mom's hair from back then. It was blonder then. He read her words again. *Well, of course,* he thought. *Sex is the only way they could have had me*. Peter felt he was in on more of the secrets of the grown-up world.

Suddenly, he felt a hand on his shoulder. It was Penelope. He almost jumped out of the chair.

"What have you got there, Nibs?"

"Uh . . . nothing." He stuffed the items back into the envelope.

"Doesn't look like nothing to me," she teased. "Oooh, you figured out the secret drawer. I've been so curious about that. You are such a clever lad."

She was standing over him now. He put the envelope back in the drawer and was about to slide it back into its hiding place.

"Come on, let me see."

Peter shook his head no.

"Pretty please?" She reached into the drawer and took the envelope.

He hated the way grown-ups could push kids around. He wondered when the time would come when he could stand up to them. Clearly, it had not arrived yet.

"Oh, how sweet," Penelope studied the photograph, "that's your mom, isn't it?"

Peter said nothing. He was afraid and confused. Afraid of saying something wrong. Afraid to show his anger. Confused because he had no idea what to say.

Penelope was reading the love note. "Ooooh-la-la. Practically X-rated. Good thing you're such a mature young man. Your dad told me about the condoms he gave you for the big party at McLeod's. You've got his beautiful dark eyes, you know. I'm sure you've been making the girls happy for quite some time now."

This touched a nerve. How dare she talk about *his* sex life? Especially when he had none. "Your mom and your dad must have been one hot item when they were together."

She fingered the lock of golden hair. He wanted to grab it away from her. "I'm hoping that he and I, well, you know, tie the knot."

She put the lock of hair and the photo back in the envelope and dropped it in the empty drawer. "How would you feel about that, Peter? We've never really had the chance to talk, you and me. I think you're a fine young man. I can't tell you how proud your father is of you. He talks about you all the time. If we got married, I'd become your stepmother, wouldn't I? I hope you don't think I'd be an evil stepmother like in a storybook. I really would love to get to know you better. Maybe you can show me around some of those games of yours up in the West Wing."

"Yeah, sometime," Peter mumbled.

She bent down, sitting on her haunches to be at eye level with him. "Maybe I should write a hot love letter like this to your dad? Think he'd like that? Of course, I'd have to make mine very different and all." She lowered her voice conspiratorially. "We absolutely can't tell him we were snooping. This will be our little secret that we saw inside his hidden drawer." She stroked the side of his face fondly, like a mom would. "Our little secret, okay?"

The word "secret" set Peter off. He couldn't stand the thought of carrying around another secret. This whole evening was just too freakin' much. "What the fuck are you doing?" he heard himself shout. "Get your hands off me. And don't you dare touch my parents' private stuff!" He couldn't look at her. "It's theirs! What the fuck are you doing here?"

"Peter, your father and I—"

"My dad doesn't love you! He still loves my mom. And she still loves him. They might even get together again. He's *not* going to marry you! He told me so. He's on to you. You just want his money. Said you're a good lay, that's all."

He could see her eyes filling with tears as he ran out of the library. He'd accomplished half of his goal—to hurt her. But not the other half—to make himself feel better.

43

In the parking lot of the television studio, Brody put his arm around Josh's shoulder as they walked toward Josh's Bentley.

Josh could hear Brody congratulating him on his excellent performance, but he was barely listening. Then he stopped suddenly and shook himself loose from Brody's embrace.

"How the hell did Jeanine know that?" Josh barked.

"Know what?" Brody asked innocently.

"About how I got Emma a transfer, that's what!" Josh started to shout. "About how I called Emma's father! And how we swore secrecy so no one would ever know! How the fuck did that TV woman know about that?"

"Easy, Josh, take it easy," Brody said. He leaned close and whispered, "My mole told me. You know, the one who's been feeding me all our inside stuff so we can keep the upper hand in this deal. Got a pal in human resources to dig around in the old files. That was a big fat pitch right over home plate, just asking you to knock it out of the park. I can't believe you didn't hit it. That was my gift to you. Josh, we've got dirt on the other side, we've got to use it."

"I made a promise to Emma's father."

"The guy's been dead for a long time, Josh."

"It was a promise about Emma. *For* Emma."

"Josh, we've done these takeovers before. You've never had a problem taking down the management. This one's no different."

"Oh, yes it is," Josh said, biting his lower lip.

"Don't you see that you lost points just now? That CEO scored big in there. And you let it happen. I wouldn't be surprised if she changed a lot of shareholder minds. The vote, Josh, the vote! Do I have to explain the takeover game to Josh Katz? Josh, you do not seem to understand the war we're in. We must be willing to do *anything* to win. Just like you crushed those fat-cat CEOs in the Burnett and Detweiler deals, you've got to crush your ex-wife any way you can. Jesus, I brought you Drew Pawling, I just brought you this tidbit. . . ."

"No! Fuck no! I told you we can play this on the up-and-up, straight and clean, and win."

"Josh," Brody said with a shake of his head, "you know the rules and you cannot change them—he who fights dirtiest wins."

Josh took a step back, as if he might be trying to avoid catching a disease. "Charles," he said coldly, instead of using the usual nickname, "I don't think I can have you on my team anymore."

Brody crossed his arms across his chest and stood up straight, to tower over Josh. "Oh, really?"

"Yes, really," Josh spat back. He turned to walk back to his car.

Brody reached out and grabbed him by the arm. "You can't fire me."

Josh pulled himself free. "Oh yeah?"

"Josh, I meant what I said. You can't fire me."

"Just watch me." He turned again. But he did not step away. He stood with his back to Brody.

Brody took a step forward so as to keep his voice low. "Josh," he said with quiet calm. Then, with almost fatherly concern, he said, "I know too much about you, much more than you think I know. If you try to get rid of me, I will be forced to do to you what you are afraid to do to Emma.

Josh, I know everything about your arrangement with Viktor Volkov. How he refinanced Anglia, how he still controls Anglia, even how he refinanced Ledgemere Farm. I know everything. And believe me, you do *not* want me to tell the Street. But if you force me to, I will. The private money you have lined up, it's Viktor's. The Street doesn't know it, but I do."

Josh turned back to face him. He felt sick to his stomach. "You're making that up," he said. "You don't know anything. You're a flack, a PR guy, you don't know the inside of my deal or anyone else's."

"Oh yeah? Try me." Brody stuck out his chin to exaggerate how he was looking down at Josh. "I have survived all these years and prospered by knowing what I'm not supposed to know. By knowing what important people desperately *don't* want me to know. I know *everybody's* dirty secrets. Everybody's! That's my business! And you know how good I am at spreading the word."

"I made you!" Josh said, raising his voice. He wanted to fire Brody right this minute, but knew he could not. Not just yet. "You wouldn't dare. I made your firm!"

"And *I* made *you*," Brody said coldly, "the social-climbing Jew from the triple-decker tenement in Mattapan. You made the deals, yes. But I made your name, your image, your fame up and down the Street. And guess what? I can unmake you too."

Brody paused. Josh stood very still, feeling trapped. Brody went on. "You can't fire me. Not just because I can ruin your rep on the street. You can't fire me because I'm the only one you can trust. You're too deep into this deal and it's the only way you can get free from Viktor."

Brody paused again.

Josh felt frozen. He felt a surge of panic that Brody might also know about the Tanya pictures and the blackmail. But that had not been on the list of his threats. He pushed that fear away for the moment.

"No, Josh, I'm not your best friend." Brody stared into Josh's eyes. "I'm your *only* friend. The only one who knows what you've got at stake. And you can't afford for the rest of the world to know that. Ever."

Josh was silent for a long moment. Then he took a deep breath. *Okay, time to make a deal.* "What do you want, Brody? Tell me what you want."

Brody too took a deep breath. He spoke slowly and deliberately. Josh could hear a faint tremor in his voice, perhaps a trace of pleading. "I want my share of points in this deal, like twenty percent of the millions you'll make before you're through. I want some capital out of this. I'm sick of begging for fees from clients like you. Getting squeezed and chiseled while you guys make tens and hundreds of millions. I want enough to retire on. And enough to make sure my kid is never a ward of the state. I'm ready to call it quits. I've had enough of never having enough." He gave a little smile, conciliatory. "Josh, it's me, Brodes, talking. Come on, let's work this one together." Brody's shoulders drooped. Suddenly he looked tired, no longer threatening. "I can help you. And you can help me. We can both get what we want. What do you say? Josh? Deal?"

Brody extended his right hand.

Josh nodded reluctantly, arms at his side. "I will *not* use that slimeball Pawling," he said bitterly, "and I will *not* fuck over my ex-wife. If you're as good as you say you are, you can help me win this one the right way."

Brody extended his hand farther, right up to Josh's clenched fist.

Josh stood, still not taking Brody's hand.

Brody kept his arm extended, hand still waiting.

After another long pause, Josh raised his right hand reluctantly and shook with Brody. Yet another partner to this rotten deal who had him by the balls. But, Josh vowed, only for a little while longer.

44

At Wilborne Hall, Tanya enjoyed a surprisingly civilized dinner. Just Viktor and her sitting across from each other at the end of the vast dining table. There were no fights, no yelling, no mention of babies, no talk of arranged marriages. They made small talk about a new and bigger yacht Viktor was thinking about commissioning. To Tanya's astonishment, it was almost pleasant. In honor of her condition, Viktor had no wine at the table and did not appear to have had a drop of alcohol beforehand. They toasted crystal goblets of San Pellegrino. It felt like a whole new start for their relationship.

Tanya left the table feeling pleasingly confused, wondering who was inhabiting the body of Viktor Volkov. She retired to "her" apartment, the suite of rooms she had slept in only a few times before.

She awoke groggy and disoriented. Instead of the nightgown she had put on the night before, she was wearing a hospital johnny plus white cotton knickers stuffed with a pad that was slightly damp. She looked down and inspected it. A big spot of blood.

She gasped.

Suddenly a nurse in a white uniform was standing over her, gently pressing a hospital thermometer into her ear.

"There now," the woman said comfortingly, "your temperature is normal again. Doctor will be by again right after breakfast to check on you. Says you'll be just fine."

Tanya tried to sit up, only to fall back down into the pillows. She felt dizzy and limp. Was that a hospital gurney and stainless-steel medical equipment on the far side of the room?

The nurse stroked her forehead gently. "Just rest and relax," she cooed. "Rest and relax, dearie."

Tanya closed her eyes and began to cry softly. She knew what had been done to her. What Viktor had done to her, using the finest medical care money could buy. She wished she could spring up, rage, and lash out. But what she felt was the huge weight of a great gray sadness pressing her down, down deep into the bed, draining her limbs of energy, pressing down on her battered heart. Rage could come later. Now, all she could muster was a trickle of tears. She drifted in a dream of sadness.

Sometime later, she was not sure when, Viktor entered the room. Without a word, the nurse left.

He stood over her, staring down with that blank expression that gave away no emotion. The ice-blue eyes of a killer.

"How *could* you?" she cried out, trying to rouse herself from the haze. "How could you do this to me? To my baby? How could you? You . . . you . . ." She was searching for a name vile enough to call him.

Viktor put his fingers to his lips. He wanted her silent.

She wanted to spit at him, strangle him, tear his heart out. But she obeyed him. She did not know why. She sucked in her breath and let her tears run out in a silence broken only by little gasps. Maybe because she knew her anger would be useless. Maybe because she just wanted him to disappear. And the more easily she let him say his piece, the sooner he would leave.

"Listen to me, Tanya. I say what I say just one time."
One finger rose in the air.

She nodded.

"Is so much you do not know. You not understand how
hard is life. World is terrible place. Cruel." He raised his
arms like an attacking bear and shouted, "Cruel!" His
arms dropped to his side. He looked down at the floor and
shuddered. "*Meer zhestok koh mneh*," he mumbled to himself. The world is cruel to me.

He looked again at Tanya. "I win great fortune. I fight
every day. Is not just for me. You understand? You my
only flesh and blood, my only family. We must make real
family. Not baby like this. Noble baby for noble family."

She whimpered.

"People like us," he motioned to the grand, vaulted ceiling of the apartment and out the window at the panorama
of the estate, "we must be stronger than ordinary people.
Is lesson you must learn. Is not just you who own fortune.
Fortune, it own *you*." He gestured at the hospital gear. "You
make mistake. But I forgive. We make fresh start. I put
new million pounds in your trust fund." He gave a questioning raise of the head.

Meekly, Tanya nodded back.

"Okay," he said. "After doctor come for checkup, you are
free. Stay or go, up to you. Driver take you back in Rolls
when you like. Okay?"

Tanya nodded again and sniffled.

Viktor turned and left the room.

She slept most of that day and the next. She did not seek
out Viktor to say good-bye when she left. On the drive
back to Chelsea, alone in the back of Viktor's Rolls with
all the curtains drawn, she sobbed and sniffled quietly
with four boxes of tissues at hand. About halfway into the
trip, she turned her heartbreak into a little project. She

started to fill up the back of the mammoth Saloon with gobs of wet Kleenex. She buried gooey balls of tissue in every compartment and crevice of the elegantly tufted limo—between the seat cushions, in the sunglasses compartments, behind the vanity mirrors, under the arm rests, in the leather portfolios, wherever she found a crack and bit of space. *Let Viktor just try to escape the tears and snot of my grief,* she thought, feeling a little moment of triumph. "Take that!" she whispered as she balled up another wet handful of tissue and looked for a new hiding place. Then her spirit crashed. She realized that Viktor would never even know what she had done. The car would be all cleaned up long before his next ride. She was powerless even to annoy her terrible father, let alone make him pay for murdering her baby.

She returned to find her parlor floor as miraculously empty of baby gear as it had been overflowing before the weekend. Lucja met her in the foyer, her eyes lowered, an air of mourning about her. Tanya leaned in and kissed her maid on the cheek. "Why don't you go home now, Lucja. I won't be needing anything."

Lucja raised her head to speak. Tanya waved her hand to signal silence as she fought back more tears. Lucja nodded gravely and fled to the kitchen and the servant's door. As Tanya fell into her big, empty couch, she remembered a detail that had not penetrated during her initial excitement. All the baby items still had had their sales tags attached. Why, of course! Viktor's goons had been able to return all the merchandise for full refunds. Viktor's charade of extravagance and generosity had cost him exactly nothing. And cost her everything. Oh, he was the miser businessman to that very core of his.

As she sat alone in her house, Tanya vowed that she would find a way to get back at Viktor. She had never thought of vengeance before. But now she did. She would get vengeance for herself. And for her baby, who never had a chance. She did not know where or how. Viktor was powerful and brutal. Overpowering, that's what he was. But she knew that somewhere, somehow she would find a way to hurt him. And hurt him horribly. She would find a way to make him feel as much pain and loss as she was feeling. She would even be willing to die trying.

She would plan. Yes, she was good at making plans. She would figure out a plan to hurt him as much as he had hurt her. *No, I will hurt him more.*

45

MONDAY, SEPTEMBER 28

ONE PERCIVAL & BAXTER PLAZA • FRANKLIN CROSSING, PENNSYLVANIA

How lucky, Emma thought, when she saw that she was the first person to show up at the employee gym this Monday. She needed the solitude after the weekend of conference calls and meetings that followed her TV confrontation with Josh. Her predawn Bloomberg check showed futures of P&B shares were trading upward ahead of the market opening. She dared not hope that the shares themselves might actually start to rise again. But if they did . . . well, best not to anticipate too much.

She relished the stillness of the empty gym. She strapped her feet into the rowing machine, began pulling, and slipped into a state of meditation. She pulled on the handgrips and set the readout for forty-five minutes. She kept her eyes shut tight. Her rowing, when it was good, had the fluid motion of her tennis game. She did not feel each of her body parts pulling, she felt the stroke moving all though her body, propelling her smoothly without her having to think about the motion. Grace equals power, she told herself, as she felt each pull going faster with almost no effort.

She tried to listen to the music in her headphones, but her thoughts overrode the melodies. She was replaying the television show. Her people had said that if it had been a political debate, she would have been the winner. Mike Saltzman, Hal Percival, the whole team of investment bankers, the proxy firm, her colleagues on the executive committee. Even Steve Upshaw had hailed her arguments and unyielding determination, although she did not trust compliments from him.

All the way home, Ned had been effusive. When Peter got back from Greenwich, he mumbled something that sounded positive as he ran up to his room. Poor kid, no way he could hide his conflicted feelings.

Hundreds of stockholders had emailed in positive responses and expressions of support. Of course, hundreds had also expressed the opposite. "Sell out now! This could be the last decent offer we'll ever get!"

Saltzman had crafted a plan for Emma to show key institutions a few projects in the confidential research pipeline. These represented the company's future growth. Like the Alzheimer's work that linked to diabetes treatments and which could end up being an enormous breakthrough for both diseases. Like the "Female Brain Chemistry Project" with its potential to unlock the mechanisms of hormones, mood swings, and neurotransmitters as they work at the level of individual synapses. There also were potential cancer blockers engineered at the genetic level. And a potential cure for ALS that used synthetic stem cells. There was promising work in regenerative medicine to regrow damaged cells into perfectly healthy ones. The list went on and on. The potential value to patients was incalculable. They were miracles in the making. The potential value to stockholders, Emma could powerfully demonstrate, was a share price well north of $120 in as little as two years' time or less.

Emma and the board were also exploring other alternatives. They had to. Emma was about to begin secret meetings with three big pharma companies to see if there was a "white knight" who would acquire P&B at the right premium and understand, because it understood the company values, what parts to preserve. This would be a last resort, but it had to be explored. Remaining independent was the best path, but she needed to have backup plans in place.

No matter how they spun it, the Anglia offer was rape and pillage as far as Emma was concerned. Barbarians intent on the total destruction of Percival & Baxter as a civilization. Emma still could not fathom why Josh had come after P&B in the first place. There were faster bucks and bigger killings out there for a raider like him.

But she knew this: Josh, who always went all-out where money was concerned, was not willing to go all-out against P&B. Or against her. Or maybe both. Clearly, someone had fed Jeanine the story of her secret rescue from Steve Farricker. And Josh had refused to use it. She had read all about Anglia's other hostile takeovers. Slander, distortions, and character assassination had been standard. No trick too dirty, no accusation too base if it meant getting the votes to oust management and clear the way for takeover. Josh Katz was known to be the embodiment of the ruthless, merciless corporate warrior. So why had he stopped short and kept his sword tucked away?

"You know the son of a bitch better than he knows himself," her mom had said. That was a theme that kept replaying in her head. Did Josh really expect her to work on his team, buying and selling pharmaceutical companies like used cars? Was he trying in some weird way to rebuild his relationship with her? As a business partner or even friend, or just as a former mate? Was it a messy combination of all of these? Entirely possible with Josh. For all his intelligence and ambition, his emotional self-awareness was often zero. Josh always knew his own mind. But often, he did not know his own heart. And she'd learned this the hard way.

Then it hit her. Suddenly, she found herself rowing even faster, more urgently, a new sweat pouring out of her. Maybe Josh was not running the show. Maybe there was someone behind the scenes. Someone who wanted the pieces of P&B for reasons Josh could not reveal or did not even know. Someone using Josh as their attack dog. That could explain his hesitancy, his ambivalence, his attempts at decency.

So then, if she could find out who had a gun to Josh's head and why, she might somehow get in between them and make Anglia go away. She might even help Josh. Wait, why would she think *that*? She had to think of Josh as the enemy. Period.

She could feel the end of her row approaching. Little pins and needles ran up and down her ankles. Not uncomfortable, just a tingling from good exertion. She opened her eyes just enough to glimpse the read-out. 1:47 remaining of her forty-five minutes. She could still pull for this finish. She thought she saw a blur of activity in her peripheral vision but paid it no heed. Legs forward, arms snapping the handle against her tummy, back, forward, back, forward. Eyes open just enough to watch the final countdown on the screen . . . :10 . . . :09 . . . :08 . . . :07 . . . :06 . . . :05 . . . :04 . . . :03 . . . :02 . . . :01 . . . :00. She slid to a final stop and felt her heart pounding gloriously. Deep breath. Slide out of footstraps. Feet to the floor. Open eyes.

Then she saw them. They were everywhere around her. The gym was packed. Some in gym clothes. Some in their office clothes. All around the rowing machine. All looking at her. She pulled the headphones from her ears. "Hi, guys," she said, breathing hard.

She reached for the towel hung over the bar that held the machine's readout. She began to dab at the sweat on her head. She fumbled with the touch screen of the iPod strapped to her arm. Pounding dance music blared out.

"Well, my secret's out, I guess," she said, still trying to silence the music. "I like old Madonna songs."

A young woman in a white coat, whose keycard said she was Betsy Gorham from the research labs, bent down and touched the screen. The music stopped. "Actually, that's Lady Gaga," she said.

Emma shrugged. She had no idea. Peter updated her playlists periodically.

"Don't worry," Betsy said with a smile. "Same thing."

Emma stood and looked around at the crowd. "Well, if you are all waiting for your turn on the rowing machine, I guess you must be pretty angry with me. Maybe we need a sign-up sheet."

No one spoke.

She raised her voice as if at a podium. Was she now making another speech at another town hall meeting? "Or maybe we need to buy more rowing machines. What do you guys think? Anybody here good at sucking up to Finance?"

Emma got the laugh she was hoping for. "But seriously, why is everybody here?"

Joe Westbrook, one of the top research scientists, stepped forward. "Emma, we came to thank you. You were great on TV Friday night. You showed us how hard you can fight. And you gave us hope that we could win."

She patted her face and again burst out with sweat. "We are in a terrible war," she said. "And truthfully, the odds are against us. But I promise you, we *can* win. We *can* beat this raider. I can't reveal just how at this time. But I promise you, if it is humanly possible for us to preserve what we have built at P&B, we will." She believed her every word. At the same time, she had no idea how she would pull it off. Just that she would.

The employees packed into the gym around her broke out in applause.

46

Peter was thinking of telling his mother about the girl he got pregnant . . . maybe. Or maybe . . . he was thinking he should tell Ned first. Or maybe . . . tell his dad on his next trip to Greenwich. Or . . . maybe not. He was thinking he should tell someone. He was also thinking he didn't dare tell anyone. He was thinking that the only thing he knew for sure was that he didn't know what to do.

He was alone in the house this evening. He had done his homework.

Ned was in Los Angeles, meeting with the collector of his *Earthborn* pieces, the guy who was putting them into the big show. Peter cooked himself a dinner of pepperoni and cheese Hot Pockets in the microwave. His favorite food after Doritos. He was going to go upstairs to play some *Armageddon II* when he heard his mom's car pull into the driveway.

Her work pressures had put her over the edge. She had become impossible to talk to. That's how stressed she was. Which was kind of weird, Peter thought, because it was *he* who used to do just about anything to avoid talking to her.

He stayed in the kitchen to meet her and see what might happen. He might try to tell her about the girl. Or not. He had no idea. He was just going to see what did or didn't spill out of him.

She walked into the kitchen and tossed her briefcase onto the table. She stepped out of her shoes. She stood for a moment and looked at him. She looked awfully tired, with dark circles under her eyes. But she smiled. She always smiled when she saw him, no matter how bad she was feeling. Peter didn't know why, he just figured that was a mom thing. Anyway, she looked tired as hell and she still smiled.

"Hi, sweetie," she said.

"Hi, Mom, how's it going?"

She raised one hand up like a traffic cop's stop signal and shook her head. "Ugh, don't get me started. Did you eat?"

"Uh-huh, no problem. Put my dish and silverware in the dishwasher and ran the rinse and hold cycle." He was not supposed to depend on Brida to clean up after him. House rule.

She smiled again and sighed. She really did look beat. Her shoulders were all scrunched up. Ned was giving her a neck-and-shoulder massage almost every night. She looked like she could sure use one tonight. Too bad Ned wouldn't be back until the weekend.

"Did you have a good day?" she asked.

He nodded.

"Come tell me. I've got to do a few emails but I want to hear all about it." She motioned for him to follow her into her study. She sat down at her desk and sighed again. Peter fell into the armchair in the corner, throwing his legs over one of the big padded arms.

"Just first let me do a little work," she said. She reached down and pushed the power button on her computer. Her screen came to life. She reached for the key fob in the desk drawer, the security token with the password that changed every thirty seconds.

"Just another day," he said. He could tell she was not really paying attention. Not that she wasn't interested in him. It was just that, well, he understood. As her log-in screen appeared, she raised her hand to type in her user name and password and the code on the token. For her password and code, he had noticed, she always typed slowly and carefully, using just her right index finger.

He stretched upward and outward from the armchair to see over her shoulder. He watched her type her codes in. Memorized them. It was easy, especially the way she did her passwords so carefully, with one-finger typing.

He had never done this before. Never.

He did not know why he did it. He did not think about it. He just did it. He slumped back again into the chair as she banged away at her emails. Had he just done something bad? Was it like *illegal* bad? He did not know. Was it as bad as getting a girl pregnant and keeping it a secret? It must be. *Maybe it's worse,* he thought.

He said to his mom's back, "I beat thirty other players this afternoon in my online war game. It was pretty cool."

She half-turned in his direction to catch him out of the corner of her eye. "Well, I guess I should be happy that you get up early to do *something*. Remember when I used to have to drag you out of bed?"

"Come on, Mom!" Why did she embarrass him like that? I mean, everybody was, like, in diapers once. That must be a mom thing, too.

She shrugged.

He could see she was paying attention to the screen and not to him. He just sat there. He and his mom could just sort of feel each other's presence while she worked. She always said she felt better just having him around. "And you like it too," she would say, teasing him, "you want your mother around so you can ignore her." He knew it was true, even though he ignored her when she said it. This would be their moment together. They didn't have to talk.

Emma muttered under her breath as she typed. Finally, she clicked her mouse and said, "Ta-da! Done." The computer screen went dark. She stood. "Do you mind if I go up and take a shower and crawl into bed? I'm really beat. We'll talk more tomorrow."

"Sure, Mom. Go ahead."

"Thanks." She crossed the room, leaned down to kiss him on his forehead. "Good night, sweetie."

Peter listened for the distant sounds of her walking around, getting ready for bed. Then silence.

He stared at his mother's computer for a long time.

Would he? Won't he?

Was he going to become a criminal? Or just a cheating liar? He didn't know.

Then, more without really thinking about it, he walked over and sat down at her desk. From the drawer, he pulled the security token, powered up the machine, and logged onto the closed, secure network of Percival & Baxter. As far as the network knew, he was Emma Conway, the chief executive officer. He figured there must be a name for this kind of crime, but he didn't think it was the kind of crime that would send him to prison.

He was not interested in her email. It was one of the shortcuts to the operations servers that he was after. After interning the previous summer in the human resources department, filing documents electronically, he knew all about the P&B system. And this summer, he had sat regularly with the tech guys in the cafeteria at the plant. That was the only fun part of his dumb job. He remembered one of the guys talking about some work he had done on the server that stored the security videos. The guy had motioned at the glass dome in the ceiling where the camera watching the cafeteria did its surveillance. "WBZ405" the guy said was the name of the surveillance files on the server. Peter opened the UNIX application that the guys had talked about to access the video records. In no time, he was scanning the videos he was interested in. The surveillance shots taken on the day of the poisoning, July 9.

Freakin' July 9! He was there—right there when it happened—and he didn't notice a thing! Not one freakin' thing that wasn't the usual boring-as-hell shit of that stupid job. He *had* to check it out.

The shots were not actually video. They were time-elapsed samples, still shots that compressed time and moved in a herky-jerky fashion. There was a time-code stamp with the date and time in the upper-right corner of every frame. The video was in color but grainy and low-res. Peter watched four screens at a time, scanning different locations around the building that day.

He thought of the expression "watching paint dry." This was about as boring. Another boring day in the most boring place on earth, as far as he was concerned, the Acordinol factory at P&B. He scanned through the camera locations and relived that day.

There was Loralee Eaton, the nut case who offed herself after confessing to the whole Internet. He watched her, with her now-famous spiky bleached-blond hair, waving at the security camera as she entered the changing room where everyone put on their white clean suits. Peter did not really remember her from the plant. But now after all the news coverage she got after her suicide, it was impossible not to spot her in the videos.

He kept scanning the images. Then at 16:02 hours, or 4:02 PM, he saw himself in the corner of the changing room getting out of his clean suit and getting ready to go home. He was wearing jeans and sneakers and his *Grand Theft Auto* T-shirt. He looked at the time in the next frame—16:34—as he was headed for the door. Then he grabbed the mouse and froze the frame. He looked at the date on the time stamp again. 07/09. July 9. That same day when the poison pills were manufactured right under everyone's noses.

He stared at the blurry image of himself heading for the exit. *Grand Theft Auto? Grand Theft Auto?* Peter squinted and thought hard. That was Thursday. He remembered wearing his *Grand Theft Auto* T-shirt to the plant that Monday. That was the 6. Then on Tuesday the 7, to show his mother and Ned that he was doing his own chores, he washed his own laundry. But of course, he fucked it up. Poured in too much of the detergent, the one with added bleach or something, and let it sit in the soak cycle too long. Bleached a big white streak out of his *Grand Theft Auto* T-shirt. He retired it to his pajama drawer. He did not wear his *Grand Theft Auto* T-shirt to work on Thursday, July 9. He didn't remember what T-shirt he did wear that day with his jeans and sneakers. But it sure as hell was *not Grand Theft Auto.*

Yet the security video said he was looking at Thursday, July 9.

But Peter knew, he absolutely *knew*, it could not possibly be Thursday, July 9. It was no later than Monday, July 6.

What the fuck was this?

Somebody must have dubbed another day's video, re-named it July 9, and faked the time code.

But who? And why?

Had anyone else noticed this? Peter assumed no. Not the P&B security people. Not the cops investigating the poisoning. It showed nothing out of the ordinary to get their attention.

Peter felt sick.

He knew he knew something.

How would he tell anyone?

Was he going to tell his mother he spied on her? That he sneaked into her computer and compromised the security of the company she was in charge of? People had been murdered. A woman had killed herself who maybe was there that day or maybe not. How could he know? Should he tell the police? Would he get arrested if he did?

Another secret. Oh fuck.

Secrets. Was he going to tell his parents that he got a girl pregnant? That he was going to be the father of a baby with some English girl whose name he did not even know? Was that, like, illegal too?

Suddenly, Peter felt sick with secrets.

He was scared and confused. He had no idea what to do. He sat for a long time, just feeling like shit about everything.

Then he figured out one thing he could do. He would go to Starbucks first thing the following morning when it was full of people using laptops. He would get on the wifi, hijack some unsuspecting jerk's email, and use the jerk's email client to send a note to the head of technology at P&B, that guy Sam Burns that the techs used to joke about in the lunchroom at the factory.

47

ONE PERCIVAL & BAXTER PLAZA • FRANKLIN CROSSING,
PENNSYLVANIA

It was long after dark when Emma got the call. Both of her assistants had gone home. She was at her desk re-rewriting her next financial presentation for the board. She was rethinking the numbers that showed how the company could rebound and get back to profitability. She was convinced that the numbers Upshaw had given her were too pessimistic.

No, she told herself, *I am not kidding myself.* I am just tweaking a couple of the sales numbers to reflect, well, to reflect what I know we can deliver, *will* deliver. She heard that reassuring voice in her head, the voice that sounded like Emma Conway but was not nice and polite. It was the voice of Emphatic Emma, the Emma who did not take shit from anyone. *"No goddammit, these numbers are not tweaked!"* Emphatic Emma insisted, *"These are what I know we can* fucking *deliver!"*

She silently thanked her foulmouthed other self and entered in the last number of her projections, the one that turned the cash flow positive at the bottom of the spreadsheet. Like magic, the negative parentheses and red number disappeared from the bottom of the cell. An unbothered, unbracketed, black, positive number took its place.

She clicked the "save" button. "Take that, Josh Katz," she muttered aloud to her empty office. Then the phone rang. It was Sam Burns, the chief technology officer. She grabbed the receiver.

"Sam," she said, packing warmth, surprise, and urgency into the one syllable of his name. "What's up?" She had known Sam Burns forever.

"Emma," he said, "can I come see you . . . uh, now?"

"Sure, come on over," she said.

"I'll be there in a couple of minutes," he said and hung up.

She continued her day's-end ritual of turning off her computer, straightening the piles of documents on her desk, and generally setting the stage for the following morning. Just a few hours from now, she thought, as she evened out corners of one especially tall stack of documents. She was just straightening her mouse pad to align with the side of her desk when Burns walked in.

She motioned for him to sit. She remembered Sam when he was the young, awkward computer geek who could fix anyone's tech problems. He would gush, in his shy, awkward way, about the future of systems technology to anyone who would listen. Sam was no longer young. His signature crew cut had gone gray. He had a slight paunch beneath his baggy, twin-pocket shirt and chinos with legs a bit too short that showed off his black socks and brown shoes. Always, for as long as she could remember, the black socks and brown shoes. But Sam Burns had lost his shyness. Years before, when it became clear that he was the most talented of the company's technology people, Emma arranged for him to get private coaching in communication and business skills. And he had blossomed into an articulate executive who could hold his own in meetings and press interviews. He still dressed like a geek. "For my professional credibility," he would joke.

"Emma," he said a bit out of breath, "I'm afraid our system has been hacked by intruders." He raised a hand in caution. "It's okay. We've already taken measures to prevent it happening again. They did no damage." He paused. "We're sure of that, Emma, we really are."

She nodded. "Okay, if you say so."

He stared into her eyes. "I do. Really. We've been very thorough. You'll see our documentation."

Emma nodded again. Yes, she would. That would be another report. She imagined another thick layer added to the growing pile.

"Emma," he said, taking the chair in front of her desk, "someone sent me an email this morning. Someone from outside the company. That's who tipped us off. My people and I spent all day checking out the sender and what he said in his note."

"Okay," she said. "Who is he?"

"A regional rep for a portable generator company. He swears he knows nothing about our systems or the note that came to me from his email client. I believe him, I spoke to him personally. It looks like he was doing his email on the wifi network in a Starbucks in Ardmore." Emma thought, *not far from my house,* but said nothing. "Someone in the Starbucks must have hijacked the guy's identity off the network to send the note to me."

Emma thought of all the people she saw in Starbucks and other public places with free wifi, all of them busy on their laptops and smartphones. Millions of them everywhere, all thinking their privacy was safe and secure. "But I thought . . ." she started to say.

Burns shook his head. "No, I'm afraid it's not difficult—if you know what you're doing. The hacker just sits there looking like all the other patrons, sniffing their online activities. He tracks one person and copies his credentials, first on the wifi, then on his email client. When that person leaves, the hacker logs back on *as that person*. That's what happened to our generator salesman."

"You mean," Emma said, "someone could send out emails as me just by sitting next to me in Starbucks?"

He shrugged. "Anyway, the email told us to check the files of the security systems. In particular, the plant surveillance videos of July 9 of this year."

At the mention of that date, she felt like she had been slugged.

"I brought back the forensic computing experts we used right after the poisoning," he continued. "They performed a new analysis of the surveillance files of July 9. They discovered that the original source data were overwritten perfectly. I mean perfectly. That's why they and everybody else missed it. Whatever you see on that video is *not* what happened that day. Unfortunately, there is no way to know what the original video images looked like for July 9. No way."

The horror flooded back over her. "And police and . . . ?"

He cut in, "FBI, FDA, local police. All notified. And Bill Renner from security is on the redeye right now on his way back from California. He'll come here straight from the airport to meet with all the investigators tomorrow morning. We've frozen everything to preserve anything and everything that might be evidence."

"And those images of the woman who confessed?"

"Like we saw, she's in there. But now we can't be sure. We can't be sure of anything about that day."

"I *knew* it!" she exclaimed, "I knew there was something wrong with that confession story, I just knew it. I had Linda Farlow triple-check it and she said it all checked out."

"It did," Burns said, sounding defeated, "from what we could tell at the time."

He took a deep breath. She could tell his next item would be the thing he was most upset about. "We did find one more thing." He stopped again.

"Come on," she said, "let's hear it."

"Well, we found the digital fingerprint of an intruder in the master folder of the research labs. It looks like they made a copy of one subfolder. The last 'created on' time and date stamp on this subfolder is just minutes after the hidden time stamp they found on the tampered video— both were done in the middle of the night on July 9, the day of the poisoning. Had to be the same intruder. Had to be."

"Well," she said, starting to get upset, "*what* did they copy?" The research pipeline was the key to the future of Percival & Baxter. The research pipeline was leverage, it was defense against a raider, it was the key to a possible defensive merger, it was everything.

"The subfolder of the 'Female Brain Chemistry Project,' with all the reports on the trials of the experimental synthetic female mood-balancing hormones. But nothing else. We'll check and check again, but it looks like that's all they copied."

"That's it?"

"Well, actually," Burns said, cringing, "it's not the first copy that someone made of that subfolder. Another copy was made in late March. Again, just that one subfolder, just one time. Emma, our security is state-of-the-art. You've seen the reports about the banks and even the CIA getting hacked," Burns said with fear in his voice. "I want you to know that, uh, that we, uh . . ." He looked down at his lap.

She recognized an employee trying to protect his job. She got up quickly from her chair and walked over to her colleague. She placed her hands on his shoulders. "Look at me, Sam," she said. He looked up into her eyes. "It's me, Emma. We'll find out what all this means."

She knew there was nothing more she could do with the network and hacker issues at this moment. "Stay calm. We need you and your team to be as clearheaded as possible. I'm looking for answers, not scapegoats. Okay, Sam?"

She patted one shoulder of the nervous man and returned to her chair. She picked up a document to signal that their meeting was over. She heard him get up. She looked at him over her papers. He was just standing there, waiting. "Let's all be calm and clearheaded," she reiterated, trying to look preoccupied with the paper in her hand, "and we'll find out what's going on here. Tomorrow, when the investigators all come back, we'll start all over again."

"Thanks, Emma," he said as he turned and left.

She felt her head throbbing. Time for a couple of Acordinol from her desk drawer. She grabbed the bottle and popped two yellow pills into her mouth. There was a kind of defiance in the way she did it. As if she were flaunting it at the poisoner, whoever she or he might be. She picked up her phone and pushed the speed-dial button for home.

Ned picked up after two rings. "Hey, slugger," he said, reading the caller ID. "Now don't tell me . . . uh . . . something's come up and you're going to be later than you thought. I mean, *even* later."

"Yup," she said softly, "afraid so."

"You want to talk about it?"

"Yes," she said, aching to spill to him. "But if I start, I won't be able to stop. It's too complicated to go into now. I'll tell you all about it when I get home."

"And when do we think that'll be?" Ned had a playful tone.

"Later," she sighed, thinking about everything she had to think about.

"Later?" Ned asked, "As in when later?"

"Later later." She smiled.

"That's what I figured. Just checking. I won't wait up for you. Love you."

"Love you too." She hung up. Just the sound of Ned's voice made her feel a little better.

Emma lost track of time as she sat scribbling notes, trying to figure out what it might mean that the day of the poisoning had been covered up. And what was the connection between the "Female Brain Chemistry Project" copied once before Anglia started buying P&B stock, and then again right after the poisoning?

Could Josh be guilty of computer espionage? Or worse, the poisonings? Would he have people murdered in order to drive down the stock price? No, not Josh. Yes, he's a greedy bastard. But not a criminal monster. Nor would he conspire with a criminal monster—at least not knowingly. Not Josh. He was too concerned about his image, his respectability, and his pretensions to being upper class. Besides, she was certain he lacked the physical courage to go into business with men who would kill him if he did not deliver what they wanted. Beneath his Wall Street bravado, she was convinced, Josh Katz was a coward.

She decided she must confront him. But because of the takeover, it would have to be in secret. Without lawyers and investment bankers and board members. Where and how was something she would have to figure out. Now she was exhausted physically and emotionally. Finally, she turned off her office lights and checked herself out of the building, waving to the lone security guard making his rounds.

When she walked into the parking lot, she saw that her Volvo wagon was the only car left. The only good thing about leaving at this ungodly hour, she thought, was that there would be no traffic on her commute home.

48

A big car was zooming up behind her out of nowhere. It had to be one of those super-sized SUVs, like a Suburban or a Hummer. Black with the brights on. The reflection in Emma's rearview mirror hurt her eyes. As she reached to flick the mirror upward, she heard the loud *crack* and felt her car tremble.

The son of a bitch had sideswiped her.

Must be a drunk.

He did it again. Harder this time.

Then a third time. Really hard. Slam! And now he kept the side of his monster SUV against the side of her wagon, pushing her toward the shoulder of the abandoned road. Slam! Off the road. Off the freakin' road! And this was that patch of Codman with the sharp S-curves and the big ditches below. She had taken this dangerous shortcut thinking she would have the road all to herself.

Panicked, she grabbed the wheel tighter and tried to slide away from the other vehicle. As she moved it kept scraping along her side, pushing, pushing, pushing the Volvo toward the edge.

This guy was trying to kill her!

Slam! Her car shuddered and slid closer to the shoulder.

Time froze. Or slowed down. Or maybe speeded up. Emma could not tell. She felt her hands sweating. But she would not let them slip from the wheel.

A riot of wild thoughts raced through her head. How

do I stop him? How do I escape? What if he rams me off the road? How safe is my car if it flips over? What if it explodes?

Slam! He did it again.

Then, next instant, she had a burst of memory coupled with a burst of action. She did everything all at once. Memories of a certain weekend flashed before her. Images, sounds, and sensations. It told her body—her hands, her feet, her eyes, her reflexes—what to do.

Years ago at Silverstone race track in Northamptonshire, northwest of London. The off-site at the car racing school, arranged by Josh's boss, J. Carter Good III, for his young investment bankers and their wives. He'd called it "team building." That letch, J. Carter, had a way of pawing all the young wives. Just short of inappropriate, which made it even creepier. He tried to pass it off as affectionate leadership. But it was like he wanted to prove he had dominion over the women of the men who worked for him. If he could have, Emma knew, he would have bedded each and every one of the wives.

During the rally course, she learned a maneuver from her instructor. And once she got the motions down, she found she was good at it. She enjoyed the thrill of it and even spent an extra hour practicing it on her own. At the end of the weekend, they gave her a Silverstone trophy inscribed, "Ace of the Hand-Brake Turn." When she and Josh were dividing up their belongings as their divorce unfolded, Emma buried the trophy in the bottom of one of Josh's boxes. That was the last time she had thought about that weekend. Until this frenzied minute.

She tried a deep breath. A shallow breath was all she could manage. Her body did her thinking, because what happened next happened through her arms and legs and eyes. Not her brain. In one instant, she eased up on the gas to slow down. The monster beside her followed suit and gave another slam. In fractions of a second, Emma slid the gearshift into neutral, put both hands down at five o'clock on the lower left of the steering wheel, then yanked the wheel all the way to the right. As the front wheels locked, she pulled up the hand brake. (Her Volvo had a hand brake! Her hand remembered before her brain did!) And she made sure to keep the locking button pushed in so it would not engage. Just as she had learned at Silverstone, her car screeched to a momentary halt and spun around to face the opposite direction. In fractions of the same second, she released the hand brake and snapped the gearshift back into drive. She peeled away from the SUV, gas pedal pressed to the floor, first along the shoulder, then onto the wrong side of the road, into the dark.

Able to breathe again, but barely, she saw in her mirror the brake lights of the SUV as it screeched to a halt. She blew through a deserted intersection. Then there was a blur of flashing lights and sounds of a siren as a police cruiser peeled out from the intersection to chase her. Her breathing stuttered, her sweaty hands released their tight grip on the wheel. She removed her foot from the accelerator, and saw in her mirror the glare of the cruiser's flashing lights bearing down. In the far distance, the taillights of the SUV disappeared into the darkness.

As her foot pressed down on the brake and the car stopped, she felt the mad frenzy ebb out of her. She slid the gearshift into park and felt the flashing lights of the cruiser surround her. She lowered her window and took what felt like the first deep breath of her entire life. She knew that the big man in the uniform approaching had come to rescue her.

49

What Emma remembered was mostly a blur. The policeman examining her battered car, she recounting her story, catching her breath, using all her willpower to appear calm, catching her breath again so as not to cry, making phone calls to confirm who she was, calling the P&B security hotline, waiting for the wrecker to take her car away as evidence, more police arriving and asking questions, inhaling deeply again so as not to cry, *not* freaking out that someone tried to murder her, riding home in the back of the cruiser, talking to Ned on her cell, catching and controlling her breathing, and *not* crying. Someone had tried to kill her. Fear and anger kept clanging in her head.

None of it seemed real until she came up the walkway of her own house and fell into Ned's arms. They said nothing. They just hugged for a long moment.

Peter was standing right behind them. As Ned closed the door, she reached for Peter. She felt him hesitate, then accept her embrace.

"Are you hurt, Mom?" he asked awkwardly, patting her on the shoulders as Emma felt his back go rigid.

"No, Peter," she said, letting go of him and feeling him relax as she did.

Ned put his arm around her waist and pulled her toward the kitchen. "*You* need a drink!" he commanded. Emma liked the way he took control of her. She was surprised that she had not yet cried. Somehow, the tears had not come.

They sat at the kitchen table. Emma and Ned shared a bottle of white wine. Peter got a can of Pepsi.

She told the story of her night backward, starting with the man (she decided to tell it that way because it had to be a man) who tried to run her off the road, and her life-saving hand brake turn. Peter's jaw fell open when he heard about her stunt driving prowess. Sitting in her kitchen with her men, she let herself get good and angry. "I can't believe someone actually tried to kill me! Some goddamn fucking bastard! He tried, oh Jesus, he fucking tried to kill me. That, that, oh Jesus, that fucker, that bastard, that that . . . I just can't believe it," she barked. Then she howled and doubled over, burying her face in her hands and breathing hard to keep from crying again. When she had regained control, she sat upright and still, mouth closed, eyes closed, breathing through her nose.

Ned and Peter sat watching her.

Peter broke the silence first. "Mom?"

She opened her eyes.

"Mom, aren't you afraid now?"

"Of course I am. But I'll be damned if I'll let them—whoever they are—know. The company will have body-guards for me tomorrow morning. We'll use them for a while, I guess. But I'm *not* going to let them get to me. Absolutely not."

"Don't you think," Ned said hesitantly, "this whole takeover thing has gotten out of hand? Maybe you should think about taking some time off. A leave of absence? Emma, do you really need to do this CEO thing under these conditions? It's just a job."

She stared at him. At this moment, Ned looked like a complete stranger to her. "What? Not a chance! Jesus, Ned. You *know* me. I mean, come on!"

"I'm just saying . . ."

"Yes, I know what you're just saying," she snapped.

Then she paused to get the outrage out of her voice. Yes, she understood he was just thinking of her safety, their safety, their happiness, their life together. "Yes, honey, I know. I know. But I *can't* quit. Not now. Especially not after tonight. If I quit, it would send a terrible signal to everyone. If the CEO were to give up at this point, the whole defense, the whole thing, well, P&B needs me now more than ever."

"We need you, too," Ned said softly. He turned to Peter. "Don't we, dude?"

Peter nodded. Of course, he loved his mom. He just didn't want to have to say it out loud.

"What would I do all day?" Emma asked, a bit of the edge returning to her voice. "I can't stay home and garden. And I certainly can't take another job." She reached across the table and took Ned and Peter each by the hand. "We all need each other and we all need to support each other in what to do together. And our lives as separate people. Your life and work, Ned. Your life, Peter, with all the things you want to do. And me. This is something I have to see through. I just do. And I need you guys to support me." She squeezed their hands. "I just can't let the bad guys win, I just can't. You understand, don't you?"

Ned and Peter nodded. "Thanks, men," she said, "I love you." She let go of their hands. She took another sip of wine. Then a deep breath. She was starting to unwind, finally.

Then she told them the story of the anonymous email from the generator sales rep and the tip-off about the video of July 9.

"So we don't know if that woman really did put the poison in the Acordinol," Emma said. The cold, wet glass felt comforting in her hand. "And we may never know. Then, another strange thing. They found out that someone copied the subfolder on this one research project." She was feeling the tension ease out of her. "Not once, but twice. Once just before Anglia started buying our stock. And again right after the poisoning. There has to be a connection."

Emma felt she would be ready to go to bed soon. She was looking forward to snuggling with Ned, then sleeping. She hoped she would sleep like a baby tonight. Not like baby Peter, who never seemed to sleep when he was an infant. But sleep like that idealized baby everyone talked about.

"I hate to say this," Ned said, "but do you think Josh could possibly be behind this?"

"I, I just don't know," she said. This was another horrible part of the puzzle she had to figure out. "He's greedy but not an assassin. He's a Wall Street guy. They have no problem with immoral; they do that all the time. Not even a glimmer of conscience. But murder? No. They're afraid of that. Not because it's bad, but because they could go to jail." She looked at Peter and said, "I'm sorry to say this about your father, honey, but it's true. He's no worse than the rest of them. But I'm afraid he's also no better."

She now felt her brain starting to shut down. "We can't trace the intruders anyway. From what the tech guys say, there's no way to know who the hacker was." She touched Peter on the arm. "Isn't that right? You're our expert."

Peter wanted to crawl under the table. "Uh, yeah, that's right," he said, hoping he wasn't visibly cringing, because he was cringing inside. "Hackers use zombie networks. They hijack computers all over the world and the people don't even know it. Then they vanish. Next time, they hijack a whole different set of computers. Then they, like, disappear again."

"Nice," Ned said, shaking his head. "That's some world we live in."

Peter shrugged as he looked at Ned, then at his mom.

No, they didn't suspect him. He did not want to talk anymore. He kept hearing Tsarina Alexandra's words, "Secrets are what make us grown-ups." Yep, he had secrets all right. With all the secrets he had, he must be sort of grown up by now.

He finished the last of his Pepsi. "I'm gonna go back to bed, okay?"

He got up and kissed Mom on the forehead.

Did she suspect him? No, he decided.

Is this what it feels like to be guilty and get away with a crime? I guess so, he thought. He was terrified to say anything, because, well, because he was sure he would squeal about his secrets and his crimes.

Emma reached up and hugged Peter close. With her head pressed against his chest, she heard his heart. She remembered how fast his newborn heart raced when she first held him. It seemed like that moment was sixteen minutes ago, not sixteen years. "Love you," she whispered into his chest.

"Love you too, Mom," Peter said. "I'm glad you're safe." He turned to leave, then stopped. "Say, Mom?"

"Yes?"

"When I get past my junior driver's license and get my regular license next year, will you teach me how to do a hand-brake turn? That is so freakin' cool!"

"No way," she said with a little smile. She was grateful to return to the little matters of home life.

"Way," Peter said. "Way! I'll keep asking you. Like you always say—persistence. I'll wear you down. Right, Ned?"

"Right." Ned smiled. Peter headed upstairs.

Emma and Ned sat in silence until they heard Peter's door close. She took Ned's hand again. "You really weren't serious about me quitting my job, were you?"

"I was going to ask you the same thing about staying in it."

She took a deep breath, squeezed his hand, then gently let go. "Ned, I can't quit. I just can't."

Ned gave a sigh and a nod.

To Emma, it looked like a mixture of resignation and support. "You still love me?" she asked with a little grin. This was a game that dated to the earliest days of their relationship. It was the teasing question Emma asked whenever she revealed an annoying habit of hers or one of the not-so-nice realities of her life.

Ned leaned across the table and gave her a soft, lingering kiss.

Emma closed her eyes. When she opened them, she was looking through tears.

50

ONE PERCIVAL & BAXTER PLAZA • FRANKLIN CROSSING,
PENNSYLVANIA

Emma spent the first half of the morning in crisis meetings with a parade of law-enforcement people.

There were local police going over the previous night's attempt on her life. They showed up with preliminary lab reports. Paint samples scraped into her Volvo and skid marks on the road, which showed that the car that attacked her was a black Ford with Goodyear tires. That narrowed the suspect pool down to several million. And it would be easy to transport, hide, or destroy the evil vehicle without leaving a trace. If the killers were professional, this black SUV was long gone. Without an insider tip or a miracle, it would likely be impossible to find them.

Then there were FBI agents returning to reexamine all the evidence, now that they would never be sure if Loralee Eaton actually did what she had confessed to. FDA enforcement teams also came to reopen their side of the same nightmare. Plus forensic computer specialists to dig back into all the P&B systems. And in all the meetings, there were lawyers, lawyers, and more lawyers.

Stationed outside her office door were her new day-shift bodyguards, Lew Dunlop and Ted Vedders. Their job would be to shadow her everywhere. They seemed like good guys, even if they wore grim expressions and had the biggest, broadest, thickest shoulders she remembered seeing away from a football stadium.

Just before lunch, she called a quick meeting of the executive committee. She gave them a summary of the situation, including the attempt on her life. "I have no intention of making myself a hero," she said, "but I also have no intention of backing out of this fight. Or letting anyone scare me out of it." She looked up and down the table at her executives. She tried to read what she saw in their eyes. She wished she could read what was in their hearts. "Are we all on the same page?"

She peered into Upshaw's eyes, looking for some confirmation of the mistrust she felt. He gave her back a look of earnest commitment. *But he's such a phony,* she thought. *He would love to sell out, cash in his chips.* She just knew it. *He's the traitor. He has to be.*

Everyone nodded and mumbled affirmatively. She asked herself, *was this obedience?* People obeyed and complied in a corporation because they had to. Where were the signs of their personal commitment? How did you probe for that? *You don't,* she thought. She realized now that she was more rattled from last night than she had thought. Someone had tried to murder her. *Calm, Emma, calm. Stick with the factual and you'll be fine. You will.*

"Now with this new information," she said, working on her monotone delivery, "and with what Sam Burns and his team have uncovered about the hacker's intrusions, we know that we *don't* know who really poisoned the Acordinol. And we may never know. The investigation has been officially reopened by the FBI and FDA. But they have made the strategic decision *not* to go public with any of this now. None of it. Not even my little, uh, incident last night. We are keeping a total blackout because they do not want to tip off, uh, the bad guys."

She stopped, trying not to wince at what she just said. "Uh, they want to be sure they don't tip off whoever did do it. So confidentiality is even more critical than ever. I can't stress this enough. Tell no one. I mean no one. No one outside this room beyond the investigators knows what I just told you. And for the sake of their investigation, no one else can know. Do you understand?"

Again, nods and mumbled affirmative phrases.

Emma stood up.

The members of the committee followed suit.

"We'll get together in a few days. With any luck, we'll know more about who actually tried to ruin us. And we'll definitely have more ammunition for the takeover defense. I'll bring you up to speed on that. In the meantime, confidentiality above all."

Emma watched as her executives filed past her toward the door.

As Linda Farlow approached her, she said, "Linda, can you stay for a sec?"

"Sure, Emma." Linda now stood by Emma's place at the head of the table. When the others had left, Emma turned and closed the conference room door. She stood with her back against it, holding the doorknob, as if to keep some force out there from getting inside.

"I think we have a leak, Linda. Someone who is helping the other side. Someone from this committee who wants to see P&B get taken over." She looked into Linda Farlow's eyes. She couldn't tell what she saw. Emma had always thought she could read character. Suddenly, she wasn't so sure. She barged ahead, anyway, doing what felt right. "Linda, I believe someone who has access to our confidential human resources files gave the tip to the TV woman. Someone gave Jeanine Holloway that information about my transfer out of Farricker's department. That had to come from someone high up in this company, someone with access to everything. Jeanine offered it to Josh Katz on a silver platter. Of course, he already knew all about it; he secretly helped arrange it back then. But he didn't use it. He made a conscious decision not to use it, not to go after me on television."

She paused, watching Linda. She could detect nothing beyond what looked like genuine concern. "Now I don't care about that event, it's so far in the past. And these days, there isn't anything anyone can say that can embarrass me. Nothing can stop me from doing what I believe in. But it's the leak that concerns me." She gave Linda a questioning look.

"Sure. Of course," Linda said. "It's the breach of confidentiality."

"Linda, do you have any clue who that leak might be? I'm not asking for evidence, unless of course you've seen or heard something. I'm just asking you from your gut. You and I have been at this company a long time. Do you have any idea who among us might be helping the other side?" She was dying to say, "Upshaw, tell me you think it's Upshaw!" But she held herself back.

Linda shook her head. "No, Emma, I just can't imagine who."

Emma thought she read sincerity in Linda's eyes, at least she hoped she did. But she wasn't sure. Suddenly she regretted bringing this up. *Too late to go back,* she told herself. "Linda, is there anyone who strikes you as, I don't know, not happy with the strategy of staying independent?"

"You mean," Linda said slowly, her gaze never wavering, "someone unhappy like . . . Steve Upshaw? Human resources reports to him, he has access to all those files."

Emma nodded gravely. "I didn't want to be the one to say it."

"He hasn't said anything in front of me," Linda said

almost in a whisper, "but we all knew he was disappointed when you got made chief executive over him. He saw himself as next in line. He's got, well, he's always had that kind of personality. I guess any of us who gets this far," she motioned at the mahogany-paneled room, "has a lot of that drive. But Steve has, well, he's got . . ."

"More than his share of it," Emma said.

Linda nodded. "Emma, is there anything you want me to do? Anything you'd like me to try to find out?"

"No, Linda, thanks." Emma felt vindicated in her judgment. Yes, she felt she *had* turned Linda Farlow into an ally, after all. "But if you hear or see something that I should know about, I'd appreciate it if you give me a heads-up."

"Of course, Emma." Linda reached forward and squeezed Emma's arm.

"Thanks, Linda."

"Anything I can do, Emma. We're all in this with you."

Emma, exhausted, sat down at the conference room table. Behind her back, she heard Linda greeting Hal Percival in the hallway.

"Hi, Hal," Linda said.

"Hello, Linda. It's so good to see you," he replied.

"You too, Hal!"

Emma stood up and was about to turn to greet him, but he had already taken a seat beside her. "No, no, please, sit down, Emma."

She sat and took a deep breath.

He looked deep into her eyes. "Emma, are you all right?"

"Yes, Hal. I'm fine. Really. Not a scratch on me." She raised her arms as if to demonstrate her sound condition. "In fact, I feel energized." She had slept like the proverbial baby and woke up feeling almost brand-new, all things considered.

"I heard you pulled off an exceptional feat of driving. Where on earth did you learn to do *that*?"

"Oh, ages ago," she said. "Lessons at a race track in England. Long story. I actually won a little trophy for that maneuver. It's called a hand-brake turn. I hadn't thought about it or done one for a hundred years. It just came back like muscle memory. I was lucky to be in my Volvo. When I reached to grab the hand brake, there *was* a hand brake to grab."

They smiled at each other. Then a moment of silence. Hal then turned serious. "Emma, this has all gone too far. You mustn't allow yourself to be put at risk like this. *We* mustn't. This is just a job. It is not worth risking your life over."

"You sound like my husband."

"Well, I'm concerned about you."

"Thank you, Hal. But I've thought this over and talked it over with my family. I've got to see this through."

"Emma, please understand that we do not expect your responsibilities to extend to personal danger. You do not need to do that for us."

"Hal, I'm not doing it for you. I'm doing it for *me*. It's what I need to accomplish for myself. I feel responsible. It's everyone and everything at Percival & Baxter. Everything that's been built here over all the years. I can't let that get washed away in a stupid, destructive deal that is about nothing but greed. I have to do everything possible to preserve and defend . . ." She paused, then said, "To preserve and defend *us*."

Hal sat back and smiled. "I knew you'd say that."

Emma felt confused. "Then why did you ask me if I wanted out?"

"If, perhaps, you did want a way out, I wanted you to have it. With everything you have done to date—after last night—you have earned the right to bow out with honor."

"Hal, this is Emma Conway you're talking to. I'm Pete Conway's daughter. When would I ever bow out of anything?"

"That's our Emma," he said, and smiled at her the way he always did.

Emma smiled back. She tried not to think about how tired part of her was feeling. And how frightened.

Suddenly, her mind felt clear. She had a plan. She wanted to see that Starbucks in Ardmore with her own eyes. And if she could find a pay phone out of sight of her bodyguards, surprise Josh with a phone call.

"Now, if it's okay with our lead director," she said brightly, "I'd like to take a little investigative field trip with my new bodyguards before that meeting of the full board this afternoon."

Hal smiled. "Of course. See you then."

51

Viktor was just about to go to dinner when the satellite phone on his desk in Belgravia lit up unexpectedly. He grabbed the phone.

"Katz, why you call now?" he asked. "We already talk once today."

"Viktor Viktorovich," the voice on the other end intoned in Yorkshire-accented Russian, "I need to talk to you. Please, Viktor Viktorovich."

Viktor could tell something was wrong. Hardacre was usually arrogant. Tonight, he sounded humble. Scared.

"What's happening, Tom? There's a problem, I can tell in your voice."

"Th-th-they know. They know everything we did." The voice had terror in it.

"What you mean, everything? Be specific." In a crisis, Viktor always grew calmer. Over the years, he had practiced behaving in the exact opposite of what people expected. It was one way he made his way so effectively in Europe. And in Russia too. When everyone was yelling, he was composed. No one could tell what Viktor Viktorovich was thinking. And certainly not what he was feeling. So at this moment, Viktor the chess player kept himself from feeling panic. He forced himself to be calm.

First, he had to get all the information. "Just tell me slowly. What are the facts?" he said in a soothing voice.

Hardacre could not see the fingers of Viktor's free hand drumming restlessly on the desk.

"Uh. . . ." Hardacre cleared his throat. "P&B knows that their systems were hacked. They know that the security videos were tampered with. They know that our Loralee woman probably did not poison their pills and probably did not kill herself. They know that the files in the Female Brain Chemistry Pro folder were copied, but they don't seem to know why. At least not yet."

Viktor was simultaneously calculating damage and risk. "But why Katz never told me any of this?"

"Katz doesn't know. No one is supposed to know. The FBI is keeping all of it secret not to endanger their new investigation. I found out from the man who runs our mole."

"So what and who they are looking for?" Viktor could tell Hardacre had more to say but hadn't yet said it.

"No one, Viktor Viktorovich. No one in particular."

Well, Viktor thought, *no suspects. That's good.* The maze of carefully built legal structures was still working. None of this could be traced back to Viktor Volkov.

"Tom, I have feeling you have something else, no?" Viktor had to find out why Hardacre was so unusually respectful.

"Yes, Viktor Viktorovich."

"So what is it? What else?"

"Someone tried to kill the woman CEO, the one who used to be married to Katz. They tried to run her car off the road. Last night, they came close to killing her, but they failed." Hardacre took a long, deep breath. "No one in my network, I swear to you, knows one thing about this. No one in my network would do something like this. Never without orders I got from you. Really, I swear on my mother's soul."

"The FBI, they are keeping this a secret too?" Viktor

asked, showing no emotion in his voice. This news infuriated him. But he would not let Hardacre know. How does this happen? Who does a thing so stupid at this delicate moment in the deal? He wondered about Sergei, the eldest son of his partner, the one who was so hot to prove himself.

"Find out everything and keep me posted. Everything."

"Yes, I-I . . . Viktor Viktorovich, yes, I promise."

"And Tom . . ."

"Yes?"

"Be strong. And don't be afraid. I take good care of you when this is over." Viktor told himself he meant it too. If it worked out that Hardacre did not have to be eliminated, he would take care of him. Maybe even let him survive to enjoy that beachside villa. Or not . . . depending . . . on what was necessary.

"Thank you, Viktor Viktorovich, thank you."

Viktor clicked off. He knew too well what he had heard in Hardacre's voice. The sound of a man who knew, but dared not admit, that he might soon be dead.

52

Emma entered the Starbucks in Ardmore, but not alone.
Lew, bodyguard number one, was following at a respectful distance. Ted posted himself outside the shop
and watched, turning his head back and forth in an arc,
like the beacon in a lighthouse. Emma wondered who
noticed the little earpieces the men wore with the curlicue
wire that wrapped around their ears. And if people did
notice, did they associate them with Secret Service bodyguards or the bruisers who guarded the velvet-rope queues
at exclusive nightclubs?

"I just want to look around," she had said from the backseat of the car, as they had parked just down the block.
Since first thing that morning, she had learned the routine.
She had no need to tell them why she wanted to do anything. They did not ask. She just told them what she wanted
to do. They did not talk unless she spoke first to them. She
just went wherever she was going. They followed, but as if
they were not there.

She stared around at the just-before-lunchtime clientele.
She heard sounds of the steaming espresso machines,
customers moving from the ordering line to the pick-up
line, waiting for absurdly complicated drinks with "half-
caff, half-skim" combinations. The elaborate formulas
baffled her. She liked plain, strong coffee with a hint of
skim. But these items seemed to matter deeply to the

patrons and the baristas preparing them. She saw people on laptops, lost in their own private bubbles of concentration, but being there to be near other people. All lost in their own bubbles, together. She thought of the hacker who had hijacked the generator salesman's email from this very coffee shop. It made her want to shout out loud that everyone's privacy and their online identities were at risk under this seemingly welcoming roof.

She remembered having checked her email from her laptop once from that very chair in the far corner. *Maybe,* she thought, *I'll have Sam Burns run some kind of check to see if my email identity has ever been hijacked.* Or maybe, she decided, she'd wait on that. Wait for things to resolve a bit and calm down. Sam and his people were slammed with really big problems now.

She turned back to Lew, who stood at the front. He surveyed the scene and tried not to be obvious about it. He gave her the faintest of nods. Someone would have to be studying very intently to have noticed her connection with them.

She walked toward the back corner where the restrooms were. And there she saw what she had thought she remembered was there—the pay phone. Yes, the shiny chrome pay phone. They still had a pay phone with coin slots and all sorts of printed instructions and advertising copy. To her it looked like a comforting artifact from a lost civilization.

She nodded in the direction of the women's room. Lew nodded back. No, he was not going to accompany her. When she came out, he was still watching the women's room door. She did not want to think about whether or not he played a mental movie of her while she was out of his sight, to gauge the time it should take for her to pee, wash her hands, and touch up hair and makeup before emerging from that door. But that must be what he did. He was vigilant. If she took too long, he would surely burst in, ignore the other women doing their business, and check the stalls for Emma Conway. Yes, that's what he would do. *Well,* Emma thought, *from now on, maybe I'll never pee alone.*

She walked to the counter and ordered a small cup of Pike Place blend with skim milk. She let the barista translate it back to her in Starbucks lingo and she nodded. She paid and asked for extra change from her twenty-dollar bill. "Could I get more quarters, please? Five dollars in quarters?" She put a dollar bill in the tips cup. Then another.

She put her coffee down on the little shelf in front of the pay phone. She knew she was just out of Lew's sight, but he knew where she was and what she was doing. Or, she assumed as much, and figured he wouldn't interrupt her as long as she did not stay out of sight too long.

She took out the piece of paper with Josh's private phone number and dialed. "Please deposit three dollars and ten cents for the first three minutes," the recording told her. Awkwardly, she started dropping quarters into the slot. She deposited a final quarter to put her fifteen cents over. This was the number Josh had given Peter and Peter had shared with her when she had insisted she be able to reach him "just in case." It had been one of the "secrets" Peter, with little prompting, had shared with his mother. She was happy that he had still not yet learned to keep secrets from her. It made her feel that their connection, which she knew was changing, was still strong.

The pay phone voice thanked her and the call went through. After two rings, Josh picked up, sounding peeved at the sight of an inbound number he did not recognize on his superprivate number. "Hello?" he snapped, "Who is this?"

"It's Emma," she snapped back.

"Emma?" he said, surprised. "I didn't think we were supposed to . . ."

"Just listen to me," she said in an almost-whisper, "I'm calling from a pay phone. For the record, this call is a wrong number or a sales solicitation." She did not say "or one of your girlfriends," although the thought crossed her mind. She cupped one hand over the mouthpiece and said angrily, "Somebody tried to run me off the road last night. They tried to kill me, Josh. They tried to *kill* me. I wanted you to hear about this from me before Peter comes for his next visit. We're keeping it quiet. But you should know I'm not giving up or backing down. I'm living with bodyguards and security details now." She felt her rage from last night mounting with her rage at his betrayals. "Is it possible that you had anything, and I mean anything, to do with some goon in a big SUV trying to drive me into a *ditch*? Any of your friends or associates, perhaps?"

Josh sounded dumbfounded. "Oh, Emma. Jesus. Emma, I, Emma, what are you talking about? My God, Emma, are you okay? You sound okay."

"Yes, I'm okay, goddammit. I'm standing here talking to you. Now answer me."

"Emma, I have no idea. My God. No idea. You have to believe me."

She resisted saying "yeah, right." Instead, she said, "This has to be related to your takeover attempt. Somebody who wants your side to win, wanted to get rid of me. Or to scare me enough to force me to quit."

"Emma, really, I . . ."

"Well, I just want you to know that I'm not quitting or letting anyone scare me."

"Emma, I have no idea. None. Really."

"Also, Josh, industrial espionage is against the law. It's

illegal to have hackers break into a company's system and steal their confidential trade secrets. You know that, don't you?"

"Yes, of course. But I don't know what you're talking about."

"Really?"

"Yes, really."

"Well, you listen to me, Josh Katz. You are not taking over my company. And if we can prove anything about your dirty dealings, and I mean anything, we will throw the book at you. Do you understand?"

"Emma, really, truly, I don't know what you're talking about."

"Just so you know, you are not going to win. Not if it's the last thing I do." She thought about saying, "And it might turn out to be." Instead, she just hung up. She took her purse, dropped her half-finished coffee in the waste basket, and headed for the door.

"Thanks, Lew, we're going back to the office," she muttered as she left the Starbucks.

53

At Viktor's insistence, he and Artyom were walking toward a remote corner of the grand, rolling lawn of Wilborne Hall. Out there, he felt sure, no one could overhear them. Each man held his own silver-plated thermos of icy vodka, provided by the butler. They stopped now and then to drink. Viktor would wait while Artyom took a slug, and Artyom would do the same when Viktor drank. They made small talk along the way to an ancient oak.

When they arrived, Viktor walked behind the tree's immense trunk and motioned for Artyom to follow. "No line of sight from the house," he whispered in Russian.

"What? You have spies looking out from your own windows?"

"No." Viktor did not want to say, "Not that I know of." But he was not sure, he was never sure. "I just cannot let anyone overhear us."

Artyom joined him in the shade of the ancient tree. "So, what's so secret?"

Viktor beckoned him closer. "Someone tried to kill the woman CEO at the American drug company," he whispered. "Tried to run her off the road. But it's nowhere in the news, the FBI is keeping it a secret." He paused and looked up into Artyom's face. All he saw was the blank expression Artyom had mastered with the police when they were young. "Artyom, do you know about this? Tell me, do you?"

Artyom took a step backward.

"Artyom, did your people try to kill that woman?"

Artyom said nothing.

"Did they?"

Still nothing.

"Did they? Tell me, my old friend."

Artyom nodded.

"I did not tell anyone to do that," Viktor said, maintaining his cool. "I gave no such order." He glared, knowing that his silent wrath inspired more fear than yelling ever would.

Artyom shrugged and took a long pull from his thermos. "Are you angry because someone tried," he said, "or because someone failed?"

"Both. If you try, you must get it done. But why did you try? Killing her would have been terrible. It's only good luck that she is okay." A murdered chief executive, Viktor knew, would risk blowing open the whole deal and ruin all of his plans.

Artyom looked down. "My fault," he said, "I was trying to help. My Sergei," referring to his oldest son, "he likes his independence. He's a genius investor, you know. He watched the American investment show. He watches them all. He saw your banker and this woman. He says this woman does a great job fighting for her side. Better than your banker does. And not just in the business way. She talked from her heart, he told me. So then the stock goes up because of her! So he decides to destabilize their side." He paused awkwardly. "Uh, or he tried to. He's still young. I reprimanded him very strongly. I apologize, eh?" Artyom stood silently.

Viktor drained the remainder of his vodka. "You make trouble for both of us," he said. But his self-control still reigned. "Artyomchik, my brother. If we get careless, we get unlucky. And then they could come for us."

"Oh no," Artyom said, wagging a warning finger. He was suddenly brighter. "They won't suspect *us*."

"Of course they will." What the hell was Artyom talking about?

"No, no," Artyom said, "this is your deal. I'm just junior partner. Not *us*. They will suspect *you*. They suspect only *you*."

Viktor showed no reaction. But he felt a shiver down his spine.

54

By the time Tsarina Alexandra sent her third private message to Katman on the FriendVault, she sounded desperate. She never typed this way, pounding the keys and holding them down to repeat, machine gun style.

"I NEEEEEED TO VIDEOCHAT W/U!!!!!! PLEASE SAY WHEN!!! PLEEEEEEEEZ!!!!! PETER!!!!!!!!!!!!!!!! KATMAN!!!!!!!!!!!!!!!!!!!!!!!!!!!!!
I NEEEEEEEEEEEEEEEEEEEEEEED UUUUUUUUUU UUU!!!!!!!!!!!!!!!!!!!!!!
NOW!!!
!!!!!!!

Tanya thought she would go mad. She had waited most of the week before deciding to tell Katman what had happened. Then, once she decided to tell him, she wanted him to respond at once. He did not. What the hell could he be doing? She sent him message after message, each one more urgent than the last, not caring how annoying or stupid she might appear. Then, finally, Katman signed on and said he was turning on his webcam.

"Where the fucking Christ have you been?" she barked at the boy who appeared on her computer screen. She sat alone in her study on the third floor of her big empty house.

"Tsarina?" Peter asked, looking like the scared teenage boy he was. "What's wrong?"

"Where have you been?" she scolded.

"Uh, I, uh . . ." he stammered.

"Oh, never mind!" she snapped. The last thing she wanted was to sound like the boy's teacher. Or worse, his mother. She did not know what to say. Or how to begin.

She stared blankly at his face.

Then she started sobbing, letting tears well up and fall, catching her breath in little gasps.

"What's wrong?" he asked, confused.

She sobbed for a couple of minutes without speaking. When she spoke at last, her voice was a feeble whisper. "Katman, will you put your arms around me?"

"Uh, I, er, I . . ."

"Just tell me you are putting your arms around me, that's all." She sounded lost. "I have no one to hug me. Please."

"Okay," he said, tentatively playing along, "I'm putting my arms around you. I'm hugging you. Can you feel it?"

She shook her head and sniffled. "Yes, I think so. Can you hold me for a while, please?" The controlled expression on her face was starting to crumble. Her jaw began to quiver. "Just hold me."

"Yes, I'll hold you," he said softly, starting to feel her mysterious upset, whatever it was.

She started to cry. Violent waves of howling, waves of shrieks that rattled and shook her whole body. Gentler waves of sobbing, pitiful and small, that gave way to bursts of little sniffles that gathered momentum and grew again into more giant waves of howling and shrieking. Then back down and up. Again. And again. No words, just the tearful language of unbearable sadness.

Finally, after a time neither could measure, she began to emerge. "Oh, Katman." She wiped her sleeve across her face. "Thank you, I had no one else to turn to." She sniffled and snorted loudly, at last able to stop the waves from overtaking her.

"Tsarina?" he asked timidly. "Can you tell me what's wrong?"

She held her breath and shook her head. *Poor boy*, she thought. *Poor me*. The wrong answer spilling out of her mouth right now would unleash the tears again. She chose her words with the greatest care, trying not to trigger Victoria Falls again. "I've lost the baby. I'm not pregnant anymore." She stopped there. Deep breath. Calm for a moment, however temporary.

"I'm sorry," he whispered.

She took another deep breath. There now. And another. Better still. "It was my father." She hung on the word, not sure if it would send her over the edge. It did not. "My father." She said it again, this time with anger. "He . . . he had me knocked out, anesthetized at his country house. And had a medical crew abort my baby." Another deep breath, still in control. "All very sanitary and safe, like in hospital. No, better, actually."

The boy gasped. "Your *father*? . . . Did *that* . . . to you?"

He looks stunned, she thought. "He murdered my baby!" she cried out and pounded her fists on her legs. Stammering through more tears, she pressed on. "He murdered my baby . . . to teach me a lesson about what it means to be *his* daughter. I hate him. I *hate* him!" she howled.

"How could a father do something like *that* to . . . ?"

She whimpered in response. She shook her head and took a deep breath. *Yes, composure*. She tried to smile at the image on the screen. She wiped her nose with the side of her hand. "I'm a mess, aren't I?" A little smile escaped along with a sniffle. "Now don't answer that. I'm getting through this. You're off the hook now, you know. Of course, I never had you *on* the hook, did I? But you see what I mean."

"Are you going to be all right? Is there anything I can do?" He sounded genuinely concerned.

"No, dear boy. Thank you." Another smile popped out, pushing a sob into the background. "Our little accident made me very happy for a time, you should know that."

"Tsarina?" he asked tentatively.

"Yes, Katman."

"Will you tell me who you are? I'll tell you who I am. Don't you think we should?"

She nodded and sniffed. "Yes, of course. What does it matter now? M-m-my mum died when I was ten. She was Alexandra Yardley, a poor baronet's daughter. My name is Tanya. Tatiana, actually." She forced a bitter laugh. "I'm . . . I'm the only child of this awful man." Sniffles starting up.

Tanya gave a shudder, then a big sigh. Suddenly composed, she said with icy calm, "My father's name is Viktor Volkov."

"Viktor Volkov?" Peter gasped again. "Viktor Volkov used to be my dad's investment-banking client. Dad said Tom Hardacre had references from him from England. Said he was lucky when Tom took the job."

"Tom Hardacre?" she asked. "What's your name, Katman? Who is *your* father?"

"I'm Peter Katz," he said. "My dad is Josh Katz. He's, like, a big Wall Street guy."

She gasped. She could not tell if her blushing showed up on the screen. She remembered her attempted seduction of Josh Katz, the whole drunken, stupid teenage episode. That man's *son* was the father of her baby! Almost her father-in-law, in a manner of speaking. This was too much. "Oh sod," she said nervously. "I, uh, met your father a few years ago at the White Elephant."

"The White Elephant?" Peter sounded confused.

"Viktor's house in Belgravia. It's a big white monstrosity. Uh, never mind . . ."

They fell into silence, staring at each other on their screens.

Finally, Tanya took a deep breath. Now she had something to think about, something that was not her grief. "Let's try to sort this out," she said crisply.

"Now, let's hear it again," said Peter.

"Tom Hardacre is no estate manager. He is one of Viktor's criminal apparatchiks," she said.

"What-chiks?" Peter asked, sounding even more confused.

"His tool, silly boy, his *operative*! I wondered what happened to him. He just disappeared one day. I thought maybe Viktor killed him for crossing him somehow. I promise you, his strings are pulled by Viktor. Surely, your father must realize this."

"Uh, I don't know," Peter said. "He just said that Tom had a great resumé as an estate manager and was one of the candidates recommended by Viktor. That's how he got the job as my dad's estate manager in Greenwich."

Tanya snickered. "Estate manager, indeed. He is Viktor's master computer criminal. I wasn't supposed to know. But tongues wag when the vodka flows, and I understand a damn sight more Russian than they realize." Then she asked, "Greenwich, isn't that the place where we met, the town with all the Disneyland mansions?"

"Yeah."

"So that's where you live, Mr. Peter Katz?"

"No, not really," he said. "It's where my dad lives. I just visit there. I live outside Philadelphia with my mom. They got divorced a long time ago."

"Well, isn't that true for just about everyone? The parents all divorced and at war with each other."

"My parents were okay for a long time. They split up when I was eight. My mom's been remarried for like three years. They used to be polite with each other and I'd just go back and forth for visits." He took a deep breath and stared hard, bringing his face right up to the screen. "But now it's awful, Tanya. Just freakin' awful. My father, he's trying to take over the company that my mom is CEO of. And my mom says her company will never sell to him. They're, like, fighting on TV. And last night, some guy tried to run her off the road when she was driving home from the office. Like, really kill her, and she did this driving maneuver that let her do a one-eighty and escape, and now she's got bodyguards. It's just too weird. And in July, somebody put poison in some Acordinol pills. That's this medicine my mom's company makes."

"Oh, yes," she said, listening intently. "Those little yellow headache pills. I take them for menstrual cramps too. I think I read about those poisonings. Just horrible."

Peter spoke faster and faster as he got more agitated. "Well, my mom got me this summer job at the factory that makes Acordinol. And this crazy woman confessed to the whole world that she put the poison in the pills on July 9. Killed herself and everything. Creeped me out 'cause I was, like, there that day. But I don't remember anything special. Anyway, I know about the security tapes they keep of the factory 'cause I used to eat lunch with the IT guys in the cafeteria. They were fun to talk to about computers." He ran out of breath.

"Tanya," he said, inhaling urgently, "I have to tell somebody about this weird shit I uncovered kind of illegally. Well, not really illegally, but it's kinda like I shouldn't have done it, but I did it, and then I found out this thing that . . ."

"Slow down, lad," she said. Her mind was racing to process it all. "What on earth are you talking about?"

"The other night, I sort of stole my mom's password to

get into her company's computer network. Well, I mean I did steal it. I was curious about the security tapes for that day. I don't know why, I just was. And I checked and double-checked because I didn't believe what I saw. It showed me there at the factory on July 9 wearing a T-shirt I stopped wearing on July 6! Tanya, somebody *faked* the security tapes and the police didn't even know it! But I figured it out. But the problem is that I was using my mom's identity and she's the freakin' CEO! That's like illegal or something. So I hijacked some guy's email in a Starbucks and sent them a message anonymously, telling them to check the tapes."

"Peter, Peter," she said, "I'm not sure I'm following you. Are you one of those computer hacker chaps?"

"No, I mean, yes, but not like that," he sputtered. "Well, sometimes, like, I can't help myself. I'm pretty good with computers. But just for fun, not to hurt anybody. I'm not exactly sure what I found, but I'm pretty sure there's some kind of cover-up about the poisoned pills in my mom's pharmaceutical company. It's the pharmaceutical company my dad is trying to take over. And I know something. But I don't know what it really means and . . ."

When he said "pharmaceutical company" for the second time, the thought hit her. Suddenly, there was an explosion of connections in Tanya's mind. Yes, her last tea with Viktor—the female orgasm drug, the American pharmaceutical company he needed to take over to complete the formula, how happy he was that the stock price had gone down, the secrecy of it all, how he made her repeat his adage about making your own luck. "Peter," she cried, raising her hand to the screen. "Stop right there!"

"Huh?"

"Peter, I think your father and my father are somehow in this deal together. And it sounds like *somebody* had people poisoned to drive the stock price down. And what you discovered, as you say, is probably the cover-up. Which is precisely the kind of thing Viktor could arrange. With the likes of Tom Hardacre doing the dirty work."

"Y-y-yes, b-b-but," he stammered, "m-m-my father would never do that." He shook his head emphatically. Tanya thought she could see tears. "Not my dad."

"Well, dear boy," Tanya said, "you had better believe it of *my* father. He has no problem murdering people who get in his way of his. Beautiful, helpless little people . . . precious little," her lips trembled again, "babies." Tanya blew her nose loudly. *There now, composure regained.* "Peter, tell me again about this . . ." She pronounced each syllable slowly and carefully. ". . . This American phar-ma-ceu-ti-cal company."

"Okay," he said, catching his breath. "It's called Percival & Baxter. My grandfather worked there and my mom does too. She became chief executive a couple of months ago when the old CEO took the first poisoned pill. And now m-m-my father's company, Anglia, is trying to, like, take it over. They're making a tender offer."

"What on earth is a tender offer?"

"When the shareholders get an offer to sell all their shares."

"Viktor has killed for lesser things," she said bitterly. "He talked about needing an American drug company's technology to get a female orgasm drug to market. This must be the company he was talking about."

"I-I-I don't know." He shook his head. "My dad would never have people murdered. And he would *never* have a guy try to kill my mom!"

"Well, *my* father would," she affirmed. "In fact, he rather told me so, though not in so many words. 'Make your own luck,' he said. Luck, indeed!" It was all becoming clear to her.

Peter sounded in a panic. "I've got to warn my dad!

Tell him about the poisoning and video and get him to talk to the police. Oh shit, maybe that's not a good idea. I don't know what the fuck to do. Uh, Tanya, what are you going to do about your father?"

Tanya stared at the screen. She was thinking, calculating. "Peter, I think I've got it. I think I have an idea. A plan perhaps. Viktor already half-confessed his crime to me. I just need to get him to do it again. If I can get him to do it again with the authorities listening, they would lock him up and throw away the key. But I need time to figure it out."

She had a moment of panic. What was she dreaming about? Viktor had wanted her baby dead. And in the next minute, he just had the child ripped from her womb. Viktor had life-and-death power over everyone around him. And he used it anyway he chose! How was she going to go up against him? How?

"Uh, Peter, just please give me a chance to plot a little."

She was grasping for bits of confidence with which to convince herself.

"Let me see, it must be in my genes. After all, I'm Viktor's daughter."

She was stalling for time, racking her brain. Yes, she must have abilities she inherited from him that she could use to turn the tables on the monster himself. She had vowed revenge, even if it meant her own ruin. She had to make this work. She absolutely had to make this work, even if it became the last thing she ever did. And yes, this boy could help. He had just told her how. The pieces began to come together.

"And you, Peter Katz, the wily and intrepid Katman, you will help me."

"I will?"

"You said you are a master at your video games, aren't you?"

"Yeah, but they're . . . like . . . *games.*"

"Think of this as a game. And you say you are a computer wizard, which means you must be a wizard on the Internet. Right?"

"Well, uh. . . ." He sounded hesitant. Why was he hesitating? She was about to bark at him, but she held back.

"Yeah, sure," he said after too long a pause, "I'm pretty good."

She breathed a sigh of relief. "Then, Peter Katz, you are going to be my Jedi Knight in shining armor and help me slay the alien invader and rescue our spaceship from the forces of evil." She hoped a display of confidence could conquer their fears. "You *can* do it, can't you?"

"Geez, I don't know. You're talking about real killers. And grown-ups with guns and money and power. Tanya," he pleaded, "I'm a kid in freakin' high school!"

"Peter, you are *not* a boy. Not anymore. You are a man. *My* man."

"Uh . . . uh . . . I don't . . . know. I don't have my driver's license yet."

Tanya brushed away his hesitancy. "I just know we can figure out how to capture my father in his dirty, murderous lies. And maybe we can also prove your dad's innocence. We'll have to prove that Viktor used him the way he uses everyone. We can do it, Peter, we can!" She was hoping against hope, fighting against her own fear and despair.

Peter held his head in his hands and groaned.

Tanya jumped up with a new realization. "His mates!" she cried. "His mates!"

"Huh?" Peter asked.

"Viktor's cronies. I've seen them. The ones who get drunk and watch *Scarface* with him and howl and fart together!"

"Huh?" Peter was confused.

"Never mind." She was remembering that night in Viktor's mansion in Moscow, when she listened in on Sergei's death sentence. "I know some of their names, where they live, and what businesses they run. Peter," she said urgently, "you really are an Internet genius, aren't you?"

He nodded with a look that Tanya read as skepticism.

"I'm going to give you a list of Russian names," she said in a tone that she hoped would give the boy confidence. "Names of Viktor's mates. If I give you those leads, can you dig up everything there is to know about them and their possible connections to my awful father?"

"Yeah, well, I guess so," he said. "There are lots of search engines. I can find out what's been written about them."

"No!" she snapped, "not good enough. We'll just find articles and blog posts and whatnot. I can do that myself! It's their criminal records we need and what the police have investigated about them. Can't you hack into Interpol and the FBI and Scotland Yard and all that?"

"Uh, no," he said, "you can't hack your way into those databases. No one can. At least I can't, not all by myself. No, Tanya, I can't do it."

"What do you mean, no? Peter, I need you to do this! *We* need you to do this!"

"Uh, I'll have to think about it."

"Criminals, Peter," Tanya insisted, "*we* need you think about criminals and where the dirt on them is kept. Think hard!"

"Okay, okay, I'll think about it."

"That's a good lad," she said, jotting down a note on paper as if he had already cracked that code. "With what you dig up, plus what you supply me on the poison pills and the deal for the pharmaceutical company . . ." She looked up from her notepad. "You *will* supply me a complete dossier on that, right?" Her mind was working now, her reason finally outshouting her fear.

"Yeah, sure," he said.

"Excellent! Soon as you deliver all that, I can work on connecting it all to Viktor. That is what they say, isn't it? Connecting the dots?'

"Yeah, sure, I'll figure something out. But my dad," he said, his lower lip trembling, "he's innocent, I just know it. I'm telling you, he's *not* one of those guys." He buried his head in his hands again.

Oh, poor lad, she thought. She remembered the way Josh Katz had treated her that night in the dark as she assaulted him with her anger at her father and her raging teenage sexuality. He was kind and firm, handling her with the chaste touch of a good parent, like the kind of father she always wished she'd had. No, she told herself, Josh Katz must be an innocent tool of Viktor's. She and Peter would join forces to prove *her* father's guilt and *his* father's innocence.

"Peter, sit up," she commanded.

He did so.

"Now listen to me. We can do anything we set our minds to."

"We can?" he said.

"We're Kroesus Kids!"

She smiled at him.

He smiled back. He looked a bit more confident, Tanya hoped. "Peter, we have resources and the connections ordinary people cannot even imagine. Our lives are charmed in that way. We were born with direct access to the people in power. It's all terribly unfair, but there it is. People like us can get to the important and powerful, the people who pull all the levers. To us, they are just a phone call or two away." She knew she was hiding her fear of Viktor, hoping to make her courage—and his—real with her bluster. It was the only chance she had.

She leaned into the screen and lowered her voice to an

urgent whisper. "We must help each other, Peter Katz, we simply *must*. We must succeed. We absolutely must. For Alexandra's sake."

He looked confused again. "Who's Alexandra?"

"Our baby girl."

55

Emma found her mother, as usual, in the garden. She was planting daffodil bulbs for next spring. "They're the very first to bloom," she said as she stood up to give Emma a hug. "Sometimes they come up right through the snow."

"Symbols of hope, I guess," Emma said. She felt tired, but hoped it did not show.

"I suppose," Diane said as she brushed the dirt off the seat of her jeans and put her gloves in her back pocket. "They're also extremely poisonous. Did you know that a good Roman soldier always carried a daffodil bulb in his kit? If he got captured, he was supposed to eat it and die with honor."

Emma forced a little laugh. "Thanks for the cheerful thought."

Diane put her hand up to Emma's cheek. "What's wrong, sweetie? You look exhausted."

Emma stepped back. "Do I really look *that* bad?"

"No, of course not. You look fine to everybody else. But I can tell when something is wrong. What is it? You want to go into the house and talk?"

Emma looked around her mother's modest yard. A light breeze rustled through the leaves, making them shimmer in the golden light of early autumn. "Nah," she said, "it's so nice out here."

"Okay, let's go sit on the bench under the big old maple."

"The bench that Dad built."

Diane nodded.

"I still miss him," Emma said. She took hold of her mother's hand as they sat down.

"I think about him every day. We were supposed to retire and get old and wrinkled together." She smiled at Emma. "I still talk to him, you know, out loud. Not in the supermarket, mind you, where people can hear me. "

"I think about him too," Emma said. She gave her mother's hand a squeeze. "I think about him a lot, what with everything that's been going on at P&B. I know what he would want me to do. And I do it. Sometimes I can almost feel him there in the building. He gives me strength."

"He'd be happy to hear that. And I know he'd be so proud of you."

They sat for a long moment, just holding hands, listening to the breeze and feeling the sunshine.

Diane broke the silence. "Okay, now tell me what's bothering you."

Emma sighed. "I-I-I don't know where to begin."

"Let me help," Diane said. "You are the embattled chief executive of a ten-billion-dollar company. You are in the middle of a life-or-death takeover war. No, it's worse than that. Pardon my French, but what you're in the middle of is one hell of a shit storm—what with poisoned pills and all. You have no nights and no weekends. You have conference rooms full of bankers, lawyers, and proxy servers harassing you around the clock. This war and the rebates are costing your company billions. It could bankrupt P&B. Twenty thousand employees are chewing their fingernails, hoping you can save their jobs. You have presentations to make to your big investors, to the proxy advisory boards, to God-knows-who-else—all to try to save your company against all odds. The vote at the annual meeting is coming. The clock is ticking."

Diane took Emma's chin in her hand and touched her cheek tenderly. She smiled as she looked into Emma's eyes. "So, tell me. What the *hell* are you doing talking to an old lady who has nothing better to occupy herself than planting daffodils?"

Emma felt little tears welling up. "I need to talk to someone who understands. But I can't break confidentiality." She felt a single tear rolling down her cheek.

"Well, you've come to the right place, honey. I don't talk to anybody but your father. And *he* would never violate the company's confidentiality policy. So I'm as good as being under your—what do they call those legal things?"

Emma sniffled as she smiled. "NDAs."

"Oh yes, I remember your father talking about those. Nondisclosure agreements. Emma, you can talk to me, honey. I won't tell a soul, I promise. Just Dad." She lifted up Emma's chin. "Okay?"

"Okay, Mom. Thanks." Emma sniffed back the last of the tears. She felt relieved. "It's about Josh . . ."

"That son of a bitch," Diane muttered.

"Yes, he is," Emma said. "But remember what you told me?"

"Sure, that you know the son of a bitch better than he knows himself."

Emma nodded. "Well, since the takeover threat first appeared, our defense team has been working with a private investigation firm."

"Sure, honey," Diane said, "I remember when that Swiss pharma made a run at P&B. Your father said they hired Kroll Associates to dig up any dirt they could find on the raiding company and their executives. Just the same way the raider was trying to dig up dirt on the execs at P&B. It's a dirty business all around, as I recall."

"Yes, well, our guys say they are very close to getting hard evidence that Anglia is a front for a Russian criminal syndicate. That Josh is their front man. They say that if they can get the evidence they need and connect the dots before the annual meeting, they could shut down the tender offer and bring criminal charges against Josh. He could go to jail."

Diane folded her arms across her chest. "Well, it serves him right."

"But Mom, even though he's been an awful bastard—"

Diane interrupted her. "No, worse."

"A rotten, no-good bastard."

"Better," Diane said, "but not good enough."

Emma took a deep breath. "He's been a rotten, miserable, no-good fucking bastard."

"Atta girl!" Diane said with a little smile, "Say it again."

"Rotten, miserable, no-good fucking bastard!"

"Good. Sometimes I can't believe how polite you are. I suppose I'm to blame. If that's true, your mother apologizes from the bottom of her heart. Honey, forget what you think your mother taught you. You've got to let fly more often. You'll live longer, I promise. A fucking bastard is a fucking bastard. There's no prize for sugarcoating the truth."

"Well," Emma said, "Josh certainly has been a fucking bastard."

"And then some," Diane added.

"But here's the thing, Mom. Something tells me that he is not guilty of doing anything criminal. He could go to jail. And it wouldn't be fair. It would devastate Peter. He loves his father. And his father—in his ham-handed, money-crazed way—loves him. He tries to love him, as much as he knows how."

"Well, he's the one who started this. You said so yourself."

"See, Mom, I'm not sure about that. You know it's hard to find out what really goes on in private equity firms like his. That's why they're called private. But our investigators have figured out that Anglia was on the verge of bankruptcy after the market crash. Then suddenly, it was back in business and doing hostile takeovers. They'd bust up companies like Detweiler Industries and Burnett Technologies and auction off the pieces. Our guys have been discovering patterns in those deals and they say they are close to proving that some really bad guys were secretly bankrolling them. There's a maze of all these offshore banking and legal charades that make it hard to discover who's really behind it all. But they say they are close."

"Well, honey, you *do* want to save P&B?"

"Yes, of course I do."

"And you *would* like to see the bad guys get punished?"

"Yes, of course. But I'm beginning to think Josh is not the bad guy. Not bad like that. Mom, when we were facing off on that TV show, he had a chance to obliterate my credibility with Jeanine Holloway's question about the transfer he and Dad arranged for me way back when."

"Yes, I saw that."

"But Mom, he didn't do it. He didn't go there. Someone from P&B tipped off the interviewer, fed her confidential information. I have an idea who the traitor might be, but I can't be sure. Anyway, Josh looked as surprised as I was when she asked the question. I watched his face. He made a conscious decision not to use that against me. That tells me he is not into the hostile takeover all the way. You should see the things he did to the men at Detweiler and Burnett. Vicious, horrible things. Distortions and lies. He stopped at nothing. And he won. But here he stopped. And it wasn't just because of me. He stopped because he knew something wasn't right about this whole thing."

"Honey, but if the guy made his own bed . . ."

"Our guys think they can prove that Josh is the front man for this Russian oligarch who still runs a secret criminal empire. He launders his dirty money and invests it in his legitimate businesses. That would make Josh an accessory to the poisoning murders and to my attempted murder and who knows what else."

"But . . ." Diane tried to interrupt.

"But I don't think Josh would do those things. In fact, I *know* it. He may be greedy, he may be a shit. Yes, he's both. But he is *not* a criminal. He would never poison people. He's a Wall Street guy. He would take people's money, yes, anyway he could. But he would not do them physical harm. That's not Josh."

"So what do you want to do?"

"I'm not sure, Mom. Once criminal indictments come out, it will be too late. So I think I need to confront him in person. Alone. Away from the lawyers and bankers and all that. I think when he finds out, he will do the right thing. He will come forward and come clean. If only for the sake of his son. Peter means the world to him."

"Well then, it's clear what you have to do."

"Really?"

"You just said it yourself. You've got to go meet the bastard in secret. Tell him the score. And give him the chance to redeem himself."

"Thanks, Mom." Emma inhaled deeply and let her shoulders drop. "That's what I needed to hear."

"That's what I'm here for." Diane got up from the bench. "He's still a fucking bastard, you know."

Emma rose, refreshed. "A fucking bastard and then some."

"That's my girl," Diane said. "Now, if you'll excuse me, I have to plant some deadly poisonous things in the name of beauty."

56

Peter looked at the list of names Tanya had given him. Her father's apparatchiks. She had other notes attached to each man—protection rackets, arms dealing, illicit nuclear materials. It was all scary shit, Peter thought. She said those were just her suspicions. But maybe Peter could use them to search for more specific proof of their criminal activities.

He had no idea where to begin. He was supposed to come up with the dirt on these guys so that Tanya could serve it up to the British cops. He felt like an idiot doing a Google search. I mean, what could he turn up that freakin' law-enforcement professionals (who were supposed to be hunting these guys down with wiretaps and search warrants) couldn't do themselves?

She thought he must have some kind of secret decoder ring for the Internet. Yes, he could hack into the odd website and make a little trouble, the way he had tried to uncover the identity of Tsarina Alexandra. But basically, he had no idea what to do other than use search engines. He typed in "Dimitri Chervonenko + Novograd." He got a few pages of nothing. Then for laughs, he added "criminal" to the string. No, he did not get a big flashing link that screamed, "Here is the inside dope on Dimitri Chervonenko, the crime boss of Novograd." But on the right side of the page, he saw what could be what he was actually looking for. In the online ads. The ads that the computer served up to match the relevance of the terms he was searching.

"They are his associates, his employees," he remembered Tanya saying, "he's their bloody *boss,* Peter!" The word "boss" reverberated in his memory. That's why the ads cried out to him. They were ads for criminal background check services. Employers everywhere do background checks on potential hires. He knew they even did one on him at P&B when he applied for his summer job, even though his grandfather and mother were longtime employees.

He did a search for "criminal background checks + international" and got a list of firms and their websites. He selected what appeared to be the top ones, then did some searching for references and reviews on them. He referenced and cross-referenced and found that one firm seemed to have the best track record and references of all. Its name struck him as kind of "duh," but then, why not? The *numero uno* guys in international criminal background checks turned out to be International Criminal Background Checks, Inc.—ICBC. Their website said they were proud to serve the US Departments of Defense and Homeland Security, the governments of most NATO nations, including the United Kingdom, where they worked for this thing called the Serious Organised Crime Agency, SOCA. There was also a link for a list of the global corporations they were proud to call their clients.

Bingo! He started checking out ICBC's services. He read through the corporate mumbo jumbo and saw that this company could dig up the deepest, darkest dirt on just about anybody anywhere, who had ever been caught doing anything wrong.

When he went to the "Get Started" page, he saw that

he would need a corporate identity to do business with them. He knew he could fake some stuff—an email identity, maybe even a fake company name. He had the American Express Centurion Card his dad got him so he could join Kroesus Kids for five thousand dollars. Well, strictly speaking, his trust fund had the card, but he could use it for an approved purchase if he got the trust officer at the J.P. Morgan private bank to cosign with his mother or father . . . oh fuck . . . and then ICBC might search his faked credentials and maybe have him arrested and . . . oh fuck!

He felt stymied. Why was he still a kid with no freakin' rights?

He looked at the ICBC website with longing. He felt that he could get Tanya what she needed here. And together, they could somehow put away her evil father, save his mother, and prove his father's innocence. But how would he get them to accept him as a customer? Sorry, kid. You want to track down some deadly international criminals? How about if you start by being able to vote and holding a grown-up driver's license?

He moused over the home page of ICBC, feeling like an Internet stalker. Then one link lit up and underlined itself. He clicked on it. ICBC Corporate Clients. He scrolled down the list, starting with Alcoa. Then he saw it! Percival & Baxter.

Bingo again!

Now he knew what to do. Tonight, after Mom went to bed, he would get on the P&B system again. He knew from his internship that there was a whole section devoted to human resources. He had been bored to death by it the previous summer. But now he could cruise the HR site and find out where and how they did background checks for hiring around the world. It shouldn't be that hard. If ICBC really worked for P&B (and being in the truth business, they wouldn't lie about it), there ought to be a place for people who do hiring to order background checks through the account P&B had with ICBC. He would submit the names for some imaginary hire in, like, Russia. And he would create a folder where ICBC could deliver their background check results. Then he would copy them and share with Tanya. ICBC promised very fast ASAP service on all queries.

He decided he had a plan now. And more secrets. But that made him more grown-up, didn't it? Okay, he was going to tell more lies. They weren't any worse than the lies he had already told. Just repeats, sort of. Okay, a few new ones. He had to do it. He was beginning to think the lies would help him and Tanya find out the truth.

57

"Peter! Peter!"

That's what he thought he heard his mother saying. That and the sound of distant knocking on his bedroom door. The sounds were like a rhythm track underneath the new Green album that screamed inside his headphones. He was lost in searches about Viktor's apparatchiks, the general searches, not the one he knew would most likely turn up pay dirt. He was waiting for everyone to go to bed so he could go down to his mom's laptop, sign on as her, and get to his real work using Percival & Baxter's account with ICBC.

He lifted a headphone off one ear. Yes, it was Mom right there, banging away. He panicked. Oh shit! Quickly, he minimized his search screens and maximized *Invitation to Death,* his new favorite online war game. He yanked off his headphones, jumped up from his desk, and opened his door.

"What's up, Mom?" he said, trying *not* to act like he was trying to act all innocent and surprised. He could see that on yet another Saturday, she had come from the office. Even though it was the weekend, she was not dressed in business casual. She was wearing one of the white silk blouses she favored and the skirt from one of her dark blue suits; this one had black piping on the hem. She was in her stocking feet. She never wore shoes inside the house.

"You finished your homework?" she asked.

"Yeah, like, hours ago. No prob." He thought she was starting to look shorter. Or maybe it was him getting taller.

"Are you winning?" she asked.

"At what?" he replied without thinking. Then he panicked. She meant the video game, dummy! "Nah, not tonight, Mom . . . uh, my reflexes are a little off."

"Can I show you something on my laptop?"

"Sure, Mom," he said. This was going to be weird, he thought. We are about to go look at her laptop together. And later, he would break in and borrow her identity again and do stuff that he had to do but wasn't supposed to do.

He followed her downstairs to the den. The laptop was open on the desk but not on. The security token was beside it. The digital numbers on the token blinked every thirty seconds as the code changed. It felt like a weird digital eye blinking at *him*.

She pushed the power button. It began booting up. She turned around to face Peter. "Why don't you turn around while I log on." That's what she usually did in his presence. "No wait, honey," she said. "Why don't you go in the hall for a sec, okay? I know you'd never look at my password. But rules are rules."

"Sure, Mom," he said. He cringed inside. He hoped his voice did not give away the guilt he was feeling. *No, Mom, I would* never *look at your password.*

He stepped out. Mom and her desk were out of view. He thought of that night when he'd cribbed her password over her shoulder. He realized now that she must have been incredibly exhausted that night to have let him sit there while she logged in. He waited, listening for the faint sound of her fingers tapping the keys. Then he had another panic. What if her password had changed? He knew they had protocols built into their system that made everyone change their password . . . was it, like, every ninety days? Or was it more often? How old was her password when he'd cribbed it? What if he couldn't get into her system tonight? What if he couldn't get the info he needed from ICBC? What would it do to Tanya's plan? Oh shit!

"Come on in, sweetie," she said when she had the video cued up. "Come look over my shoulder."

Yeah, right, he thought.

"This is a piece of the security tapes from the plant the day the Acordinol was tampered with," she explained. "The shots were taken over the course of the day labeled 07/09. Look at it and tell me something."

"Okay, Mom." What he wanted to do was to flee. To his room, out into the street. Anywhere, really. He had to pretend he knew nothing. Absolutely nothing.

She clicked the "play" button. The herky-jerky video, taken from the camera in the ceiling, showed Peter and several other workers walking back and forth in the changing room. She clicked "pause" again.

"There, Peter. Look right there." She pointed at the screen. "What do you see?"

He knew this video by heart. He had studied every frame over and over that night. But he could not let on anything about it. He had to play dumb. He had to lie to his mother—again. He told himself it was okay. He had no choice. It was for everyone's good. "I, uh, see me at my job. That's the changing room outside the production floor. That's me, all right." The less he said, the less likely he was to slip up and say the wrong thing.

"Yes, sweetie. But look at what you're wearing. Look at your T-shirt."

"*Grand Theft Auto,*" he said and pressed his lips shut. *Don't say too much*, he told himself. *Don't say anything more than you have to.*

"I remember that T-shirt," she said, "don't you?"

"Uh, yeah."

"But don't you remember when you ruined it? You

wanted to show us you were doing your own laundry the way we asked you to. Ned and I were sitting in the kitchen after dinner. It was earlier that week. *Before* Thursday the ninth. Remember? You walked out of the laundry room holding *that* T-shirt with the big streak all bleached out. You said you were going to retire it to your pajama drawer."

"Oh yeah, I remember." God, he so wanted this moment to be over! He wondered, was it lying when you didn't say anything? He wasn't sure.

"That's what I thought," she said. "I may be living a crazy job, but I still pay attention to my boy." She stood up and turned to him. "This tape is labeled 07/09 but it can't be you on that date. Because in the video, your *Grand Theft Auto* T-shirt hasn't been ruined."

"Uh, that's right." Did he sound lame? Or worse, like he was hiding something? Mom seemed okay to him, like he wasn't doing anything she thought was wrong.

She put her hand on his arm. "Honey, I want to arrange for you to talk to the investigators about your T-shirt. I'm afraid I can't tell you anything more than that. But they need to hear you confirm that that picture is not you on the ninth of July. It must be sometime before then. It's important, okay? Just answer their questions."

"Okay, Mom." She was being normal, he decided. Nothing was up. "Whatever you need."

She sighed. "I'm tired, Peter, really tired." She turned and clicked through the steps to turn off the laptop. "I'm going to bed now. And so should you."

He looked at the security token beside the laptop. The numbers on it blinked and changed. He knew they were not alive and accusing him, but it felt like it. The laptop screen went black. Emma turned off the desk lamp.

"Come upstairs," she said, "and turn off those video games, would you?"

"Sure, Mom," he said as he followed her. He hoped she

would go to sleep quickly. He hoped her password had not changed. He hoped he could get Tanya the information they needed. He was sick of telling lies. But what else could he do?

58

WEDNESDAY, OCTOBER 7

Tanya decided to make her two key phone calls from her bedroom. First, she got comfortable on the padded window seat with the view to Sloane Gardens.

The first number she got from her "call sent" list. "Perrrrrcy! Percy Montifer, it's Tanya," she cooed.

Percy mumbled pleasantly back.

"Percy, I'm so grateful I caught you in an idle moment." As she said it, she conjured up his lackadasical presence and thought, *when does Percy not have an idle moment?* "Oh, how lucky for me," she jabbered on over his mumblings.

She stood up and stared at the bell gable across the street, as if her attention to it would reinforce her enthusiasm.

"Percy," she said urgently, "Percy, I've decided that you and I *do* need to get serious about each other. I'm sorry about . . . well . . . I'm sorry about absolutely everything. I don't know what I was thinking. I've been such a childish, willful, silly girl. But I want you to know that I'm growing up. Really, I have done a lot of thinking. And I think we should have a proper night on the town and be seen by absolutely *everyone*. Go back to the original scene of the crime, as it were, where I first treated you so badly. That's right, the Soho Bar at the Groucho Club. I want to make it all up to you in front of everyone. And I do love their

Rose Petal Bellinis and, if I'm not mistaken, you like the Albemarle Fizz. See? Of course, I remember! Please, let's make a new start. Yes, yes, tonight. At eight. Perfect, see you there. Oh and Percy? What I said about my vagina dentata? No teeth, luv, honest. See you at eight, then."

She rang off. Percy wasn't such a bad sort, really, weak chin and all. He just had that limp, ethereal quality that inspired in her . . . a yawn.

She dialed again. The next number from her directory of actual and current contacts. "Alban! Yes, it's me. Have I caught you at a good time? Are you well? Remember the party I was going to give you and your lovely fiancée? She was such a lovely gi—"

She was not surprised to hear that Alban had broken up with the gap-toothed American beauty, whatever her name was. She wondered what two exes should say to each other under these circumstances, but told herself to get down to the business at hand.

"Listen, Alban, I'm afraid I must cut to the chase, as it were. I have an urgent and very serious favor to ask of you. Matter of life and death, actually. Not for me but some other poor souls, I'm afraid. Alban," she lowered her voice and got very solemn, "Alban, I have to talk to your grandfather in the House of Lords. Now, please. Let me explain. Alban . . . *Alban*, is your grandpapa still a member of the Intelligence and Security Committee? Oh my, how fortunate. So then, uh, he would know the Home Secretary? Ah yes, of course. And the top directors of the SOCA?"

She had done research and discovered the government's Serious Organised Crime Agency, SOCA. They would be the ones to trap Viktor. Alban's grandfather would undoubtedly know the top-ranking officials. "Alban, I need his help. Yes, quite seriously. I need his help catching a truly awful criminal. I can't just ring up SOCA and ask for some operator at the call center, now can I? I need to talk to a top investigator about crimes of international proportions, that's why. It's a terribly serious matter, and it involves my father. I'm afraid I mustn't say anything more to you as it might put *you* in danger. But if you could arrange for me to meet him soon, I could share the matter with him and get his counsel. He's used to carrying around state secrets and whatnot, I'm sure. Please, Alban, can you put me in touch with him? Oh, thank you, thank you! I shall sit here with the phone in my lap and I won't go anywhere 'til I hear from you. Oh, thank you, Alban, thank you very much, indeed!"

She collapsed onto the soft padding in the window seat. Her heart was pounding. What in the bloody hell did she think she was doing? What on earth made her think that she could go up against all-powerful Viktor? She felt her palms turning sweaty. As she wiped her hands upward against her thighs, they came to rest on her tummy. She pressed her hands against the place where her baby should have been. "You're the reason," she said softly to the baby that wasn't there. "You are the reason I *must* go up against Viktor and win."

Later that evening, she sent Peter a chart of all the connections that would lead to Viktor's getting locked up. "Do you see, Peter?" she said to his image on her screen. "See how the arrows go from Alban to his grandfather to SOCA to the trap they will set for us? All the dirt you're digging up on his mates? It's all coming together. You really are an Internet genius. Do you see?"

"Yeah, sort of," Peter said. "I got incredibly lucky that my mom's password hadn't changed. I got into this ICBC company. The names you gave me came back with these, like, long histories of criminal activities."

"Peter," she said, "this is even better than I'd dared

hope for. Perfect, actually." She drew more arrows from the criminal associates to Lord What's-His-Name and SOCA down to Viktor Volkov at the bottom.

"You see, we have already started off lucky," she explained. "Alban's grandfather knows everyone important, everyone we will need. I just have to convince him. I have all of your wonderful research on the poison pills and Percival & Baxter. Together we have tracked Viktor's French pharmaceutical company. And you did wonderful digging on the names of Viktor's filthy associates. It's a very compelling dossier we have assembled. With my memory and your research, it's a map of criminals from Tortola to Riga. The people Lord Chelmsford will contact for me can arrange my undercover sting to trap Viktor into confessing. I've been reading up on this. It doesn't just happen in spy novels, you know. The spy novels get it from real life."

"Can you really do it, Tanya?" Peter asked. "This guy's, like, a big government official."

"I think if I can disarm the skepticism he's bound to have about me, I'll give him a bit of a shock. He's a Trinity boy like Alban, after all, and they never grow up fully. They have a weakness for female dramatics. I think I can bring him around."

She had no idea if what she was saying was even remotely plausible, let alone possible. But she felt that if she could not get Peter to believe in her, she would have no chance with Alban's grandfather.

"I've got to get to work now, luv," she said. "Got to prepare for the performance of my life." She had no idea how she would do it, except that she would begin by creating scripts for herself. Yes, like writing a play.

59

Tanya followed the instructions to come to the Peers Entrance at the House of Lords. She passed through the Gothic doors and found herself in what looked like the entrance to a gentlemen's club—red leather sofas and a stand-up desk with a green-glass–shaded library lamp—attended by an austere man of indeterminate middle age in tailcoat and white bow tie. The Keeper.

"Tanya Volkov to see Lord Chelmsford. I have an appointment."

After consulting his notebook, the Keeper looked up. "Yes, Miss Volkov, Lord Chelmsford is expecting you," he said with great formality. "If you please, up the staircase to the Royal Gallery. Lord Chelmsford takes private meetings at the back of the gallery near the door to the queen's robing room."

She smiled nervously. The Keeper did not smile back.

She had dressed in a classic black-and-white Chanel suit, one that harked back to the suits that made Coco Chanel a legend. She'd completed her take-me-quite-seriously look with black stockings and timeless black Ferragamo pumps with bow and medium heel. And from Prada, a simple black handbag and a laptop briefcase. She had her dossier in a paper file and on the computer in order to deliver her evidence in whichever form Lord Chelmsford might find more convenient.

She signed in and was shown to the security checkpoint, smaller but not much different from the ones at airports. She got her photographic visitor's badge, had her bags sent through the moving belt to be scanned, and walked through the personnel scanner.

Here I am, she thought, *in the inner sanctum of the British class system.*

Beyond was the sweeping staircase leading to the main floor of the House and the grand chambers around it. She could not help thinking of Viktor's bitter observation that the ruling classes were the criminals who had won. He called them hypocrites and she knew he was right. She wondered why she thought she could seek justice from them. *Because,* she told herself, *you have no one else. For better or worse, these people are your only hope.*

She walked through the grandeur of this great Gothic wonderland, where every inch of wall, ceiling, and cornice was richly decorated.

The Royal Gallery was an immense room. Chilly even on a warm day like this. Around the perimeter were tables and chairs, where peers were meeting and talking with visitors. Above loomed gigantic battle paintings, nearly fifty feet long—Trafalgar and Waterloo. Many dead bodies. *Was it glory,* Tanya wondered, *or just gore?* There, at the far end, were clusters of red leather sofas with low tables before them, all very separate from each other. Two men sat waiting by themselves, one white-haired and elderly, the other gray and sixtyish.

She approached cautiously. "Lord Chelmsford?"

The two men stood.

"Yes, Miss Volkov," said the gray man, "Lord Chelmsford has been expecting you. I'm Mr. Braithwaite, his assistant. Please sit down."

She was clutched with fear. She hoped it did not show

too much. She sat and smoothed her skirt over her knees several times, a nervous habit. "Thank you so very much for seeing me, Lord Chelmsford," she said. "And Mr. Braithwaite. Thank you very much, indeed."

She hoped she sounded humble and grateful. Because she was.

Lord Chelmsford nodded graciously and said nothing. She could see traces of Alban in the ancient aristocrat—the straight blond hair gone to thinning white, the high cheekbones and jutting chin, the haughty eyes. And the mouth; oh, the mouth. It was the mouth of an ancient miser, cruel and withholding. The thin lips had almost vanished. The withered slit was like an old prune with a nasty gash cut into it. Sitting before this preview of Alban in sixty years, Tanya felt lucky not to be spending the rest of her life with her former Trinity beau. She looked into the old man's eyes. She saw nothing. Just a blank wall of cold reserve. He folded his arms across his chest. Mr. Braithwaite pretended to smile.

"Uh, Alban and I used to . . ." she said, attempting familiar charm.

"Yes, I know," the lord said curtly.

She smiled. "At Trinity where you were as well, if I am not . . ."

"Yes, I was at Trinity. We've been Trinity for centuries. And Eton." Lord Chelmsford did not smile back. He clenched his jaw tighter.

So much for old school ties. She fidgeted in her chair. She had anticipated difficulties. She had rehearsed different strategies before the mirror, even wearing her full outfit, talking out loud to the imagined lord. She had not anticipated the Braithwaite chap. She supposed he was there to do the dirty work; or more likely, *all* the work, given the way the class system worked.

She decided to try the direct approach she had practiced. "Do you know who my father is?" She swallowed hard on the word "father." She felt that empty cramp in her womb again, as if her phantom baby were beckoning her, trying to ask her what had happened, and why she wasn't still growing inside her. She often got this cramp when she said or thought the word "father" or, worse still, "Viktor."

"Yes, certainly," Lord Chelmsford said. "Alban told me all about your unusual request. Naturally, Mr. Braithwaite and my staff have prepared a rather detailed background file for me. Most of it merely repeats what I already knew firsthand. Your father is a noted investor with large estates in Britain. I happen to have met him at several social events. I must say, I admire his energy and drive." Lord Chelmsford unfolded his arms and started drumming the fingers of his right hand on his thigh. Slowly and softly. *Enough to be noticed,* Tanya thought, *but not enough to be overtly rude.*

Suddenly, her mind went blank. All the approaches she had carefully rehearsed vanished. She could remember not one word of the dialog she had labored over for this meeting.

Panic set in.

She could feel herself sweating—her hands, her armpits, her feet, her forehead. She looked at her left foot tapping nervously out of her control, as if it were someone else's left foot. Suddenly, she was remembering cries and whimpers of the Sergei chap she'd heard Viktor condemn to painful death for his betrayal. *Her* betrayal, this pathetic attempt at betrayal she was about to botch, would be far worse than poor Sergei's. How much more awful would *her* punishment be?

Her mouth went dry. She had no idea what, if anything, might come out if she tried to speak. She blurted a sound that was supposed to be the pronoun "I" but it sounded like an odd squeak. She licked her lips, took a deep breath and started again, having no idea what she was about to say.

"I, uh, I can prove that he has committed serious crimes and I'm prepared to become an informant for Her Majesty's government. I'm prepared, eager actually, to get a confession out of him so that he can be brought to justice."

There.

She'd said it.

She said it badly, but she said what she had come to say.

"My dear young lady," the lord said quietly, "I happen to know several people who have invested with your father at Guardian. They tell me they have done very well indeed. I assure you, the people I know do not invest with criminals."

She leaned forward. Utterly off script now, she felt certain she would get sent packing any minute. So now she had nothing to lose. No doubt, he'd call Viktor and tell him about this interview as soon as she left. And Viktor would plan his revenge. He would make her pay so badly she'd welcome her own death. Yes, that's what he would do.

Feeling terror and dejection, she spilled out words in between gasps that held back tears. "I know what you're thinking. You're thinking I'm a silly girl. One of the girls Alban bedded and cast off. You're thinking, why is she wasting my time? Why did my grandson press me to have this interview? You're thinking, how can I get rid of her? She is a pitiful mess. Incoherent, irrational, quite possibly mentally unbalanced."

She sat back, again pressing her skirt nervously over her knees. "That must be what you are thinking now. Isn't it, Lord Chelmsford?" At least she had kept herself from crying. But barely.

"Why, yes," he said, "I'm afraid so."

Then he did something she recognized. He smiled ever so slightly. It was the same smug little smile she knew from Alban. The smile that came whenever Alban experienced a petty triumph over someone. A triumph he absolutely did not deserve but took as proof of his innate superiority. "I think that's a fair summary," the lord said. The slit in the prune curved upward at both ends.

Like Alban at his worst, he was hateful and supercilious.

Suddenly, she felt more on solid ground. The old man was feeling familiar to her. Maybe he was not so formidable, after all. Maybe she had a chance. Her practiced routines began to come back. She decided to try the Grovel. Alban had always warmed to a good groveling.

"Lord Chelmsford," she pleaded. "I am helpless, I admit it. May I appeal to your magnanimity, your nobility, the privilege and social responsibility of your position? Would you . . . could you possibly . . . arrange . . . with *all* your power and your vast network of intimate connections at the highest levels of government, a way for the proper authorities to help me entrap my father into confessing his horrifying crimes?"

"Young lady," the lord harrumphed, "it sounds like you are trying to settle a personal matter with your father. Family vendetta is not something that Her Majesty's government can address."

Braithwaite nodded. "Indeed."

"Of course, that *is* true." Tanya expected this. She had set it up. She wanted him to know that she was not just being civic-minded. She was personally driven, passionate about going through with this plan. "May I share a very personal matter with you?"

She thought the two men looked horrified at the prospect

of a hysterical young woman sharing God-knows-what. And this was precisely what she wanted. It gave her courage. She hoped she could open up her emotional floodgates wide enough to drown them. She sniffled and choked, feeling her lower lip quiver. "Let me tell you that my father—my father," her voice cracked with real emotion. "My *father*," she paused again to collect herself and swallow a sniffle. "My father had my baby aborted. Ripped from my womb!" Tears, real tears. "Without my consent. Utterly against my will." Pause to reach for handkerchief in handbag. Sniffle. Blow. Refold handkerchief. "He tricked me. Invited me to be his guest for the weekend. At his great house in Kent. He had me doped up." She looked up at the men for a reaction. She could detect none. Nothing. After all those waterworks. Nothing. "He is guilty of murder, as far as I am concerned. *Murder!*" She looked down into her lap to recover her composure and prepare for her next move. She had hoped for a bit of empathy, but no matter.

"Miss Volkov," Braithwaite offered with practiced courtesy, "we are very sorry to hear that. But as I said, I'm afraid this is not a matter for—"

"No, no please, that's not the crime I'm here about." She sniffled one last time and forced a smile. Deep breath. *There now.* She reached into her handbag, deposited the wet handkerchief, and pulled out three bottles of Acordinol. Back on script. Frightened as ever, but back on script. She was sure they saw her hand shaking, but she knew what she planned to do and that gave her a little boost. Just as she had practiced, she placed the bottles on the low table and lined them up in a row. So what if her hand quivered? "I assume you've seen all the publicity about the poisoned Acordinol pills? The poor souls who died in the States? Yes?"

The men nodded.

"I believe it has been established, although not with one hundred percent certainty, that none of the poisoned medicine was imported to Britain. But the manufacturer has posted the tainted lot numbers on its emergency website on the chance that someone who purchased a bottle in America brought it here inadvertently."

She poked at the bottles with her index finger. "One of *these* bottles is from that poisoned lot. One of *these* bottles has deadly pills inside. The deadly lot number ends in 4271." Tanya stared deeply into their eyes with this lie, just the way she had practiced in the mirror, telling her falsehood over and over while training her eyes not to waver. She felt certain she had perfected the steady look of truth. At least she hoped so. "Can you inspect these lot numbers and tell me if you can determine which one has the poison? Please, can you decipher them?"

Braithwaite picked up one bottle and turned it around in his hand. He kept it at the tips of his fingers, as if the bottle itself might be poisonous. He turned the bottle around, at a loss to determine which printed numbers might be the lot number and which numbers meant something else. He handed it to the lord, who did a similar inspection and handed it back to his aide. Braithwaite answered for the two of them. "No, Miss Volkov," he said and put the bottle back beside the others. "This is really not a matter for us to address."

Tanya ignored the brush-off. "Now, suppose you had a headache." She opened the bottles one by one, then spilled a mess of pills onto the desk. She scooped them up and mixed them together in the palm of her hand. Then she offered her hand, first to one man, then the other. "Would *you* take two of these? Would *you*?"

Lord Chelmsford sat back against the red leather sofa

and shook his head ever so slightly. Braithwaite gave a thoughtful *tsk-tsk*.

"Would you like *me* to take two pills to show you? Just two pills at random?" With her other hand, she reached for two pills and brought them up near her mouth.

"No, Miss Volkov," the lord snapped, "please do *not*. Not here, not now."

She stared into his empty blue eyes, this time without the itchiness that telling lies made her feel. "*This* is the crime I'm talking about. My father is about to take over the company that makes these pills so that he can steal a molecule that's in development in one of their laboratories. It will happen in a matter of days. Just a few days from now! He told me so. My father had his thugs put poison in the Acordinol pills to drive down the share price of this company. And it worked. He said this to me. I'm sure I can get him to admit it outright. If you can provide police experts to record his confession secretly we can catch him. We can do it at my house in Chelsea. But we *must* act now. There's a thing called a tender offer. It's an election and it's going to give Viktor the victory he wants in less than a week."

"My dear Miss Volkov." The lord shook his head and sighed.

"It's Yardley-Volkov, m'lord," Tanya insisted. "I'm much more British than Russian. The Yardleys, you know . . ."

"Yes, I know all about the Yardleys." He nodded. A bit less impatiently, it seemed to her.

She sat up straighter. "As a British subject, it horrifies me that we would harbor a criminal like him on our shores. He may have his elegant offices in Canary Wharf and his great houses, but I promise you, behind his façade of respectability, he directs an illicit empire. He has an army of computer hackers, money launderers, extortionists, thugs, and murderers working. Right under our noses. I have seen them, met them at his parties, and heard for myself the way they talk about their evil exploits. I have documentation."

"Young lady," the lord said, "your father is an important investor in companies that are vital to our national interests." He paused before adding, "Miss Yardley-Volkov."

She took that as progress. "His criminal roots are well documented in the media."

He shrugged. "Slander is the stock-in-trade of our tabloid press, I fear."

She leaned forward onto his table. "That's why I'm coming to you and not to them. Evidence is exactly what I can provide, if only you will help me. He is behind the poisoning of these Acordinol pills and a thousand other crimes. He has told me so. He is *this* murderer," she said, touching her belly, "and a murderer many times before that. Behind his respectable British façade, he makes a mockery of everything we hold dear. If you don't believe this, then I will just take two of these pills." Tanya moved the two pills up to her lips this time.

"Please do *not* do that," Braithwaite insisted. He reached across the desk and took her hand firmly in his and pulled it away. She let the pills fall back onto the table.

Braithewaite leaned in to Lord Chelmsford. He cupped one hand over the old man's ear and whispered something.

Braithewaite said, "Miss Volkov, would you give us a moment to consult, please? May I ask you to wait in the Prince's Gallery?"

Tanya rose from the chair. She picked up her handbag but left her laptop case on the floor. Her knees felt wobbly, her ankles weak. Hoping she did not totter, she made the long walk out to the adjoining Prince's Gallery. She took a gigantic breath. Had she done it? Were they calling Viktor right this minute? Was she about to be arrested for impugning "an important investor" who had made the lord's rich friends even richer? She could not sit again. She paced back and forth.

After what seemed like forever, Braithwaite appeared beside her. She had not heard him approach.

"Miss Volkov, please come back," he said and motioned for her to follow him back to the sofa where the lord sat. He motioned for her to sit as he took his place beside his master.

"Miss Volkov," Braithewaite began.

Tanya interrupted him, afraid they were about to dismiss her—or worse. She started to plead, "Please, hear me out, please! Before you make up your minds, please read the dossier I have brought."

"Miss Volkov," Braithwaite said, raising a shushing finger to his mouth, "please."

"Sorry," she said and held her breath.

"Miss Yardley-Volkov," Braithwaite said, enunciating her combined surnames carefully, "we are prepared to examine the dossier you spoke about."

Not quite believing what she knew she heard and still fearful that it might be a trick, she reached into the laptop case at her feet. Inside she carried her MacBook and printouts of the documents she had assembled with Peter—the whole story of the poisonings and the impending takeover of Percival & Baxter, the maps of Viktor's associates and their criminal associations around the world.

With her hand inside the case, she forced herself to speak with all the calm she could summon up. "Do you prefer to see the dossier on paper or on the laptop?"

"Paper, thank you. We are, uh, traditionalists," Braithwaite said. He looked and sounded nervous to her.

"Yes, paper, please," Lord Chelmsford said with a sigh.

"Not the computer," he muttered more to himself than to the room.

If this was a trick, Tanya thought, it was too late for her to save herself. She had tried to go up against a man who always got his way, the one who always had all the power. What a fool she had been! But then, she felt a strange serenity about accepting her awful fate. At least she had tried.

But if this was not a trick, then maybe, just maybe, she *could* bring Viktor to justice.

She grabbed the folder and lifted it out of the laptop bag. "After you've examined these documents, do you think we could get SOCA to take a look?" This was her hope, her fantasy, the impossible dream she had imagined as the perfect outcome. Either that or being thrown to Viktor and tortured to death.

She put the folder on the table and slid it within reach of Lord Chelmsford.

"We have already spoken to the director of SOCA," Braithwaite said, "and he has assigned an investigator to review this immediately."

Tanya started crying softly. Yes, it was possible, just maybe possible, that she could bring Viktor to justice for murdering her precious baby girl.

60

Mike Saltzman was due in Emma's office in a minute or two. In his email, he said he had big news. To Emma, he had finally started to look like the eighty-year-old man he was. *No, lately, even older,* she thought. Gone was the youthful vigor, the visible delight he took in the twists and turns of the takeover war. He just looked tired and old.

Emma knew that she looked beat as well. Ned had been kind enough not to comment on the dark circles under her eyes. And he had made a sweet little joke about the new streaks of gray that seemed to be appearing daily in her hair—something about sexy "older women." But she knew she looked like hell and would continue to until they got to the end of this ordeal. She dared not say it to anyone, but the possibility of losing P&B might come as a relief, if only because it would mean that it would all finally be over.

Saltzman bounded into her office. She had not seen that spring in his step in a couple of months. And he had that fire back in his eyes. With a little flourish, he waved the thick folder in his hand and placed it in front of her.

"Here it is," he said. "We've got the links to the Russian crime network documented. This deal is backed by the biggest protection racket in all of Russia and the former Soviet republics. It took a lot of work to break through all the veils and the maze of money laundering, but we have it. We got our big break from a fellow at J.P. Morgan. One of our bankers on the deal team knew him from their days in the Barclays training program. The Morgan guy started talking about the Anglia takeovers. How the big banks loved being in their syndicates. How Anglia over-collateralized them in return for their participation. They got their high fees but with much lower risk. It gave the Kroll team the lead they needed."

"What do you mean, overcollateralized?" she said.

"It's like lending a mortgage for a house. Your bank puts up two million dollars. But suppose the house is worth five million dollars? They have an extra three million dollars of collateral with only two million dollars at risk. Anglia was generous with the big banks that way because the prestige of having the big banks being involved helped sanitize the deals. Gave them the cover of respectability."

Saltzman went on, "The guy pulling the strings is really the Russian oligarch—a mobster, if you ask me—Viktor Volkov. There are layers to this. He's got a lot to hide. He has been backing the Anglia takeovers. We have this evidence now. With what our investigators have uncovered with the new tip and some code cracking in the offshore banking world, we can shut down Anglia's offer. And where, before, we were just going after Anglia with lawsuits, we can now file complaints and present evidence that will lead to criminal proceedings. It's game over." Saltzman paused and looked at her.

She said nothing. All she felt was fatigue, weariness deep in her bones.

"Emma, I said it's game over for Anglia." He extended his right hand to shake.

She flipped open the corner of the folder, turning the pages inside. "But isn't the FBI still working on who did the poisonings and rigged that woman's suicide, and the doctored tapes?"

Saltzman shook his head yes. "That will come soon enough. In the meantime, just give us the word to go public with what we have and we can shut down the deal. The big banks will run from Anglia like it's radioactive. The tender offer will collapse. And once the feds get through with him, Katz will be toast. I hope he likes wearing orange jumpsuits."

She saw the sparkle in Saltzman's eyes that had been there when she first met him. "Emma," he said, "we've won." He extended his hand farther across the desk.

She stood and took it, clasping her other hand over his and squeezing them.

Yes, there was drama in this moment.

"You saved the company," she said, letting what he said sink in, letting her mind relax a bit from its state of high tension, letting burdens lift from her heart for the first time since that awful day in July. "Mike, you saved the company, you saved P&B." She let go of his hand and sat down. She did not know whether she wanted to laugh or cry. She felt herself breathing hard. It was finally over. "You saved us," she said. "You really saved us."

Saltzman shook his head. "No, Emma, you did. You saved the company. We just gave you the backup you needed."

Relief, exhaustion, exhilaration flooded over her. She fell back into her chair.

Saltzman picked up the folder. "I'm going to go drop this bomb. And end this war." He turned and started walking away.

Suddenly, she felt like something grabbed at her throat. "No, wait, Mike!"

She realized she had no time to feel relief or release. She would have to save the victory celebration for later. She was thinking about the conversation she had had with her mother. The conversation about Josh. Yes, of course she was thrilled that Saltzman had found the evidence they needed to stop the takeover. Yes, P&B was saved. That had been everything. The only thing she cared about doing.

But, she suddenly realized, there was something more.

She was more certain than ever that Josh was not, *could not,* be a criminal. Why did she care about that bastard? She thought it must be for Peter's sake. Yes, he loved his father, with all his faults. He would be devastated. Yes, there was Peter. And even more, there was that goddamn sense of decency of hers. At a time like this, it felt like the worst burden in the world. But there it was, looming over her, demanding that she prevent injustice. Even injustice for the son of a bitch who had caused her so much heartache. Of course, she could say none of this to Mike Saltzman. At least not until she herself had figured out what to do. She needed to stall for time. Just a little bit of time.

"Uh, Mike?" He stopped in the doorway and turned around. He raised his eyebrows in a question.

"Uh, Mike," she said, racing to assemble her thoughts, "before we pull the trigger . . . we, uh . . ." She went for the only delaying tactic that would be credible. Because it would be true. "We have to go to the board with this ASAP. That's why I want everything checked beyond a doubt. Can you have your sources just check it all again one more time? For the board?"

"Emma, every day we get closer to the annual meeting, the vote. It is ten days away. Just ten days."

"That's why we have no time for even the smallest mistake. Please, Mike."

She did not have a plan yet. But she knew she had to do *something* with Josh to let him prove his innocence. Let the bastard get punished for everything he did do, but not for things he didn't do. She had to stall Mike Saltzman. "What's another twenty-four hours at this point?"

He shrugged with what looked like disappointment. "Well, I suppose . . ."

"Give it one more day of extra, redundant due diligence, Mike, just one more day. All right? Then we fire all the ammunition we've got."

"Okay, Emma," he said, "you're the boss."

61

It took Tanya three calls to get through to Viktor. She found him at Wilborne Hall, scene of the crime. She remembered lying in the hospital bed, groggy from anesthesia and heartbroken from her abortion. *His* abortion.

"Papa?" she ventured, "Papa, it's me."

"Yes?" he answered coolly.

"Papa, I have thought about everything." She paused. She sniffled. "Papa, I have thought about everything . . . and I understand why you did what you did." She paused again. She did not want to overplay her hand.

Viktor said nothing.

"I-I-I think we can make a new start. I mean, what I mean is . . . I was wrong and you were right." She took a deep breath loudly into the phone. "There, I said it. Did you hear me? I said *I* was wrong and *you* were right."

"Yes, I hear."

"See, I've made a real effort to clear my mind of girlishness. I understand now what you said about my responsibilities. About *our* responsibilities."

"Is good," Viktor said.

"You should also know that I've changed my mind about Percy Montifer. I'm seeing him again. He's not so bad, actually. In fact, he's rather a dear. Charming in his hopelessly toffish way. I thought you might want to know."

"Really?" he asked, sounding surprised. "I am glad to hear this."

Tanya was fairly certain that Adeline would have already called him with the news.

"Papa, I think I can accept him." She spoke slowly, working at sounding serious and in no way defeated. "Yes, in fact, I know I can. I can accept him as my husband. I just need a little time is all. Papa, I want to make you happy. To make us happy."

She waited for a response, but got none.

"Papa, why don't you come to dinner when you get back to London? We can talk. Come to my house. I promise you a real Russian buffet. All the things you like. No English tea sandwiches, honest. We can talk like father and daughter. Make a new start of it."

She paused. Again he said nothing.

She let her voice catch in her throat. "I'm . . . I'm all alone in the world. You're the only dad I've got. Please, Papa?"

"Tanya," he said with gravity, "you very angry with me last time I see you. Very angry. I understand why. I think you still angry, no?"

"Yes," she said, "but less than before." She exhaled noisily, her emotional exhaustion was real. "Less every day. Really. What matters is the future. *Our* future. That's the lesson you tried to teach me."

"Okay," Viktor said flatly. "I come tomorrow night."

"Perfect," she said softly. "I've hired Orlov, your favorite caterer."

"Orlov is good. I come at eight," he said and hung up.

Tanya gave an immense sigh. She put the phone down on her kitchen table and turned to the man in the ill-fitting suit sitting beside her. "Tomorrow, Inspector Jenkins, at eight. Does that give you and your technicians enough time to install your equipment?"

The fiftyish civil servant with the bald head and fat double chin said, "Yes, certainly. More than enough time."

"And you really can jam his cell phone so he can't receive any calls?"

"Oh yes, we certainly can. We do that as a matter of course. We don't like any surprises or interruptions in these kinds of sessions."

"I'm so grateful to you and SOCA," she said nervously.

"Thank you," Jenkins said, "but we haven't done anything yet."

62

All day, Peter had been thinking about London time, five hours ahead. He checked out pictures of Tanya's street online so he had a mental image of the place. The old brick houses, the Dutch-style gables, the park in Sloane Square, the cars with steering wheels on the wrong side and odd-looking license plates. But he had no way to imagine the action that was supposed to unfold. This could be the biggest day in his life and her life, maybe the most dangerous. Yet he could not tell a soul. This Tanya had him wrapped up in so many freakin' secrets.

He was alone in the house. Mom was at the office, working all weekend again. Ned was in Los Angeles, doing meetings for his upcoming exhibition.

He'd called Tanya on his cell at the time they'd agreed upon. "Hey, Tanya, I'm going to go see my dad later today. I'll get there around nine your time. I'm going to ask him about the poisonings just like we said. He's going to be shocked when I tell him what we know. He's innocent and he's going to say so. He'll have proof, I'm sure. He would *never* be part of killing those people, never. I know he's innocent, Tanya, I just know it."

"I'm sure you're right, Peter," she said, hoping with all her heart that he was. She was almost as determined to get proof of Josh's innocence for Peter as she was to get proof of Viktor's guilt for herself. She feared for Peter's safety. Even more than for her own. He was going to be surrounded by enemies, she would be surrounded by police. "Now be sure to watch out for Tom Hardacre," she cautioned. "He's bad, all bad."

"Yeah, I know. Did I tell you about the time he blew off the head of a raccoon with his pistol?"

"No, and you don't have to tell me now. Just be sure not to say anything in front of him. Not a thing."

He felt a sudden wave of fear wash over him. He had to sit down. Holding the phone at his ear, he fumbled for one of the chairs at the kitchen table. He fell back into it, almost tipping over. His breathing had gone shallow, his breaths coming rapidly. "Uh . . . is your plan all set? Did they . . . uh?"

"Peter, I can't tell you. I'm afraid I can't tell you anything." She ached to tell him everything, but Inspector Jenkins had cautioned her repeatedly and pledged her to absolute secrecy. "It would be dangerous for you if you knew anything. And dangerous for me too. Do you understand?"

"Yeah, I think so." He saw his foot tapping nervously. It felt like it was connected to someone else.

"What if Tom Hardacre gave you the third degree?" she asked. "Put a gun to your head? You'd tell him what you know, you'd have to. But if you don't know anything, you can't tell him anything."

He thought of all the fun he'd once had with Hardacre, playing with computers. It made him shudder. "Gee, I guess you're right."

"Oh, I know I'm right." He heard her sniff back a tear. "Peter, I'm so frightened."

"Me too," he said. His foot stopped tapping.

They shared a long moment of silence, with just the sounds of their breathing.

"Peter?" she said finally.

"Yes, Tanya?"

"We have to go through with this on our own."

"I know." His foot started tapping again.

"I won't call or text you. And you cannot call or text me. If either one of us were to ring up the other at the wrong moment, well, it could blow us both to bloody hell. This is our last call. Until we are both safe again."

"I understand."

"In fact, Peter, as soon as we hang up, you should delete my numbers and contact information from your phone, the one you take to Greenwich."

"You're right. And the call log too." The phone in his hand suddenly felt menacing. "No traces from me to you."

Another pause. Silent fear on both ends.

Again, Tanya broke in first. "Peter, I want you to know that I'm giving you a great big kiss. Mmmmwaaah! Peter," she said softly, "remember the night you made me pregnant?"

Peter gulped. "Uh . . . yes," he said, thinking, *how could I forget?* He remembered everything. Absolutely everything. Sometimes he couldn't stop thinking about that night, playing all the sensations over and over in his head. Remembering how close they were, joined together, how she led him around, teaching and guiding him, but still made him feel like he was leading her.

"You were strong and passionate, Peter."

"I guess so," he said hesitantly.

"You *were,*" she insisted. "You were a real man for me. You're still a man for me." She paused. "Do you understand?"

"Yes, I guess I do." He didn't know what to make of this. It's not like they were about to go steady or get engaged or anything. He would just follow her again.

"We must make a pact, okay?"

"Okay," he said.

"This is our pact. If you feel afraid, you must feel me beside you. I'll be there. And if I feel afraid, I will think of you beside me and feel your strength. We will make each other fearless and strong. Is that a deal?"

"Yes," he said. He liked the deal. Tanya treated him like a man. No one else did. "It's a deal."

She giggled suddenly. "You know, you're lovely and big. I'm talking about your willy. Bigger than most men. You should know that. Do you know that?"

"Well, I guess I do now." Peter felt a smile spreading across his face.

"When all this is over, would you like to come visit me in London? We can shag day and night in every single room of my big house. Would you like that?"

He gulped, "Uh, sure." Suddenly, he had a hard-on straining against the zipper of his jeans.

"Peter, I will keep you inside me. And you must keep me inside you."

"I will," he said and he did feel her presence. It was like a warm glow somewhere near his heart.

"Brave, Peter. We must be brave for each other. Promise?"

"Yes, Tanya, I promise."

There was another silence. Then at the same moment, they clicked off.

63

Peter called the charter helicopter service from the landline in the kitchen. The number was in the speed-dial directory.

"Mid-Atlantic Charters," the woman said.

"Hi, Jennifer, it's Josh Katz's son." Pause. "Peter?"

The operator responded warmly. "Well, hello, Peter, haven't heard from you in a few weeks."

"Yeah, you know, like, school and everything. Say, uh, I know, uh, it's short notice, but can I get a charter to take me to my dad's in Greenwich this afternoon? Uh, it doesn't have to be, like, fancy or anything, like the S-76 he uses."

"Let's see," she said. He heard her clicking at the computer. "Here we go, I've got a Bell 407 that's open this afternoon. We could have it in Philly at three. Will that work?"

"Sure, Jenn, that's great, uh, cool." Peter worked hard at sounding relaxed and casual. Inside he was anything but. "Now, uh, here's the catch. It's for a surprise birthday party for my dad. He's not, like, expecting me. So, uh, we can't tell him that I'm coming, okay? Can you put it on his account but don't bill it 'til, like, day after tomorrow or something? I don't want to spoil the surprise for him."

He figured that with a regular, big-spending client like Josh Katz, the service would be happy to do whatever his son asked for. He just didn't want to sound like an entitled jerk when he asked. Then he clutched inside. He wasn't lying well enough. Nobody arriving in a freakin' helicopter could surprise anybody. "Uh, what I mean is, I've got to get there before he comes in from Manhattan tonight. That's why I gotta get there this afternoon so we can all surprise him." As he was spilling these extra lies, he knew he was telling her too much, but he felt he had to tell her something.

"No problem, we won't spoil your surprise," she said. Jennifer was just a voice on the telephone, but he felt like he knew her, sort of. And that she sort of knew him. "You're a good son. Your dad must be very proud of you."

"Uh, thanks, Jenn," he mumbled, relieved that she had bought it all and asked no questions. "See you guys at three. Thanks again, Jenn."

"Hope your dad enjoys the surprise."

"I hope so too." He felt a chill at the double meaning of their words as they hung up. Peter decided he was getting pretty skillful at lying. He was not sure if this was a good thing. But it seemed to him it could turn out to be an important skill in the world of grown-ups.

He scribbled a note on the kitchen whiteboard—"Gone to Dad's. Took the helicopter. Usual thing. I'll explain later. Love, Peter." This way, with an old-fashioned note on the wall, he did not have to discuss this trip with Mom or Ned or ask permission. He told himself this was not a lie. Just a necessary avoidance of a problem.

He called the cab company they used when neither Mom nor Ned could drive him and got a reservation for a pick up to get him to the heliport by 2:30.

64

Tanya stood in her open front door as Viktor's Rolls pulled up to the curb. She could actually feel the presence of Jenkins and his team, hidden inside. Jenkins had spent a long time with her, explaining everything, especially the last step, the agreed-upon signal that would trigger them to appear and take Viktor away. And that would be only when she had both his specific confession of guilt and his admission that Peter's father was innocent. Jenkins reassured her repeatedly that she was completely safe from harm. Still, she felt afraid. How could she not? Even if he carried no gun, he could still kill her with his bare hands.

Viktor did not wait for the driver to open his door. He bounded out. The bodyguards took up their usual positions, one guarding the sidewalk by Tanya's front door, the other leaving for the mews behind the house. But then, instead of Viktor going up the sidewalk to her front door, he turned back into the car.

Then Tanya felt herself go nearly blind with panic. Adeline Montifer climbed out of the Rolls, holding on to Viktor's outstretched arm. The two were smiling, waving at her.

Tanya ran toward the curb. What the hell should she do? She had to get Adeline to leave and get Viktor inside by himself. This was something that had never even crossed her mind. And it would ruin everything. That woman was about to ruin *everything*!

She'd have to improvise. Somehow. Have to be persuasive and emphatic and be completely cool and composed. She slowed her pace as she neared them. "Well, hullo you two," she said cheerily, "welcome to Sloane Gardens." Tanya felt her smile muscles straining. She prayed it did not show.

Viktor took Adeline's left hand and lifted it in the air.

"Look, Tanya," he said proudly.

Adeline gave Tanya a little smile, then looked down.

The diamond Tanya saw on her third finger was enormous. The square-cut gem's hundreds of facets glittered in its setting. Viktor raised Adeline's hand higher, closer to Tanya's face.

"You see?" he said, beaming, "already you make our family happy." He let go of Adeline's hand. "Tanya, you know Adeline make me happy, very happy."

Tanya felt her throat starting to close up. *No, no,* she thought, fighting her body's panic responses. *A good face, I must put on the good face.* She forced another smile. *There now, if life has taught you anything,* she told herself, *it's how to be false and utterly convincing.*

"Adeline," she said fondly. She leaned in to give the woman a polite, arm's-length hug and an air kiss. The bit of contact helped ground her. She let go and took up Adeline's hand to admire the giant rock. "Why, it's just gorgeous," she said. "Congratulations, you."

"Thank you very much," Adeline said brightly as she turned her hand this way and that, "I do hope you approve."

"Oh, mightily," Tanya said, "heartily, utterly, most completely." For an instant, she feared that her false smile might freeze into place and stay this way forever. She let go of Adeline's hand.

"You could have ring like this too," Viktor said. "From Percy."

Tanya felt her stomach tying itself into a knot.

"Up to you," he added. "You make up own mind. You always do."

"Yes, Papa," she said. What if she were to treat this as a game? She was good at games. And today, she was determined to win. "Papa, you know you have no one to blame but yourself on that score. I take after you in being stubborn and independent." She turned to Adeline. "I fear I am very much my father's daughter." She gave Adeline her best English smile, and got an identical one in return. *No,* she thought, *hers is even better than mine. She's had twenty years more practice at it.*

"Tanya," Viktor said, taking Adeline's hand again, "Adeline will be family for you. Like mother, partway. Like sister, partway."

"Why yes, of course," Tanya said.

Then, in hopes of catching Adeline off guard, she leaned in and gave the woman a firm, full-contact, completely wraparound bear hug. She could feel Adeline stiffen. Then Tanya let go of her, feeling she had scored a point against the opposing team. "Has Percy seen the ring?" she asked with wide-eyed innocence.

"Not yet," Adeline said, "you are the first. Well, outside of the man at Cartier, of course." She smiled again, a bit more warmly, it seemed to Tanya.

Tanya smiled back and decided, *now, it's time to act.* "Adeline, I'm so pleased for you and Daddy. And I'm so looking forward to us getting to know each other, really getting to know each other. But tonight, well, I need a little alone time with Papa. Any other time, I'd be thrilled to have you join us. But, well, I do beg your forgiveness and hope you understand. Please?"

She turned to Viktor. "Daddy, I'm so glad you brought Adeline here, but I feel we do need to talk over a few things, just father and daughter." She turned again to Adeline. "It's just getting our house in order, as it were, for the future." She raised her eyebrows and tried to give Adeline a beseeching look. She felt pretty sure Adeline would cooperate.

"Why, of course, I understand," Adeline said pleasantly.

Tanya took Adeline's two hands in hers. "Thank you so much. I do hope you let me make it up to you soon." She gave a little squeeze and let go.

Adeline said, "Of course, luv." She turned to Viktor. "I'll go back to Belgravia and wait for you there."

Viktor nodded and kissed her on the cheek. He opened the door of the Rolls and said to the driver, "Take Lady Adeline home. I call you."

Tanya kissed Adeline on the cheek, a real kiss. "Thanks awfully, Adeline. We'll talk soon."

"Yes, soon," Adeline said as she folded herself into the backseat.

65

Tanya and Viktor faced each other in her doorway. She wished she could get rid of the anxiety that Adeline's sudden appearance had caused her. She *so* hoped he could not tell how rapidly her heart was still pounding.

She bent down and planted a light kiss on his cheek. "You and Adeline look very happy," she said.

"I want you to see this," he said.

"I'm so glad you brought her," she said warmly, starting to feel that she could actually be convincing with him. "But we do need to have our talk. Just the two of us. Don't you agree?"

He nodded.

She led him into the dining room. "For you, *Papachka,*" she said with a gracious sweep. It was a magnificent Russian feast—stuffed cabbage, blinis, roasted hens, kasha—in elegant chafing dishes, stretching down the long dining table.

She watched him nod in approval.

"Help yourself, Papa." She handed him a large plate. Viktor took heaps of everything. Tanya limited herself to a few ladylike portions. They sat facing each other at the empty end of the table.

"I have wine, if you'd like," Tanya said. "Or vodka on ice?"

Viktor shook his head no. He reached for the crystal water pitcher and poured for himself and Tanya. As he poured, Tanya remembered, he drank water *that* night at Wilborne Hall. *I wonder if he too is remembering that now.*

They ate in silence. Viktor chewed and swallowed with gusto. Tanya picked at her bits, spending her energy moving them around.

Soon, Viktor cleaned his plate and sat back.

She wondered if he'd belch the way he did with his mates. But he did not. She then recalled that he had never belched around Mummy either. Delicately, he put a hand to his mouth, but no sound came out. He then took another drink of water. "So," he said, swirling the ice cubes in his glass, "you want make new start?"

"Yes, Papa, I do. I told you, I have thought and thought about everything. And now I begin to see the wisdom in the things you have done."

"All things I do? *All?*"

"Yes. Yes, all." Tanya did not hide the sadness she felt. It would make her performance more believable. "I can't say I am happy about losing the baby. I am very sad. I think I will always be sad. But everyone has sadness in their lives."

"Yes, everyone have sadness." He nodded. Then he asked, "You not angry? You must be very, very angry. I understand. I am angry too, all my life." He pointed to himself. "Many things make me angry. Even today."

"Yes, I was angry," she said softly, "but every day, it's a little bit less. And the more I think about our fortune and what it means, the less I feel the anger. I know now it will fade in time."

"Everything fade with time."

She could sense he was testing her. But she had prepared herself and rehearsed the possible scenarios. Or so she hoped.

"Tanya," he said, jabbing his right index finger at her, "I *no* ask you to forgive me! Understand?"

Was he trying to trap her? She answered softly, putting

as much resignation into her voice as she could, trying to make him feel that she was submitting to his superior knowledge. "I know, Papa. Forgiveness doesn't matter. I think that is one of the lessons you were trying to teach me. Especially about money." She paused. Sat up straight. A pose of strength to show him she understood. Staring into his eyes, she announced, "Feelings do not matter."

"That is cold thing to say, my daughter."

She could feel him testing her. "Yes, Papa, money is a cold thing. A very cold thing. But isn't that your lesson to me?" She was no longer afraid. If he killed her, so what? She stared at him, determined not to be the first one to blink.

"Yes," he said, "that is lesson I teach." Finally, he looked away.

She knew she could do this. "I have found that cold place inside me." She tapped above her heart. "I am *your* daughter, after all. So I must have it."

He tapped the same spot on his own chest.

Tanya now sensed it was time to switch on the next emotion—wide-eyed admiration. But she had to use restraint or he wouldn't believe it. "*Papatchka,* you once told me how you saved yourself from that bully in the orphanage. I remember. You said you killed him to save your own life. And I'm glad you did. I'm grateful. I feel proud of your courage. It must have been so frightening to be beaten by a boy so much bigger than you."

He nodded.

"What was it like to kill him? What did it feel like?"

"No feeling. He try to kill me, I kill him back. Simple. Sometimes someone has to die, that's all."

"Then killing, it's not always wrong, is it?"

Viktor snickered.

She said, "Like kings and prime ministers, right?"

She knew theirs was the double standard that infuriated him.

"Yes," he softly roared. "I say this many times! Kings, prime ministers, presidents, generals, they kill all the time. You read news every day. They never *stop* killing. And they are heroes. Big shots with medals!"

He was with her, she thought. She felt her confidence building. "I see that now, Papa. It's all lies and hypocrisy. They are just bigger liars and bigger hypocrites, that's all. When the Soviet Union collapsed, you saw opportunity and you seized it. You never told me the whole story, only bits and pieces. Will you tell me now?"

He nodded. She leaned forward to show him she would hang on his every word.

He told her about his street-gang days, fighting his way up the ladder of thieves and swindlers, of muscling into the protection rackets. His narrative rambled a bit.

She listened as if fascinated, occasionally prompting him with the names of associates and places from the lists she and Peter had documented. She felt as if she could feel the recordings being made by the unseen technicians in nearby rooms. And again, she feared that Viktor could too. What if he were suddenly to stop, spring up, and kill her? Any minute, he might do it, pull out a gun and shoot her or pull out a knife and slash her throat. Or grab her head and snap her neck in one violent motion. But however he did it, it would not matter. The men just out of sight would capture his killing on camera and lock him away.

But he kept talking, seemingly lost in memories.

His first big takeover—the steel company, with the kidnapping and extortion of the fleeing former Soviet minister. He laughed about how he had frightened the man and how the official groveled with gratitude when Viktor spared his life. He had even given the man some shares in the new company.

He paused. Took a deep breath.

She felt it was a good moment to change the subject, lest he feel this was an interrogation and not their intimate father-daughter get-together. Viktor, she'd been instructed, had to be made to feel that he was telling his stories voluntarily. And to feel *he* was in control.

"As I told you," she said, breaking in on a comfortable moment of silence, "I have decided I rather like Percy."

"Is good," Viktor said.

"I find the Montifer grandness rather endearing, don't you?" She reached out and gently touched his arm. "It's poignant, actually, when you see how frail their condition has become. We would breathe life into their bloodline. And with the education you have given to me, well, I do know how to be a true British aristocrat, don't you agree?"

He nodded.

"Yes, *Papachka,* I think Percy Montifer probably is the right choice for me. He is definitely suitable. Actually, perfectly fine. I understand now everything you once said, yes, everything. And I'm sure I'll make beautiful babies." She wagged a finger at him. "After all, we do know I'm fertile." Then she panicked. Could he detect the bitterness in her saying this? But she bit down and stayed cool. "Yes, I'll marry him, just the way you wanted."

She stood up and leaned across the table. Put her hands on his shoulders and planted three firm kisses on his cheeks. She patted him before she sat down again. "With my qualities, your fortune, and the Montifer credentials, I'll bet there's nothing *we* can't achieve in Britain, *our* family. That's what you want, isn't it, Papa?" She reached across the table again and took his hand in hers. "It's what you wanted all along. I was too willful to understand what you dreamed. But that's all past."

When Viktor squeezed her hand in return, Tanya was delighted. Even happier when he brought it up to his mouth and kissed it three times. She took their clasped hands and placed them on her tummy. "Yes, your grandsons right here. I can just feel it." She kept his hand against her as if she already had a tiny rugby team in her womb. "And we'll call the first boy Victor after you, would you like that? Victor, Lord Montifer?"

"Maybe," he said. "Maybe." She thought he looked happy with her, happier than she had ever seen.

She let go of his hand. She might just have him hooked now. She cleared her throat. "Uh, Papa, there is one thing. And you said you would help. Dear Percy, well, I fear he may not ever be very exciting in the bedroom. So I was wondering about that orgasm drug you said you were developing. I dare say, when I become Lady Montifer, I'm likely to be one of your best customers. You did offer me orgasm after orgasm, didn't you?"

"Yes," he responded with a smile. "Soon drug be ready, we hope."

"How soon?" Tanya asked, putting a little heat in her voice. "You know, you can't keep us young women waiting forever."

Viktor nodded. "We making progress. Maybe this month we get technology we need, then make laboratory trials, then clinical trials."

"But if you don't have it, how are you going to get it?"

"We buy American company. They don't know this, but their research lab has formula we need. So we sell off rest of assets, make maybe hundred million. But then we make billions giving women orgasms." He smiled.

"Oh, lovely," Tanya cooed, "however do you do it, *Papachka*?" She leaned forward. "I know I've been silly with boys and shopping. But now I'm putting that behind me." She took his hands again. "I want to learn about your business, I really do. So I can tell my sons from their earliest days the story of the empire they will inherit."

She smiled at him and leaned in closer. "Tell me, Papa, how do you take over a big international corporation? It seems like such an impossible and hugely expensive thing. Don't you have to make public offers and negotiate back and forth? I haven't seen a thing in the press about it." She gazed into his eyes. "I've started reading the *Financial Times,* you know. Aren't you proud of me? I haven't seen your name once."

"I have banker in America. Is important nobody should know is me behind deal."

"A banker? Who is he?"

"Called Anglia."

"Ohhh, yes. I do remember reading something about Anglia Partners. Isn't that the Mister Katz, I, uh . . . uh . . . met a few years ago. I'm still embarrassed about that night." She winced, an act she had practiced in front of the mirror. "Really? The same Mr. Katz I . . . , from that night? I do apologize . . . again!"

Viktor waved the thought away. "Yes, is same Katz."

Tanya mirrored her father and also waved Katz away. "And the company with the formula, is it Pomfret & Something, yes?"

Viktor shook his head no. "Percival & Baxter is name of this company."

"Ah yes, but isn't that the company that makes those yellow headache pills, the ones that poisoned those people in America? See? I do keep up with some business news."

Viktor nodded again.

Tanya shook her head. "That's terribly sad about the pills that killed those poor people."

"Yes, is very sad."

"But, as they say, maybe every cloud does have a silver lining. And that did make their stock go down." She pointed downward. "Which made that company a good buy for us?"

Viktor nodded.

Tanya leaned on her elbows, jaw in her hands, eyes wide with admiration. "My *papachka* is not lucky in business, you say. You've told me all along that a strong man makes his own luck. Tell me, Papa, tell me for your grandsons how you make your own luck." She sat back and patted her tummy again. "Tell your boys."

Viktor sat back too. "Yes, I make things happen all over the world."

"Like the poisoned pills?"

Viktor nodded.

Tanya felt a pang. She needed him to admit his guilt in words, not just a gesture. Jenkins had gone over this point five times.

She inhaled, then asked hopefully, casually, "You had your people poison the pills to make the stock go down so then you could buy this company for a good price?" She knew her tone was awed and admiring. And the next line she had practiced more times than she could remember. "You poisoned the pills to make *our* fortune bigger, didn't you?"

"Yes, everything for us. I do this and much more. For us."

"And your banker, Katz," Tanya again asked, making herself sound puzzled and naively curious, "did he help you?"

Viktor waved away Katz yet again. "Katz do nothing, nothing. I use him to front deal is all. I call him smart Jew, but he is stupid."

"That's odd, how could that be?" she asked.

"Ach," Viktor said dismissively, "he know nothing."

"So Katz is stupid," she reiterated. Then added, "And innocent?"

"Yes," Viktor said, "Katz stupid and innocent."

Hoorah! This was the admission Jenkins had insisted

Tanya get in order to help Peter. It had been the last one required before his men could move in. And she had done it. Actually, truly had done it! Now, time to wrap it up. She turned her head to the right and coughed twice into her right fist.

Five agents burst into the room, all with guns raised at Viktor's head. Viktor jumped to his feet, but had nowhere to go.

Tanya gasped at the guns.

"Viktor Volkov," Jenkins spoke crisply as his men frisked and handcuffed Viktor, "on behalf of Her Majesty's government, we are taking you into custody for murder, conspiracy, securities fraud, and other crimes. We have statements on high-definition video and audio. You have the right to remain silent."

He stood quietly as a second set of cuffs were snapped around his ankles and a chain snapped to the handcuffs. The short chain forced him to stoop.

Jenkins said, "Thank you, Miss Volkov. Her Majesty's government thanks you for your cooperation."

Tanya heard the technicians clattering in the background, taking down their equipment. She was staring at Viktor. He stood silent, held in place by the stolid goons with their guns.

She turned back to Jenkins. "It was all my pleasure. And I'm pleased I was able to do my duty as a citizen to capture a murderer. "

Viktor started cursing in Russian. The agents took his arms roughly and began walking him out toward the kitchen door and the mews behind.

Tanya stamped her foot and screamed at Viktor's back. "I will never forgive you! Never!" She was about to shout in Russian. But before she could, she started crying, and she could not speak. She was too exhausted.

She heard doors close, a car start, then another, and another. One by one, the cars drove away. She took a deep breath. Her tears stopped. Viktor was really on his way to jail.

66

Viktor sat in manacled silence in the back of the police car. He was calming himself after his shock and attempting to collect his thoughts. He concentrated on slowing his breathing. He could feel his heart responding, slowing down to a more normal beat.

There now.

He had broken his own golden rule, he thought. He had let his desire for warmth and connection overrule his natural caution. He had fallen victim to his idiotic need, not so much for this wretched daughter, but his need from childhood to fill up the emptiness of the boy with no close family. The need for someone of his own blood to love him.

His dream of a dynasty was dead. This he knew for certain. But maybe, he thought, the lesson here was that, sooner or later, all children disappoint.

But how did I go so wrong tonight?

Then it hit him—*I did not drink.* If he had been drinking like a man, he would never have fallen for this trap.

Yes, Tanya had planned this craftily.

He felt a cold wave of clarity wash over him. He needed to regain his strength and presence of mind. He was still Viktor Viktorovich, father to himself, the man of his own making.

He would find a way out.

He would come back stronger than ever.

He always did.

He just needed time to plan his next move.

He closed his eyes to block out the police car and the events of this dreadful evening.

He willed himself to be somewhere else.

Anywhere that was not here, not now.

His thoughts drifted back to that day at the orphanage when he killed the king bully. The first time he took a life. He was also a Viktor, Big Viktor. The bully had hated Little Viktor because he shared his name.

"Smorchok!" he'd scream as he pummeled Little Viktor. You shriveled little mushroom! *"Nedonosok!"* You pathetic runt! "How can you be Viktor, you nit, you thumbnail, you filthy tadpole? Vitunya the little turd, that's you. Only I am Viktor, you do not deserve to live!"

But on that day, Little Viktor fought back, summoning strength he did not know he had. Using his speed, he knocked the big boy's feet out from under him and brought him crashing to the pavement. He pummeled his head against the curb. Again and again and again. He kept smashing the head, getting vengeance for all the beatings Big Viktor had given him. He pounded that head against the curbstone until the cracking sounds turned to splats. He saw his tormentor's eyes roll backward, heard the gurgle of blood drowning out breath. He felt Big Viktor go limp. In that instant, he saw a living terror turn into dead meat.

At first, he'd panicked. "I did a bad thing, I did a bad thing," he gasped. More fear and guilt and shame than he had ever known. Something dreadful would happen to him because of this. If only he could turn the clock back—just a few seconds. He so wanted to bring Big Viktor back to life. Even let Big Viktor beat him again, if only he would not be dead.

But Big Viktor just lay there.

Little Viktor fell to his knees and began to cry.

Suddenly he felt himself being lifted up. He felt claps on the back and heard his name cheered. The other boys were thanking him, calling him a hero.

He could still see that moment as if it had happened yesterday.

And who was the boy carrying him on his shoulders in triumph? It was Artyom. His only true brother, his only true family, the only one he would ever know.

Tonight, a terrible mistake. *Let the hypocrites call what I have done crimes. But in all my life, all I have ever done is what I had to do. I have done nothing wrong.*

67

Peter stepped out onto the helipad at Ledgemere. He waved to the pilot as the bird whooshed up and clattered away into the sky.

Ordinarily he would have asked to sit in the cockpit with the pilot on the flight to Greenwich. He would have watched his every move and practically flown the aircraft with him. But not this time. This trip, he sat in the back, thinking. And worrying.

As the water views and city panoramas of New York zoomed past below him, he was oblivious. First, he had to figure out how to talk to his dad in complete confidence. The library, his dad's sanctuary, that was the place, he thought. With the doors and windows closed. Then, how to break the story to him in pieces? *Oh shit*, he thought, *how come I never told anyone about the pregnancy? That will be a huge bombshell, and that's before I even get to the stuff that's really scary.*

And then, what do I expect Dad to do? Call the FBI? Call P&B? Call his lawyers? Call them all? Make like a statement on the news? Maybe that too.

It crossed his mind a couple of times that he might be wrong about his father's innocence. But he dismissed that. No way. Un-fucking-thinkable. Once his dad heard what the real deal was, he would know the right thing. His dad was no murderer!

As he neared the big house, his worst fear hit him. Tom

Hardacre walked out of the caretaker's cottage and gave him a big wave. They met about halfway between the cottage and the main house. Tom gave Peter a fond pat on the shoulder.

"Good to see ye, lad," Hardacre said. To Peter, he looked genuinely glad to see him. That was creepier and scarier than if he had acted like the bad guy Peter knew he was. Hardacre was obviously a supertalented liar. "Why the unplanned visit?" he asked. "We would have had Cook prepare all yer favorite foods from scratch." Tom grinned. "Like Doritos and Hot Pockets."

Peter hoped the smile he returned was convincing.

"Seriously, lad, to what do we owe the honor of yer visit?"

He had thought about this. "I need help with my math homework," he said without batting an eyelash.

"Where's yer rucksack?" Tom asked.

Peter had thought of this too. "My homework's online. Dad and I can access it on his computer."

Peter took a step toward his father's mansion.

Hardacre took a step and blocked Peter's way. "No PlayStation? Thought you never went anywhere without yer PS2."

In the stress of leaving and the distraction of his trying to figure out stuff on the helicopter ride, he had not thought of this one. "Uh, broken. The motherboard finally went."

"Well, you've sure got enough extra ones up in the West Wing," Tom said. He motioned toward Peter's suite of rooms on the second floor.

"Guess so," he said. He had an entire closet full of spare video-gaming devices of every kind. All those guilt presents from his dad. His mother and Ned let him keep only one device at home. And when he got in trouble, they would take it away. At Ledgemere, you'd have to call a moving van to put all his games out of reach.

"Ye stayin' for dinner, I assume. Cook's makin' something French that I can ne' pronounce."

"Uh, yeah, sure, of course." The conversation was running out of steam. From what he could tell, Tom was acting pretty normal. Not like he suspected anything. "Uh, Tom, I gotta go see my dad. It's important. Got a test coming up day after tomorrow. Catch ya later, okay?"

Tom shrugged okay and headed back into the cottage. Peter sighed with relief. That wasn't so bad.

He hurried into the mansion by the side door under the big wisteria vines. When he walked into the library, he saw that fat guy, Charles Brody, with his dad. They were standing by the tall windows that looked out over the lawn and the helipad. They must have gone over there to see who arrived.

"Peter," Dad said, "why didn't you call me? I'm always happy to see you. But you know I've got a ball-busting schedule."

Peter had no idea how much business stuff his dad and Brody had to do. They could be another five hours. And he couldn't think of a smooth and casual approach. So he just walked up to his dad and looked at him hard, right in the eyes. "Dad, can I see you alone? Really, it's important."

Dad looked at Brody.

"Dad, *please*."

"Hey, no problem, Josh," Brody said, giving Josh a pat on the back. He reached forward and shook Peter's hand. "Good to see you, Peter. As always." As he turned to leave, he gave Josh the telephone pantomime motion—three fingers curled, thumb and pinky extended like a phone. He mouthed the words "call me."

Peter stood still and silent while Brody made the long walk down the length of the library to the door. In Peter's ears, the noise of Brody's shoes on the hardwood floor seemed like the loudest thing he had ever heard.

When Brody closed the library door, Josh opened his mouth to speak.

Peter raised his hand in alarm. He put one finger over his mouth, then pointed to the closed door of the library. They could still hear Brody's footsteps on the marble floor beyond the library. Peter held his hand up like a crossing guard signaling stop. The clicking sounds of Brody's shoes got fainter and fainter until they disappeared.

Peter lowered his hand.

"Peter!" Dad said with irritation, "what is wrong, kiddo? Can't you see I'm . . ."

Peter raised his stop sign hand again. He whispered, "I have to talk to you in *private*. I have something to tell you. It's about P&B and the poisoned pills."

"Okay," Josh whispered in return. He pointed to the two visitors' chairs in front of the desk. He sat down in one and motioned for Peter to follow.

Peter slid his chair very close to his father. He had the feeling that his dad was not taking him seriously, like he was bothering him with some stupid teenager crisis. He leaned into his father and whispered, "Dad, I have a lot tell you."

Dad nodded okay and leaned in closer.

"Dad, do you know about the anonymous tip Mom's company got? The tip that told them to take another look at the security videos on the day of the poisoning?"

"Yes, Peter," he whispered, matching his son's low volume, "Mom called me. She said they may never know who really poisoned the pills and all the investigations are open again."

"Dad, *I* gave them the anonymous tip. It was me. *I'm* the one who found out that the security tapes had been tampered with. I did. I'm the one and I did it by doing a bad thing. I broke into Mom's computer. I stole her password. I went snooping on the company system under her identity.

She doesn't know it yet. She'll kill me when she finds out." Peter was rushing to spill all of it as fast as he could.

"I looked at the security files and everything. I knew something was wrong because the July 9 video had me wearing my *Grand Theft Auto* T-shirt and I wasn't wearing it on July 9. I ruined it two days before. When P&B took a second look, they discovered that somebody had hacked into the system and switched the video of that day for a few days before. That's when I was wearing *Grand Theft Auto*."

Dad raised a hand to interrupt.

Peter shook his head. He was on a roll. He had to talk faster and faster. He was afraid he would not be able to get it all out. "There's more. It gets worse."

He took a deep breath. "I got Viktor Volkov's daughter pregnant. It was her idea, not mine. We met at that party at Scott McLeod's, remember?"

Dad stared at him. He looked confused.

"I didn't know her name, just her Kroesus Kids avatar, Tsarina Alexandra. But that's who she is. Tanya Volkov. She's, like, twenty-one and she's English, like, way English. I was her sperm donor. I didn't know. Honest. She was going to have a baby girl and raise her all by herself and it was okay 'cause she's so rich and everything. But Viktor didn't want her to have the baby so he drugged her and gave her an abortion and now she's not pregnant anymore. I never told *anyone*. Not Mom, not you, not anybody. Not till right now."

Peter finally took a breath. He could see Dad wanted to say something, but he had to get everything out first. He raised his index finger and charged ahead. "But you see, Tanya found out that one of Viktor's companies in Europe needs some kind of science from P&B for a female orgasm drug and her father had the poison put into those pills to drive down the stock price of P&B so you and he could take it over. But you had no idea, right, Dad? Nobody's supposed to know that you are doing the takeover for Viktor, right? That's a secret, right? But you have to tell me—please tell me—you didn't know about the poison pills, right?"

"No," Dad said, shaking his head. He put a hand on Peter's leg to stop him for a moment. But there was no stopping the rest of the story.

"And Tom Hardacre, he manages Viktor's computer-crime stuff. That's his real job and who he really is. That's why he and I could build computers together, that's why he knows so much. And you are stuck and you don't know the whole story. But I do. And I'm not sure how they did it, but they got into all the computer networks. And maybe they also murdered that woman Loralee and rigged it to look like suicide and posted all those notes under her name. Geez, I know how to do some of that. . . . I mean, I wouldn't do it, but I could hack my way around and do some shit like that, so I'm sure this Viktor or Tom or somebody who works for her father could do it too. And I'm pretty sure the guy who tried to run Mom off the road must also work for them, don't you think?"

Again, Dad raised a hand to try to slow him down. But he rambled ahead. Nothing could stop him now. "But I told Tanya that you are innocent. That this Viktor was just using you as a front. And she says that's just the kind of thing he would do. She hates him now. Really, she does. And I came here because I know you can prove you're innocent. Right, Dad? Right?"

Peter had to stop. He was gasping for breath. He was also crying. Great big tears.

Dad leaned forward and wrapped his arms around him. "That's right, Peter, I didn't know," he whispered as he patted Peter's back. "I didn't know any of this."

He let go and walked to the telephone behind his desk. "I'll call the police," he said in a normal voice. "The FBI, I guess. I don't know who to ask for, but we can find out."

Peter watched him pick up the handset and put it to his ear. He looked down at the console. Peter did too. There were no lights on any of the lines. The computer monitors were all black. "Oh fuck!" Peter cried, realizing the worst, realizing that he had totally screwed up.

The library door opened. Tom Hardacre burst in with Brody behind him. Peter saw a pistol in Hardacre's hand, the one he'd used to blow apart the raccoon. Hardacre was pointing the gun directly at *him*.

"Just stay where ye are," Hardacre said. The smiling charm Peter had seen minutes before was gone. He was acting just like the evil guy Tanya said he was.

"That's right," Brody said. "I'm afraid calling the FBI or anyone else is not in the plan, Josh." He had a handgun too and he pointed it at Dad. To Peter, Brody looked uncomfortable handling it. Still, it was a real gun.

"Put yer cell phones on the desk," Hardacre barked. "Peter, I saw your iPhone in your pocket. Let's have it." Peter took it out and deposited it on his dad's desk.

"I don't have mine on me," Josh said coldly.

"Brody, check him," Hardacre said.

Holding the gun gingerly in his right hand, Brody patted his left hand over Dad's pants pockets. The only thing he found was his wallet. He drew it out and dropped it next to the iPhone.

"You want to steal that, Brody, huh?" Dad asked.

"Nah, that's all right. You can keep it. It makes you taller when you're sitting on it, doesn't it, little man?"

"Let's get moving," Hardacre said. He stepped forward and grabbed Peter roughly and held his head by the chin. "You'll excuse me, *master,*" he said. His breath smelled awful. He pressed the gun barrel against Peter's head. "You'll do exactly as I say," he snarled at Dad, "or I'll put a bullet through yer boy's head."

Dad made a fist.

"Nah-uh-uh, Joshy," Brody said. He thrust his gun in Dad's face and grinned. "I work for Viktor. Tom works for Viktor. And you work for Viktor. Even Emma's best friend inside P&B works for Viktor, even though she doesn't know it. That bitch Linda Farlow. She was my mole, Josh. Emma will have a canary when she finds out it wasn't Upshaw. But what's the difference? They'll all be looking for jobs soon anyway. We can't have you messing up the plans, especially when we are so close to completing the deal. The proxy votes are being counted as we speak. P&B will be toast before you can say miracle cure."

"Now, come with us," Hardacre said as he rubbed the gun harder against Peter's head, "and don't make any trouble." He led them out of the library, back to the kitchen, and down the stairs to the cellar. "If yer wonderin', Josh, I've sent the staff home. You, Mr. Katz, have decided to take one of your surprise getaways to a tropical island, one of those really expensive and exclusive destinations. You left suddenly on that helicopter, in case ye didn't know. That's the official story." He gave a nasty little snort. Peter thought it was the most evil sound he had ever heard.

At the base of the stairs, Peter saw that the safe-room door had been opened. It was totally dark inside. The only light was what spilled in from the hallway. Hardacre and Brody shoved Peter and Dad inside. They stood in the doorway, pistols aimed. Hardacre suddenly shifted his pistol from his right hand to his left. He held the barrel steady, right in line with Peter's head. Peter couldn't see the right hand but he knew that the place where Hardacre was reaching was where the safe-room door's control panel was.

Hardacre would be setting the code to close and lock. Peter heard the mechanism that moved the door rumbling to life.

As the door moved on its tracks across the opening, Hardacre said, "You two will have an unfortunate accident. There'll be no air in here and no escape. All the systems will be shut down, all the alarms are on test, all the power off. And by the time anyone finds ye, ye'll be . . ."

The door slid into place. Then darkness, deeper and blacker than any night Peter had ever known. The locking mechanism went *click, click, click*. Then, dead silence.

68

When Emma saw Peter's note on the whiteboard in the kitchen, she felt shaken, scared even.

Gone to Dad's. Took the helicopter. Usual thing. Explain later. Love, Peter.

First, when did he ever make an effort to let her know his whereabouts beyond "out"? Second, why didn't he use text or email or voice mail? Third, he had not asked permission to go. Which, of course, explained the note on the whiteboard.

She called Peter's cell phone and got voice mail.

Then she called Josh's personal cell. It too went straight to voice mail.

Then she called the landline at Ledgemere. Voice mail there, as well.

Blaring alarms were going off in her head. She went to the speed-dial directory of her home phone, one of the databases meticulously maintained by her "totally digital" son. She scrolled through, found the helicopter charter service, and called.

"Mid-Atlantic Charters," the woman said.

"Hello," Emma tried to sound calm, "this is Emma Conway. I'm the mother of Peter Katz. You know, the boy you ferry back and forth to Greenwich, Connecticut, for his father, Josh?"

"Why, Mrs. Conway," the woman said cheerfully. "Yes, of course."

"Of course *what*?" Emma wanted to scream, but instead said through gritted teeth, "Did, uh, my son Peter just charter a trip to his father's house?"

"Well, uh . . . I, uh . . ." the woman stammered. Emma could not imagine why she would be stonewalling her.

"Excuse me, but I happen to *know* he took a helicopter to Greenwich this afternoon. I just need to confirm that it was with you people. Yours is the only service his father uses, to my knowledge. Now *please,* just tell me where my son is!"

"Gee, I guess you don't know about the surprise. Peter asked me not to tell anyone about the surprise." The woman had a playful tone in her voice that made Emma even angrier.

"What surprise? What on earth are you talking about?" When Emma heard herself shouting at this stranger, she stopped and took a deep breath. "Please, I need to find my son. Immediately."

"Oh, I'm sorry," the woman said. "Your son asked me not to tell anyone about the surprise birthday party for his father later today. He was very sweet about it."

More alarms went off in Emma's head. Josh's birthday was in April, not October. Peter knew that as goddamn well as she did! *What was he lying about? And why?* "But you did take him to Greenwich? Just answer me, please!"

"I'm so sorry," the woman said, sounding even more contrite. "Oh yes, he touched down at the helipad at Ledgemere Farm at . . . ." Emma heard her clicking at the computer keyboard. "It was at 15:51 hours, uh, that's 3:51 PM. Our Bell 407 has since returned to base."

Emma looked out her kitchen window at the bodyguard in his car parked by the entrance to her driveway. He would sit there until his replacement for the night shift arrived. If she took her car anywhere, he would follow her.

And he would insist on accompanying her to wherever she was going. Especially by helicopter. No good. As chief executive, she was not supposed to take a personal meeting with the man trying to take over P&B. Not without the lawyers and investment bankers present. But as the mother of Peter Katz, she *had* to go to Ledgemere right away.

"How quickly can you get me to Greenwich?" she asked urgently. "How soon can you get me there? Please, this is an . . ." She stopped herself before she could say "emergency" or any of the other terrifying thoughts racing through her head.

"You'll want to depart from Penn's Landing? Same as your son?"

"Yes," she snapped, then added with forced politeness, "Yes, thank you, uh, please, yes."

"Well, I can have that same Bell 407 waiting for you in," keyboard keys clicking, "three-quarters of an hour."

"I'll be there, yes!"

"Uh, ma'am," the woman interjected awkwardly, "shall I, uh, put this trip on Mr. Katz's account as well?"

"Yes!" Emma said, her voice rising involuntarily. She stopped herself from screaming, "Yes, goddammit!" at the woman. Collecting herself, she then said calmly, "Yes, thank you for your help."

"I hope the surprise party is a lot of fun," the woman said. "Your son seems like a very nice young man."

"Thank you," Emma said as she hung up.

Next she scrolled to the cab company Peter used when she and Ned were both unavailable.

"Where do want to be picked up?" the dispatcher asked, "at your house as usual?"

She could not have the cab pull up to her front door.

"Uh," she stalled, "I'll be at the corner of Williamson and Youngsford." She would walk through her backyard, through the backyards of two neighbors, and out to the corner. She went upstairs to change out of her business clothes into jeans, sneakers, a jersey top, and a waist pack instead of a purse.

69

Josh stood beside his son in the darkness of the safe room, just touching the boy's arm to know where he was.

Josh tried opening his eyes wider. But this wasn't like waking up in the middle of the night when you could make out gray shapes after your eyes adjust. It was utterly black. Josh wished he had memorized the layout of his own safe room. Even more, he wished he had learned the technology that controlled it. But he did not have a clue. He had never bothered. The safe room was just another trophy. He had to have one because all his competitors had one.

He took Peter by the hand. At least he could *try* to lead his son to safety. "Here, Peter, take a step backwards with me. I'm pretty sure the couch is just behind us."

"Yes, Dad," Peter said softly, "I think you're right."

He felt Peter let go of his hand.

After three tentative steps, Josh felt the couch touch the back of his legs. "Got it," he said and sat down slowly. Peter was already seated. He realized that his son had known all along where the couch was.

This was the blackness of hell Josh had glimpsed when he thought Viktor might have done the poisoning.

Well, I had it coming, he thought.

But now he was taking his boy with him. He was making his son pay for his mistake. How had he fucked up so badly, fucked up absolutely everything?

It was money. The money had fucked him up. Money had made him blind. Money had made him stupid. Goddamn fucking money. He thought money was everything. And now it was nothing.

"Dad?" Peter sounded like he might start to cry.

"Yes?"

"What's going to happen to us?"

"I-I-I don't know." Josh cringed. Normally, he would never have allowed himself to admit such a thing. Josh was proud. Josh was arrogant. He had to be. In the deal business, no one got respect if they didn't flaunt their arrogance. Fuck you, *I* know best, you don't know shit. Arrogance was a skill, an art form. Like a tennis serve or a golf swing. You practiced arrogance to make it part of your essence. In the deal business, you were nobody without swagger.

But when Josh heard the steel door of the safe room slam shut, his arrogance vanished. The elaborate façade that was Josh Katz, Wall Street titan, just evaporated. *Poof.* Gone.

"Dad?" Peter's voice was tremulous.

"We should try not to talk, Peter. It uses up oxygen."

"I'm scared."

"I know, I know," Josh said, covering his own panic.

"Dad, I'm really scared. Are you?"

"Yes, Peter." Suddenly tears filled his eyes. "I'm scared too. I'm scared too."

"Dad, I know where the override controls are for the door."

"You do?"

"Maybe I could feel my way to it and, like, change the programming."

"Maybe, son. I don't know."

He felt Peter get up from the couch, heard him crawling on the floor, and fumbling with a wall panel on the other side of the room.

Then he heard Peter sob. "What's wrong, Peter?"

The boy sniffled. "Tom turned off the power. All the power. Disconnected the batteries too. There's no juice anywhere."

Josh knew that should have set off the alarm but it had not. Hardacre was thorough. Beforehand, he would have called the security company to put the alarm system on test, probably for days. Long enough for him and Peter to die here. Josh moved his mouth to say what he had just thought, but the words would not come out.

"Dad, I think we're stuck here." He was sobbing.

Josh could hear him crawling back toward him.

"I'm sorry, son."

Josh had never felt so helpless. He felt a pain deep in his heart. Not for himself. He had lived a lot. His pain was for Peter. A boy whose life his stupidity would cut short. A boy, he realized, he had not really gotten to know. A kid who had not gotten as much fathering from him as he deserved. He felt empty and inadequate. He said simply and sadly, "I'm so, so sorry."

In the absolute darkness, Peter curled up next to him. Josh hugged him.

"Dad?"

"Yes?"

"I love you."

"I love you too, son."

"It's all my fault," Peter said through tears.

"No, Peter." Josh held his son tighter. "It's all *my* fault."

70

As worried as she was, Emma still had to admit that the view from the helicopter was spectacular. The panorama of the Manhattan skyline and New York harbor not far below was enough to make her momentarily forget her troubles. She realized now that it wasn't just the thrill of the fancy flying machine that made Peter's eyes light up when he said "Dad's helicopter."

As they flew north-northeast over Westchester County, she studied the densely packed mosaic of yacht clubs, beach clubs, country clubs, old mansions, and new megahouses hugging the coast, competing for every possible slice of water view. If the Manhattan skyscrapers were built for making staggering sums of money, she thought, these suburbs were built for spending it. Especially Greenwich, she noted, as its excess of fancy rooftops, walled-in lawns, pools, and tennis courts came into view.

As the helicopter came in to land, she got her first view of Ledgemere Farm. There was nothing remotely farmlike about it. The formal gardens and fountains, the rows of topiary, tennis courts, paddleball courts, pools, vast rolling lawns, the towering brick wall that sealed off the property along the curving road, and the dense, old-growth forest that separated it from the golf club on the other side. Trees blew around it as the helicopter touched down on the cement circle. The pilot turned off the motors, hopped out, opened the passenger door, and offered Emma his hand as she stepped out.

"I'll be an hour, I guess," she said. "Maybe two, I'm

not sure. But my son and I will definitely be going back to Philadelphia together."

The handsome pilot nodded. He had a retired-military look, she thought. She wondered if he was Danny, the Gulf War veteran Peter used to talk about. She realized she had been so preoccupied she had forgotten to ask. Well, on the flight home, Peter would certainly be more interested in talking to the pilot than to her, so she would be sure to find out. Emma smiled. "Thanks so much," she said, "it's a beautiful ride."

"Yes, ma'am," he said, smiling back. "It's a tough job but somebody's got to do it."

Emma started walking across the grass toward the imposing mansion. She stopped for a moment to take in the whole property—the sweep of grounds, great house, and outbuildings. Just as Peter had said, the caretaker's cottage was about the same size as her house. And her house, she felt, was more than anyone really needed.

There were many big estates along the Main Line in Philadelphia, but Emma had never dreamed of living in any of them. To her, Josh's mansion looked as big as the 30th Street Station. Well, not quite. But it was huge, and it did look old and very, very English. She could imagine how Josh would have been smitten by it. He always had that weakness for the trappings of British aristocracy. When they'd moved to London, she had watched how he'd studied their clothes and mannerisms. Knowing Josh as she did, she had decided that what he was really looking to borrow was the unshakable self-confidence and the guilt-free entitlement that seemed to be bred into the British upper class. They didn't merely *think* they deserved their superior status, they assumed it was their absolute right.

She remembered Josh giving her a tour of Mattapan and the triple-decker tenement where he grew up. It had looked cramped and depressing, just as he had told her. An awful place. Nothing like the Conway family's lovely suburban home, where Emma and her brothers had grown up taking it all for granted.

For Josh to wake up every morning here in the middle of this overblown movie set of British grandeur must be a constant reminder . . . of . . . she asked herself . . . *of what*? If she and Josh had somehow stayed married, she would never have agreed to buy a place like this, no matter how much money they might have had.

She turned toward the turreted carriage house modernized into a garage, with bays for six cars. She counted them. Six. Emma groaned. Her mind, she recalled, used to turn off when Peter breathlessly recited the lineup of Josh's fancy automobiles. Her gaze went back over the acres of immaculately tended gardens in the distance. He must have as many groundskeepers as the golf course next door. Then something hit her. This was late afternoon on a weekday in early October. She knew from her own bits of gardening that this was a busy time for tending plantings to prepare them for the coming winter.

There was not a single gardener in sight.

She spun around.

Not anywhere.

The estate appeared to be completely deserted. She walked up to the mansion's back door. It looked medieval beneath a Gothic arch. An ancient wisteria vine climbed up to stained glass windows above. She tried the heavy cast-iron handle. It was unlocked. She stepped inside. By the doorjamb was the alarm terminal. She braced herself, waiting for the siren to go off. Nothing happened. She looked closely at the panel. No lights on. The system appeared to be completely off.

She walked from the vestibule down a corridor. The

kitchen was enormous, with four sinks, two oversized prep islands, two restaurant stoves, a wall of built-in refrigerators. The countertops were covered in different colors and textures of granite. Again, empty. No lights on, just the fading afternoon sun pouring through the windows.

She shouted hello several times. No answer. She walked to the light switch, an elaborate panel with a confusing array of buttons and a keypad. She poked at the buttons. Nothing worked. In the pantry, she saw a lonely, old-fashioned light switch. She snapped it on and off several times. Nothing. The power in the house must be completely off. Or out. But why? There had been no electrical storms today. Besides, Peter had told her about all the elaborate backup generators the estate had.

She hurried from the kitchen to the main staircase. Wide stone steps winding down into the cavernous foyer, like the steps of a city hall or public library. She shouted upstairs for Peter. He might be up in his West Wing. She got no response. She ran up the stairs and turned right, as Peter had described the place to her over and over again. Through the second doorway, she found his first video arcade, jam-packed with flat screens and consoles. Then the second room, even more packed than the first. Then the TV room, with walls covered in flat screens, the floor littered with gaming consoles. Beyond that, Peter's bedroom, undisturbed and uninhabited. No drawers left open, no clothes strewn about. Peter had not set foot in this room today. She ran back through his gaming rooms. No screen savers flickered, not a single light or diode glowed from any of the machines.

She shouted Peter's name into the silence. She felt panic in her voice. She grabbed the handset of the phone on the wall. No dial tone.

She shouted Peter's name again. Where *was* he?

She grabbed her BlackBerry from her waist pack and frantically jabbed 911. "Greenwich Police, please, I need the Greenwich Police," she told the operator. "I'm at Ledgemere Farm. My son is supposed to be here, but the house is empty. The power is off. The alarms are off. The phones are dead. Something is terribly wrong. I need help, right now!"

The clerk spoke slowly over the rhythmic beeping of the recording device. "Please, ma'am, slow down and tell me again where you are."

"Uh . . . I'm at the Josh Katz residence. Ledgemere Farm. I'm not sure what the street address is. It's a big estate next to a golf course. Here in Greenwich. Ledgemere Farm, that's its name."

The operator clicked some computer keys. "Yes, I have it," he said.

Emma was almost shouting. "My son! He's supposed to be here! But there's no one here. The house is deserted!"

"Ma'am, I have to ask you," the man said with practiced calm, "who are you and how did you get into the house?"

"I came by helicopter. The pilot, he's still here, he's waiting on the helipad. Do you want me to have him call you? That's how I got here, how I got in. My name is Emma Conway. I'm Mr. Katz's ex-wife. Our son, Peter Katz, took the same helicopter charter service earlier today. He told me he'd be here. He fibbed about his father's surprise birthday, but that's not 'til next April. Something's wrong. He's not in the West Wing where he should be. . . ." Emma's words were spilling out faster than her thoughts. "My son, he's supposed to be here! Please, send the police, please!"

"Yes, ma'am, we have just dispatched a cruiser. It should be there in just a few minutes."

Emma felt a sense of unreality. She heard herself running down the stairs, phone at her ear. She started thinking about the safe room. Yes, the safe room. Suddenly, she knew that's where Peter was. She *knew* it! It was in the basement. Somewhere. Peter had gone on and on about the safe room. The bad guys, whoever they were, had locked him in the safe room. She just knew it.

"Now, ma'am," the operator said, "it says in our notes that the property is gated as well as alarmed."

"I told you," Emma barked, "the alarm is off. And I don't know anything about the gates. Just tell the police to break in if the gate is closed. I told you, there's something wrong here. I'm going to the basement to check the safe room." The pulsing beep of the recording annoyed her, angered her. "Damnit! Please just send the cops!"

She found the stairs to the basement. But it was dark down there. "I'm going downstairs to check on the safe room," she said breathlessly. "Are the police on their way?"

"Yes, ma'am."

"Tell them to come in through the back door. It's got big vines above it. Tell them to come *down*stairs, that's where I'll be." Peering into the darkness below, she decided that holding the BlackBerry was no way to navigate. "Just please tell them to get here and help me," she exclaimed hurriedly. She clicked off and tossed the device back into her waist pack. Spreading her arms to hold the banisters on both sides of the stairs, she stepped hurriedly down into the darkness.

She stopped at the bottom and waited for her eyes to adjust. She saw dark gray right around her and pitch-black in both directions beyond. On the wall in front of her, she could just make out the shapes of framed pictures. Lots of framed pictures, pictures Peter had told her about, where the keypad that unlocked the safe room was hidden. There was not enough light for her to find the special photo of the men in white suits by the big car in front of the mansion.

The faint reflections on the picture glass made the images impossible to make out.

She took five steps into the blackness to the wall. She dragged her hand across it to find an empty space between picture frames. She pounded on the patch of wall.

"Peter!" she screamed, pounding furiously. "Peter! Are you in there? Peter! Josh? Peter? Peter, answer me!"

Nothing.

She pounded again and shouted.

Again, nothing. All she heard was her own heavy breathing. Her head hurt. Her eyes strained. She began pulling at the framed pictures, ripping them off their hooks one by one, dropping them on the floor, not caring that glass cracked and broke at her feet.

Then she found it. The picture frame that did *not* pull away. The one that was bolted to the wall. Just like Peter had said. She caught her breath and patted the sides of the special frame that would not come loose. Yes, this had to be the one. Carefully, she slid the frame upward. It moved smoothly along tracks holding it against the wall. In the dim gray, she could just see there was a screen of some kind built into the wall. Then she remembered the flash-light function on her BlackBerry. Why hadn't she thought of that earlier? She fumbled with the device buttons in the dark, then the screen lit up, a cold gray beacon.

She remembered what Peter had told her when he inadvertently spilled out what was supposed to be a secret, a secret that he said he had promised to keep. Josh's birthday, backwards and inside out. Frantically, she started to work the date in her head, 04-14-1965, into a combination. Then her heart sank. *Of course, you idiot,* she thought. The power was off. The combination would not work.

She pounded on the wall in frustration. Once, twice, three times. She took a deep breath.

Then she heard a faint pounding sound in return. Yes, she was sure she heard it.

"Peter! Hold on, sweetie! The police are on their way!"

She turned and ran upstairs at full speed. *The gate,* she thought, *the gate!* She threw her smartphone back into her waist pack and bolted out of the big back door. She saw the front gates in the far distance. No sirens yet. Nothing. She sprinted breathlessly over the gravel to the iron gates, the only break in the giant brick walls that blocked out the street beyond.

The police cruiser arrived with lights pulsing but no siren. Two policemen got out and faced her on the other side of the towering wrought-iron gates.

"Can you open up for us, ma'am?" the taller cop asked, standing beside the open driver's-side door.

Emma grabbed at the stainless-steel box that held the two gates together. She tried to shake it. It did not budge.

"See any switches or levers?" the second cop asked.

Emma inspected the steel box again. No buttons, no latches, nothing. A goddamn steel box that was trying to hurt Peter. She tried to rattle it again. Nothing would budge.

"The works must all be inside," the first cop said.

"I told you!" Emma tried not to yell. "The power is off! Nothing works!" She stared at the policemen. "You've got guns! Shoot it open! For God's sake, shoot it open!"

The second cop shook his head and started speaking into the mouthpiece of his radio. "We'll get Fire to come over and break it open," he explained.

"There may not be time," Emma pleaded. "There's no air in there where my son is. Just please, shoot the lock open. Just try, please! My boy is in there with no air, I just know it!"

The taller policeman shook his head wearily. "Ma'am, can we see some identification, please?"

She took a deep breath, trying not to explode at the man. She dropped her shoulders and exhaled. "Yes, of course." She reached for the wallet in her waist pack and pulled out her driver's license. The recent near-deadly run-in on Codman Road came back in an ugly flash. These cops were here to rescue her just like that one back there. She handed her license to him through the gate. "I'm Emma Conway," she explained, forcing herself to sound completely contained. "As I told your 911 man, I believe my son is trapped in the safe room in the cellar of this house. It's my ex-husband's house and my son visits here once a month. He's told me all about it." She watched the cop examining her license. "Officer, I'm the chief executive of Percival & Baxter, you know, the pharmaceutical company. Have you heard of it?"

He nodded. "Yeah, of course. Isn't that the company that had the, uh . . . ?"

Emma finished his thought. "Yes, that's the one. We're in the middle of an investigation, a confidential investigation with a number of agencies. FBI, FDA. Uh, I came here by charter helicopter." She pointed to the helicopter sitting idle on the helipad in the distance. She saw confusion on the faces of both policemen. She reached for her BlackBerry. "Here, just a minute," she said as she speed-dialed her office.

"Emma Conway's office, may I help you?" Stephanie had picked up on the first ring. "Emma?" Stephanie said. She recognized the caller ID. "Where are you? We've been looking all over for you. The bodyguards called in and said you vanished from your house."

"Stephanie," Emma said urgently, "I'll explain all that later. Listen, I'm in Greenwich, Connecticut, right now. I'm at the house of my ex-husband—"

"The man from Anglia Partners?" Stephanie sounded

incredulous. "Emma, Mike Saltzman has been trying to reach you for hours. And Mr. Percival and the board—"

Emma cut her off. "Yes, Stephanie, I'm sure they have. We'll get to all that in a minute. Right now, I'm going to hand the phone to the Greenwich police who are here with me. I want you to confirm who I am and my relationship to Mr. Katz. Stephanie, this is important. I think Peter is trapped in the house and we have to get these police inside. Please, Stephanie!" Her voice cracked. "Just tell the police everything. But be quick about it, please!"

She handed her BlackBerry through the iron gates to the first policeman. He listened and shook his head repeatedly. "Uh-huh. Yes. Uh-huh. Uh-huh. Yes, I know we can trace the call to confirm. No, that's all right, I don't have to speak to him. Uh, thank you. Yes, she will call you back soon." He clicked off the call and handed the device and her license back through the gate.

"It's okay," he said, "Ms. Conway."

"Do you see?" she asked. "Can you use your gun to shoot open the lock? Please? We need to hurry." With pleading in her voice. "My son is in there, I just know it!"

He waved for Emma to stand well aside.

She walked over to the brick wall and stood just inside the column that held the hinges of the iron gate. She heard their shoes on the gravel. Then two deafening blasts. Then the rattle of steel. Then the creak of the doors opening.

She lunged forward to see the two men moving the giant gates.

"Meet me in the house," she said, starting to run. "Take a right and down the stairs. I'll be in the basement, where my son is!" She bolted across the gravel to the house, through the big door, leaving it open. She was down the stairs in what felt like a single heartbeat.

"Peter!" She banged on the same spot on the wall. "Peter,

we're coming! Help is here!" She could have sworn she heard another faint bang in return.

The heavy footfalls of the policemen sounded behind her. Beams from their flashlights lit moving spots around her. She pounded on the wall again. "He's in here! I heard him knock! In here!"

"Fire will be here in a few minutes, and two more cruisers," one cop explained as he shone his flashlight beam around the halls and doorways of the cellar. "They can break into the wall."

She spun around to face him. "The power! If you can turn on the power, I know the combination. I can open the door. It's sealed with some crazy tech system. It may take them too long to break in. It's supposed to be impregnable. My son tried to explain it to me. Can't you just find the switch that turns the power back on? He told me the combination."

The second cop searched the corridor to their right. "I'm looking for the furnace room with the mechanicals," he called over his back. "The main power switch is usually there."

Emma and the first policeman stood in silence and listened to the second policeman rooting about. "Think I found it!" he shouted.

Suddenly, lights went on overhead. Emma had to blink to readjust her eyes. First thing she saw was the litter of broken glass and picture frames at her feet. She had never in her life destroyed things that way. Then she saw the panel on the wall at eye level. One little green diode blinked above the keypad. She saw the rectangle of numbers one through nine. Zero below. Beside that, an "Enter" key and a "Cancel" key. She took a deep breath. *Think, Emma, think,* she told herself. Josh's birthday. Backwards and inside out.

She took the policeman's arm. "Officer, do you have a pencil and a piece of paper? Please?"

He nodded and produced a little notepad and pen from the clip on his belt.

"Thank you!" she almost shouted.

First, she wrote Josh's birth date in the standard day, month, year format:

04141965.

The she wrote it backward:

5691410.

Then she asked herself what "inside out" actually meant. *Uh, uh, start in the middle.*

She wrote:

1

Now, go left? Or right? She didn't know. Then she thought, if they let Josh choose his own combination (with the technician's prompting, of course), how would he turn his backwards birthday inside out? We read left to right. And Josh is right-handed. So his first move would be the number on the right. She wrote:

14

Then left:

149

Then right:

1491

Then left then right:

1491605

She was breathing hard. She held the notepad up to the wall and punched in the numbers quickly. Then slammed her finger onto the "Enter" key.

Nothing.

The green diode continued to blink, blink, blink.

"Fire should be here in a few minutes," she heard the cop say.

She shook her head no and attacked the notepad again, this time starting the inside-out sequence with the number on the left first:

1946150 . . . Enter!

Nothing.

How can that be? He'd said backwards and inside out. She was sure. But maybe she wasn't so sure. Did he say inside out and backwards? Now she wasn't sure what he said. All the stress was getting to her. Suddenly, she wasn't sure of anything. *Don't think that way, Emma. Get back on track. Okay.* She would have to try it both ways. First, from the left inside out, then backwards. If that didn't work, then from the right inside out, then backwards again. "Fuck," she mumbled, cursing Josh's birthday digits and his goddamn birthday too. She started scribbling the numbers angrily on the notepad.

Just then, the wall made a clunking noise. A seam appeared in the shape of a doorway. And with a muffled whoosh, the hidden pocket door slid aside.

Peter stepped out. Then Josh. They were drenched in sweat and gasping for breath. They had circles under their eyes, as if they hadn't slept in days or had been crying.

Before Peter could clear the doorway, Emma threw her arms around him. She hugged him and held him with a ferocious hunger. She had feared the worst. She had imagined the world without her boy, without his life going on ahead of him. She had felt her heart about to freeze. Now she clutched him tight—to feel his body heat, to warm her frightened heart, and convince herself that he really was all right.

She felt Peter accept her embrace and hug her back for a long, soothing moment. Then he started squirming. "Hey, Mom, it's okay, it's okay," he said. To Emma, he still sounded scared. His attempted escape from her embrace felt halfhearted to her, as if he were doing it for show and didn't really mind being swallowed up in her arms. That was enough for Emma. She let go of her hug and cupped his cheeks in her hands to hold his face before her.

"It's okay, Mom," he said. She felt he was trying to sound nonchalant, but he still sounded frightened to her. "When I saw the diode across the room start blinking, I knew that somebody got the power back on. So I crawled over to turn on the lights and open the door." He took a deep breath. "I had a feeling it was you."

Emma could feel tears in the corners of her eyes. She fought back a sniffle. "Young man, you are in deep yogurt."

"Yeah, I know." He smirked as he kissed her forehead. "*Very* deep." Mother and son reached out and hugged each other again. "You heard me banging on the wall, honey. And I heard you bang in return, that's how I knew you were in there! That's how I knew!"

Peter shook his head. "No, Mom. It's soundproof in there. I explained that to you before. We didn't hear anything. How could we?"

"But I heard you bang on the wall after I did."

"No, we didn't hear you. We never banged on the wall. Honest, Mom. Good thing you turned the power back on. It was getting hard to breathe in there."

71

Josh was shocked that Emma gave him a hug right after she finished with Peter at the safe-room door. "You're not supposed to die in there," she said as she let go of him. "*I* want to be the one to kill you." Then she started to pound him with her fists over and over. "How dare you?" she shouted. "How dare you put Peter in danger like that? You selfish bastard!"

Josh raised his arms. "Emma, Emma, I'm sorry, I'm sorry, Emma, Emma, stop for a sec, stop! Stop, please." He grabbed her wrists. "I can fix this. Just give me a minute, will you? There's a lot to explain. Just give me a chance. Please! I've got to make a phone call first. Please, Emma, let me go!"

"You bastard," she muttered, still trying to slug him. "How could you do this to him? What the hell kind of a father are you?"

Peter stuck his face between them. "He's a good dad!" he insisted. "He didn't mean for it to happen. Honest, he didn't. It was my fault for not thinking about how Hardacre must have had the place bugged."

Emma stopped hitting. She and Josh turned to Peter at the same moment.

"Listen to me, you guys!" the boy shouted. "*I'm* the one who has to make a phone call. I gotta call London! It could change everything! I couldn't tell you about it before. Just let me call Tanya in London. She could have gigantic news for this whole mess."

"Who's Tanya?" Emma asked, visibly confused.

The policeman stepped into the middle. "Hold on a minute, this is a police investigation. Somebody just tried to kill you two. We've got to get statements from everyone. I've got investigators and a crime-scene crew on the way."

"I know, Officer . . ." Josh looked at the cop's name badge, ". . . Officer Drummond. Please, I think I can help us do this in a businesslike way. Let's go upstairs to the library. We can sit down calmly. We'll have phones and computers. There are some calls I have to make before you guys escort me to wherever I'm going. One call in particular I should make right away."

"And I have to call Tanya in London!" Peter insisted. "I have to call her *now*! Tom Hardacre took my phone. She's probably been texting me and calling me. I gotta find out about her! It's important!"

"Who is this Tanya you keep talking about?" Emma demanded.

Josh put his hand on Peter's shoulder. "Please, son, let me do this first. Okay?"

Peter lowered his head and muttered "okay."

"Thanks, Peter," Josh said. He reached out and hugged him. Hugged him like he had never hugged him before. Hugged him in a way he would want to hug him again and again for as long as they lived. He felt sure Peter was feeling the same thing. Hoping so. "Thanks, son."

More cooperative than a moment before, Peter said calmly, "Okay, Dad, I'll wait. No prob."

As soon as the light had miraculously come on in the safe room, Josh had started making his mental list of "make goods." This was the second time he had stared into infinite blackness. And this time he had almost made his son pay for *his* mistakes. This had to be the worst thing a person could do. No way he could forgive himself. Sitting in the pitch-black without hope, he had cried for his son. When he walked out of the safe room with a new chance at life, Josh knew he *had* to do what was right, no matter what it cost him.

As rumpled, sweaty, and frightened as he was, he felt the need to take command. Not to play the alpha male the way he would have done in a deal negotiation. But to try to make up for all this. To begin his atonement for all the evil he had allowed by looking the other way. He was sure he'd be going to jail for his unwitting part in the Acordinol murders. But he told himself he'd take what he had coming like a man. Maybe, he thought, for the first time in his life.

He escorted everyone into the library and motioned them to the visitor chairs in front of his big desk. He watched Emma nervously patting Peter on the shoulder and running her hand down the length of his arm, as if re-assuring herself that he was here and all right. Peter seemed to accept her affection without his usual embarrassment.

Josh cleared his throat to get his tribunal started. "Before I begin answering Officer Drummond's questions, I have to make one important phone call." He walked behind his desk, glanced at all the terminals and screens flickering with activity. He pushed his desk chair aside and stood over his console.

"Emma, this is for you."

He picked up the handset and pushed one of the speed-dial buttons.

"Joe Willoughby, please," he said, "it's Josh Katz calling. Yes, yes, I know he's been trying to reach me. Well, I'm back now. Sorry for the inconvenience. It's important that I speak to him right now. Yes, thank you." He waited a long moment, watching Emma watch him.

"Hello, Joe! Yes, yes. Everything is fine." He was performing for the room, especially for Emma. "We did have a little excitement but it's over. I'll explain later. Listen, I need you to do something for me right away, I mean right away, right this minute."

Josh cleared his throat again. "Joe, I want you to withdraw the P&B tender offer immediately. It's off. The whole deal. The tender offer, the new board slate, the proxy contest, all of it. Kill it. Stop it. Pull the paperwork. Rescind it, unregister it, whatever is required. Anglia is pulling out of everything. Do you hear me?" The takeover attorney's protests sounded distantly in his ear. The only sounds he was listening for would come from the people who sat before him. "No, I don't care what it costs. Just make it all stop. Call the SEC, call the proxy solicitor, call everyone, file all the necessary papers. Immediately."

He listened for another stretch. "Yes, Joe, I know this will make Anglia look stupid. I know, I know." He stared at Emma, who was watching him. "No, I don't care how it looks."

He listened for another bit. "I don't care about my credibility. Yes, I know it'll be a cold day in hell before Anglia can mount another deal. Joe, I just did spend a cold day in hell. Call off the deal. Just call off the whole fucking thing. I'll explain later. Okay? Thanks, Joe, thanks."

He made a show of listening again. "No, I haven't lost my mind. I understand what I'm doing. I understand completely. And Joe, one more thing. I'm going to need a criminal lawyer. Yes, I know your firm only does corporate law. I've got some new troubles and I'm going to need the best criminal lawyer you know of. Yes, just have him call me. Yeah, here at Ledgemere. Thanks, Joe. 'Bye."

Josh put the handset back.

He looked straight at Emma. "There now," he sighed and took a deep breath. He raised his shoulders, then let them drop. He lowered his head. "I'm sorry for everything, Emma. Really, I am. I hope that begins to help."

"That's a start," she said coldly.

Josh reached for his desk chair, his place of authority. He gave it a push and sent it rolling behind one of the flat screens. There was now no place for a big boss to sit behind the fancy desk.

He took a seat on the visitor's side of the desk with the others. "Now comes the hard part." He felt his shoulders slumping. He felt sure he looked as defeated as he felt. "I have to admit that I am guilty. I did not make the decision to take over Percival & Baxter." He stared into Emma's eyes. "It wasn't my idea, it was never my idea."

She stared back. "Then whose was it?"

"I was taking orders from a Russian, Viktor Volkov. He bailed out Anglia Partners after the subprime crash. Nobody was supposed to know. That's, uh, why they call it 'private equity.' I had everything I owned in the firm." He shrugged and gestured to indicate the house they were in and more. "When the market crashed, my valuations nosedived. I was leveraged like crazy, thirty to one on some deals. Just the way everyone else was. But, uh, my deals were, uh . . ." His voice trailed off for a moment as he tried to push away memories of the market crash.

He cleared his throat. "Viktor refinanced it all. Half a billion. Even this house. As long as I had to pay back his loan, he was calling the shots. He told me what companies we were going to take over, what companies we would sell, what companies he would keep for himself."

"Why P&B?" Emma asked.

Josh shrugged. "I had no idea why. Peter told me just now it was something about a drug for women that he wanted to steal. The thing is . . . I think I'm guilty. I didn't know anything about the poisonings. Really, I didn't. That's the truth, you have to believe me. But I think my role must make me . . . yes, I'm guilty as hell."

. . .

Peter jumped to his feet. "No, Dad! You're *not* guilty! I-I have to call my friend in London! Please? If I still had my cell phone, I'm sure I would've heard from her by now. She's supposed to have major, *major* information by now. At least I hope she does." He looked at his watch. "She should've done it by now. I don't have my speed-dial list but I can access it on the computer. Can I go log on, Officer Drummond? Please?"

The cop nodded. Peter ran over to a computer beside the Bloomberg terminal. He logged in, clicked through a few screens, then tapped the "enter" key. The speaker on the phone on Josh's desk started ringing with an outgoing call. From the odd buzzing sound it made, it had to be an international call.

"How'd you do that?" Drummond asked.

Peter almost blurted that he and Tom Hardacre had set up the system that connected all the computers and the phones. Then he thought the better of it. "A little programming, that's all," he said, telling himself it was one more secret he ought to keep to himself.

The phone buzzed and buzzed and finally went to a voice-mail greeting. A young woman's voice spoke in perfectly rounded upper-class English. "This is Tanya. I'm sure you know what to do. I shall call you back just as soon as I'm able. Thank you very much, indeed." The line beeped.

Peter heard his words spill out in a rush. "Tanya! Tanya! It's Peter! Everything is all right here. I'm here at my dad's in Greenwich. I mean, we're all right. We thought we might be goners, but we're all okay. Tanya? Tanya, what happened to you? Are you all right? Tom Hardacre took my phone and almost killed my dad and me so, like, you need to call me on my dad's landline, okay? And Hardacre disappeared and this guy Brody did too. Both of them. Geez, Tanya, we have to talk. Is everything all right? Are you there? If this number's not on your read-out, it's US area code two zero three." And then he gave her the direct line.

Mom asked again, "Peter, who on earth is this Tanya?"

He thought for a moment about his necessary secrets and decided he had to speak slowly. If he rushed, he would get himself in trouble. "She's . . . uh . . . the daughter of Vikktor Volkov, the Russian no one's supposed to know about." He took a deep breath. "Mom, she's the girl I got pregnant who I didn't tell you about, but Viktor had her baby aborted, and I didn't tell you about that either."

He saw the shock on Mom's face. He raised his hand like a stop sign, like a peace offering. "But I will. I promise. I'll tell you the whole thing. Just not this sec, okay?"

Mom said, "Peter, what the . . . ?" She was rising out of her chair.

Dad touched her arm. She sat down.

"Please, can I get this out?" Peter said, his eyes darting back and forth between Mom and Dad. "Tanya was planning a secret operation. She couldn't tell me anything more about it because she knew I would run into Tom Hardacre when I came here. So we had two secret operations going on. Hers was, like, more secret because she was, uh, like, working with the British government, at least she hoped she would, and we were going to . . ."

The phone on the desk started to ring. Peter grabbed it. "Tanya? Tanya? Is that you?"

He held the phone tighter to his ear, nodding and saying an occasional "uh-huh" as he listened.

"Yeah, the police are here. You should have the British police contact our police." He nodded in the direction of the Greenwich cop, performing for the people before him the way Dad had just done. "Oh, you mean SOCA is already working with the FBI? That's what they told you?"

He listened some more, nodding emphatically. "Geez, Tanya, that's amazing news. That's freakin' amazing. Here, let me put you on speakerphone." He pushed the button, placed the handset back in its cradle, and clicked the volume level up to the highest level.

"Go ahead, Tanya. We've got Officer Drummond of the Greenwich Police here. And my mom, Emma Conway, and my dad, Josh Katz. This is Tanya Volkov calling from London."

"Hullo, everyone!" Tanya shouted, making the speaker go fuzzy. Peter quickly adjusted the volume down.

"We can hear you fine, Tanya," Peter said, modulating his own voice downward, "no need to yell."

"Well, all right, then," Tanya said brightly, "I'll take a more civilized tone."

"Tell everyone your news, go ahead."

"Well, the news is this: At about tennish last night, GMT, Viktor Volkov was taken into custody by SOCA, that's the Special Organised Crime Agency of Her Majesty's government. A special-operations team undercover at my house got his confessions on tape. Viktor confessed to planning the murders of those innocent people who took the poisoned Acordinol pills. He confessed to all the bloody machinations to take over Percival & Bixley. . . ."

"Percival & *Baxter*," Peter corrected her.

"Uh, Percival & Baxter, thank you, Peter. Viktor confessed that the poisonings were done to drive the share price down in order to buy Percival & Baxter on the cheap. He wanted to steal a molecule in development in one of their labs and combine it with other compounds from one of his pharmaceutical companies. He said it would make the first orgasm drug for women, something better even than a female Viagra."

Peter saw Mom glare at Dad.

Dad shrugged again. He mouthed the words "I had no idea."

Tanya went on. "The SOCA men took him into custody last night. They inform me that he is to be prosecuted for this and a host of other crimes. And they assured me that your FBI, the French Sûreté, and the Russian Federation are all interested in prosecuting him. He will spend the rest of his life in prison, they assure me."

"Now tell us about my dad," Peter said eagerly. "Tell us about my dad!"

"Well, during his confession, I asked Viktor repeatedly, under the guidance of the SOCA authorities, mind you, if Mr. Katz had any knowledge of the poisoning plot or any of the other wrongdoing that he, Viktor, had engineered. Viktor was specific that Mr. Katz knew absolutely nothing about any it. He said he had kept Mr. Katz in the dark deliberately. He exonerated Mr. Katz fully. Viktor used Mr. Katz the way he used many, many others. Which is to say, very badly indeed."

"Can you repeat that, Tanya?" Peter asked.

"Yes, Peter, with pleasure. Viktor was emphatic that Mr. Katz is completely innocent of any guilt or complicity in his crimes. He specifically and repeatedly used the words 'innocent' and, I'm afraid, 'stupid' to describe Mr. Katz."

Peter looked up from the speakerphone. "Hear that, Dad? That's what I told you we were working on but couldn't tell you about. Tanya couldn't tell me either because it would have put me at risk. And if I didn't know what she was doing, then Tom Hardacre couldn't torture it out of me. She had to keep it secret to protect you and me. But she was working on it all along!"

"Peter! Peter!" Tanya called over the speakerphone. "Please pick up the telephone, I want to talk to you privately."

Peter grabbed it. "I'm here, Tanya," he said. He turned his back.

"I'm so happy, luv," she gushed. "I feel like this awful weight has been lifted from my chest. From my heart, actually. I'm so glad you're safe. You are safe, aren't you? No harm done? Right as rain and all that?"

"Yeah, I'm okay." He loved hearing her voice.

"You are very brave, Peter, you know that? You are a very brave man."

"And you are too. Uh, brave, I mean," he added quickly.

Tanya giggled. "We are both a couple of brave souls, aren't we?"

"Yeah, I guess we are."

"You know, Peter, I was worried about you. When my texts and messages got no answer, I got very worried."

Peter lowered his voice. "Yeah, I figured you would be. I was worried about you too." He wished to hell he had his own phone back. He hated to have this conversation in front of everyone.

"Peter?" she said softly.

"Yes, Tanya."

"Remember when I told you that you should come visit me in London and stay with me in my house?"

"Yeah," he whispered, "I do."

"Well, I meant it, I really did. How soon can you be here? I do *so* want to see you."

Peter cupped his hand over the phone. "And I really want to see you too." God, he wished he had some privacy. He had to lean forward so no one could see the bulge in his jeans.

"So when can you fly to London?"

"Geez, I'm in school now." He was sure he was blushing. "My next break isn't until Thanksgiving. That's, like, in a month and a half."

"Oh sod! You're a man now, make some excuses, figure something out. Look, together we found a way to put away one of the world's most dangerous international criminals. Surely, you can figure out how to steal a few days away from your—what do you call it?—your high school."

"Geez, well, since you put it that way."

"Peter, I haven't had a good shag since our night at Kroesus Kids. Your lady awaits. You have a duty, an obligation to fulfill."

"Uh, okay, I'll figure it out. Somehow."

"Make it soon, luv."

"I will. I will."

"That's my man. Mwwwwah!" Then she hung up.

Peter took a deep breath. He looked down. His jeans were almost flat. In a minute or so, he could turn around and face his mother.

Josh heard the BlackBerry in Emma's waist pack start to buzz oddly. She pulled it out, looked at the screen, and answered immediately.

"Mike Saltzman," she announced, clearly for the benefit of the people around her. "Yes, I know. Anglia has called off the takeover, I know. I was sitting here with Mr. Katz when he called their takeover attorney." She turned and looked at Josh. "Yes, of course, we can still sue Anglia. Let's discuss that tomorrow at my office. We've got some loose ends to tie up here in Greenwich, then I'm going to take the helicopter and get the hell out of here."

A woman shouted from the hallway. Josh recognized Pen's voice and felt a warm glow. She ran into the library, straight into Josh's arms.

"Josh! Josh! Are you all right?"

She kissed him all over his face. She stroked his hair and his cheeks. "You're all right, you're all right! I was trying your cell over and over! And no one answered. I was going to call the police. And then as I got here I saw the police cars going in. They told me. Oh, Josh, you're all right. And Peter! Peter!" She reached for the boy and gave him a hug. "You're all right too!"

"Oh, hi, Penelope," Peter said, wiggling out of her embrace but smiling. "Yeah, we're all right."

She turned to Emma.

"You must be Emma," she said, extending her hand. "I'm happy to meet you. I'm Penelope Longstreet, Josh's girlfriend."

"No," Josh said, taking Penelope's two hands in his. "Penelope's not my girlfriend, she's my fiancée." He pressed her hands against his chest. "That is, if she'll still have me."

Penelope sighed and pulled their hands to her own heart. She kissed his fingertips. He leaned forward and kissed her forehead. "Don't answer yet," he whispered.

"I have one more bit of unfinished business," he announced as he walked back to the big desk that used to be one of the symbols of his wealth and authority. He reached for the secret compartment. He turned the knob backward, forward, backward, then opened the little drawer. He extracted the envelope with Emma's love letter and the lock of her hair.

He walked over to Emma and handed it to her, looking at Pen all the while. "Emma, this doesn't belong to me anymore. It belongs to our past."

He waited for her to peek inside the envelope. "You kept this?" she asked, looking confused.

"I think," he said, turning again to Pen, "that was one of my mistakes. One of many, I'm afraid. Emma, you moved on before I did. You and Ned are very happy together, I can tell. But now it's time for me to move on too. Even though it may be too late. Pen, tell me, is it too late?"

She came to him and wrapped her arms around his shoulders. "No, Josh, it's not too late. Not for me."

"You may want to reconsider," he said. "I've got some serious troubles ahead. Scary ones. I doubt I'll be able to afford Ledgemere anymore. And Anglia Partners is toast. I don't know what I'm going to do anymore. That's the ugly truth. You sure you want in on that?"

She nodded emphatically. Tears were starting. She tried to sniff them back. "Hey, remember the deal we made the day we met? The rich guy and the model? Seeing through the money and the makeup? Well, that's still on. It never changed, Josh."

"Uh, excuse me," Officer Drummond said. "We have an investigation to conduct."

"I'm sorry," Josh said. "May I go upstairs and clean up first? I'm not going anywhere, you can be sure of that."

Drummond nodded. Through the library windows, Josh saw police and technicians busy taking photos and inspecting the grounds.

Another cop walked into the library through the garden door. "We found a body in the garage," he announced. "Fat guy in a dark blue suit. Somebody blew his face off. I called CSI, the medical examiner, and the body-bag guys."

Drummond nodded.

Josh winced. "Must be Brody," he said. "That's Charles Brody, the PR guy I told you about. Must be that Tom Hardacre did not want anyone around who could identify him."

"Ewww," Peter said, turning pale and cupping his hand over his mouth, "I saw Hardacre shoot a raccoon in the face. It was gross and it smelled awful."

"Same thing here, kid," the cop muttered as he turned and walked back out to the garden.

Josh thought Brody got what he deserved. But he still felt sorry for the man's life. He'd spent his life sucking up to people who just used him. And all he got was a bullet in the face. He realized, after all their years together, he had no idea if Brody was married or divorced or widowed, or even straight or gay. And Brody's son, the retarded young man in the group home? Josh made a mental note to find out about him once the dust had settled.

He took Penelope by the hand and headed upstairs to freshen up for his new ordeal.

Emma stood up from the chair and addressed Drummond. "Officer, do you mind if I go outside for a while?" She raised her BlackBerry. "I've got a million calls to return. And I should let the helicopter pilot know that we're going to be here for a while."

"Sure," he said, "go ahead."

"I'm not going anywhere, I promise."

"I know," he said, and turned to ready his digital recorder and notepad.

Emma turned to leave, then turned back to Peter. "Peter, can I ask you a question?"

"Sure, Mom."

"You told me that the combination was your father's birthday backwards and inside out. Isn't that right?"

"Yeah, that's right."

"Well, 'inside out' means starting from the center number, right?"

Peter nodded.

"I did that. I turned it backwards. Then I took the first number to the right? Right?"

He nodded again.

"Then the number to the left?"

"Yup, Mom."

"Peter, I tried that! And I'm telling you, it didn't work.

It didn't work any way I tried it. I know your father's birthday—oh-four, one-four, one-nine-six-five. And I promise you, it did not work."

He smiled at her. Was his smile sheepish? Or guilty, she wondered. "No, no, Mom. Dad's combination uses the European formula. It's *day* first, then month, then year. I guess I shoulda told you."

She stared at him. Then she shook her head and turned to go outside, muttering to herself, "Pretentious jerk."

PART THREE

DECEMBER 2009

72

Tanya snuggled close to Peter. The layers of ornate linens on her canopied bed were strewn about like wreckage after a storm. Her collection of baby dolls was gone. The day after Viktor had been taken away, she had them put in storage.

"I did promise you we'd shag in every room in my house," she said as she unwrapped her legs from his, "even the bedroom."

Peter gave her a little peck. "And you had condoms in candy dishes in every room."

"De rigueur."

"De what?"

"Nothing, my sweet." She sat up straight and looked deep into the lovely dark eyes of her Kroesus Boy. "Tomorrow, you go back home, luv." She took a deep breath to hold back a tear. "And very soon, you will begin to forget about me."

He sat up and kissed away the tear. "No, I won't Tanya. You and I, we . . ."

"Ssssh." She silenced him with a fingertip over his lips. "You'll always be my lad. And we'll always have our secrets."

He kissed her fingertip. "I know, I know. Secrets are what make us grown-ups, right?"

She smiled.

"Tanya," he said, sounding adorably hesitant and boyish, "even though we're not gonna, like, get married or anything, I want to say something."

"What?" She knew what it would be.

He took hold of her shoulders and looked searchingly into her eyes. "Tanya, I, er, uh, I love you, Tanya. There, I said it. I love you."

"I love you too," she said.

They shared a soft kiss. Then it hit her. For the first time ever, she felt something deep inside her. Something she had never felt before. Yes, finally she felt that *she* loved Tanya too.

73

Josh watched the real estate agent's Subaru go down the long gravel road, pass through the open gates of Ledgemere Farm, turn, and disappear into the world beyond.

He put his arm around Penelope's waist. "She says she has three hedge-fund guys already salivating to make an offer."

"Will you miss it?" she asked.

"Nah. Being a lord of the manor wasn't at all what it was cracked up to be. I think we're gonna have a great time together, you and me. Just being," he paused to emphasize the Boston accent, "just being *nomm-ull.*"

"*Nomm-ull*?" she smiled. "Like *uthuh* folks?"

"Well, not exactly. After all the wreckage clears and all the legal wrangling over the loans and assets gets settled, after I sell off everything that was Anglia Partners, I'll still own a nice little chunk of Percival & Baxter. That's mine." He paused. "And yours." He paused again. "*Mrs.* Katz."

They went back inside.

"With that smart CEO they've got," he said, "and all that good stuff in the pipeline, that stock is going to rocket."

"So," Penelope said, "Emma is going to make us rich all over again?"

"Not quite," he said. "Sid would call it 'comfortable.' I'm going to have to work somewhere. And of course it can't be on Wall Street. That's going to be the deal with the government, part of my one hundred percent cooperation, turning over every Viktor-related business record and computer file, except for the hard drives Hardacre took with him."

Josh was not surprised that the authorities had been unable to find even a trace of the wily Yorkshireman. He just evaporated into the ether. Like the zombie networks he ran, the forensic investigator had said.

"I'll work too," Penelope said. "But I don't mind. Nothing's wrong with being a couple of working stiffs."

"No, not a thing. You know, my lawyers tell me Peter saved my ass. If he hadn't done everything he did with Tanya and SOCA, I'd be a candidate for an orange jumpsuit. Pen, I don't know how I can ever repay him."

She took his head in her two hands. He loved the way she did that. "You don't have to," she said, "that's the whole point. You *can't*. He's your son. He loves you. That's why he did what he did. All you have to do now is be his dad. Give him what he needs to find his confidence. And you guys will be best friends for life."

"I hope so," he said.

She gave him a little kiss and let go. He took her hand and led her to the center of the grand entrance hall that would soon belong to someone else.

"I'll never forget the first time I saw you." He took a step back, pointed at the carved ceiling, then at the floor. "You were standing right here."

"Of course, you can't," she smiled, "and you never will."

74

At her desk, Emma reached for one of her piles of paper. A medium-tall pile that had grown with one document upon another. She finally had asked Stephanie to stop straightening the piles so that the right angles lined up perfectly. She liked the piles to look a little messy, like the projects themselves. With bits out of order and pieces sticking out here and there. As if crying out for attention and improvisation and sudden solutions you had no idea you could pull off. Like life.

Oh sure, there were problems of all kinds and a new crisis every day landing on her desk. But it was nothing compared to what she had just lived through. She welcomed each new day with all the challenges it brought. She felt she could manage her way through almost anything now.

With Percival & Baxter's stock on the rise again and the worst of the losses behind them, the company could focus on rebuilding Acordinol. The latest studies showed that, as a result of the company's conduct during the crisis and the new security measures and safeguards, trust in P&B products had not just rebounded, but risen to levels even higher than before the poisoning. P&B's other established businesses were humming and there were many good things in the research pipeline. New Alzheimer's therapies and diabetes work showed progress. The regenerative bone and skin tissue projects were also looking like they might do amazing things someday.

As for the virtual molecule of synthetic dopamine that had started it all—it turned out there were reactivity problems the lab found while trying to build the real molecule. And so the computational chemists had to go back to their virtual drawing board. Even if Volkov had won and been able to steal the molecule, his female Viagra would not have materialized as he'd hoped.

The week after Emma's trip to Greenwich, Linda Farlow barged into her office. She hinted at having been the leak. "I didn't break any laws, Emma," the bitch had said with a smirk. "And you can't fire me. Because I quit." Then she turned and strode out.

How wrong she had been about Linda. Yes, that was a blind spot she would have to watch for. She was too eager to see justice done for everyone, too eager to right the world's wrongs. It was her guilt, she thought. She was blinded by her guilt about the advantages she'd had over Linda. Her guilt wouldn't let her see what the woman was really like. That and the feeling that somehow their kinship as women in the corporation would make them . . . well, that was wrong too.

And Steve Upshaw—whom she had been all set to confront, accuse, convict, and fire—had resigned to take a divisional presidency at Roche the very afternoon she was on the helicopter. Yes, she admitted to herself and to no one else but Ned, her people instincts were not quite perfect. For starters, she had to stop apologizing to the world for the good things fate had granted her.

With a few quiet minutes alone between appointments, she looked out over the forest of the P&B land preserve. The leaves were almost gone. "I'm here, Dad," she whispered. "And it's going to be all right. All of it."

She heard the chirp of her personal cell from her purse. She peeked inside. It was Ned. She grabbed for it.

"Hi," she said softly. She felt glad no one was around. She whispered playfully, "Hey, aren't you the hot new ceramicist who's getting all that attention for his *Earthborn* pieces? The ones *The New York Times* called 'the power of testosterone fused with clay'?"

"Yeah, that's me," Ned replied. "You remember me, I'm the guy with the great hands, the hands he can't keep off his hot wife."

"Mmmm," Emma said.

"You know," he went on, "since we have the house to ourselves tonight, I thought I'd make us a feast. I'm thinking oysters, caviar, champagne, truffles, figs, chocolate, and more champagne . . . what do you say?"

"I say yum. And I'm talking about the man as well as the meal."

"Well," Ned said, "the main course is you. Can I tell you exactly how I'd like to devour you?"

Emma thought she was blushing. Good thing she was still alone. "Please do."

Ned started describing what he would do.

"Mmmm," Emma said, closing her eyes as he went on.

"Then I want to bury my face between your breasts and slowly . . ."

Emma opened her eyes. And saw Hal Percival standing before her. She sat up straight, holding the cell phone closer to her ear. Ned went on. Emma looked at Hal, raised two fingers and mouthed the words "two minutes."

Hal smiled and took the seat across.

On the other end of the call, Ned's descriptions kept getting sexier.

Emma replied, for Hal's benefit, as if she were having a business conversation.

"Yes, I could get behind that," she said as Ned went on with more details.

Looking at Hal and feeling awkward, she said flatly, "Hmm, sounds like a good strategy." A pause, a nod. Then, "Definitely an approach we could try out in research."

Ned kept going. And Emma listened politely, keeping eye contact with Hal.

Finally, she said crisply, "Sounds like a plan." Hoping she was not blushing, she clicked off the call and put the phone back in her purse.

"Emma," Hal spoke before Emma could formally greet him, "I want you to be the first to know that I have decided to retire from the board of directors."

"That's terrible," she said and she meant it. "Hal, we need you more than ever."

Hal shook his head no. He raised a hand to stop Emma from making whatever argument she was about to make.

"You know, Emma, the lawyers and investment bankers say that in these takeover battles nobody's right or wrong. It's all about money and control. Nothing else. The companies and what happens to them and the people inside them, none of that matters. That a company is just an empty vessel whose only purpose is making money." He sighed and looked out the window. Then he turned back to Emma. "I think, after all we've been through, I've finally come around to that point of view. There's no meaning to any of this beyond the money. Haven't you come to the same conclusion?" Hal sat back.

Emma leaned forward, studying this man she thought she knew.

Then she burst out, "Bullshit, Hal. Bull-*shit!* I don't believe that. Not for a second." They stared at each other. "And neither do you!"

"You're right," he said, cracking his crooked little smile. "But I am quite serious about retiring and there will be no convincing me otherwise."

He stood up to leave.

Emma stood, not sure what bomb he would drop next.

"Emma," he said in his most formal manner, "I have decided to put the Percival family shares, the largest individual interest in the company, into a new philanthropic trust. And I am appointing you the head trustee. Because I know you will make sure that, while this company does well for its shareholders, it will also do its share of good for the world."

Emma did not know what to say. "Hal, I . . ."

Hal just smiled. He extended his hand. She took it. Then he clasped his other hand over hers. "This company is in your hands now. I want it that way. And your father would have wanted it too. Emma, you've earned it."

ABOUT THE AUTHOR

GLENN KAPLAN is the author of *The Big Time*, a nonfiction book based on interviews with top executives that examined the dynamics of success in the world of big business. He spent more than twenty years in advertising agencies, creating campaigns for Fortune 500 companies, and is now a creative director on the client side. His first novel was *All for Money*. His second novel, *Evil, Inc.,* was a *New York Times* bestseller. He lives in New York City with his family.

Epilogue

Woodrow had been spending nearly as much time at his wife's chapel/wedding venue as he had the River City Police Department lately. But it wasn't just because he was visiting her. It was because he was a guest invited to all the weddings that had been taking place there over the past several weeks.

Since Luther Mills was dead, the eyewitness had returned to town. Rosie Mendez with her beautiful brown eyes and chocolate-colored curls had married Clint Quarters in the chapel with Landon Myers serving as his best man just two weeks before his own wedding to the assistant district attorney, Jocelyn Gerber.

Then Hart Fisher had wed the evidence tech, Wendy Thompson. The chief smiled as he thought of how adorable Hart's little girl Felicity had been as the flower girl, and how happy she had been to get Wendy as a mom and Wendy's parents as her already doting grandparents.

Tyce Jackson's nuptials had been the most elaborate of all of them—of course. But his socialite bride, the judge's daughter, hadn't been the bridezilla Woodrow had warned his wife she might be. Tyce was the one who had wanted every detail to be perfect for the young woman he called his princess bride. He'd been a groomzilla.

Woodrow smiled over the thought. Then the change in music drew his attention to the rear of the church as the bride appeared, clutching the arm of the man giving her away. Parker grinned as he escorted Keeli Abbott down the aisle.

Parker was more like his mother than any of the other kids. Every bodyguard he'd matched up with the person the chief had hired him to protect had fallen in love. Or maybe they'd already loved each other and just hadn't been aware until Parker had played Cupid and put them together.

Spencer Dubridge, standing at the altar next to Hart Fisher, grinned when he saw his bride. When she reached the end of the aisle, he pulled back her veil to reveal her beautiful face. She was glowing with happiness and from her pregnancy—although the A-line design of her lacy white dress concealed most of her baby bump.

A-line...

Woodrow smiled at his wife, who stood beside him in the front pew. She was rubbing off on him. He was beginning to know as much about wedding gowns and bridal bouquets as he did about law enforcement.

Maybe it was time he considered retiring. And he

knew just the man to take over for him: the groom. He'd talked Spencer out of quitting River City PD for the bodyguard business. River City had more than their share of bodyguards and now two new branches of the Payne Protection Agency would soon be opening.

Nick was going to start his own franchise. He was already hiring former colleagues away from the FBI for his team. And Garek and Milek Kozminski would soon share a franchise, employing ex-cons who'd turned around their lives the way the former jewelry-thieving brothers had turned around theirs.

What Spencer was starting here with Keeli was more important than the bodyguard business. They were starting a family.

Woodrow pulled his wife close as he looked around the chapel that was filled with their family. Like every wedding guest there, he knew there was nothing more important than love and family.

* * * * *

She lunged forward, slamming him against the brick wall
at his back, her forearm against his throat. "Who are you?"
she snarled.

Stunned, he didn't resist her. Clearly, Rachel had some
serious self-defense training, which only furthered his
certainty that this was a woman who believed herself to be
in mortal danger.

"I told you," he rasped past her forearm. "I'm Marcus Tate."

"That's your name. Who are you?"

"I don't understand—"

"How did you follow me without me spotting you? How
do you know I look in shop windows to check my six? For
that matter, why are you here? Why did you think you could
take down some bad guy who might be following me?"

Ah. He didn't usually talk about his job, and certainly not
with civilians. But this situation was not usual in any way.
"I'm a soldier," he gasped.